«I Don't Belong Anywhere». György Ligeti at 100

Contemporary Composers

General Editors
Massimiliano Locanto
Massimiliano Sala

Volume 4

Publications of the Centro Studi Opera Omnia Luigi Boccherini
Pubblicazioni del Centro Studi Opera Omnia Luigi Boccherini
Publications du Centro Studi Opera Omnia Luigi Boccherini
Veröffentlichungen des Centro Studi Opera Omnia Luigi Boccherini
Publicaciones del Centro Studi Opera Omnia Luigi Boccherini
Lucca

«I Don't Belong Anywhere»
György Ligeti at 100

EDITED BY
WOLFGANG MARX

❦

BREPOLS
TURNHOUT
MMXXII

The present volume has been made possibile by the friendly support of the

ernst von siemens
music foundation

© BREPOLS 2022

All rights reserved. No part of this publication may be reproduced,
stored in a retrieval system, or transmitted, in any form or by any means,
electronic, mechanical, photocopying, recording, or otherwise, without
the prior permission of the publisher.

D/2022/0095/241

ISBN 978-2-503-60240-0

Printed in Italy

Contents

WOLFGANG MARX
    Introduction vii

Ligeti's Music

BENJAMIN R. LEVY
    Condensed Expression and Compositional Technique
    in György Ligeti's *Aventures* and Beyond 3

BRITTA SWEERS
    Listening to *Lontano*: The Auditory Perception
    of Ligeti's Sound Textures 27

PIERRE MICHEL – MARYSE STAIBER
    Rediscovering the Meaning of Words with Hölderlin:
    About *Drei Phantasien* by György Ligeti 49

MANFRED STAHNKE
    The Dove and the Bear: 'Galamb Borong'
    and the Connection to 'Ars Subtilior' 71

PETER EDWARDS
    Analysing the Concerto for Violin and Orchestra:
    Apparitions of the Past and Future 93

Context and Reception

EWA SCHREIBER
    Listening (to) Ligeti: Tracing Sound Memories
    and Sound Images in the Composer's Writings 113

MÁRTON KERÉKFY
    'Functional Music' and *Cantata for the Festival of Youth*:
    New Data on Ligeti's Works from His Budapest Years   135

BIANCA ȚIPLEA TEMEȘ
    Mourning in Folk Style:
    Ligeti's Reliance on Romanian Laments   161

JULIA HEIMERDINGER
    György Ligeti's Film Music beyond Stanley Kubrick   179

READING LIGETI

VITA GRUODYTĖ
    Letters from Stanford:
    György Ligeti to Aliutė Mečys   199

HEIDY ZIMMERMANN
    More than Printing Scores:
    Ligeti and His Post-1960 Publishers   225

JOSEPH CADAGIN
    «Everything Is Chance»:
    György Ligeti in Conversation with John Tusa,
    28 October 1997   247

ABSTRACTS AND BIOGRAPHIES   273

INDEX OF NAMES   281

Introduction

György Ligeti is among the most important composers of the second half of the twentieth century. After fleeing to Austria in the aftermath of the failed Hungarian uprising against the communist regime in 1956 he quickly emerged as a highly innovative composer whose music offered alternatives to the then predominating, Darmstadt-endorsed total serial style: most famously his micropolyphony, but also his play with nonsensical sounds and language as well as the 'pattern-meccanico' style. The complex, multi-layered rhythmic patterns in his later works (such as the Piano Études) and his juxtaposition of different tuning systems (for example in his concertos for violin and horn) are also core aspects of a composer who reinvented himself several times during his career (despite there also being constants in his stylistic development). There is also his interesting early Hungarian music, much of which has been 'rediscovered' only recently — not least in the context of the recording of his complete works for Teldec and Sony (a feat achieved by virtually no other composer of the last decades).

Yet Ligeti did not only communicate through his compositions; he was also a frequent speaker and writer about music — not just with regard to his own works but also discussing the music of other composers, or more general issues of musical culture. His collected texts cover two volumes, including a number of highly-rated musicological and analytical articles (for example on the music of Webern and Boulez), yet also reflections on the general development of art music and, of course, comments on his own music as well as his life. He was a welcome speaker on the radio or at live events, as well as a sought-after composition teacher during his years at the Hochschule für Musik in Hamburg.

Ligeti was a composer with multiple identities: a Hungarian born as a member of a minority in Romania, a jew being a member of another minority within that minority, later acquiring an Austrian passport while spending much of his time in Germany. «I don't belong anywhere», he once said in an interview with Marina Lobanova, only to add immediately «I belong to the intelligentsia and culture of Europe»[1].

---

[1]. Lobanova 2002, p. 396.

2023 marks the centenary of Ligeti's birth. Unlike in the case of some other composers, his music has continued to be performed regularly since his death in 2006. His *Le Grand Macabre* is among the most regularly staged operas of the last half-century (only behind some works by US minimalist composers such as Philip Glass and John Adams). He also continues to be the subject of research; there is hardly a year without an academic conference dedicated to him taking place somewhere. The Ligeti Collection at the Paul Sacher Foundation in Basel which houses Ligeti's sketches and papers has been the source of many new analytical and biographical discoveries, including some presented in this volume.

Ligeti's centenary appears to be an appropriate moment to take stock of the relevance this composer has in the contemporary world, to assess where he 'belongs' today and how our views of his œuvre and our understanding of his position in musical and cultural history have evolved. What do Ligeti and his music have to say to us in our post-postmodernist age? Why do his works still fascinate us so much, and has our approach to them changed in recent years (particularly since his death)?

The first part of this book, 'Ligeti's Music', offers new insights into a selection of Ligeti's works, ranging from the early 1960s to the 1990s. Benjamin R. Levy opens this section with a discussion of the compositional evolution of *Aventures* and *Nouvelles Aventures*. Drawing on his extensive sketch studies in the Paul Sacher Foundation in Basel, he demonstrates the close links between Ligeti's initial verbal «jottings» and their later musical manifestations. The early jotting stage was far more than a mere 'brainstorming' for ideas as its impact on the music can be shown in detail in the score. Levy also discusses literary connections indicated by the jottings, as well as influences the musical ideas (particularly the «condensed expressions») developed in relation to *Aventures* and *Nouvelles Aventures* continued to have on Ligeti's works for decades, up to the Violin Concerto.

In the second chapter Britta Sweers reassesses *Lontano* not on the basis of the creative process but rather from the recipient's point of view. She argues that auditory perception has often been neglected in the analysis of Ligeti's music. Based on two empirical studies with (mainly) third-level students she found that listeners' reactions to *Lontano* had little to do with the dominant discourse around the piece which — just like in the case of *Aventures* and *Nouvelles Aventures* — is centered on the composer's extensive statements and sketches. Instead the responses were dominated by negative emotional categories, expressing tension and loss of orientation. Observing that Ligeti's compositional style pushes «human psychoacoustic sound perceptions to an extreme» she concludes that both acoustic and psychoacoustic approaches as well as aurally based sound analysis have to be integrated into research on Ligeti which is still dominated (too much?) by a focus on compositional intention.

Introduction

Ligeti's musical response to a poetic text in the *Three Fantasies after Friedrich Hölderlin* is the topic of Pierre Michel and Maryse Staiber's contribution. The three pieces are not traditional 'settings' of given texts; Ligeti left out many lines and words of the poems and diluted the already fragmentary texts further. The authors — a musicologist and a Germanist — closely analyse particularly the first and third *Fantasies*, outlining how Ligeti's closeness to Hölderlin's «in-between status» let him find poignant ways of musical expression. Sensing a kindred spirit in Hölderlin, Ligeti experienced an aesthetic crisis especially at the time of writing the *Fantasies* in the early 1980s. He felt torn between the old and the new, tradition and innovation, and responded in a characteristic way, highlighting complexities and ambiguities in the texts.

Manfred Stahnke focuses one of the more traditional aspects of Ligeti's œuvre, investigating a possible connection between his Piano Étude no. 7 'Galamb borong' and the rhythmic complexities of the 'ars subtilior' style around 1400. Taking the Latin ballad *Angelorum psalat* by the late 14th-century composer Rodericus as an example, Stahnke details the additive polyrhythmic textures of this highly complex music and its possible links to Ligeti's étude. This — among many other, simultaneous influences form popular and traditional musics which Stahnke also acknowledges — may well have been on the composer's mind when writing the études. Stahnke was first a student and later a teaching assistant of Ligeti's in Hamburg (his text contains many memories of this period) and had introduced Ligeti and his composition class to this piece in the early 1980s.

Peter Edwards's chapter on Ligeti's Violin Concerto provides a perfect conclusion to this section as he asks questions not dissimilar to those posed by Levy and Stahnke in particular. Focusing especially on the concerto's first two movements he explores «the extent to which the innovations of the present are reliant on the past». Looking at harmonic glissandos, the parallel use of different temperaments by different instruments, the Lydian mode and polyphonic textures Edwards identifies links to previous composers, styles and periods. Special attention is paid to Harry Partch's thinking about tuning systems and his approach to composition in comparison to Ligeti's, yet Edwards senses Partch's influence also in the way in which Ligeti uses the marimba in the concerto.

The book's second part is dedicated to the 'Context and Reception' of Ligeti's works. How was Ligeti shaped by the sound and the music all around him, and how did he talk about it later? Ewa Schreiber reflects in her chapter on how important the 'soundscape' was for Ligeti at different stages of his life — despite the common focus on visual metaphors (such as spiderwebs, crystals, labyrinths) in the Ligeti literature. Particularly during the final decades of his life Ligeti often mentioned the importance of aural memories that shaped his world, such as the clacking of his father's typewriter, the sounds of different languages, the noises of the street and of certain specific places, or the role of radio and records (and their limitations in terms of technology and availability). This is related to the aural impressions the style of certain composers made on Ligeti, and the role of his aural imagination for his own creative process.

This is followed by a listing and assessment of the composer's functional music, a particularly neglected part within his already neglected early output. Márton Kerékfy's chapter benefits from new material that has become available since Friedemann Sallis published his monograph on Ligeti's early music in 1996 — with the Paul Sacher Foundation and Hungarian archives providing the bulk of those sources. Kerékfy offers detailed lists and contextual information on Ligeti's marches, dances and marching songs, folk song arrangements, arrangements for instruments and incidental music. He also discusses the circumstances of some pieces' commissioning, the contexts of their performances and their reception.

Growing up in Transylvania Ligeti was exposed to Romanian folk music, while later he returned to the country to study traditional music in Bukarest and Cluj-Napoca. Bianca Țiplea Temeș investigates the influence this engagement had on his musical style, particularly the 'bocet' (dirge) used at Romanian funerals. Temeș links it to the descending lament lines that play such a central part in many of Ligeti's works, and about which entire books have been written[2]. The case for this link is strengthened by the balancing presence of upward tetrachords in both the folk songs and several of Ligeti's pieces, although Țiplea Temeș also acknowledges that the composer's style is influenced from many different musical genres, periods and styles at the same time.

Everyone interested in Ligeti knows the story about Stanley Kubrick's use of his music in *2001: A Space Odyssey* and some of his later movies. Much less well known is that Ligeti's music has featured in many other films over the years. These include art house films, mainstream productions and even TV series. Julia Heimerdinger analyses in her text which of his works have been used most often, and reflects on the most likely reasons for the choice of these pieces in genres as diverse as martial arts film, psycho thriller, ghost story, tragicomedy and documentary. She also discusses the interaction of Ligeti's music with that by other contemporary composers in some of these movies.

The last part of this volume, 'Reading Ligeti', is dedicated to newly discovered or widely unknown primary sources related to Ligeti's life and music. Vita Gruodytė recently discovered in a Lithuanian archive letters exchanged between the composer and Aliutė Mečys in 1972. The two of them lived together in Berlin at the time and normally had no need for

---

[2]. BAUER 2011.

Introduction

epistolary communication, except for a period early in that year when Ligeti spent a few months at Stanford University. The extracts of the letters published here offer a rare view into the composer's private life and his habits. Ligeti shares his impressions of the American way of life, his daily struggles with infrastructure and technology, professionalism and higher education in the US, as well as his compositional plans (particularly regarding his opera project) and a comparison of performances of his music conducted by two then very young, rising conducting stars: Zubin Mehta and Seiji Ozawa.

The Paul Sacher Foundation recently acquired the Ligeti archive of Schott Music, Ligeti's long-time publisher in Mainz. Heidy Zimmermann, the curator of the Ligeti Collection at the Foundation, evaluates the correspondence between Ligeti and his editors at Universal Edition, Peters/Litolff and Schott with regard to the gestation process of new works, the relationship between the composer and the staff, the extent and duration of revisions during the editing process, and also the way in which the composer approached the (re-)publication of some of his older works. There are interesting 'nuggets' of information emerging from this correpsondence, such as Ligeti's disgust about the NS past of one of his publishers (although he only became aware of it *after* switching to a competitor).

The volume concludes with the transcription of an extended interview for BBC Radio 3 that Ligeti gave in 1997. His interviewer was John Tusa, and unlike a later interview with Tusa from 2001 this one was ultimately not broadcast. Ligeti talks about several of his pieces — particularly those written after 1980 —, his engagement with tuning systems and 'dirty' sounds (with an interesting account of his visit of Harry Partch in California in 1972 — something not mentioned in his letters to Aliutė Mečys), the person and poetry of Sándor Weöres, the music of Romanian keening women (acknowledging the influence outlined in Bianca Țiplea Temeș' chapter), the dialectics of change and determinism and others.

***

I am very grateful to Roberto Illiano, Massimiliano Sala and Fulvia Morabito of the Centro Studi Opera Omnia Luigi Boccherini for their cordial collaboration and support. Heidy Zimmermann from the Paul Sacher Foundation always facilitates access to its Ligeti Collection and — in addition to writing a chapter herself — was very generous in making sketches, pictures and other material available for this volume. Gora Jain from the Forum für Künstlernachlässe in Hamburg kindly gave us permission to use some of Aliutė Mečys's paintings and drawings of Ligeti (including the cover picture). Claire Taylor-Jay supported the editing process of some of the texts. However, I am most grateful to the contributors from all over Europe and the US who shared their latest research and accompanied the gestation process of this volume with great patience (everything moves slower in times of a pandemic…). Their essays help explain our time's continuing fascination with Ligeti, the regular performances of his music and the ongoing engagement with his thoughts and texts. Ligeti may have believed that he doesn't 'belong anywhere', yet these texts are making the case that he does indeed 'belong everywhere' — and will continue to do so during his second century.

Wolfgang Marx
University College Dublin

Bibliography

BAUER 2011
BAUER, Amy. *Ligeti's Laments: Nostalgia, Exoticism, and the Absolute*, Farnham, Ashgate, 2011.

LOBANOVA 2002
LOBANOVA, Marina. *György Ligeti: Style Ideas, Poetics*, Berlin, Ernst Kuhn, 2002.

Ligeti's Music

Condensed Expression and Compositional Technique in György Ligeti's *Aventures* and Beyond

Benjamin R. Levy
(University of California, Santa Barbara)

György Ligeti's works *Aventures* and *Nouvelles Aventures* are complicated and at times almost self-contradictory pieces. The composer himself has referred to them as being, «concentrated and expressive — expressive and deep frozen»[1], and has described their structure as «semantically incomprehensible, yet in terms of affect, clearly understandable»[2]. The quick juxtapositions of contrasting material in these works can be alienating, shattering any continuity; yet the fragments that remain point tantalizingly towards a wider, yet unrealized context, hidden from the audience. In his description of these pieces, Richard Steinitz remarks on both the «profusion of detail» and also a level of abstraction in the «stylized behavior» of the characters, noting a curious effect of this apparent paradox: that the performers' «extravagant behavior seems all the more truthful because it is archetypical and has no location»[3]. And so these works are emotionally charged, yet distant and restrained; they are communicative but resist specific meaning. Moreover, these pieces speak to a full variety of human experiences, but present these experiences in a highly condensed and abstracted way — often as brief, stylized excerpts, which neither imply a clear chain of cause and effect nor establish a unified narrative viewpoint, but which nevertheless remain somehow dramatic and evocative. How, then, does Ligeti balance such conflicting ideals? And how might we, as listeners, begin to make sense of these compositions?

This paper draws on a study of the sketches, held at the Paul Sacher Foundation, to help elucidate the compositional method through which Ligeti developed rich and expressive

---

[1]. Ligeti 1983, p. 44.
[2]. Ligeti 2007, vol. II, p. 197. Translations are the author's unless otherwise noted.
[3]. Steinitz 2003, pp. 130-131.

musical categories, and then pared this material down in the events of the score, constraining explicit references to these types and ensuring this ultimate balance between familiarity and alienation — between representation and abstraction. Moreover, I argue that this was pivotal for Ligeti's development, because it was in these pieces that he first explored ideas to which he would return throughout his career. As such, I hope to show how these moments of condensed expression extend beyond the immediate context of the pieces in which they were developed and work as meaningful reference points for later compositions, in cases even imparting some of their expressive connotations to ostensibly abstract works.

Ligeti's sketches for these works are extensive and fascinating documents which allow for the reconstruction of the basic framework of his compositional approach[4]. As was typical for the composer, an early stage of the process involved the creation of five different layers of material, with each of these basic types containing multiple subtypes, as summarized in Table 1.

Table 1: Type-Layers and Subtypes Used in the Sketches

I.	Voiceless-Whispering Layer [hangtalan-suttogo réteg]	8 Subtypes
II.	Sparse Stationary Layer [ritka mozdulatlan réteg]	7 Subtypes
III.	Humorous/Erotic Layer [humoros/erotikus réteg]	9 Subtypes
IV.	«Speech»-Layer [«beszéd»-réteg]	11 Subtypes
V.	Expressive Layer [expresszív réteg]	7 Subtypes

The sketches for these subtypes include verbal descriptions — what Jonathan Bernard calls «jottings» — where the composer freely associates different musical and extra-musical ideas with these basic types[5]. These descriptions include frequent references to musical styles or genres (especially to the parts of a requiem and to operatic conventions, which are idiosyncratically mixed in these works), to literary or artistic works, and to everyday experiences, often connecting these to performance techniques. In two typewritten sketch pages, in particular, Ligeti assigns the basic material layers Roman numerals, and the subtypes receive lower-case letters and prose descriptions. At a later stage, however, he revised these letters into Arabic numerals, reordering subtypes within each layer. Throughout the extensive process of rearranging material, which included breaking up the original concept of the work into the finished versions of both *Aventures* and the second movement of *Nouvelles Aventures* and returning to finish the sequel after completing the Requiem, this system of Roman and Arabic numerals retained its importance, and is an important key to the expressive meaning of the work.

---

[4]. The sketches for these pieces are housed in the Music Manuscripts of the György Ligeti Collection of the Paul Sacher Foundation, Basel. Aspects of several of these sketches are discussed in Levy 2017, with a greater focus on the compositional technique of individual works but with less on their intertextual connections.

[5]. Bernard 2011.

Condensed Expression and Compositional Technique

A subsequent stage of composition involved an extended continuity sketch, mixing graphic and verbal elements and assembled from several sheets of paper, connected lengthwise, end to end. An excerpt from the continuity sketch is given below as Ill. 1. The pages are lain out like the score with information on the vocal parts towards the top, and for the instrumental forces towards the bottom, all moving chronologically from left to right with approximate timings in seconds underneath (although these, too, go through drastic distortions). The continuity sketch orders the material of the piece into different numbered sections and contains diagrams showing the contour of different musical gestures, or textures. The continuity sketch also contains references back to the Roman and Arabic numeral system, described above, and links the early verbal development of material types to the finished score of *Aventures* and the second part of *Nouvelles Aventures* with a high degree of correlation.

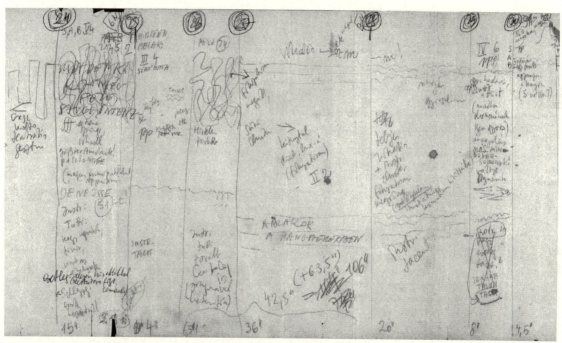

Ill. 1: Detail from the Continuity Sketch for *Aventures*, Material Segments 24-27, György Ligeti Collection, Paul Sacher Foundation, Basel. Reproduced with Permission.

Indeed, a significant portion of the final compositions — including *Aventures* and both movements of *Nouvelles Aventures* — are clearly derived from these verbal sketches and draw on this network of ideas for their dramatic effects. The beginning and ending of the work appear to be conceptually in place from this early stage of composition, fixing the dramatic arc of the work from the tentative «interjections» and «sighs» [III: interjections, Seufzer] of the opening to the desolate ending, «mute, but wanting to speak, struggling» [18: néma, de szolni kivan, erölködik]. Many of the titled segments, or set pieces, within the works are also sketched out in these pages. Most strikingly, however, the language found in these jottings is remarkably similar not only to the titles of these passages, but in many cases to particular expressive markings or performance directions given in the scores themselves. Examples in the following discussion will show these to be the starting point of Ligeti's processes of condensed expression: taking the rich world of associations plotted out verbally and incorporating it into the subtext of individual gestures, the associated compositional techniques, and the nuanced performative aspects of the score.

Condensed Expression in *Aventures* and *Nouvelles Aventures*

A few of the passages from *Aventures* and *Nouvelles Aventures* will demonstrate the abundant connections between verbal ideas in the sketches and their manifestations in the score. Some of the set pieces of *Aventures* and *Nouvelles Aventures* have specific subtitles that can be traced back to the sketches. In some cases, these connections occur through explicit reference to the system of Roman and Arabic numerals found in the continuity sketch, and in other cases through peculiar and specific language used in the descriptions and corresponding performance directions. The Allegro appassionato section of *Aventures* (bar 49ff.), for example, relates to subtype v4 in the sketch (see Table 2, below), and the interruption, «La Serenata» (bars 56-57), relates to subtype III4. These can both be seen explicitly in the part of the continuity sketch excerpted above in Ill. 1, along the top of the page in material segments 24 and 25.

Table 2: Subtypes v4 and III4

Subtype v4

passionnée, extreme Sprünge, Exaltation, nagy szenvedélyek – tutti, tömör, sok különféle mozgas egyszerre, kitöltve
passionate, extreme leaps, exaltation, great passions – tutti, concise, many different directions at the same time, filling in

Subtype III4

serenata, pleng-pleng-plang (elöbb becsukott szajjal szavak) – dimm-bimm-binng, tkt-frf-bmb – nyelvpengetés, pzzi, peng-BLENG – sotto voce
serenata, pleng-pleng-plang (with the mouth closed before the words) – dimm-bimm-binng, tkt-frf-bmb – tongue plucking, pizzicato, peng-BLENG – sotto voce

The voice parts of the Allegro appassionato consist of large leaps in alternating directions and is a type of texture that Ligeti reuses explicitly in the Sequentia (Dies irae) movement of the Requiem[6]. The expressive marking, «con tutta la forza – exaggerating, as if possessed»[7], and the *ffff (possibile)* dynamic make clear the emotional charge of these gestures, and perhaps suggest the dramatic ensemble finales of an opera. Additionally, a technical feature helps explain the idea of «filling in» mentioned in the sketch. The leaps create pairs of clusters voiced in different registers, for instance, in Ex. 1, the upper notes of the soprano initially fill out a cluster from $A\flat 5$ to $E\flat 6$ and her lower notes form another cluster two octaves lower. Moreover, the instruments pick out notes from the voice parts (for example, the flute uses the upper notes of both the soprano and alto, combining them into a different compound line) adding to the sense of «filling out» chromatic regions through these exaggerated leaps.

Ex. 1: Vocal Pitches, *Aventures*, Allegro appassionato, bars 49 and 51-53.

The passage marked «La Serenata» in bars 56-57 also follows the sketch's wording in both performance directions (*sotto voce, quasi pizz.*) and in many of the syllables for the vocal line. The vowels are all marked as nasal, and along with the humming *m* and *ng* sounds, involve closing the mouth as indicated in the sketch, while the accented harder consonants, glissandi, and quasi-pizzicato markings help convey the sense of a plucked instrument that could accompany a serenade — in Ligeti's retrospective libretto to the works[8], he strengthens this connection and grounds it in a specific operatic context, by having the baritone dress, at times, as Don Giovanni. There is already a sense of ironic distance from having the vocalists mimic instrumental sounds, but this is heightened further by the abrupt contrast from the previous texture, and set within this fragmentary context, the expressive point of reference is put through an additional level of remove.

---

[6]. Ligeti's sketches for the Dies irae specifically reference this section of *Aventures*. See LEVY 2013.

[7]. «con tutta la forza – übertreibend, ausser sich», following Cardew's translation in the supplement to the score.

[8]. See LIGETI 2007, vol. II., pp. 201-225.

Many of jottings for the subtypes in Layer II carry associations from the requiem mass, and in this regard, it is significant to remember that Ligeti was working on his Requiem just after *Aventures* and alongside the composition of *Nouvelles Aventures*, as this suggests a level of associative and intertextual connection. The typical movements of the Requiem appear in descriptions of Subtypes 112 (lux perpetua), 113 (benedictus, Agnus), 114 (Gloria), 115 (requiem), and 117 (dies irae). Several of these appear in the transition out of the Allegro appassionato and in the following passages, shifting the underlying referential frame from the operatic world to that of the requiem. The continuity sketch shows the dense cluster of the Allegro appassionato clearing up and continuing or flowing into the material of 112, marked with reference to the «lux» idea and diatonicism, above «windows» of rest in the instruments (see Ill. 1, above, text in segment 27 reading «sűrű cluster → kitisztul / diat. lux-á / (folyatosan[?]) / 112 / ablakok a hangszerokben»). This shift towards lightness is marked in the score at bar 65, where the instruments briefly drop out and return, with dolce, legato lines and leaps that become less extreme and angular — the initial flute line — D, E, C, F♯, B, A — even hints at a diatonic collection (as do moments of Ligeti's own *Lux Aeterna*), although the larger context remains highly chromatic. While this might be a slight difference at first, it initiates a narrowing of the cluster, a slowing and lightening of the texture that lasts until bar 89 and fits with the associations of the sketch. Moreover, this subtle shift sets up a more dramatic contrast between two other requiem-associated subtypes.

After some intervening material, Ligeti returns to subtypes from the same layer, hinting further at their underlying associations[9]. The «Gloria» of 114 is realized in bars 99-103, where, as suggested by the «cones» of the sketch description (see Table 3), the singers use megaphones in a kind of proclamation — a loud sustained chord in the high register. This is immediately followed by the «Requiem» of 115, an echo which receives the marking «solemne, funebre» as the alto and baritone shift to their lower registers and the harpsichord, piano, and double bass sustain a low cluster as the voices die out. The movements of Ligeti's own Requiem make use of registral contrasts associated with a progression from darkness into light, and while the breadth of the imagery described in the sketch does not fully come through in such a brief pair of gestures, there is certainly something striking about this contrast as conceived and presented that gives this a crushing weight, if not the extended symbolic associations with a Requiem[10]. Most of all, though, this stripped-down presentation — each event a single chord — is at the heart of Ligeti's technique of condensed expression: retaining enough of the original expressive content so as to remain suggestive, but remaining on the edge of intelligibility, not venturing into overtly semiotic meaning.

---

[9]. The intervening material is discussed in Levy 2017.

[10]. The registral associations of light and dark are present in many of Ligeti's works and sketches, see Salmenhaara 1969.

Condensed Expression and Compositional Technique

Table 3: Subtypes II2, II4 and II5

Subtype II2

visszafojtott, misztikus, fenséges, belsö fény, arado vilagossag, lux perpetua
restrained, mystical, sublime, inward light, radiating [áradó] brightness, lux perpetua

Subtype II4

kiherdetés, Vasari kikialtas (tölcsérek, csövek – filtr.), Gloria, reggel
proclamation, Market cries (funnels, tubes – filtering), Gloria, morning

Subtype II5

funebre: mély, vonszolt, komoly, mély regiszter, requiem, mély nyugvopont
funebre: deep, lugubrious, grave, deep register, requiem, deep resting point

Although the first movement of *Nouvelles Aventures* was composed later, there are some indications that the layers and subtypes inform it as well. For example, the first movement's *Hoquetus* (bar 28) has precedent in some of the wording of subtypes IV9 and V5. More direct connections, however, exist in the second movement of the work, which continues the continuity sketch and sequence of material segments of *Aventures*. For example, wording for the soprano's «Grand Hysterical Scene» first occurs in handwritten annotations to subtype V5, and the continuity sketch associates this passage with subtype V7 as well. Indeed, many of the ideas in these two subtypes (Table 4) bleed together. Extending through several interruptions, it lasts from bar 8 to bar 28 of the second movement, and it is easy to read this as a climactic, quasi-operatic mad scene, where the soprano, as if possessed, transcends her earlier dramatic and impassioned singing styles, crossing over into shrieks, cries, convulsions, and the sounds of unbridled emotions[11].

Table 4: Subtypes V5 and V7

Subtype V5

exaltalt, ideges hoquetus – dramatikus – dialogusok-örült – jeu extatique – benne hisztérikus koloraturak, igen rikacsolo, gonosz madarak, ördögi hoquetus
ördögi haha – komplex ritmuseloszlas többrétegben (alretegek) – konvulziv, nem akarja abbahagyni (NB: ostinato elmosasa több réteg altal) – ez a darab egyik dramai csucspontja) – esetleg konvulzivba tartott hangok is – extreme Sprünge – grotesque? – atkozodasok

---

[11]. Ligeti had considerable knowledge of the operatic repertoire, and the kind of parody found in *Nouvelles Aventures* is similar to that discussed in Everett 2009 in relation to *Le Grand Macabre* and Donizetti's mad scenes.

exalted[?] nervous hoquetus - dramatic – dialogues-pleased – ecstatic play – internally hysterical coloratura, quite screeching, evil birds, diabolical hoquetus
diabolical haha – complex multilayered rhythmic dispersion (sublayers) – convulsive, not wanting to stop (NB: ostinato blurred by other layers) – this is one of the dramatic climaxes of the piece) – perhaps sounds sustained in convulsions– extreme leaps – grotesque? – cursing

Subtype v7

gatlastalan, teljes attörés, szabadjara engedva, stilizalt orditasok, egyben (tömör) panic, rémület, szenvedélyes irtozat, kiabalnak, vonitanak, visitanak, sirnak, hörögnek, – szadista exerciroztatas – feszes – rakiabalas
uninhibited, completely breaking through, letting loose, stylized shouting, in a (compact) panic, terror, vehement horror, crying out, howling, shrieking, weeping, fuming – sadistic exercises[?] – strict – yelling

The two main interruptions to the «Grand Hysterical Scene» can also be traced definitively to the sketches. The first is the untitled passage in bar 14, which changes character decisively, switching to the baritone and alto, in unpitched repeated syllables in slightly conflicting rhythms, but with the same text. The continuity sketch relates this passage to subtype iv9, a kind of litany or recitation (Table 5). The second interruption is labeled as a chorale (bars 19-21). Although not identified with a subtype in the continuity sketch, it is labeled «koral» and relates back to Subtype i16. *Nouvelles Aventures*, then, continues this characteristic mixture of operatic and sacred genres through fragmented and discontinuous moments, briefly familiar modes of expression, which are never allowed to develop and never seem entirely in place.

Table 5: Subtypes iv9 and i16

Subtype iv9

szavalo-felolvaso, litaniazo – mindeghik énekes sajt egy hangjan ~~harom~~ *két* különbözö hang), rétegek, attört technika, - mindegyik énekes kissé mas jellegben, tempoval – mindenki megtartja jellegét és tempojat (kb.) *(ritka hoquetus?)*
recitation-reading aloud, giving a litany – each singer has a line of ~~three~~ *two* different tones), layers, penetrated technique – each singer a little different in character and tempo – everyone maintains their character and tempo (approx.) *(sparse hoquetus?)*

Subtype i16

koral – koralvariaciok
chorale – chorale variations

Condensed Expression and Compositional Technique

*Recurring Motifs and Musical Meaning:
The Demonic Clocks and Panicked Chase*

The remainder of the paper will be devoted to two passages that have particularly rich and wide-ranging associations. Both passages come from *Nouvelles Aventures* but have significance beyond the pieces themselves, expanding the network of intertextual relationships past the immediate works, or the contemporaneous Requiem, and into more diverse contexts through the later decades of his career. This kind of intertextuality has been noted with regard to the *lamento* motif, where Ligeti draws on an established musical topic[12]. Here, I argue that Ligeti's own more idiosyncratic musical references can work in similar ways, and, if we sensitize ourselves to their presence, can help us make sense of some of the discontinuous moments of Ligeti's later works. In fact, scholars such as Carolyn Abbate and Byron Almén have suggested that musical rifts and disruptions are critical to achieving a broad sense of narrative in music, and Ligeti's use of abrupt changes, frequently in connection with specific musical materials, opens the door to meaningful interpretations in similar ways[13]. In particular, the techniques and musical characters employed in the following examples become recurring motifs in Ligeti's works, lending their content to other pieces, including later instrumental works, where these expressive connotations might not be obvious.

The «Horloges Démoniaques» section of *Nouvelles Aventures* (Ex. 2, p. 12) is a passage often mentioned in the literature because of its connection to the stories of Gyula Krúdy — in particular a story Ligeti remembers as featuring a widow living in a house surrounded by irregular ticking sounds of clocks and other old machinery, and which he cites as inspiration for his meccanico style[14]. This material is found in sketches for the original conception of *Aventures* as material segment 54, which draws on subtype IV3 (Table 6), and further pages of sketches are devoted to working out its construction in detail. In these sketches Ligeti pays particular attention to balancing two types of rhythmic parameters. First, he tracks the strings of repeated notes (i.e. the number of repeated notes before a singer changes pitch and syllable). Values between one and five are used an approximately equal number of times; single notes and strings of four notes are used eight times each and all other values are used seven times each[15]. The second rhythmic parameter monitored in these sketches has to do with the rhythmic

---

[12]. On this kind of topical analysis, see Ratner 1980, Allanbrook 1983, Agawu 1991, or more recently Mirka 2014 and Frymoyer 2017. On Ligeti's use of the *lamento* motif in particular, see Steinitz 1996 and on the lament more generally, Bauer 2011.

[13]. Abbate 1991; Almén 2003.

[14]. See Ligeti 1983, p. 17; for more on Krúdy's importance and the sense of dissolution or disruption in his style, see Lukacs 1990, pp. 160-161, Frigyesi 1998, p. 110, and George Szirtes's introduction to Krúdy 1998.

[15]. Following the sketch, this calculation connects the last three notes of the soprano in bar 32 to the first two notes of bar 34, together as the value 5, even though it is split by the grand pause in bar 33.

Ex. 2: *Nouvelles Aventures*, movement II, bars 31-35. Reproduced by kind permission of Peters Edition Ltd., London.

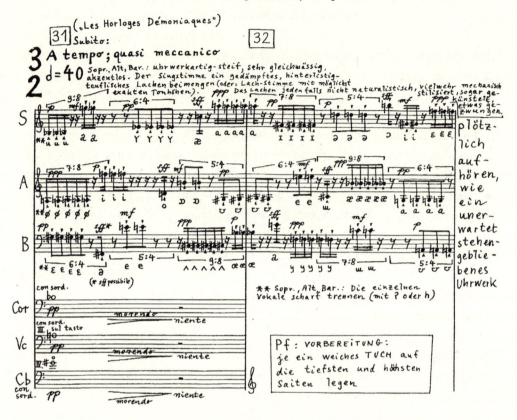

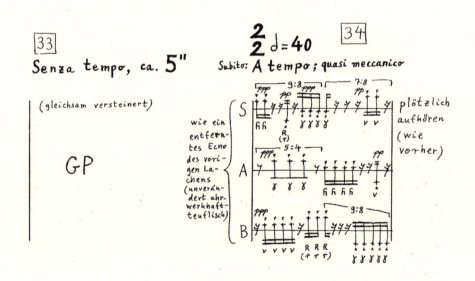

subdivisions used in successive beats — here Ligeti roughly balances all of the divisions between quintuplets and nonuplets, using each between four and six times. For both parameters, Ligeti avoids repeating the same value within a voice on successive beats. This focus on changing values (both of the strings of notes and the speeds of subdivisions) ensures a level of unpredictability and thus results in the ironic subversion of the normal function of a clock — a consistent feature of the way this technique is used in later compositions. Another feature of the sketch is the idea of «voice removal» — a significant handwritten addition in the margins of the sketch. In the passage, when the voices return after the general pause, they have moved from pitched to unpitched material and from vowel sounds to breathy or noisy, consonant sounds. This kind of interruption, and return to abruptly transformed material is typical the use of «demonic clocks» material in later pieces, and forms a parallel with the extra-musical basis for this topic.

Table 6: Subtype iv3

Subtype iv3

makogas – stacc – rész: b,p,k,t, stb. – gonosz órák *Stimm-elvonás?*
gibbering-staccato-section: b,p,k,t – evil clocks *voice removal?*

Malfunctioning clocks and transfigured reappearances both have precedent in Krúdy's *The Adventures of Sindbad*. Temporal order in these stories is deliberately confused through a combination of actions, dreams, and reminiscences and the free flow between life and afterlife, and clocks are often a symbol for the nearness of death or the loosening of temporal structure through dreams or the supernatural. For example, in one striking passage, Krúdy's narrative backtracks to announce: «It was at this time, one autumn night... when clocks that no one could remember working began to move their hands, and when doors on unoccupied floors of occupied houses started creaking as if in pain because someone behind them dared not cross the threshold — it was then that Sindbad rose from the dead»[16]. Moreover, the characters in these stories often disappear and reappear in changed ways, for example when Sindbad the ghost recalls a youthful love affair and then visits the same woman, now in her old age, and correspondingly when she beholds him as a ghostly apparition. This kind of transfigured reappearance is an often-overlooked feature of the clocklike passages in Ligeti's music, and it carries a kind of uncanny expressive force, drawing on the content of these novels and imparting it to the musical material through the mimetic imitation of disorderly clock sounds, their interruption, and sudden, transformed reappearance.

While this section of *Nouvelles Aventures* is the most direct expression of this type, it is not the earliest. References to «demonic clocks» go back at least as far as the prose sketches for the

---

[16]. Krúdy 1998, p. 81.

unfinished *Variations concertantes* (1956), and the prehistory of the idea also includes *Poème symphonique*, the work for 100 metronomes from 1962. The demonic clocks motif occurs in the earlier *Aventures* as well, embedded into the «Conversation» section (bars 38-46). In the «Conversation», the material types are shared by all the voices and are derived from mixing various subtypes together. Rather than using these subtypes directly, Ligeti extracted features from them and reorganized them into five new categories, which he assigned letters from A-E, and then developed additional subtypes, now described as «characters» and labeled with Arabic numerals. This new organizational system can be traced into the score through consistent performance directions; in Ex 3, for instance, E10 is always delivered with a pinched nose as a «derisive-caustic remark» [spöttisch-gallbittere Bemerkung] and D3, developed from the demonic-clocks idea, always reads, «stiff like clockwork, indifferently» [uhrwerkartig-steif, teilnahmlos].

This passage was developed in the sketches as a «Polyphonic Trio» [Polifon Trio], and Ligeti has also compared it to a Bach Invention[17]. Here the construction of the music, revealed by the sketches, references Bach's imitative polyphony, even while the subtitle in the score and aspects of the material suggest a context closer to spoken language. Each voice uses the entire string of characters only once, but in a different order, so the three-part invention is not exact, however moments of imitation do occur, including all three voices using D1 at the beginning, and imitation between D3 and E10 at the end (see Ex. 3, bars 44-45, p. 15). This passage, then, demonstrates another type of intertextuality — referring to baroque imitative polyphony on the one hand, while also suggesting the back and forth of a conversation between the various subtypes that have been deployed elsewhere in the piece. This is, perhaps, the most elaborately worked-out example in these pieces, using multiple subtypes and drawing connections to diverse associative contexts, both inside and outside the piece, exemplifying the richness of Ligeti's method of condensed expression[18].

Once Ligeti has developed the features of the demonic-clocks motif, he reuses them freely in later works. Ligeti has compared his Cello Concerto (1966) to *Aventures*[19], and so perhaps it is not surprising that it is the first purely instrumental work to incorporate the topic in this form. Towards the end of the Concerto's second movement (bars 57-66), Ligeti begins to alternate between passages marked «mechanisch-präzis» that reflect the demonic-clocks motif with its polyphony of repeated notes moving at conflicting speeds, and passages of contrasting material constructed through different techniques. Like its use in *Aventures*, after each episode

---

[17]. LIGETI 1983, p. 45.

[18]. It is likely that other sections of *Aventures* (e.g. *Action dramatique*, bars 108-13) and *Nouvelles Aventures* (e.g. movement I, bars 30-39), which feature a mixture of recurring expression markings, were composed in a similar manner, but there is less in the sketch records to help reconstruct the process.

[19]. See, for example, LIGETI 2007, vol. II, p. 244.

CONDENSED EXPRESSION AND COMPOSITIONAL TECHNIQUE

Ex. 3: *Aventures*, «Conversation», bars 44-46, annotated. Reproduced by kind permission of Peters Edition Ltd., London.

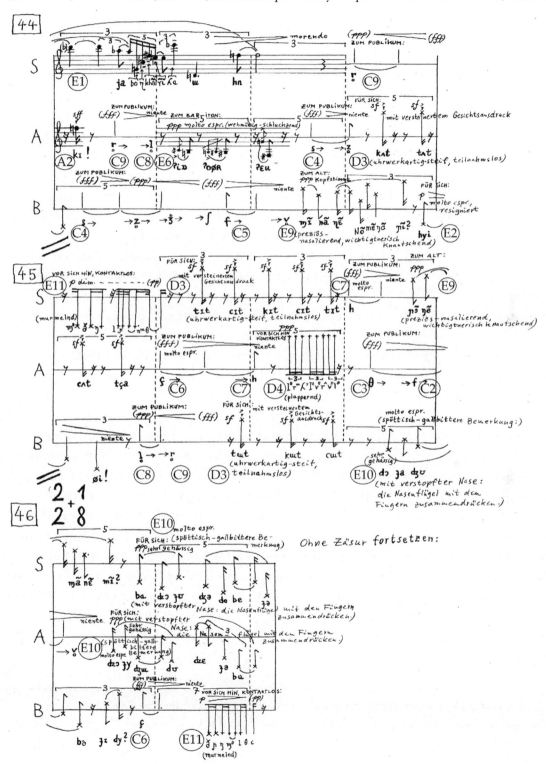

of contrasting material, the reentrance of the clocks motif is altered: different lengths, changed pitch content, orchestration, and articulations.

This legacy of reuse continues through the end of the 1960s, in the third movements of the String Quartet no. 2 (1968) and the Chamber Concerto (1969), and in *Ramifications* (1969-1970). In the former two works, the clocks idea forms the bulk of a movement through streams of repeated notes that change in speed and orchestration, veering into different degrees of temporal disorder. In *Ramifications*, however, it occurs only at the very end of the movement, almost completely unprepared (bars 110-114), giving way just as abruptly to the final measures of silence. After the majority of the piece uses net-structures and directionally clear pattern-meccanico figures[20], the sudden appearance of the clocks motif is startling, but perhaps the expressive effect established in *Aventures* can help us make some sense of this confounding ending. The unsettling arrival of irregular clock sounds signals that temporal order has been put out of place, and perhaps in an even more ominous sense — in keeping with the grim humor found in Krúdy — that time has run out on the piece. Finally, the meaning of the clocks motif is brought back into the realm of dramatic music with the opera, *Le Grand Macabre*, where it appears at Rehearsal #57, in the form of a metronome, later intensified and distorted by the different forces of the orchestra. Here it accompanies Nekrotzar's pronouncement that the world will end at midnight; since this event never comes to pass, the use of the motif here carries the same connotations of the unreliability of time and the nearness of death — the same sentiments that might be sensed implicitly in instrumental examples like *Ramifications*, are once again made explicit through the libretto of the opera.

Returning to *Nouvelles Aventures*, the passage immediately following «Horloges Démoniaques» has similarly wide-ranging implications for Ligeti's later compositions. This passage does not have a subtitle in the score, but the sketches link it to subtype v6 (Table 7) and the idea of a «chase». Perhaps because it is not verbally identified in the score, it has received less commentary compared to the demonic clocks, but this type of melody is also reused frequently in his later works. In the melodic construction of this passage (shown in Ex. 4a), each instrumental part voices a chromatic hexachord, through quiet running figures in lockstep rhythms and parallel semitones, spread across multiple octaves — realizing many features described in the sketch. Ligeti carefully designed the basic pattern to avoid repeated pitch successions, so that, for example, if F goes to F♯ first, Ligeti will not use that succession again until all of the other possibilities have been exhausted. In his sketches he often tracks this with semicircular, fan-shaped diagrams, which I have reconstructed in Ex. 4b.

---

[20]. CLENDINNING 1993 and ROIG-FRANCOLÍ 1995 both discuss this aspect of Ligeti's compositional style. The well-known pattern-meccanico technique also has connotations of malfunctioning machinery. However, the construction differs from the specifically clocklike material I am discussing here, and, I contend, its meaning is shaded differently.

Condensed Expression and Compositional Technique

Table 7: Subtype v6

Subtype v6

panic, rémület , hajsza (de halk) – sokoktavas orgonaszerü felrakas, **pppp** possible, tutti, gyorsan mozog – ének is néha harom oktavaban bele
panic, terror, chase (but quiet) – many octaves, stacked up like an organ, **pppp** possibile, tutti, quickly moving – singers also sometimes in three octaves

Ex. 4a: *Nouvelles Aventures* II, bars 36-39. Reproduced by kind permission of Peters Edition Ltd., London.

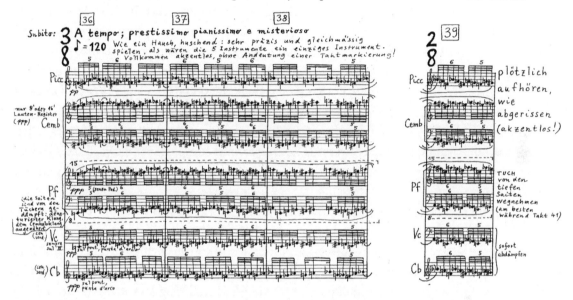

Ex. 4b: Pitch-Succession Chart for the first 30 notes of the Piccolo Melody.

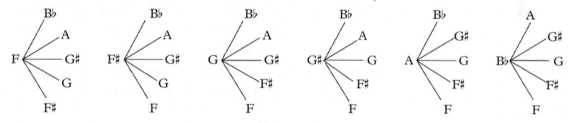

While this idea is less directly mimetic than the demonic clocks, there are still ways in which its construction is an effective analog and fitting representation of the imagery associated with a panicked chase[21]. There is the speed of presentation, but also the tension generated

---

[21]. Observations on analogy, conceptual blending, and cross-domain mapping in ZBIKOWSKI 2017 reinforce the cognitive basis for this kind of musical analogy.

by semitone clusters spread to wide registers, and most of all, the restlessness of the pitch successions, arranged for minimal repetition and creating a sense of disorientation: never settling into motivic patterns or establishing memorable melodic landmarks. These speak to the idea of a chase, and especially to the accompanying panic, confusion, and terror of being lost. Moreover, in the dramatic action of the piece, the singers begin a process of freezing «as if turned to stone» and returning to exaggerated gestures and excessive motions, alternating between these two states from here to the end of the piece, emphasizing internal racing of the mind as much as the physical chase.

There is also a literary connection enriching the imagery of this kind of frantic chase, this time coming from Franz Kafka rather than Krúdy. Ligeti's sketches for *Ramifications* reference «Brunelda in the car, the police perusing Karl Rossmann», [Brunelda a kocsiban, Karl Rossmannt üldözik a rendörök] thus linking the idea to a scene from Kafka's *Amerika*. The passage in question sets up a paradoxical geography, where Rossmann, fleeing the police by running down the straight main road, not knowing where the side streets might lead, is somehow overtaken by his acquaintance, Delemarche, who has taken a longer and more circuitous route. Delemarche then leads Rossmann back to Brunelda's apartment (and his earlier predicament), through a winding series of inner courtyards, staircases, and complex passageways. This literary context also suggests a connection to another pervasive image in Ligeti's musical thought: that of the labyrinth.

In another scene from the same novel, centering on the desperation of Theresa — one of the few sympathetic characters Rossmann encounters — shortly before her mother's death; Kafka describes the streets of the city as long and straight, and contrasts this with the labyrinthine interiors: «the corridors of these tenements were cunningly contrived to save space, but not to make it easy to find one's way about; likely enough they had trailed again and again through the same corridor»[22]. The result is that they lose track of which buildings they have been to, possibly even revisiting the same ones again and again. Here, the divorce between interior and exterior terrain becomes a metaphor for a psychological state: inner thoughts restlessly darting back and forth, but losing any sense of greater purpose or outward direction. This is aptly captured in Ligeti's musical construction by the constant and rapid changes of direction, never repeating the same succession, yet somehow always remaining trapped aimlessly but frantically within the same cluster.

Like the demonic clocks, this musical motif is reused extensively in later pieces — diverging slightly from the original construction and branching out into closely related effects and new shades of its original meaning. Ex. 5 provides instances of the reuse of this type of material in several of Ligeti's works. Again, the first reuse comes in the second movement of the Cello Concerto, where these types of melodies first occur at letter K (Ex. 5a, bar 41). Parallel

---

[22]. KAFKA 1996, p. 155.

CONDENSED EXPRESSION AND COMPOSITIONAL TECHNIQUE

Ex. 5: Pitch-Succession Melodies in Later Works.

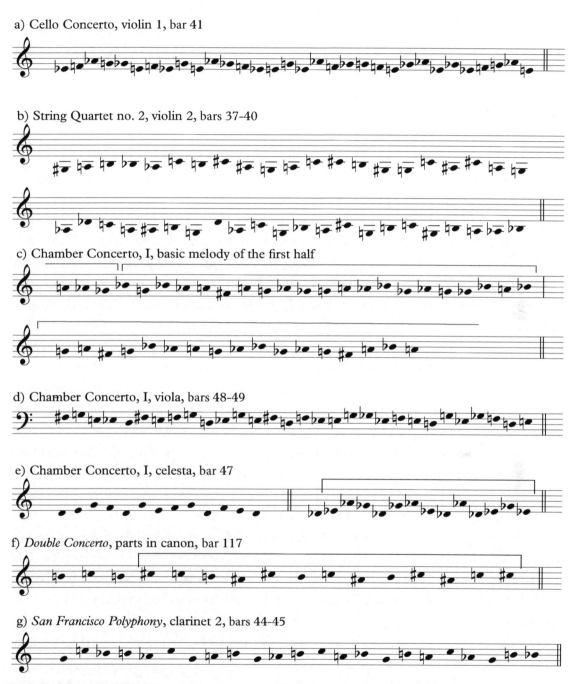

melodies begin on C♯, D, and E♭ and are doubled in octaves by various instruments. Here the pitch-succession property is handled in a slightly looser way — the melody on E♭, for instance, allows two repetitions and omits one succession over the first 32 notes.

In the String Quartet no. 2, the chase motif occurs in the fourth movement (bars 37-40), as an intervening passage between the *presto-furioso* accented chords, and the quiet, sustained signal harmonies, which make up the bulk of the movement. Here the melodies are similar but not in parallel, the rhythmic lockstep is changed to conflicting triplets and sixteenths, and the dynamic level is fortissimo rather than pianissimo. The melodic construction, however, is the same (violin 2, shown in Ex. 5b has only one repetition and one omission), as is its role in the movement as a whole, as a brief, frenzied outburst, but one which is fated to return to the previous material.

The first movement of the Chamber Concerto develops this type of melodic construction in new ways. The opening of the piece uses an intertwined melody expressing a cluster from F♯ to B♭. Here the instruments enter simultaneously, but on successive notes of the basic melody, creating a micropolyphonic canon, in keeping with the sense of a chase or pursuit; the bass clarinet starts on the first note, cello on the second, flute on the third, and clarinet on the fourth. From the fourth note to the 24th (see Ex. 5c) the melody creates a complete cycle of unrepeated pitch successions. The notes from 24 to 41 also contain no repeated pitch successions, and, if taken with the introductory notes, 1-4, they complete another exact cycle of all possible successions.

The melodies that begin the second half of the movement apply the same concept to different kinds of clusters. The strings use a chromatic cluster from D to G, while the celesta takes interlocking diatonic and pentatonic clusters in the same range (Ex. 5d-e). Each of these clusters, whether chromatic, diatonic, or pentatonic, is articulated through a pitch-succession melody, although as the piece goes on these melodies themselves are subjected to variations, shifts, and internal retrogrades[23]. While the slower canonic presentation in this movement is a more dreamlike kind of disorientation, the effect is closely related, and we might consider that the expression marking of this movement — *corrente*, literally 'flowing' or 'running' — could even be a vestige of the original connotations of this technique.

Following the developments of the Chamber Concerto, several works from later in Ligeti's career continue the expansion of this technique, often integrated into more involved orchestral textures and less strictly applied, but still maintaining the connection between this kind of melody and the expressive associations of disorientation and bewilderment. The canon toward the end of the Double Concerto (Ex. 5f), after an initial neighboring figure, uses a complete pitch-succession melody on the cluster from A♯ to C♯, before allowing this cluster to expand and spiral out into increasing disorder.

---

[23]. CLENDINNING 1989 discusses some of these internal retrogrades and variations of these melodies in her analysis of this movement.

The consistent connotations of this type of melody are clearest, however, in *San Francisco Polyphony*. Ligeti has described this work as having been inspired by the confounding landscapes of the city, where straight streets were forged through impossibly steep hillsides, where the architecture and varied neighborhoods hint at fragments of the city's history, and the comings and goings of the fog cast things into and out of obscurity in unpredictable ways — while Kafkaesque terror may be replaced by wonder and exhilaration, the image of being lost and racing through a city of impossible topographies remains the same. As such, it is not surprising that in portraying the city, the composer would draw on his previous experiments toward this end. Ligeti has suggested that the density of the opening suggests the city's fog, from which individual melodies may momentarily emerge[24]. As the opening cluster begins to narrow, and the lines come into clearer focus just before the molto sostenuto section at letter K (bar 46), the accelerating instrumental lines use the same basic properties of pitch-succession melodies. Imbedded in a texture of similar melodies, Ligeti is not as strict as with the original applications of the technique, although he is still clearly guided by the same principles; for example, the melody excerpted in Ex. 5g omits 5 possible successions, but shows only one repetition (G-B). Melodies such as these stand in stark contrast to moments later in the work, where incessantly repeated pattern-meccanico figures are presented in strictly regular directions are reminiscent of minimalism and help depict other facets of the city, especially its modern and industrialized side.

Even in the first movement of the Violin Concerto, decades after *Aventures*, melodies rooted in this basic principle can be found, contributing their effects as part of Ligeti's late style. The diatonic melody in the violins at letter F (also marked by the accented notes of the piccolos, with other instruments in parallel fifths), shown in Ex. 6a (p. 22), uses a Machaut-influenced technique: a melodic *color* of 17 notes and rhythmic *talea* of 7 units (the unequal beats of the bar), to create the interplay of two non-coinciding patterns[25]. While this guarantees a degree of varied repetition, the construction of the melody itself will add another dimension. When examined in light of the previous analyses, we find that the basic ostinato melody contains no repeated pitch successions through its first statement. Here, however, Ligeti has added an additional constraint: only the pitch-successions using perfect fourths or fifths and major seconds are used, all other successions are avoided. Given this constraint, the melody uses 17 of the 22 available successions (Ex. 6b, p. 22).

In the Violin Concerto, Ligeti was aiming for an amalgamation of different influences and reference points, some decidedly modernist and others alluding to more traditional sources.

---

[24]. LIGETI 1983, pp. 66-67.
[25]. For more on the use of repeated patterns of different lengths in Ligeti's later music, see BAKKER 2013.

Ex. 6a: Ostinato Melody, Violin Concerto, movement 1, bars 34-38.

Ex. 6b: Pitch-Succession Chart for the Ostinato Melody.

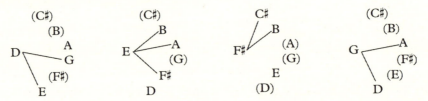

Condensed Expression and Compositional Technique

Many of the features of this passage suggest folkloristic materials: diatonic collections, common melodic intervals, a limited range, and instruments moving in parallel fifths. The asymmetrical meter of 2s and 3s evokes the Balkan and African rhythmic patterns that had long been a source of fascination for Ligeti, as well. But Ligeti was also wary of quoting or referencing traditional musics too directly, and sometimes struggled with this balance[26]. The use of modified pitch-succession melodies may have helped him avoid falling into more direct imitation. Countering these more familiar pitch collections, are the disorienting directional changes and lack of repeated pitch successions, which keep these melodies elusive and intangible. The defamiliarizing effect of these melodies, then, contributes to the sense of balance between recognizable and ungraspable elements that was a crucial feature of Ligeti's late style, just as much as it was for the semantically charged, yet unlocatable world of *Aventures*.

Conclusion

As should be clear from the examples above, the materials developed in sketches for *Aventures* and *Nouvelles Aventures* formed a stockpile of ideas, only part of which were realized in the pieces themselves. Ligeti often worked out the material for these subtypes with great care and meticulous attention to detail. However, in their first musical expressions they are often fragmentary, suppressed to a few brief measures, and surrounded with contrasting material. In their original context, Ligeti achieved a certain power by charging these moments with more significance than their often-brief appearances allow them to express. What is more striking, however, is that Ligeti continued to use this repository of techniques and dramatic effects throughout the following decades, shifting this internal system of veiled references and hidden meanings into a source of broader intertextual connections between disparate pieces. Alongside the more familiar *lamento* motif and pattern-meccanico textures, the musical ideas from these works return across decades of Ligeti's oeuvre, helping imbue meaning to some of the disjunctures found in his works and contextualizing some of the pathos, irony, and humor that can be felt in his music. Ligeti's system of condensed expression allowed him to walk a fine line between abstraction and signification in these individual works, but it is also central to another seeming paradox: from the examination of these fragmentary and incomplete moments, a continuous line begins to emerge across many of Ligeti's compositions.

---

[26]. SCHERZINGER 2006 discusses Ligeti's association with types of African music in greater depth; KERÉKFY 2013 examines the quotations of folk music that were present in the original, discarded first movement of Ligeti's Violin Concerto.

Bibliography

Abbate 1991
Abbate, Carolyn. *Unsung Voices: Opera and Musical Narrative in the Nineteenth Century*, Princeton, Princeton University Press, 1991.

Agawu 1991
Agawu, V. Kofi. *Playing with Signs: A Semiotic Interpretation of Classic Music*, Princeton, Princeton University Press, 1991.

Allanbrook 1983
Allanbrook, Wye Jamison. *Rhythmic Gesture in Mozart: «Le Nozze di Figaro» and «Don Giovanni»*, Chicago, University of Chicago Press, 1983.

Almén 2003
Almén, Byron. 'Narrative Archetypes: A Critique, Theory, and Method of Narrative Analysis', in: *Journal of Music Theory*, XLVII/1 (Spring 2003), pp. 1-39.

Bakker 2013
Bakker, Sara. *Playing with Patterns: Isorhythmic Strategies in György Ligeti's Late Piano Works*, unpublished Ph.D. Diss., Bloomington (IN), Indiana University Press, 2013.

Bauer 2011
Bauer, Amy. *Ligeti's Laments: Nostalgia, Exoticism, and the Absolute*, Farnham, Ashgate, 2011.

Bernard 2011
Bernard, Jonathan W. 'Rules and Regulation: Lessons from Ligeti's Compositional Sketches', in: *György Ligeti: Of Foreign Lands and Strange Sounds*, edited by Louise Duchesneau and Wolfgang Marx, Woodbridge, Boydell Press, 2011, pp. 149-167.

Clendinning 1989
Clendinning, Jane Piper. *Contrapuntal Techniques in the Music of György Ligeti*, unpublished Ph.D. Diss., New Haven (CT), Yale University, 1989.

Clendinning 1993
Ead. 'The Pattern-Meccanico Compositions of György Ligeti', in: *Perspectives of New Music*, XXXI/1 (Winter 1993), pp. 192-234.

Everett 2009
Everett, Yayoi Uno. 'Signification of Parody and the Grotesque in György Ligeti's *Le Grand Macabre*', in: *Music Theory Spectrum*, XXXI/1 (Spring 2009), pp. 26-56.

Frigyesi 1998
Frigyesi, Judit. *Béla Bartók and Turn-of-the-Century Budapest*, Berkeley (CA), University of California Press, 1998.

FRYMOYER 2017
FRYMOYER, Johanna. 'The Musical Topic in the Twentieth Century: A Case Study of Schoenberg's Ironic Waltzes', in: *Music Theory Spectrum*, XXXIX/1 (Spring 2017), pp. 83-108.

KAFKA 1996
KAFKA, Franz. *Amerika*, translated by Willa and Edwin Muir, New York, Schocken Books, 1996.

KERÉKFY 2013
KERÉKFY, Márton. 'A Folkloric Collage Jettisoned: The Original First Movement of György Ligeti's Violin Concerto (1990)', in: *Mitteilungen der Paul Sacher Stiftung*, no. 26 (April 2013), pp. 39-45.

KRÚDY 1998
KRÚDY, Gyula. *The Adventures of Sindbad*, edited and translated by George Szirtes, New York, Central European University Press, 1998.

LEVY 2013
LEVY, Benjamin R. '"Rules as Strict as Palestrina's": The Regulation of Pitch and Rhythm in Ligeti's Requiem and *Lux Aeterna*', in: *Twentieth-Century Music*, X/2 (2013), pp. 203-230.

LEVY 2017
ID. *Metamorphosis in Music: The Compositions of György Ligeti in the 1950s and 1960s*, Oxford-New York, Oxford University Press, 2017.

LIGETI 1983
György Ligeti in Conversation with Péter Várnai, Josef Häusler, Claude Samuel, and Himself, translated by Gabor J. Schabert, Sarah E. Soulsby, Terence Kilmartin and Geoffrey Skelton, London, Eulenburg, 1983 (Eulenburg Music Series).

LIGETI 2007
LIGETI, György. *Gesammelte Schriften*, edited by Monika Lichtenfeld, 2 vols., Mainz, Schott, 2007 (Veröffentlichungen der Paul Sacher Stiftung, 10).

LUKACS 1990
LUKACS, John. *Budapest 1900: A Historical Portrait of a City and Its Culture*, New York, Grove Press, 1990.

MIRKA 2014
The Oxford Handbook of Topic Theory, edited by Danuta Mirka, Oxford-New York, Oxford University Press, 2014.

RATNER 1980
RATNER, Leonard G. *Classic Music: Expression, Form, and Style*, New York, Schirmer, 1980.

ROIG-FRANCOLÍ 1995
ROIG-FRANCOLÍ, Miguel. 'Harmonic and Formal Processes in Ligeti's Net-Structure Compositions', in: *Music Theory Spectrum*, XVII/2 (Fall 1995), pp. 242-267.

SALMENHAARA 1969
SALMENHAARA, Erkki. *Das musikalische Material und seine Behandlung in den Werken Apparitions, Atmospheres, Aventures und Requiem von György Ligeti*, Regensburg, Bosse, 1969 (Acta Musicologica Fennica, 2).

SCHERZINGER 2006
SCHERZINGER, Martin. 'György Ligeti and the Aka Pygmies Project', in: *Contemporary Music Review*, XXV/3 (2006), pp. 227-262.

STEINITZ 1996
STEINITZ, Richard. 'Weeping and Wailing', in: *The Musical Times*, CXXXVII/1842 (August 1996), pp. 17-22.

STEINITZ 2003
ID. *György Ligeti: Music of the Imagination*, Boston, Northeastern University Press, 2003.

ZBIKOWSKI 2017
ZBIKOWSKI, Lawrence. *Foundations of Musical Grammar*, Oxford-New York, Oxford University Press, 2017.

Listening to *Lontano*: The Auditory Perception of Ligeti's Sound Textures

Britta Sweers
(Universität Bern)

György Ligeti's music has been perceived as accessible and recognizable, not least due to its specific use in film. Ligeti became probably one of the most listened-to New Music composers internationally when his music was adapted into popular culture (even if unasked) thanks to Stanley Kubrick's *2001: A Space Odyssey* (1968). As Christopher Platt, music editor of the *New Yorker* magazine, remarked in 2008:

> György Ligeti is one of those composers whose music you probably know even if you think you don't. Large chunks of it, weird and wild and other-worldly, helped carry the lone pioneer through the ultimate barrier towards the end of Stanley Kubrick's film *2001: A Space Odyssey*[1].

Due to the surreal and visually open image of the psychedelic Star Gate sequence in particular, set to *Atmosphères* (1961) and Requiem (1963-1965)[2], the audience was almost inevitably forced to *listen to* and experience the sound of music similarly without narrative. Rather than serving as a mere emotional or atmospheric background sound or stimulation, Ligeti's music thus became a central component, equal to the surreal visuals of this sequence. This prominent utilization in popular culture might be one reason why Ligeti's music has been widely regarded as having transgressed various boundaries. It has stimulated imaginations and allowed an unbiased aural approach independently of any knowledge of New Music theory or discourses related more specifically to Ligeti or New Music. This is likewise evident in his works having become part of school music education in German-speaking contexts[3].

---

[1]. Platt 2008. See May 2020, pp. 23-25.
[2]. See Steinitz 2003.
[3]. Bullerjahn 1989.

Set against this background, it appears surprising that Ligeti's composition *Lontano* (1967) has partly instead been met with rejection by listeners, thereby contradicting the descriptions of the piece in the dominant Ligeti-related discourses. Analyzing the range of associations related to *Lontano*, this article explores the dichotomy between these discourses and auditory perceptions, as well as psychoacoustic issues. As I argue here, an adequate analysis of Ligeti's works needs to combine discursive, score-based, aural, and acoustic perspectives more strongly in order to reach a more comprehensive understanding; this becomes specifically apparent in the case of *Lontano*. This gives the listener and his/her imaginary musical perception a stronger authority over pre-determined descriptions and terminology that could restrict, rather than support, a listener's perception of the works.

Listening to *Lontano*: A Sound Experiment

In 2005, I helped to conduct an associative experiment on synesthetic music perception at the University of Music in Rostock (Germany). The focus was on Ligeti's eleven-minute work *Lontano*, which has been described as a harmonically structured cluster composition shaped by a mixture of micropolyphonic/floating and homophonic/static instrumental sound textures. In particular, the specific setting of up to forty voices, harmonically meticulously through-composed and using a compositional technique described as micropolyphonic, results in constantly changing tone colors, as well as in sound clusters in which individual instrumental sounds are no longer recognizable. These distorted tone-color impressions are likewise caused by the instrumental voices having often been placed at extremely high or low pitch levels[4].

The composition has been framed by various associative suggestions by Ligeti himself, ranging from Albrecht Altdorfer's (ca. 1480-1538) painting *Die Alexanderschlacht*, to John Keats's (1795-1821) poem 'Ode to a Nightingale' (1819) to Giovanni Battista Piranesi's (1720-1778) *Carceri d'Invenzione* (1760-1761). Each of these works is shaped by complex and transforming spatial textures and has also been associated with synesthetic perceptions of different levels. Ligeti further mentioned more abstract yet colorful and imaginative impressions of «floating crystals» and the stained-glass windows of the Sainte Chapelle in Paris[5], while many authors who have subsequently discussed the composition have also described it as a «sound sculpture»[6], shaped by «harmonic crystallizations»[7]. *Lontano* thus appeared ideal for an analysis of aural

---

[4]. See Engelbrecht – Marx – Sweers 1997 for a more comprehensive discussion.

[5]. Ligeti in Nordwall 1971, p. 90.

[6]. Dibelius 1984, p. 6. See Engelbrecht – Marx – Sweers 1997 for a detailed overview of related discourses.

[7]. Ligeti 1984b [1967], p. 22.

synesthetic and associative musical perceptions. We expected colorful associations, maybe also references to the changing textures and tone colors so comprehensively discussed in literature[8], especially by those students with a synesthetic disposition.

The group consisted of twenty-five students (20-25 years) who had trained professionally in different classical music disciplines (e.g., violin, piano, flute, percussion) and in school music education. The culturally mixed group (twelve German, one Scandinavian, one Belgian, and ten East Asian — mainly South Korean and Chinese — students) was unfamiliar with Ligeti's compositions or related discourses. The students, who listened to a high-quality stereo device in a large room, were asked to observe and describe their immediate sentiments during the listening process — in written form, but also in images. In order to relativize our findings and to distract the participants from *Lontano* as our primary object of investigation, we embedded the excerpt into a sequence with four other samples that likewise created sound textures: *Lontano* was preceded by minimal-influenced music (the intro of Mike Oldfield's *Tubular Bells* (1973)) and computer-based sounds (the beginning of part 1 of Jean-Michel Jarre's *Oxygène* (1976)). It was followed by a Romantic composition (a section of the Andante from Aleksandr Borodin's Symphony No. 2 (1876)) and a sound recording of Balinese *suling sunari*[9].

The impressions of the latter samples were as expected, i.e., highly varied and full of colorful concrete descriptions. Yet the reactions to *Lontano* were striking. In contrast to the aforementioned compositions, which were often described with positive associations, the comments on *Lontano*, similarly clearly relating to emotional categories, were blurry, abstract, partly distanced, and remarkably negative: «the music does not touch me»; «one watches a threat»; «In a movie: the moment when someone is about to kill him- or herself»; «something exciting: a crime»; «a wood that is cut down — dinosaurs»; «increasingly less space in my head»; «like in hell»; «flickering like a desert sun»; «hornet swarm»; «volcano» (describing the music at letter G); «factory»; «pain». Some remarks fell into a category of industrial and stress-related noise, evident in remarks like «a train drives into a station – tinnitus», the latter word apparently directly relating to the sound of the high strings. Several described their feelings as «highly uncomfortable», some towards the extreme that, they added after the experiment, they would have liked to run out of the room. Except for one student who spoke of a «contrast of different colors», none of the students mentioned any impressions similar to how Ligeti's work has been associated in literature[10] — neither concrete works nor anything as colorful as the descriptions of texture in Ligeti discourses. Some more specific descriptions that emerged especially during the discussion after the experiment came close to Ligeti's Kafkaesque

---

[8]. See ENGELBRECHT – MARX – SWEERS 1997 for details.
[9]. Also described as «heavenly pipes», *suling sunari* are four-meter-long wind-blown bamboo pipes.
[10]. See ENGELBRECHT – MARX – SWEERS 1997 for a comprehensive discussion.

description of his childhood dream of a spiderweb in which his bed was entangled[11]. It almost appeared that Ligeti's emotional associations of sadness were reflected in the extreme fear and pain mentioned by the students. It was also evident that many students rejected the work, which became apparent in a comment on the subsequent Borodin example: «Finally – music».

An Auditory Re-Study of *Lontano*

The experiment sketched above points to a dilemma that I could not yet articulate at that time. In retrospect, I can see that I was confused because none of the students' impressions had in any way paralleled either Ligeti's association or those prominent in the Ligeti discourse that related to colorful sound textures, timbres, and spatial aspects in *Lontano* and similar compositions from the same period, such as *Atmosphères*. How could the students so strongly deviate from the thoroughly fascinating discourses addressing the aforementioned issues? Was this maybe also shaped by the non-Western socialization of half of the students? Interestingly, Bullerjahn[12], falling back on an earlier experiment[13], had already pointed to similar results in a strictly European context — while students recognized Ligeti as a composer, they did not necessarily also voice stronger associative impressions when listening to *Lontano*.

In order to re-evaluate these findings, I repeated the associative experiment with thirteen mostly culturally European experimentees in spring 2021. Given the restrictions of the COVID-19 situation, participants listened to the work individually, either on a private stereo device or in digital format (which meant that I could not control the actual sound quality) while taking notes. This individualized situation allowed for more discussion, thereby adding more qualitative aspects, as well as bringing in a more heterogeneous yet predominantly academically advanced group (with at least an MA degree and/or long-term experience in music). The group included nine musicologists or scholars of culture, one art historian, one historian, one musician, and one administrator. Despite the more evident openness towards New Music (although only two persons were loosely familiar with the specific *Lontano* discourse), the results strikingly resembled the previous group in some aspects, while also adding further facets:

• *All prominently experienced a transformation process at the beginning.* Partly associated with nature-related events, such as a sunrise and green meadows, this part received the *most colorful, precise, and positive responses.* Several participants described this section, which especially at the beginning is still shaped by an identifiable pitch, as being subsequently disturbed or even

---

[11]. Ligeti 1967, p. 165.
[12]. Bullerjahn 1989, p. 22.
[13]. The experiment was conducted by Meissner and is described in Meissner 1979.

destroyed by the increasingly dissonant sound. One participant — who not only identified as a synesthete but also provided the most comprehensive associations — described extremely colorful associations for the beginning («Morning mist, just before sunrise, wide, flat landscape; gray with light pastel colors that shimmer here and there; the sun rises; gold, reddish, shimmering air»), which then transform into a horror movie («black castle, fire»), with her previously colorful imagination completely turning into versions of dark gray and black.

• *Those sections that shifted towards noise qualities were met with the strongest rejection or comparably «gray» associations*, while dissonant sections were either experienced negatively or mostly associated with insects (and likewise negatively perceived). This group also repeatedly mentioned hornets or insect swarms in relation to the high-pitched section at letters E-F. Rejection was also apparent, maybe even specifically invoked due to the lengthy high-volume sections.

• *Dissonant, noise-related sections were repeatedly described in technical terms, as if listeners stepped out of their associative mode* («interference»; «siren»; (again) «a train driving into a station»; «helicopter»). This was also evident in those sections where instruments play extremely high or low or use specific bowing techniques («strings: tremolo scratchy, separately audible»; «unclean intonation»; «a bit annoying in the high passages»). Repeated associations for the high sections were likewise «heat», «sun», «desert» (seven respondents).

• A wide range of *negative emotional categories dominated* (seven mentioned «fear», others «threat» or «darkness»; additional remarks were «rotten smell»; «it dies and is in pain»; «very terrible»; «What is happening? I am afraid»; «stalking, threat, predator»; «destroyed landscape»; «an atmospheric change of weightless, oppressiveness, and alarm»; «zoom into a window, death, it smells of decay, fear, imprisonment, we zoom further into the burning room, there is a door, a locked door, behind it we hear screaming, there is someone...»). Eight participants likewise listed feelings of tension and four of «coldness».

• Those familiar with the Ligeti discourse *struggled to match the literature with aural experiences* («I try to imagine a sound sculpture; don't hear it»). Furthermore, if *spatial issues* were mentioned at all, they were mixed with emotions («emptiness», «expansion», «suspense»; the synesthetic participant described experiencing emotions instead of colors). Rather than three-dimensional impressions, participants mentioned a *loss of orientation* («A sudden flight, rise, navigation then fall, as in a dream... the loss of reference», «impression of simultaneous distance and proximity, dissonance, uncertainty, fear»), partly interrelated with a feeling of *inner distance* («the music takes me nowhere»; «flatness»). This is also reflected in the following description of the ending: «Then new figures emerge from the fog, silently, without faces, they slide past us and turn their backs on us: faceless». Three other participants associated the ending with a feeling of «uncertainty» and «no redemption», while another, who had associated the composition with the destruction of the environment and civilization, added «drawing back, unspoken sacrifice so that this civilization can live in wealth».

• The issue of *discovery, partly as a process of an inner exploration*, again combined with fear («the fear of what will be discovered in front of you or inside you») or overcoming this fear («The sound is a curtain; behind, it can be different. Do not be afraid! He just wants to play!») was likewise repeatedly mentioned. The category of fear is even apparent in one description of the ending that clearly parallels Ligeti's suggestions, although the experimentee did not know about the Altdorfer association that Ligeti specifically related to bars 145-149, letter BB: «A ray of light breaks through this diffuse [structure], despair, unborn souls scream, complain, moan, limbo, light yellow, gray, they move on».

• *Only a minority mentioned predominantly positive associations*. One person (the only one completely unfamiliar with Ligeti's works) described the music as a processual transformation («Life develops from a core — different areas of life emerge and are individually presented; colors emerge, surfaces...»; «Paintings of the Creation with different timbres»), and only related the music to the idea of «frozen time» by mentioning that «time seems to stand still».

In summary, the predominant category of «fear», that has rarely ever been mentioned in the Ligeti discourse, stuck out again, although this group received the music more positively than the previous one, some describing it as «great music» and «fascinating», which was also evident in their large range of associations. The contrasting reactions to passages with clear pitches versus noise-like clusters, in which instruments could no longer be identified, were likewise evident. While it is still necessary to verify and differentiate these observations with a larger group of listeners, these patterns nevertheless suggest that the initial experiment might not have been a failure, but rather already pointed to discrepancies regarding the description and analysis of Ligeti's works. This includes an evident difference between uninfluenced auditory perception and the central Ligeti discourse. Given the dominant focus on the analysis of musical scores, this is likewise intertwined with a discrepancy between notated music and auditory perception, which requires a re-analysis of actual acoustic and terminological concepts.

Terminology and the Predominance of Spatial-Structural Associations

An initial answer regarding the discrepancy between the Ligeti discourse and auditory perception can be found in Julia Heimerdinger's Ph.D. thesis, in which she meticulously analyzes how Ligeti himself strongly shaped the language of the discourse surrounding his works[14]. For

---

[14]. Heimerdinger 2013.

example, recurring features of his language were expressions like «Textur» (texture), «Klang» (sound), and «Klangfarbenkomposition» (lit. sound-color composition). Further keywords were «Gewebe» (fabric), «Statik» (statics), «Zustand» (state), and «Veränderung» (transformation)[15]. As Heimerdinger outlines, this likewise includes specific descriptive phrases: «Ligeti further describes spatial effects, e.g., of an "increasingly contracting, web-like sound" and an "imaginary space" [...], of "vibrating", "flickering", and of something "floating"»[16].

Having been developed out of a lack of an adequate vocabulary for related aural experiences, particularly in the case of *Atmosphères*, these concepts, including expressions like «Klangflächenkomposition» (lit. sound-surface composition) to describe a cluster technique that positions timbre in the foreground, subsequently became central in Ligeti-related discourses, especially in a German-speaking context[17]. This process was further shaped — and also indirectly controlled — by an initially small group of authors who wrote almost exclusively about Ligeti in the 1960s to 1980s, including Harald Kaufmann, Josef Häusler, Erkki Salmenhaara, Ove Nordwall, Monika Lichtenfeld, and Constantin Floros[18]. These authors — who were also in direct contact with Ligeti — particularly utilized the aforementioned concepts, although it is «difficult to decide, whether and when expressions, images, and analogies were evoked by the music itself or adapted from Ligeti»[19]. As Heimerdinger further elaborates[20], this vocabulary, as well as the predominant analytical focus on structure and the lack of potential alternative approaches, has rarely been questioned.

This vocabulary includes key associative phrases that are strongly entangled with spatial-structural descriptions, such as Ligeti describing his works as rather static objects where «time is as if frozen»[21]. Similar spatial-structural associations by authors writing on Ligeti were likewise apparent in the description, for example, of *Lontano* as a «three-dimensional object», as Ulrich Dibelius remarked in the liner notes to a recording of *Lontano* by the Sinfonieorchester des Südwestfunks Baden-Baden from 1969:

> The metier of the composer thereby assimilated something of the imaginary
> world and the formal intentions of the visual artist. For it was no longer a question
> of inventing points of sound, sonorous lines and their derived progressions and

---

[15]. See *ibidem*, p. 131.

[16]. «Desweiteren beschreibt Ligeti räumliche Wirkungen, z.B. von einem sich "immer mehr zusammenziehenden, netzartigen Klang" und einem "imaginären Raum" [...], von "Vibrieren", "Flimmern" und etwas "Schwebendem"». *Ibidem*, p. 137.

[17]. *Ibidem*, p. 178.

[18]. *Ibidem*, pp. 143-149.

[19]. «Es ist schwierig zu entscheiden, ob und wann Begriffe, Bilder oder Analogien nur durch die Musik evoziert werden oder ob sie von Ligeti übernommen wurden». *Ibidem*, p. 161.

[20]. *Ibidem*.

[21]. «[...] die Zeit ist wie gefroren». Ligeti in BOULIANE 1988, p. 21.

superpositions, but rather of proceeding straight away from complex phenomena, from a quasi-three-dimensional mass of sound, whose construction could no longer be made up of numerous single ingredients mixed together for a total effect[22].

From a compositional perspective, it might be obvious that, rather than being taken as literal descriptions, expressions such as «three-dimensional mass of sound» need to be taken as an allegorical description of, for instance, compositional hierarchy — with the first dimension being understood as the melodic-linear movement, the tonal-harmonic side the second dimension, and the third dimension being timbre and sound. This specific vocabulary is likewise apparent in Dibelius's description of *Lontano* as a «musical landscape with unfathomable depths of perspective»[23]. Dibelius even speaks of «sound sculptures»[24], i.e., «almost tangible structures of curves, arches, bays, reliefs, profiles, stretches of material either diminishing or becoming more compact»[25], the difference between sound sculptures and visual sculptures being that the former are not static and constantly change.

None of this equals a visual three-dimensionality. However, these descriptions have so strongly permeated into public Ligeti-related discourses that they are easily taken as (authorized) literal representations, having inevitably been merged with associative descriptions. This might be one reason why the associations of the initial experiment came as such a surprise; apparently, the Ligeti discourse is not self-evident. Furthermore, as Heimerdinger points out, many expressions were often not appropriately used, which calls for a cautious approach towards the terminological discourse:

> In addition, there are also problems with the terms "sound", "sound structures", "sound surfaces", "cluster", "sound ribbon", "sonic complex", "complex sound", "sound fabric", and "texture", which have repeatedly been confused and have been utilized with changing meanings[26].

---

[22]. «Das Metier des Tonsetzers nahm dadurch etwas von der Vorstellungswelt und den formalen Intentionen des Plastikers an. Denn nicht länger ging es darum, Klang- oder Tonpunkte, Linien sowie deren sich verzweigende Verläufe und Überlagerungen zu erfinden, sondern gleich von komplexen Phänomenen, einer quasi dreidimensionalen Klangmasse auszugehen, deren Zusammensetzung aus einer Vielzahl einzelner Ingredienzien durch ihre absichtsvolle Verwischung zum Summeneffekt unmöglich mehr nachzuvollziehen war». Dibelius 1984, p. 5.

[23]. «[...] eine aus Klängen gebaute musikalische Szenerie mit unauslotbarer Tiefenperspektive». *Ibidem*, p. 12.

[24]. «Skulpturen aus Klang». *Ibidem*, p. 6.

[25]. «[...] fast haptisch wahrzunehmende Gebilde aus Rundungen, Wölbungen, Buchten, Reliefen, Profilen, sich verjüngenden oder an Kompaktheit zunehmenden Materialbänder». *Ibidem*.

[26]. «Darüber hinaus gibt es aber auch Probleme mit den Begriffen "Klang", "Klanggebilde", "Klangfläche", "Cluster", "Klangband", "klanglicher Komplex", "komplexer Klang", "Klanggewebe" und "Textur", die immer wieder miteinander vertauscht und zudem mit wechselnder Bedeutung benutzt werden». Heimerdinger 2013, p. 131.

Terminological confusions might not be surprising, given that work with tone colors had already been a central component for Impressionist composers like Claude Debussy and was discussed particularly in Arnold Schoenberg's *Harmonielehre* (1911), which remained, however, extremely vague[27]. While subsequent discourses nevertheless particularly made relationships with the compositional practices of the Second Viennese School, Ligeti's work with tone colors (*Klangfarben*) or timbres fell back much more directly on acoustic and psychophysical aspects of sound and noise perception. Eliminating the melodic line (which had still been apparent as an audible 'line' in the Second Viennese School but also in serialism) through the noise-related effects of micropolyphonic clusters, which have also been described as *Klangflächen* (sound surfaces) in German, Ligeti indeed brought timbre and tone color to the foreground. However, Ligeti himself rejected too overt an exact categorization into some of the aforementioned expressions:

> The other request: recently, misunderstandings have been increasing, and I have been classified more and more in the group of «timbre composers». That bothers me, because the invention of new timbres (as well as the color of «movement» or «texture») was never an end in itself for me, but only a means of design[28].

Despite these, and his own remarks about compositional structure, Ligeti rather emphasized or even encouraged a more associative perception of his compositions. For example, as he remarked in the program notes to the premiere of *Atmosphères* in 1961:

> In this [...] form there are no events, [...] only states; no contours, no shapes, just the unpopulated [...] musical space. The timbres, the actual carriers of the form, become — detached from the musical shapes — intrinsic values[29].

---

[27]. On the one hand, this provides a definition of *Klangfarbenmelodie* (lit. sound-color melody) as a sequence of «Klangfarben, deren Beziehung untereinander mit einer Art Logik wirkt, ganz äquivalent jener Logik, die uns bei der Melodie der Klanghöhen genügt» («tone colors whose relationship to one another works with a kind of logic, quite equivalent to the logic that is sufficient for us for [the recognition of] the melody based on pitch»). SCHOENBERG 2011, p. 503. On the other hand, Schoenberg left it open whether he meant orchestral sound colors or overtones, for instance, or whether this was an abstract philosophical concept. See SCHMIDT 2001 for further details.

[28]. «Die andere Bitte: In letzter Zeit häufen sich die Mißverständnisse und ich werde immer mehr in die Reihe der "Klangfarbenkomponisten" eingeordnet. Das stört mich, denn die Erfindung neuer Klangfarben (wie auch der "Bewegungs-" oder "Textur-Farbe") war für mich nie Selbstzweck, sondern nur Mittel der Formgestaltung». Ligeti in HEIMERDINGER 2013, p. 130.

[29]. «In dieser [...] Form gibt es keine Ereignisse, [...] nur Zustände; keine Konturen, keine Gestalten, sondern nur den unbevölkerten [...] musikalischen Raum. Die Klangfarben, die eigentlichen Träger der Form, werden — von den musikalischen Gestalten gelöst — zu Eigenwerten». LIGETI 2007.

Moreover, Ligeti was very clear that his music should not be understood as explicitly programmatic music but as open, especially for those uninitiated into New Music discourses[30]. *Lontano* in particular took this approach, as well as the relationship to score and sound perception, to a new extreme. Not only can the resulting sound not be deduced from the score alone anymore, it also assumes noise qualities that were judged negatively by the experimentees. Yet the range of answers likewise confirmed the limitations of the existent discursive focus on sound textures. Ligeti's emphasis on openness might thus call for the stronger integration of an aural perspective into the analytical process.

Ligeti in Concert Reviews:
Descriptive Approaches and Acoustic Perceptions

Aurally based descriptions, which can be found especially in concert program notes and in reviews of live performances, almost inevitably place the emphasis on other issues than the score-based discourses do. These include not only the difference between score and auditive perception, but also more descriptive components, repeated references to Kubrick's *2001: A Space Odyssey* movie, and (psycho)acoustic aspects. For example, musicologist and music journalist Martin Hufner's description of *Lontano* in the program notes for a concert at the Staatsoper Hamburg in 1998 almost reads like a 'how-to-listen' within a concert room. Yet, maybe also in the face of the dominant Ligeti discourse, it similarly reads like an apologetic explanation for the seemingly simple depiction when Hufner points out that «What can here be read like a technical description of musical processes is in the end, however, the result of a highly expressive music»[31], and continues with a more score-oriented depiction that is nevertheless «impossible to verbalize», as he concludes:

> You can[not] translate this language back into human verbal language, because it is music; but this music is able to generate a lot of hearing and somehow also generate "compassion" without one knowing exactly what this "something" actually is[32].

The challenge of describing Ligeti's work is also evident in other reviews. As Service remarked in relation to a performance at the City of Birmingham Symphony Orchestra's *Floof!*

---

[30]. See Bullerjahn 1989 for a comprehensive discussion.

[31]. «Was sich hier lesen mag wie eine technische Beschreibung musikalischer Vorgänge ist jedoch im klingenden Resultat eine hochexpressive Musik». Hufner 1998.

[32]. «Man kann diese Sprache weder in die menschliche Wörtersprache zurückübersetzen, denn es ist Musik; aber diese Musik ist in der Lage, sehr viel Gehör und irgendwie auch "Mitgefühl" zu erzeugen, ohne dass man genau zu sagen wüsste, was dieses "Etwas" eigentlich ist». *Ibidem*.

Listening to *Lontano*

Festival in 2003, «The piece hovers at the edge of audibility and comprehension. Here, its dense textures and darkly glowing melodies created a thrilling, shimmering musical experience»[33]. In other cases the descriptive emphasis is set on the less disturbing passages, as is evident in this quote: «Already the first delicate tones of Ligeti's atmospherically dense piece *Lontano* put the hall in a kind of limbo. Petrenko masterfully managed to let the flowing, finely balanced sound swell up and down again. The music, which unfolds as if coming from afar, finally disappears into nothing»[34]. In contrast to the associations mentioned in the experiments, negative descriptions are mostly avoided in reviews and in the discourse.

Besides some emotional impressions that, however mollified, clearly parallel the experimentees' reactions (e.g., «A powerful sound image with depressing sections»[35]) and references to Kubrick's *2001* movie (by description of the works as spheric, cosmic, planetary impressions), a further central issue in reviews has been the acoustic experience. Ligeti himself not only spoke of «sonorous net structures» (*klangliche Netzstrukturen*), but also addressed explicit acoustic aspects when talking about the intermediate space between sound (*Klang*) and noise (*Geräusch*), with sounds being «veiled and blurred by the complex interweaving of the parts»[36]. As the experimentees' descriptions of the beginning of *Lontano* indicate, this is clearly perceived and partly addressed in a highly varied vocabulary.

The importance of auditive perception likewise became apparent during the analysis process that led to the publication *Lontano: Aus weiter Ferne*[37]. During the writing process we had the opportunity to listen to *Lontano* in two live concerts. It was only here that the actual acoustic dimensions of Ligeti's work, with its interchanging tone colors, became audible, compared to which recordings sounded almost bland — despite high-quality stereo devices — and it might be a further issue of investigation how far an incomplete rendition (even in digital format) plays a central role for negative auditory reactions. Along with the fact that research subjects repeatedly indicated that they were overwhelmed by the sound experience, this nevertheless calls for a stronger integration of physical and psychoacoustic aspects of timbre and noise in the analysis of Ligeti's work.

Ligeti as a Sound Artist

Ligeti's specific work with timbres addresses a variety of issues related to the description and categorization of non-tonal sound and noise. Modern composition has addressed related

---

[33]. Service 2003.
[34]. Kolbe 2016.
[35]. «Ein mächtiges Klanggebilde mit bedrückenden Abschnitten». Dpa 2009.
[36]. «Die Klänge wurden durch die komplexe Stimmverwebung verdeckt und verwischt». Ligeti 1984a, p. 30.
[37]. See Engelbrecht – Marx – Sweers 1997.

aspects from a large range of perspectives. Central discourses occur most prominently in electronic music, in which reflections on sound — here created with electroacoustic means — shift physical and psychoacoustic aspects, as well as auditive analytical questions, to the fore. The best-known approach is probably *musique concrète*, which detached recordings from their original context by arranging and transforming the sounds into compositional works[38]. Another has been the soundscape composition approach developed at Simon Fraser University. Composers like Raymond Murray Schafer have been explicitly working with *environmental sounds and noises* that are transformed by the whole spectrum of analog and digital possibilities without, however, «obliterating the sound's recognizability»[39], which is also transferred to acoustic instrument-based compositions. Ligeti can be viewed as representing another extreme in this spectrum. Still utilizing traditional (instrumental, orchestral, or vocal) means, his compositions have pushed *human psychoacoustic sound perceptions to an extreme* by shifting the attention to sound and noise per se, rather than to melody and harmony — thereby, however, evoking a different associative level. It was clearly apparent that our research subjects got lost or shifted towards negative perceptions whenever noise qualities started to dominate over identifiable tone colors. How strongly this nevertheless resulted in a recognizable «Ligeti sound»[40] is also reflected in the following *Guardian* review:

> The essential Ligeti sound is achieved by scoring of massive complexity and detail, fluctuating with immeasurable subtlety; more fancifully, it suggests the murmurings of a distant exotic religious ritual[41].

Given the central role of timbre and noise aspects for the «Ligeti sound», it thus appears useful to further integrate a sound-acoustic perspective as a central component in the analytical description of Ligeti's compositions. This, moreover, also relates the works more strongly to other timbre-related discourses, including popular music. For example, Brockhaus demonstrated in his study on *Kultsounds* that in the case of popular music, while the structure is important, it is not the central innovative level[42]. Rather, innovation in popular music has always occurred on the level of timbre and sound texture[43], which requires a different analytical focus on, for example, the actual nature of the individual timbres or the integration of spatial effects like reverberation, each also requiring a more physical acoustic language. While this is already

---

[38]. A method Ligeti likewise used in compositions like *Glissandi* (1957) and *Artikulation* (1958).
[39]. TRUAX n.d.
[40]. SHAVE 2012.
[41]. FORD 1974.
[42]. BROCKHAUS 2017.
[43]. E.g., «popcorn sound», the sound of a specific synthesizer (e.g., the Yamaha DX7 or the Hammond organ) or an electric guitar type.

apparent with electronic music that shares common experimental and technological approaches with popular electronic music, despite different intentions and foci[44], it also applies to directions more strongly tied to notated music, as in the case of Ligeti. For example, Beurmann and Schneider, who were among the first to apply stronger acoustic and psychoacoustic perspectives to Ligeti's works, remarked in 1991, «The opposition of "sound" and "structure" is by no means obvious or as natural as the often-practiced comparison of "two-dimensional" homophony and "linear" compositional techniques might suggest»[45].

Already outlining here the challenges posed by the discursive patterns that were only later analyzed in more detail by Heimerdinger[46], by pointing to the discrepancy between the limitations of musical perception and the composed work, the authors emphasized the importance of a deeper understanding of related acoustic and auditive processes. The study thus became especially significant for working with sonographic measurements, here in the case of *Atmosphères*. Elucidating the central role of the altered transient process[47] at the beginning, the study subsequently illustrated from an acoustic perspective the different qualities of the clusters and their constantly altering contours. Beurmann and Schneider[48] consequently recommended speaking also of different levels of energy or intensity rather than just of static tone color, which appears as too limited regarding the acoustic specifics of timbre.

In contrast to basic parameters — like frequency (pitch) and intensity (volume) — sound is considered a secondary parameter that still cannot be objectively measured and depends on subjective impressions. Tone color (or timbre) is a parameter of a single tone that is composed of a fundamental and a specific sequence of individual partials. The latter can be manipulated — in Ligeti's case mostly through micropolyphonic settings and textures. While the specifics of what determines a tone color or timbre remain subjects for further research[49], it is evident, for instance, that not only the composition of basic tones and related overtones and volume play a significant role, but also the transient process — the time-related development of the sound

---

[44]. E.g., while popular music often focuses on individually recognizable sounds, sound compositions in electronic and art music often address more abstract issues.

[45]. «Die Opposition von "Klang" und "Struktur" ist also keineswegs einleuchtend oder so selbstverständlich, wie es die oft geübte Gegenüberstellung von "flächiger" Homophonie und "linearen" Satztechniken nahelegen mag». BEURMANN – SCHNEIDER 1991, p. 311.

[46]. HEIMERDINGER 2013.

[47]. The transient (process) describes a general acoustic feature of sound. The beginning of a sound is shaped a short burst of energy of a few milliseconds that is also visible in an initial wave of high amplitude.

[48]. BEURMANN – SCHNEIDER 1991. In a recent study on the musical analysis of sound mass compositions, ANTUNES – FEULO DO ESPIRITO SANTO – MANZOLLI – QUEIROZ 2021 added further insights into the psychoacoustic aspects of Ligeti's works.

[49]. See, for instance, SIEDENBURG – SAITIS – MCADAMS – POPPER – FAY 2019.

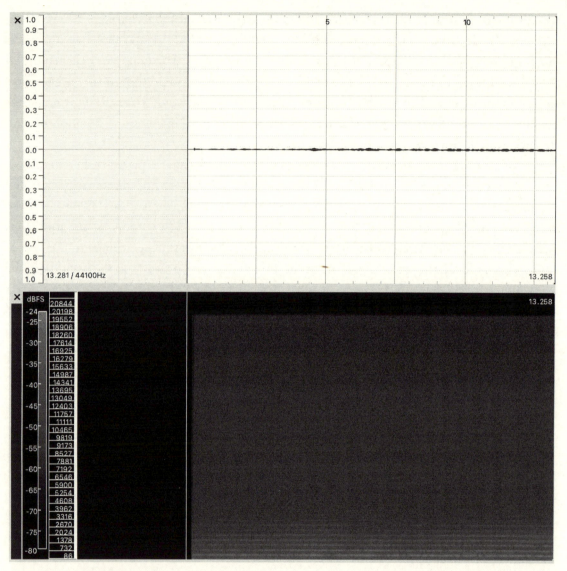

Fig. 1: Beginning of *Lontano* (sonic visualizer): a low volume level (above) and still recognizable frequency lines. Pitch is still recognizable (below).

spectrum and volume during the first split seconds of a tone. Without the transient process during the first split seconds, timbres cannot be identified.

Many of Ligeti's works play with exactly these processes. For example, as is audible at the beginning of *Lontano*, one cannot only still identify the flutes as such, but also their pitch and harmony at the beginning (Fig. 1) — which was also the part that met with positive and highly imaginative responses by the experimentees. However, the flute quality increasingly disappears — not only due to minor alterations of pitch, but also due to long sustained tones

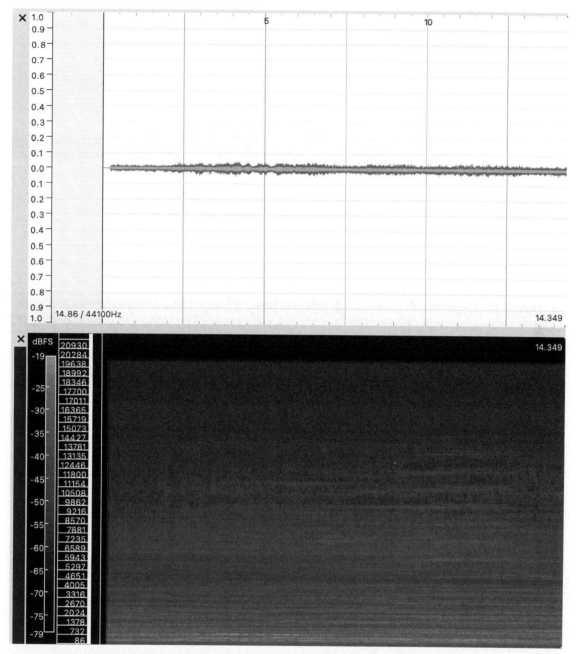

FIG. 2: *Lontano*, Letter B: transformation point at the beginning. While frequency lines are still recognizable, the overall sound becomes more compact and merged towards a noise spectrum. Yet the volume level is still moderate.

that create phases without transient processes, and thus increasingly without recognizable instrumental timbre qualities which brings out the «flickering» effect of the narrow, dissonant intervals more clearly. Yet given that this passage (letter B; FIG. 2) still evokes a melodic

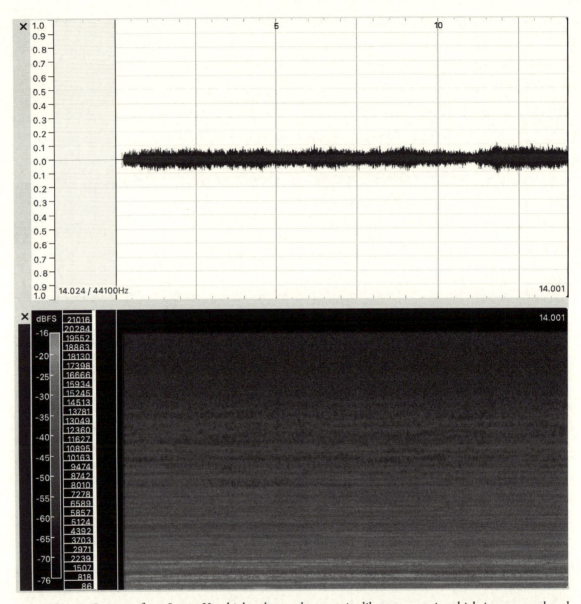

Fig. 3: *Lontano*, from Letter Y: a high-volume, almost noise-like spectrum in which instrumental and precise pitch recognition is no longer possible. One of the passages that evoked predominantly negative responses.

impression and is played at a moderate volume, it was still met with strongly associative responses. Subsequently, the instrument quality increasingly disappears, in extremely high or low registers, when large numbers of instruments (the same as well as different ones) play simultaneously, thereby resembling different noise and high-volume qualities (Fig. 3). These segments also provoked the most negative reaction and marked the spots where the experimentees got lost on an associative level, evident in their more technical vocabulary. Each of the initial timbre qualities are thus transformed, to the extent that, partly, the exact tone color can no longer even be named. It appears that this leaves the listener almost without orientation, while the emerging noise spectrum — visible in the spectral analyses — tends to evoke either unspecific or more negative environmental associations, also depending on the energy level — too-long sequences of noise-resembling passages of strong volume intensity were in particular often met with extreme rejection — and the nature of the sound textures.

Similar effects can be observed with vocal works like *Lux Aeterna*, where vocal qualities are transformed towards an instrumental sound quality. For example, the idea of a distinct human soprano voice is diffused by dissonant harmonies, as well as by a deleted transient and a decay process of the sound. However, the timbre and/or noise quality still appears less confusing in vocal works like *Lux Aeterna* than in *Lontano*[50].

This field of tension that was apparent in both experiments, as well as the discrepancy between score and acoustic perception, can be further framed by Pierre Schaeffer's reflections on the electroacoustic sound work as formulated in his *Traité des Objets Musicaux* (1966)[51], which has shaped sound-related discourses beyond *musique concrète* until the present day. As Schaeffer outlined, an *objet sonore* or «sound object» is not to be made equal with the sounding body itself[52]. Rather, it can create different *objets sonores*; e.g., the sound produced by a violin does not necessarily always signify a violin. Exactly this happens in *Lontano* as well. The emerging sound no longer signifies either the original orchestra or the score, due to the previously outlined specific physical and psychoacoustic processes. This, in combination with the — in terms of duration — *dominating* extreme registers and intensity levels, might further explain why so many 'non-initiated' listeners reacted so extremely negatively to *Lontano*. On the other hand, it also accounts for the more unspecific associations. It can be assumed that the experimentees might have mentioned further positive aspects of noise-resembling passages in a live context, although the range of associations during the second experiment, in which the sound quality could not be controlled, was still amazingly broad. Given the central role of exactly these psychoacoustic experiences in *Lontano*, this calls for a stronger awareness of general high-quality renditions of New Music, not only in an experimental situation but also in a pedagogical context.

Outlook

The two experiments demonstrated that Ligeti evidently changed our perception of music on multiple levels. In the light of the previously discussed observations, we can ask whether

---

[50]. However, given that the human voices are still in a more limited range compared to the instrumental extremes in *Lontano*, they still appear as more easily accessible to the human ear.

[51]. SCHAEFFER 1966.

[52]. *Ibidem*, p. 223.

it could therefore be that the Ligeti discourse has become too fixed, rather than serving as a framework open to expansion. In the case of *Lontano*, the piece evidently deviates from and maybe even limits normal auditory perception. Given the importance of every analytical approach, an analysis of Ligeti's works might therefore benefit from a broader range of perspectives, also given the fact that, as Beurmann and Schneider indicated, Ligeti had good psychoacoustic knowledge[53]. In the face of the introductory experiment, I would like to particularly emphasize two analytical aspects for future research on Ligeti's work.

Firstly, *a stronger integration of an acoustic and psychoacoustic vocabulary* could provide a deeper understanding of, for example, what happens in the case of timbre alteration. Expanding the descriptive vocabulary allows a more specific explanation and visualization of, for instance, *why* timbre qualities alter and disappear (e.g., by shifting towards unidentifiable noise qualities). It also helps the listener and analyst to *articulate impressions more specifically* (e.g., by relating 'flickering impressions' to the acoustic specifics of dissonant effects *beyond negatively connoted judgments*). It likewise supports an *identification and understanding of extreme reactions* more clearly and in a more descriptive way (e.g., as *Lontano* utilizes extreme instrumental registers and volume ranges)[54].

Secondly, I argue for *a stronger position of aurally based sound analysis*, especially in those cases where score and acoustic perception strongly deviate from each other. This, however, requires further methods, such as a stronger integration of descriptive transcriptions, which has become an important tool in the form of so-called 'listening scores' in electronic music analysis[55]. It might also include a *more open space for associative reactions*, which could lead away from a discourse that has been too strongly pre-determined and would render the listener a stronger authority — to the extent that analysis of multi-layered compositions is incomplete without aural impressions.

The experiments confirmed that the aural experience of *Lontano* is extreme and overwhelming. It could be hypothesized that works like *Atmosphères* and especially *Lux Aeterna* have been met with more open responses, because timbre-wise they are more homogenous and less noise-like. This, however, requires further experimental studies, also on the actual auditory process, because, excellent recordings and cinema stereo devices notwithstanding, *Lontano* in particular illustrates that Ligeti's music needs to be experienced through active listening, most ideally in a live concert context. The latter point particularly applies to the micropolyphonic orchestral compositions, with their constantly altering sections that cannot be fully represented

---

[53]. Beurmann – Schneider 1991, p. 329, footnote 23.

[54]. Good examples of this approach are Antunes – Feulo do Espirito Santo – Manzolli – Queiroz 2021 and, with regard to *Continuum*, Douglas – Noble – McAdams 2016.

[55]. A good example is Ligeti's electronic work *Artikulation* (1958), which was realized as a listening score by Rainer Wehringer (Wehringer 1970), an approach that could also be expanded to acoustic compositions.

by analog and digital recordings. This is also because Ligeti's works push the fundamentals of acoustic phenomena, psychoacoustic sound perception, and seemingly obvious assumptions about 'music' to extremes. As the case of *Lontano* illustrates, the related challenge concerns scholars, journalists, musicians, and audiences alike; finding adequate words for the experience of Ligeti's music is difficult and fascinating at the same time.

Bibliography

ANTUNES – FEULO DO ESPIRITO SANTO – MANZOLLI – QUEIROZ 2021
ANTUNES, Micael – FEULO DO ESPIRITO SANTO, Guilherme – MANZOLLI, Jônatas – QUEIROZ, Marcelo. 'A Psychoacoustic-Based Methodology for Sound-Mass Music Analysis', in: *Proceedings of the 15th International Symposium on CMMR*, 15-19 November 2021, edited by Tetsuro Kitahara, Mitsuko Aramaki, Richard Kronland-Martinet and Sølvi Ystad, pp. 135-144, <https://cmmr2021.github.io/proceedings/pdffiles/cmmr2021_16.pdf>, accessed May 2022.

BEURMANN – SCHNEIDER 1991
BEURMANN, Andreas E. – SCHNEIDER, Albrecht. 'Struktur, Klang, Dynamik: Akustische Untersuchungen an Ligetis Atmosphères', in: *Für György Ligeti. Die Referate des Ligeti-Kongresses Hamburg 1988*, edited by Constantin Floros, Laaber, Laaber-Verlag, 1991 (Hamburger Jahrbuch für Musikwissenschaft, 11), pp. 311-334.

BOULIANE 1988
BOULIANE, Denis. 'Geronnene Zeit und Narration', in: *Neue Zeitschrift für Musik*, CXLIX/5 (May 1988), pp. 19-25.

BROCKHAUS 2017
BROCKHAUS, Immanuel. *Kultsounds. Die prägendsten Klänge der Popmusik 1960-2014*, Bielefeld, transcript, 2017.

BULLERJAHN 1989
BULLERJAHN, Claudia. 'Assoziationen für Kenner? Zu Ligetis außermusikalischen Anspielungen, erläutert am Beispiel des Orchesterstücks *Lontano* (1967)', in: *Zeitschrift für Musikpädagogik*, LI (September 1989), pp. 9-23.

DIBELIUS 1984
DIBELIUS, Ulrich. 'Konsequenzen eines Klangbildners: Zur Musik von György Ligeti', in: Liner notes to *Ligeti*, Wergo WER60095, 1984, pp. 5-14.

DOUGLAS – NOBLE – MCADAMS 2016
DOUGLAS, Chelsea – NOBLE, Jason – MCADAMS, Stephen. 'Auditory Scene Analysis and the Perception of Sound Mass in Ligeti's *Continuum*', in: *Music Perception*, XXXIII/3 (2016), pp. 287-305.

Dpa 2009
Dpa. 'Umjubelt: David Fray in Hamburg', 15 October 2009, <https://www.mainpost.de/ueberregional/kulturwelt/buehne/umjubelt-david-fray-in-hamburg-art-5328431>, accessed May 2022.

Engelbrecht – Marx – Sweers 1997
Engelbrecht, Christiane – Marx, Wolfgang – Sweers, Britta. *Lontano. «Aus weiter Ferne»*, Hamburg, Von Bockel, 1997.

Ford 1974
Ford, Christopher. 'György Ligeti: «I always imagine music visually, in many different colours»', in: *The Guardian*, 7 May 1974, <https://www.theguardian.com/music/2016/feb/02/from-the-classical-archive-gyorgy-ligeti-interveiw-1974>, accessed May 2022.

Heimerdinger 2013
Heimerdinger, Julia. *Sprechen über Neue Musik. Eine Analyse der Sekundärliteratur und Komponistenkommentare zu Pierre Boulez' «Le Marteau sans maître» (1954), Karlheinz Stockhausens «Gesang der Jünglinge» (1956) und György Ligetis «Atmosphères» (1961)*, Ph.D. Diss., Halle, University of Halle, 2013, <https://opendata.uni-halle.de/bitstream/1981185920/7919/1/Sprechen%20ueber%20Neue%20Musik.pdf>, accessed May 2022.

Hufner 1998
Hufner, Martin. 'György Ligeti: *Lontano* für großes Orchester 1967', program note for a concert of the Philharmonisches Staatsorchester Hamburg, 1998, <https://www.musikkritik.org/1998/10/gyoergy-ligeti-lontano-fuer-grosses-orchester-1967/>, accessed May 2022.

Kolbe 2016
Kolbe, Corina. 'Funkensprühendes Dirigat: Petrenko zurück in Berlin', in: *Musik Heute*, 15 September 2016, <http://www.musik-heute.de/13838/funkenspruehendes-dirigat-petrenko-zurueck-in-berlin/>, accessed May 2022.

Ligeti 1967
Ligeti, György. 'Zustände, Ereignisse, Wandlungen', in: *Melos*, xxxiv/5 (1967), pp. 165-169.

Ligeti 1984a
Id. 'Bericht zur eigenen Arbeit', in: Liner notes to *Ligeti*, Wergo WER60095 (1984), pp. 29-30.

Ligeti 1984b [1967]
Id. '*Lontano*', in: Liner notes to *Ligeti*, Wergo WER60095 (1984), pp. 22-23.

Ligeti 2007
Id. '*Atmosphères* (Einführungstext zur Uraufführung)', in: Id. *Gesammelte Schriften. 2*, edited by Monika Lichtenfeld, Mainz, Schott, 2007 (Veröffentlichungen der Paul Sacher Stiftung, 10), p. 180.

May 2020
May, Andrew. *The Science of Sci-Fi Music*, Cham, Springer, 2020.

MEISSNER 1979
MEISSNER, Roland. *Zur Variabilität musikalischer Urteile. Eine experimentalpsychologische Untersuchung zum Einfluß der Faktoren Vorbildung, Information u. Persönlichkeit*, 2 vols., Hamburg, Wagner, 1979.

NORDWALL 1971
NORDWALL, Ove. *György Ligeti. Eine Monographie*, Mainz, B. Schotts Söhne, 1971.

PLATT 2008
PLATT, Russell. 'Clarke, Kubrick, and Ligeti – a Tale', in: *The New Yorker*, 12 August 2008, <https://www.newyorker.com/culture/goings-on/clarke-kubrick-and-ligeti-a-tale>, accessed May 2022.

SCHAEFFER 1966
SCHAEFFER, Pierre. *Traité des Objets Musicaux*, Paris, Éditions du Seuil, 1966.

SCHMIDT 2001
SCHMIDT, Matthias. 'Klangfarbenmelodie', in: *Österreichisches Musiklexikon online*, 2001, <https://www.musiklexikon.ac.at/ml/musik_K/Klangfarbenmelodie.xml>, accessed May 2022.

SCHOENBERG 2011
SCHOENBERG, Arnold. *Harmonielehre*, Leipzig-Wien, Universal Edition, 2011.

SERVICE 2003
SERVICE, Tom. 'Floof! Symphony Hall/CBSO Centre, Birmingham', in: *The Guardian*, 3 June 2003, <https://www.theguardian.com/music/2003/jun/03/classicalmusicandopera.artsfeatures>, accessed May 2022.

SHAVE 2012
SHAVE, Nick. 'Ligeti, György: A Uniquely Modern Voice', in: *BBC Music Magazine*, 20 May 2012, <https://www.classical-music.com/composers/gyorgy-ligeti/>, accessed May 2022.

SIEDENBURG – SAITIS – MCADAMS – POPPER – FAY 2019
Timbre: Acoustics, Perception, and Cognition, edited by Kai Siedenburg, Charalampos Saitis, Stephen McAdams, Arthur N. Popper and Richard R. Fay, Cham, Springer, 2019.

STEINITZ 2003
STEINITZ, Richard. *György Ligeti: Music of the Imagination*, Evanston, Northwestern University Press, 2003.

TRUAX n.d.
TRUAX, Barry. 'Soundscape Composition', n.d., <https://www.sfu.ca/~truax/scomp.html>, accessed May 2022.

WEHRINGER 1970
WEHRINGER, Rainer. *G. Ligeti. Artikulation. Elektronische Musik. Eine Hörpartitur von Rainer Wehinger*, Mainz, B. Schott's Söhne, 1970.

Rediscovering the Meaning of Words with Hölderlin: About *Drei Phantasien* by György Ligeti

Pierre Michel – Maryse Staiber*
(Université de Strasbourg)

The Three Fantasies after Hölderlin (1982) for a mixed choir of sixteen voices function as a bridge between the 1960s/70s and Ligeti's later trajectory. The composer himself highlighted the importance of Hölderlin's work in the aesthetic context of the late 1970s and early 1980s. In a 1984 talk with musicologists[1], he also cited two other composers: Heinz Holliger (see his *Scardanelli Zyklus*) and Luigi Nono (with his string quartet *Fragmente-Stille an Diotima*).

A cursory look at the score (or even a first listen) may evoke a previous stage in Ligeti's writing, especially the counterpoint in *Lux Aeterna*[2] (here, the first pitch heard in the work is also an F…) and the microtonalism of *Clocks and Clouds*, but numerous features diverge.

The polyphony of these pieces, although dominated by imitations and canons, is characterized by great diversity. To observe the dialogue between the text and the composition, we propose to combine a variety of approaches to reading and writing. We will emphasize Ligeti's many cuts in Hölderlin's poems and consider the way in which the poem is read when proceeding in the same manner as the composer, i.e., removing a number of lines, if not stanzas.

We will seek to highlight interesting occurrences in the relation between text and music, and to establish whether a coincidence between the respective approaches to poetry and music can be identified.

---

[*]. The authors thank Olivier Class for the realization of the musical examples with Finale. Translated from French by Jean-Yves Bart, with support from the Maison Interuniversitaire des Sciences de l'Homme d'Alsace (MISHA) and the Excellence Initiative of the University of Strasbourg.

[1]. Kolleritsch 1987, p. 132.

[2]. Michel 1985, pp. 128-138.

Another novelty in this work lies in the diversity of musical gestures. In addition to contrapuntal and heterophonic episodes, the music is also rich in highly assertive homorhythmic passages, particularly when Hölderlin's text is being foregrounded. On several occasions during the *Three Fantasies*, the choir moves in large chord clusters through the clearly marked scansion of rhythm.

On Ligeti's Return to a Real Poetic Text

Last but not least, these *Fantasies* mark a return to text, an element that had been absent from Ligeti's choral and vocal works since the 1960s, with the exception of the Latin texts in Requiem and *Lux Aeterna*, whose meaning was not a key factor. Here we leave behind the imaginary language of *Aventures*, the 'vocal' tones of *Clocks and Clouds*, and come back (durably, as this would extend beyond the *Fantasies*...) to a very distinctive setting of poetical texts to music, to Ligeti's appropriation of a poetry he had loved since he was young:

> Rather than transpose his poems in music, I wanted to elaborate linguistic, emotional and pictorially vivid features which resonated with certain musical ideas, images and concepts. There are associations of musical ideas [...], but they are not settings in the Schubertian or Wolfian sense — to mention just the two most distinguished composers of songs. [...] I did not simply want to write straight "settings" of the poems, as that would just have led to the same kind of re-duplication that we see in a large number of literary operas. Following the texts slavishly and inventing music to go with them — that is an undertaking I find just too primitive and superfluous. [...]
>
> I in fact behaved with complete passivity: I used fragments of text wherever music appeared of its own accord, and conversely I omitted parts which did not inspire any music — above all in places which are abstract or imaginary. If you look at what I used, you will see that there are nothing but concrete, sensual images — nothing philosophical, or only what is also indirectly conveyed through images[3].

Noticeably, Ligeti dwells here on the concrete impact of words, to the detriment of abstract and philosophical dimensions, and occasionally favours a figurative dimension, reflected in the general expression, if not in the forms of these *Three Fantasies*.

In a letter to Constantin Floros dated 2 August 1983, Ligeti stresses that he did not simply choose Hölderlin's fragments because he loved his work; he contrasts their «marvellous imagery and emotional aura» with the poetry of Sándor Weöres[4]:

---

[3]. KOLLERITSCH 1987, pp. 132-133, translated into English by Maryse Staiber, and (for the second paragraph) LOBANOVA 2002, p. 263.

[4]. FLOROS 2013, pp. 113-115.

Rediscovering the Meaning of Words with Hölderlin

> The fact that I choose Hölderlin: it is not just that he is one of my favourite poets. For the "setting" I actually chose those poetic fragments for their marvellous imagery and emotional aura. (In the past I have written choruses on Hungarian texts, on poetry by Sándor Weöres, where the element of verbal imagination is the most important element, while in the Hölderlin poems the field of imagery had greater resonance for me.)[5]

An examination of the selected poems — respectively *Hälfte des Lebens* (The middle of life), from the odes and hymns of 1799-1802, *Wenn aus der Ferne* (If from the distance) and *Abendphantasie* (Evening fantasy) from the maturity years (1798-1800) — and of the musical work reveals a large number of different relationships between text and music; sometimes the poem disappears into the music (the first stanza of the first poem, the entire second poem) while being symbolically 'exploited'.

A few pertinent elements in both poetic and musical terms will serve as signposts here, including the concepts of autonomy, heteronomy, fragment, distance, emotional remoteness and isolation, separation (themes that were dear to Ligeti), and opposition, for instance between anabasis (an ascending movement) and catabasis (the descending chromatic sequence on *traurig*), etc.

Given the innovative character of the writing of the first poem, and the innovative potential of the composition, this study focuses on a comparative poetic and musicological study of the *First Fantasy*, and to a lesser extent of the *Third Fantasy*. Regarding the *Second*, which although it expands on themes that are dear to Ligeti (distance, loss), is less original than the other two in both poetic and musical terms, we will mostly consider its canons at the unison and micro-intervals in relation to a poetic text that is also more conventional.

Perhaps Ligeti attempted to highlight Hölderlin's 'modernity' with his musical setting, to bring him closer to us, while drawing on older texts in his search for a new balance, at a time where the composer was experiencing an identity crisis and a creative crisis.

We observe a particular interest of the composer for moments where the poetic text shifts away from a confident stance, a drive towards 'beauty and harmony', and turns to solitude, melancholy, loss, distress and exile.

First Fantasy

The *First Fantasy* is particularly interesting both poetically and musically. The poem *Hälfte des Lebens* is the shortest of the three texts, and here Ligeti only cut out two lines, unlike in the other texts where he made far more extensive cuts.

---

[5]. *Ibidem.*

In a recent publication on the genesis of the work, Vera Funk drew on Paul Sacher Foundation documents to uncover Ligeti's initial plans for these *Fantasies*, consisting of a cyclical structure with a single musical motif repeated in all three pieces for greater unity[6]. This idea was apparently later scrapped, as it is not found in the final version.

The Text and Overall Form

The textual material of this first *Fantasy* is strikingly characterized by sharp breaks, oppositions, if not a tendency to split into fragments. Extraordinarily potent evocations are introduced in these breaks, in a quick succession of highly disparate images. Ligeti's cut after the fifth line (see the bracketed passage below) reinforce the evocative power of this sequence by removing the original verb phrase and the complement:

Und trunken von Küssen	And drunk with kisses
(Tunkt ihr das Haupt	(You dip your heads
Ins heilignüchterne Wasser.)*	Into the hallowed, the sober water.)

*. Ligeti cut out the bracketed passage. English edition: Hölderlin 1980.

Here, Ligeti abandons the complement altogether, focusing on the evocation of kisses, conveying an image of being drunk on the fullness and beauty of life (with its plentiful fruits and wild roses)[7]. The dimension of purity and sanctity (expressed by the neologism «heilignüchterne Wasser») disappears as a result of the composer's cut, and we directly turn to an elegiac expression of the distress and solitude of a lyrical I: «Weh mir, wo nehm» ich…?» (But oh, where shall I find?). This cut makes the musical sequence more abrupt and dramatizes the exile, the roaming of the human being on earth, abandoned and prey to winter. The musical treatment reinforces the idea with an overlap of the two texts and a contrast in the writing for the beginning of the second stanza (which is far more vertical).

If we look at this *First Fantasy* as a whole, we find that in its general form it is organized around an alternation between complex polyphonic sequences (in which the text is unintelligible) and passages where the homorhythm of voices and nuances highlight far more intelligible bits of the text. We examine this in greater detail below through an analysis of the three moments (the first is divided into two sub-parts) that stand out upon listening, precisely characterized by:

---

[6]. Funk 2017.
[7]. For a complementary reading of this work, see Lichtenfeld 1987, p. 123.

Rediscovering the Meaning of Words with Hölderlin

1 - Polyphony (inherited from Ligeti's previous works):
2 - New musical gestures facilitating the understanding of snippets from the text:
3 - A complex polyphony, close to heterophony, with a final emphasis on «klirren die Fahnen» (Weathercocks clatter) (*tutta la forza*).

The Musical Transposition of a Blend of Diverging Elements from the Poem

1A: bars 1 to 13

The beginning of the *First Fantasy* (*Hälfte des Lebens*) (bars 1 to 13) provides an illustration of this divergence. This part corresponds to the following lines:

Mit gelben Birnen hänget	With yellow pears the land
Und voll mit wilden Rosen	And full of wild roses
Das Land in den See	Hangs down into the lake

Here we are in the presence of the same melodic imitation among the sopranos, altos and tenors, including micro-intervals. This common melody is presented in two different rhythmic forms, alternating between ternary (sopranos 1, 3, altos 1, 3, etc.) and binary subdivisions (sopranos 2, 4, altos 2, 4, etc.). There is a strict canon (melody and rhythm) between some voices, but each new entry comes in the form of couples of voices (one in a binary rhythm, the other in a ternary rhythm). This rigorous canon does not last: each section successively loosens the canon and then departs from it (see for instance the lengthening of rhythmic values on *Rosen* during bars 5-7 on G sharp then A flat), in an order reversed from that of the initial entries. The tenors, which initially appeared third, exit the canon first by ushering in a first entry in tutti on E flat (bar 6). Then comes the turn of the altos on B flat (see Ex. 1) and of the sopranos on C sharp (bar 8).

In this passage, two texts are sung simultaneously, somehow highlighting the entire realm of the living (generously given to us by nature, creation): unlike in the poem, where elements appear in succession as the text unfolds linearly, the music, through the overlap of different parts of the text sung by the sopranos, altos and tenors on the one hand, and the basses on the other (see Ex. 1, p. 54), creates a different structure to simultaneously evoke this bounty, this abundance of the realm of the living, ruled by harmony and a sense of plenitude.

While the writing for the sopranos, altos and tenors is fairly unified owing to the canon, the basses play a specific role: as they sing «Das Land in den See», they adopt the same rhythmic device using pairs of voices (bars 3-6), but with an ascending melody, culminating in the first entry in tutti (to which they contribute in part) of the tenors on «In» as the basses end their phrase on «Land». The following entry of the four basses on «In» (end of bar 7) coincides exactly with the (aforementioned) entry of the altos on «Das Land». This beginning, which may seem quite simple, actually proves to be remarkably subtle in its diversity.

Ex. 1: *Drei Phantasien nach Friedrich Hölderlin* (1), altos 1 and 2, basses 1 and 2 only, up to beginning of bar 8.

As the passage continues, the sopranos, altos and tenors are again subject to canonic writing (bars 9-12), but this time with only two voices per section, which creates a sense of dislocation.

The following transpires from the analysis of this first sub-section:

- the text is sung in full by the sopranos and altos;
- it is distorted by the tenors: «Mit gelben Birnen hänget / Das Land»;
- it is sung by the basses only beginning at «Das Land»; then, in bars 9-10, the basses sing «hänget» (from line 1) followed by «Das Land» (from line 3) after «in den See», switching the order of words around.

1B: bars 13 to 17

This passage corresponds to lines 4 and 5 of the first stanza; the composer cut out lines 6 and 7.

Ihr holden Schwäne (bar 13)	You lovely swans,
Und trunken von Küssen	And drunk with kisses
([Tunkt] ihr das Haupt	(You dip your heads
Ins heilignüchterne Wasser.)	Into the hollowed, the sober water.)

In this kind of transition leading to the second stanza, Hölderlin displays a particularly noble poetic register that might have resonated with Ligeti: «Striving for high art is very important to me»[8].

Regarding this cut, it can be hypothesized that Ligeti meant to 'say' something through the cut (lines 6-7: «Tunkt ihr...»): the swan, a highly symbolic animal and the (sober/refreshing) water are connected, leading to a syntaxial fragmentation (lacking coherence, as it stops at «Trunken von Küssen» (And drunk with kisses), and the neologism «heilignüchterne» disappears. This cut can likely be explained by the excessively abstract and philosophical evocation of these lines, if not their foray into the realm of the religious and sacred (see Ligeti's quotation in the introduction).

This section connects with the preceding one against the backdrop of the basses still singing «Das Land in den See» (the land [...] / Hangs down into the lake), and then already «Weh mir» (But oh) with the tenors, in a kind of lamentation: the basses are initially lagging, and subsequently (alongside the tenors) ahead of the other sections.

Note here the (vertical) confluences of vocal sounds in bars 14-17 around «Küssen» and «Weh mir» at a point where two parts of the poetic text overlap — indeed, «Weh mir» belongs to the beginning of the second stanza. For clarity, we reproduce in Ex. 2 some of the voices from the vocal group that represent the different texts sung in bars 15 to 17 (see p. 56).

Climax (Second Stanza), bars 18-27

A first section, in bars 18-21, confers great verticality on the following lyrics from the three first lines of the second stanza, sung homorhythmically by the entire choir, without caesurae:

(Weh mir), wo nehm' ich, wenn	But oh, where shall I find
Es Winter ist, die Blumen, und wo	When winter comes, the flowers, and where
Den Sonnenschein	The sunshine

---

[8]. Ligeti 1985, p. 126.

Ex. 2: *Drei Phantasien nach Friedrich Hölderlin* (1), soprano 1, alto 1, tenor 1, basses 1 and 4, bars 15 to 17.

This is a very dynamic passage, *Tutta la forza, con dolore*, with an intensification of sound owing to the fact that two sections begin (altos and basses) and the two others (except for soprano 4) join them for the crescendo in bar 19, leading to a very strong nuance (***fffff***) — see TABLE 1. This moment arguably stands out as the expressive climax of this *First Fantasy*.

TABLE 1
TEXT DISTRIBUTION BARS 18-27

	Bars 18-20	Bars 20-22	Bars 23-24	Bars 26-27	End of bar 27
Sopranos	Bar 19: *und wo Den Sonnenschein?*		*Die Mauern stehn*	*... stehn*	
Altos	*wo nehm ich, wenn / Es Winter ist, die Blumen, und wo / Den Sonnenschein?*		*Die Mauern stehn*	*... stehn*	
Tenors	Bar 19: *und wo Den Sonnenschein?*		*Die Mauern stehn*	*... stehn*	
Basses	*wo nehm ich, wenn / Es Winter ist, die Blumen, und wo / Den Sonnenschein?*	*Und Schatten der ...*	*... Erde ?*	*Sprachlos und*	*Kalt*

Rediscovering the Meaning of Words with Hölderlin

What follows, starting from the end of bar 20 (see Table 1), again features a backdrop of basses («Schatten der Erde»), and then a concentration of the entire choir with empathetic, *tutta la forza*, homorhythmic accents in A flat on the words «Die Mauern stehn». From a poetic standpoint, after the plenitude, the lyrical subject is surrounded by walls and left to his own devices: the music itself also suggests a sense of closing in (with the reduction to a single note sung on several octaves before «stehn»). The poetic and existential context is more concrete here, and its musical equivalent appears to be the homorhythm as well as the limitation to the A flat.

Und Schatten der Erde? (barely intelligible)	And shade of the earth?
Die Mauern stehn (bars 24-27; clearly intelligible)	The walls loom

The ensuing transition of the basses on «Sprachlos und kalt» (Speechless and cold) matches the intensification of the elegiac dimension in poetic terms, culminating, with the loss of words and the grip of the cold, in a point of non-return, an extreme existential disarray. The end of bar 27 constitutes a sort of articulation (which anyone familiar with Ligeti's music in general will recognize: a small sustained cluster on A sharp/B) between what precedes and what follows (indeed, the canon in the following section also begins on these two pitches).

Long Final Section (bars 29 to 50)

im Winde	in the wind
Klirren die Fahnen.	Weathercocks clatter.

In this long passage, the listener can only make out the beginning of the text: «Im Win...», and the end, sung homorhythmically on «klirren die Fahnen» (Weathercocks clatter). In the poetic evocation, despite the disappearance or loss of language, the world does not fall entirely silent: there are still sounds coming from actual elements and objects (the wind howling, the weathercocks clattering), violent, strident, aggressive sounds. While language, understood as communication between human beings, has vanished entirely, dissonant sounds and meaningless noises remain.

Musically, the entire passage is characterized by a single overarching evolution, with altos, tenors and sopranos singing increasingly restless rhythms while the basses provide a static backdrop on the vowel A until the final words sung with the others: «klirren die Fahnen» (Weathercocks clatter). The writing in bars 29 to 36-37 is based on the steady stratification of ternary and binary rhythms between the voices (one voice in ternary rhythms, another in binary rhythms); this common thread in the overall sound is however not systematic in this passage either. In its complexity, the writing foreshadows Ligeti's later work, as do bars 12 to 20 in the third *Fantasy*. In detail, we find that:

Firstly, the «couples» of voices (alto 1/alto 2, alto 3/alto 4; tenor 1/tenor 2; tenor 3/tenor 4) are regulated by a very precise overall pattern of sorts in bars 29-35, allowing for a final vertical coincidence by groups of two voices (ending on *F* at bar 33 on altos 1 and 2; at bar 34 on altos 3 and 4 then tenors 1 and 2, and at bar 35 on tenors 3 and 4). We reproduce the parts of altos 1 and 2 for a better visualisation of this phenomenon:

Ex. 3: *Drei Phantasien nach Friedrich Hölderlin* (1), altos 1 and 2 only, bars 29-34.

Secondly, after these convergences on *F*, the hierarchies are reversed within the couples: at the end of bar 33, alto 2 comes in and is imitated by alto 1 (see Ex. 3), and the same goes for all other couples of voices, including among the sopranos (from bar 34 on: imitations between soprano 2 and soprano 1, and then soprano 4 and sopranos 3).

Rediscovering the Meaning of Words with Hölderlin

This reversal (a phenomenon that is reminiscent of some of the devices at work in Wolfgang Rihm's musical setting of Paul Celan poems[9]) reoccurs when the binary/ternary superimposition disappears within the «couples» after some time and gives way to a stabilisation of the rhythm around the semiquavers (bars 36-38) at the point where Ligeti asks for «neutral vocals» (the legato is gradually left behind starting at bar 36). Then, we have the progressive appearance (still unstable by bar 39) of a new wave of imitations in two groups (sopranos on the one hand and altos on the other, end of bar 39 and bar 40), led by soprano 1 on the one hand and alto 1 on the other (we have only mentioned two voices for each section here, but voices 3 and 4 can be inferred from the above).

Ex. 4: *Drei Phantasien nach Friedrich Hölderlin* (1), sopranos 1 and 2, altos 1 and 2 only bars 38-41.

---

[9]. Michel – Staiber 2015.

This sequence triggers an overall acceleration (agitation: crescendo) starting in bar 41, coinciding with an increasingly heightened dislocation (starting in bar 44) of the vocal parts with numerous silences, the addition of micro-intervals and a gradual decrease in the number of sounds in the phrases (5, then 4, 3, 2 and finally a single note — *C*), in a vast crescendo. Such complex processes are frequently found in Ligeti's work[10].

All these elements combined (from bar 29) are more reminiscent of heterophony than of ancient counterpoint, especially as this passage also includes a slower layer of alternating, overlapping sustained bass notes.

In her dissertation Jane Piper Clendinning insists on the implication of complex patterns and explains that «the final section [...] features a combination of pattern-meccanico and microcanon — a melodic line strongly influenced by pattern-meccanico techniques is set in microcanon in eight parts entering at quarter notes intervals»[11].

To be more specific regarding the vocal and sound dimension of this part, we observe the appearance of the final syllable «de» («Win-de») on the different voices starting at bar 35; in bars 38-40, the composer states that the legato should be ended and a switch made from the vowel *e* to a neutral vowel. The «Win-de» sound becomes «he-he-he» at bar 40: this hardening, which is initially moderate on «he», is pushed further with «ke» (bar 41), leading to a transformation of the vocal sounds, which become highly articulate as the vast crescendo unfolds. Phonetically, «ke-ke-ke» (bar 41) foreshadows the later strongly aspirated consonant of «Klirren». This development on the vocal sounds «de, he, keke» appears to have been of particular concern for the composer, who clearly intended to highlight this sense of stridency, of violence over a fairly long stretch of time. This free expansion around the poetic text intensifies the dramatization of the final sequence of the poem, its existential disarray; as the closing words «klirren die Fahnen» (bars 49-50) are clearly intelligible, it is likely that Ligeti wanted to emphasise them; he notes in the score that the vocal sounds must resemble cries («wie zwei Schreie»), while strictly respecting the indicated pitches («jedoch in genauer Tonhöhe»).

Distance/Emotional Remoteness/Lamentation: On the *Second Fantasy*

A connection is made straight away with the *First Fantasy* through the expression of a lamentation («Wehe mir» in the *First Fantasy* and «Ach! wehe mir!» in the *Second*); as the composer repeats these words on several occasions in the *Second Fantasy* (bars 43-48, 53-55), we get the sense that this is a recurring motif.

---

[10]. Michel 1995.
[11]. Clendinning 1989.

Rediscovering the Meaning of Words with Hölderlin

The poem is used very partially (numerous passages are omitted) and madrigalisms are evoked on «Nachtigall» (nightingale) (bars 27 ff.) in the form of vocalisations. Different passages of the text are often superimposed (as if in a counterpoint) and coincide on part of a sentence or a word, set to music in a clear, homorhythmic manner.

The stanzas succeed one another without caesuras, but some openings stand out as on «Wars Frühling?» (Was it in spring?) and «Ach! wehe mir!» (But ah! woe is me!), probably for emphasis.

Some passages of the text are highlighted by the homorhythmic writing and thus more intelligible:

- «Und dunkler Zeit wir uns gefun(den)?» (And darkened years once more we're meeting) tenors 3 and 4, basses 1 abs 2, bars 18-19;
- «Wars Frühling? War es Sommer?» (Was it in spring? in summer?) (tutti);
- «Ein seelig Dunkel» (A blissful darkness) bars 34-36, partly homorhythmic writing. «Hoher Alleen» (made by tall avenues) bars 38-39, tenors and basses 1 and 3;
- «Ach! wehe mir!» (But ah, woe is me) bars 43-48, different sections then tutti at 47;
- «Ach» (composer's addition, tenors and basses, bars 54-55) then «Traurige» (Sad) (bars 54-56);
- Wenn aus der Ferne (If from distance) (bars 57-60, sopranos): Ligeti added these words here as a reprise of the initial text on a second important motif, distance, which plays a key role in his music and presents itself here as a call-back to the initial melodic motif. Ex. 5 shows both presentations in the soprano 1 part, for the first bars and bars 57-58.

Ex. 5: *Drei Phantasien nach Friedrich Hölderlin* (II), bars 1-2 and 57-58, soprano 1.

This *Second Fantasy* is probably the most traditional out of the three, despite the rather frequent occurrences of micro-intervals: it may even evoke some choral works by Brahms (*Fünf Gesänge*, Op. 104). The sound is fairly round, with canons at the unison forming a continuous flow: the melodic movement (E, D, C sharp, in a descending movement) of the initial canon recurs in different rhythmic presentations (see Ex. 5); variations and transpositions of this three-note conjunct, descending motif, which could very well be perceived as a tonal element, are proposed. The composer himself, who had just written his Trio for Violin, Horn and Piano, openly acknowledged this traditional dimension:

> I imagine highly emotive music, of high contrapuntal and metric complexity, with labyrinthine branches and perceptible melodic forms, but without any "back-to" gesture, not tonal but not atonal either[12].

This overall sound is strongly evocative of the traditions of romantic music, with occasional consonant harmonies (bars 16-18, basses and tenors), more or less exposed open fifths (bars 11, tenors/basses; bar 55, basses), and even the 'BACH' motif in canon in bars 39-41 (on G – F sharp – A – G sharp).

In addition to the main canon, there are almost always complementary elements: the flow of the music does not rest on a single overarching process (as is often the case in *Lux Aeterna*), but always on at least two elements that can be contradictory.

The non-canonic passages frequently include micro-intervals that are more or less homophonic, as in the tenor and bass parts in bars 10 to 13 on «erwartet die Freundin dich» (your girlfriend awaits you now).

The form of this *Second Fantasy* is characterized by a high degree of continuity and more or less pronounced build-ups, with dynamic climaxes reached for example in bars 26-27 on «Wars Frühling? war es Sommer?», in bars 35-36 on «Ein seelig» and on bars 46-48 on «Ach! wehe mir!».

The *Third Fantasy*: A Certain Intermediality

Here, in addition to the worlds of poetry and music, a pictorial dimension comes into play, as the composer alludes on multiple occasions to his long-time infatuation with a famous painting by Albrecht Altdorfer, *Battle of Alexander at Issus* (*Alexanderschlacht*)[13]. This intermediality was emphasized by Ligeti himself during the discussion that followed Monika Lichtenfeld's presentation at the 1984 symposium of Graz (see note 1). Art historians have used the term polysensoriality in reference to the 1529 painting, in which different worlds are superimposed (East/West, setting sun/rising moon, night/day) — antagonisms and contrasts that clearly appealed to Ligeti.

This *Third Fantasy* is more compact and denser than the *Second*, and also far more dynamic, with a rapid succession of elements. Fig. 1 shows the overall form of this part, highlighting moments of greater intensity, such as the passage from bar 4 to 24 («unzählig/der Zauber»).

---

[12]. Ligeti 2007.
[13]. Painting shown at Munich's Alte Pinakothek.

Rediscovering the Meaning of Words with Hölderlin

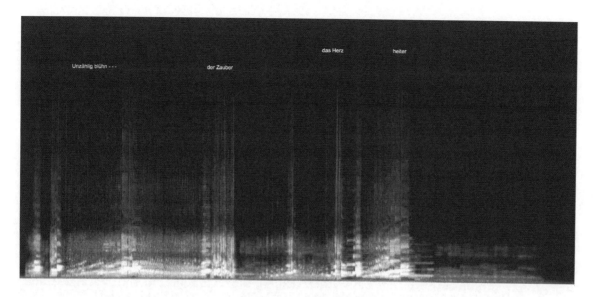

Fig. 1: *Drei Phantasien nach Friedrich Hölderlin* (iii), graphic representation using E-Analysis.

Of the three *Fantasies*, this is the one where the text is overall most intelligible and where the poetic images are the most accented.

A first listen reveals a few contrasts in the writing: the words «Unzählig blühen die Rosen» (There countless roses bloom) trigger a canon in the entire choir, where each new entry rises by a semitone; the phrase «dorthin nimmt mich» (O there now take me) is scanned on a simple, catchy, accented quaver rhythm (bar 11); also, «Purpurne Wolken» (Crimson-edged clouds) gives way to a complex heterophony (bars 12 to 21).

Another comment by Ligeti arguably sheds light on precisely the latter passage:

> In the *Abendphantasie* the association of Altdorfer's *The Battle of Alexander at Issus*, the vast scenery of cloud formations pierced by rays of sunlight plays a role: that could be quite random on my part — I don't know if Hölderlin saw the *Battle of Alexander*[14].

Also worth mentioning are the words «dunkel wirds» (darkness falls), sung by the altos and basses in low registers; the phrase «Du ruhelose, träumerische!» (you the dreamy, wild / Unquiet) coinciding with an unstable, restless passage; «...ist dann das Alter» (All my late

---

[14]. Excerpt from a letter to Constantin Floros (FLOROS 2013, p. 114). In the discussion that followed Monika Lichtenfeld's presentation (Graz 1984, see KOLLERITSCH 1987, p. 133), Ligeti noted the importance of this painting, which had first been pointed out by Ulrich Dibelius. In her article «Canon as an agent of revelation in the music of Ligeti» (BAUER 2019), Amy Bauer observed that Ligeti also mentioned this painting in reference to his work *Lontano* (LIGETI 1983, p. 93).

years) in a low register with sustained notes, ending with an overall descending movement (with micro-intervals) with the indication «morendo poco a poco al niente» and a long hold on the final vertical interval.

Remarks on the Music

Overall, this *Third Fantasy* is a less continuous, fluid piece than the first two; it features sharper articulations and outlines, with numerous homorhythmic passages, synchronous accents, etc.

A few specificities of the polyphonic writing are worth noting: A few elements stand out: at the beginning (bar 4), starting from «Unzählig blühn die Rosen» (There countless roses bloom), among the basses, the imitation sung by all voices on different degrees (rising by a semitone at each entry). Furthermore, on the words «die goldne Welt» (the golden world) in bars 8-10 (canon at the unison, basses then tenors), the texture becomes increasingly stable, with longer rhythmic values; the end of this passage is characterised by loud *ff* superimposed accents on «Welt» and «O!» (added by the composer).

The «Dorthin nimmt mich» (O there now take me) in bar 11 clearly stands out with its rhythmic pattern in accented quavers, reflecting the poetic idea of being transported into another world, another realm. It is worth recalling Ligeti's own statement in his notes on this work here:

> What I have in mind is a spiritualized, strongly condensed art form. I am trying, beyond every kind of modernity, to recreate in music something of today's sense of life[15].

The following section, which is based on a non-canonic counterpoint built around three-tone motifs (bar 12) highlights the word «Purpurne» (Crimson-edged). This initially non-canonic passage often ends with canons (for instance for basses 4 and 3, end of bar 15 and the following bars), with occasionally overlapping voices. The complexity and scope of the musical development on «Purpurne» (bars 12 to 20) is arguably an indication and confirmation of the significance of the imagery of the crimson clouds in the sky of Altdorfer's painting; the word «Wolken» is emphasised briefly but strikingly (*ff*, long final sustained note). Ex. 6 shows the end of this evolution leading up to the emphasis on «Wolken». This passage is slightly evocative of heterophonies from other cultures in which Ligeti was interested at the time[16].

---

[15]. LIGETI 2007.
[16]. See MICHEL 1995, pp. 119-130.

Ex. 6: *Drei Phantasien nach Friedrich Hölderlin* (III), bars 19-21, sopranos and altos only.

The following transition is characterised by homophonic blocks on the words «und möge droben // In Licht und Luft zerrinnen mir Lieb» und Laid! — / Doch, wie verscheucht von thöriger Bitte, flieht / Der Zauber» (and up there at last let // My love and sorrow melt into light and air! — / As if that foolish plea had dispersed it, though, / The spell breaks) that stand out quite clearly and function as articulations from a high point that comes practically in the middle of this *Fantasy* to a darker and quieter passage on «Dunkel wirds und einsam» (darkness falls, and lonely): Ligeti highlights the image of the spell breaking to depict a nocturnal,

Ex. 7: *Drei Phantasien nach Friedrich Hölderlin* (III), sopranos, altos and tenors only, bars 33-36.

lonely universe. At the line «Unter dem Himmel, wie immer, bin ich. —» (Under the heavens I stand as always. —), the presence of a lyrical «I» and the allusion to the sky disappear. Only solitude and darkness remain, hence the musical articulation from very vivid blocks to a highly polyphonic passage of low, dark musical tones, subito lento.

On the words «zu viel begehrt» (with «O» added by Ligeti) / Das Herz» (For the heart demands / Too much) (bars 34-36, see Ex. 7), the writing becomes more vertical again, with often strong nuances. The use of male falsettos in this passage (first tenors and basses, bar 34, then bar 37, then 39 for bass 1 solo, then basses in 46 on the «-ter» syllable of «Heiter», as in an echo) resonates with the text's evocation of the rush of youth, suggesting the idea of an overwhelming, too intense desire — this part is not sung by the female vocalists. In Ex. 7 we can see that the male vocalists sing the entire line «Zu viel begehrt das Herz», whereas the female vocalists, which are delayed by a bar, sing «O das Herz»; note the addition of the interjection «O» (for the sopranos only) and a reduction of the text for the female vocalists, on a more emotional register than the text sung by their male counterparts.

After a new canon on different degrees (in an ascending chromatic movement) in bars 39-43, entrusted to the altos and sopranos on «du, ruhelose, träumerische...», we reach a new dynamic climax on the words «friedlich und heiter» (for serene contentment) (bars 42-46) which are sung in succession with great intensity (*tutta la forza*). Rather than a sense of peace and serenity, a deep tension between reality and dream persists. The desire to attain some kind of peace remains a dream, a fantasy, and is not embodied in reality. In this sense, Ligeti points to the sense of existential disarray that runs through Hölderlin's poetic writing and makes him our contemporary, while reinforcing the contrast between «ruhelos» and «friedlich und heiter ist dann das Alter» (Unquiet / All my late years for serene contentment).

After «Heiter», which is neatly divided into two syllables in bars 45-46 (*tutta la forza*), there is a gradual limitation of the number of voices on the words «das Alter» (bars 49ff.), which are sung by the altos, tenors and basses in dark, low registers (suggesting old age), and eventually (bar 53) only by the tenors and basses in a *morendo poco a poco al niente*, as is often heard in Ligeti's work.

Conclusion

This interdisciplinary study brings us to three final questions:

1) How can Ligeti's trajectory explain the return to ancient texts?

While Ligeti evoked the idea of an aesthetic crisis[17], we are of course reminded here of Wolfgang Rihm's *Hölderlin-Fragmente* (1976-1977)[18], which, a few years prior to the *Fantasies*,

---

[17]. *Ibidem*, p. 196.
[18]. Rihm 2013, pp. 27-29.

proposed a more traditional approach to composition, mediated in particular by the impact of the young German composers sometimes associated with the «New Simplicity» movement on cultural life[19].

A key question raised in the *Third Fantasy* and throughout the cycle, stands out: How can there be a return to beauty and spirituality after 1945? This in turn is evocative of a question that arises in all artistic forms. Revisiting Hölderlin's complex work involves dealing both with the ancient world (Greek and Roman Antiquity) and the modern: this work is close to us in the themes it addresses: exile, wandering, disorientation, worry, existential disarray — all characteristic of modernity. Ligeti himself appears to have always felt a kinship with Hölderlin: «What is essential to me in Hölderlin's art is the tension between a domesticated, almost classical form (ancient metrics, balanced language) and an excessive emotional content»[20].

2) As Hölderlin himself famously put it by asking «und wozu Dichter in dürftiger Zeit»[21], we may also consider this: what is the good of being a composer «in a time of distress»?

These *Three Fantasies* reflect a time of crisis, a pivotal time when the composer could not and did not want to adopt a clear-cut positioning between the ancient and the new. As in Hölderlin's poetic writing, he situates himself in an in-between space, allowing him to look for new compositional paths while drawing on ancient devices (canon, madrigalism, etc.).

This is why the music of the *Fantasies* cannot be pigeonholed (being neither tonal nor atonal), in the same way that Hölderlin cannot easily be categorized, as he looked both to the distant past (Greek antiquity) and to the future (he was fascinated by the new values of the French Revolution and the new vision of mankind) — in his writing the combination of ancient and the new is pushed to the breaking point, leading to fragmentation. Ligeti made many cuts and worked with poetic fragments, highlighting oppositions, antagonisms. The *Three Fantasies* exemplify a new global conception of a music that reflects this complexity — hence its in-between positioning: «I imagine highly emotive music, of high contrapuntal and metric complexity, with labyrinthine branches and perceptible melodic forms, but without any "back-to" gesture, not tonal but not atonal either»[22]. Ligeti's musical treatment highlights Hölderlin's modernity while striving for a new balance.

3) What is the contribution of our interdisciplinary approach, consisting in a comparative study of the poetic text and the music?

---

[19]. DARBON 2007.
[20]. LIGETI 2007, French translation in *L'Atelier du compositeur*, p. 286.
[21]. HÖLDERLIN 1980.
[22]. LIGETI 2007.

Rediscovering the Meaning of Words with Hölderlin

By evidencing compositional processes based on an idiosyncratic interpretation of selected poems, which Ligeti treats as fragments, we have shown that the scattershot, fragmented character inherent in Hölderlin's poetry is intensified, even though an attention to meaning remains on display. Ligeti's approach is very different from those of Luigi Nono or Wolfgang Rihm. Musically, his *Fantasies* exhibit a sense of continuity (in that they are more or less linear, fluid). The poems are not broken down into bits of text: there is a respect for the poetical text, whose meaning is not destroyed, even though some sequences are not clearly intelligible. Through his choices in the treatment of the three poems, Ligeti brings Hölderlin closer to us, making him our contemporary, emphasising contrasts and the themes of solitude, exile and existential disarray.

Bibliography

BAUER 2019
BAUER, Amy. 'Canon as an Agent of Revelation in the Music of Ligeti', in: *Contemporary Music and Spirituality*, edited by Robert Sholl and Sander Van Maas, Abingdon-New York, Routledge, 2019, pp. 109-127.

CLENDINNING 1989
CLENDINNING, Jane Piper. *Contrapuntal Techniques in the Music of György Ligeti*, Ph.D. Diss., New Haven (CT), Yale University, 1989.

DARBON 2007
DARBON, Nicolas. *Wolfgang Rihm et la Nouvelle Simplicité*, Notre Dame de Bliquetuit, Millénaire III, 2007.

FLOROS 2013
FLOROS, Constantin. 'Ligeti's *Hölderlin-Phantasien* – A Letter from the Composer', in: *New Ears for New Music*, translated by Kenneth Chalmers, Frankfurt am Main, Peter Lang, 2013, pp. 113-115.

FUNK 2017
FUNK, Vera. '«Einen Anfang finden». György Ligetis Skizzen und Entwürfe zu den *Drei Phantasien nach Friedrich Hölderlin* für sechsstimmigen gemischten Chor a cappella', in: ZGMTH / *Zeitschrift der Gesellschaft für Musiktheorie*, XIV/2 (2017), pp. 263-283.

HÖLDERLIN 1980
HÖLDERLIN Friedrich. *Poems and Fragments*, translated by Michael Hamburger, bilingual edition with a preface, introduction and notes, Cambridge, Cambridge University Press, 1980.

KOLLERITSCH 1987
György Ligeti; Personalstil – Avantgardismus – Popularität, edited by Otto Kolleritsch, Vienna, Universal Edition, 1987 (Studien zur Wertungsforschung, 19).

Lichtenfeld 1987
Lichtenfeld, Monika. '... «und alles Schöne hatt' er behalten» – Fragmente zur Ligetis Ästhetik', in: Kolleritsch 1987, pp. 122-133.

Ligeti 1983
György Ligeti in Conversation with Péter Várnai, Josef Häusler, Claude Samuel, and Himself, translated by Gabor J. Schabert, Sarah E. Soulsby, Terence Kilmartin and Geoffrey Skelton, London, Eulenburg, 1983 (Eulenburg Music Series).

Ligeti 1985
Ligeti, György. 'Entretien avec Edna Politi', in: *Contrechamps*, no. 4 (April 1985), pp. 123-127.

Ligeti 2007
Id. 'Drei Phantasien nach Friedrich Hölderlin', in: Id. *Gesammelte Schriften. 2*, edited by Monika Lichtenfeld, Mainz, Schott, 2007 (Veröffentlichungen der Paul Sacher Stiftung, 10), pp. 285-286 [translated by Catherine Fourcassié in *L'Atelier du compositeur. Ecrits autobiographiques. Commentaires sur ses œuvres*, Geneva, Contrechamps, 2013].

Lobanova 2002
Lobanova, Marina. *György Ligeti: Style, Ideas, Poetics*, Berlin, Verlag Ernst Kuhn, 2002.

Michel 1985
Michel, Pierre. 'Les rapports texte/musique chez György Ligeti de *Lux Aeterna* au *Grand Macabre*', in: *Contrechamps*, no. 4 (April 1985), pp. 128-138.

Michel 1995
Id. *György Ligeti compositeur d'aujourd'hui*, Paris, éditions Minerve, 1995 (Musique ouverte).

Michel – Staiber 2015
Michel, Pierre – Staiber, Maryse. 'Wolfgang Rihm et la poésie de Paul Celan', in: *Paul Celan, la poésie, la musique – Avec une clé changeante*, edited by Antoine Bonnet and Frédéric Marteau, Paris, Hermann, 2015, pp. 453-471.

Rihm 2013
Rihm, Wolfgang. 'La langue comme occasion pour la musique', in: *Fixer la liberté?*, texts selected by Pierre Michel, and translated by Martin Kaltenecker, Geneva, Contrechamps, 2013, pp. 27-29.

The Dove and the Bear: 'Galamb Borong' and the Connection to 'Ars Subtilior'

Manfred Stahnke
(Hochschule für Musik und Theater Hamburg)

Beginning in the 1980s, a discussion about new or unusual methods of rhythmic organization flourished in the Hamburg composition class of György Ligeti. From very early on, the music of Conlon Nancarrow (1912-1997) belonged to this discussion firsthand; Ligeti had discovered his works in Paris in the summer of 1979. When I came back to the class in October 1980 from the USA, I could add some more of the Nancarrow Studies for Player Piano[1]. I had found Studies 1, 27 and 36 in Hamburg, at the Institute for Musicology, in early summer 1979. This was the earliest Nancarrow vinyl recording that was released, and I copied it to a music cassette. The vinyl also contained Ben Johnston's *Sonata for Microtonal Piano* (1960-1964), which I had originally set out to find as I wanted to study with him, from summer 1979, in Urbana-Champaign, Illinois. I also gave this piece from the 60s, with its strong hint of popular music from the US, to Ligeti. Johnston (1926-2019) had been one of the closest co-workers and promoters of Harry Partch (1901-1974). From the 70s on, Partch, the modern inventor of «just intonation», became a central influence on Ligeti's harmonic thinking. But in this essay, I will concentrate on Ligeti's thinking about time construction and will only glimpse at his new scales in so far as they are important for his seventh piano étude, 'Galamb borong'.

Originally, Nancarrow's polymetric thinking came from a direct jazz reference; he tried to envisage the swing of jazz. A jazz trumpet player himself, his distance from bar lines led to his success when using paper rolls for the pianola, his mechanical piano. In this regard, Nancarrow is not far away from the experimental works of the 'Ars subtilior' era around 1400, which were also far away from bar divisions. Here, a freely flowing cantus was achieved through new

---
[1]. On MILLER 1976.

expressions of durations (triplets, quadruplets, additive rhythm, and displaced syncopation). This complex rhythmic world of great flexibility existed only for a very short time in Europe, from around 1370 to 1420; it was developed by Jacob de Senleches from Flanders and his colleagues, and was named «Ars subtilior» by musicologist Ursula Günther (1927-2006)[2]. I will relate this music to Ligeti.

In 1979 a student from Puerto Rico, Roberto Sierra, came to the class and brought salsa from the Caribbean. Even more important was Sierra's discovery in 1982 of Central African animal horn music of the Banda Linda, an immediate sensation in Ligeti's class[3]. Simha Arom, whose first vinyl record was *Musiques Banda* in 1971, had analyzed the hocketing pulse layers via multitrack recordings. Arom, originally a horn player from Paris then a self-taught ethnologist, who became a close friend of Ligeti, made these recordings of an initiation rite in the Central African Republic. We compared this music with the medieval hocketing technique. Soon the young musicologist Annette Kreutziger-Herr brought us music by Johannes Ciconia from around 1400; I remember the tapes spinning on Ligeti's Revox machine. Ciconia's canonic chanson *Le ray au soleyl* in 4:3:1 proportions became a hit in the class. I copied some of the transcriptions of the Codex Chantilly (edited in 1982 by Gordon Greene)[4], which included Solage and his astonishing chord progressions in *Fumeux fume*, Senleches with his endlessly, softly flowing *En ce gracieux tamps*, and Rodericus with *Angelorum psalat*. In this essay I will deal with a rhythmic feature of this ballade and show a possible connection with 'Galamb borong'.

Within the group around Ligeti, a vocabulary of very different times and world regions amalgamated towards new forms of thinking. Ligeti and his class searched for new — or rather, old — rhythm and harmony, almost manically foraging through radio programs of the time about old or non-European music, like Radio Bremen 2 or Radio DDR 2. We exchanged music cassettes with Ligeti; his secretary, Louise Duchesneau, distributed copies of pieces Ligeti wanted to let us hear from his newly found treasures, and vice versa. Balinese and Javanese time and scale organization, analyzed by Jaap Kunst[5], were as fascinating as the extremely long-stretched polymeters from the High Andes (explored by ethnomusicologist Max Peter Baumann)[6], or polyphony from New Guinea and the Solomon Islands, such as the tendency towards equidistant heptatony in Malaita (studied by Hugo Zemp)[7].

---

[2]. GÜNTHER 1963, p. 112.
[3]. AROM – DOURNON-TAURELLE 1971.
[4]. GREENE 1982. Codex Chantilly. S. Uciredor ('Rodericus'), *Angelorum psalat*, Bibliothèque et archives du château de Chantilly, MS 564 fol. 48v. Cliché CNRS-IRHT, © Bibliothèque et archives du château de Chantilly, copies from the manuscript with kind permission.
[5]. KUNST 1973.
[6]. BAUMANN 1982.
[7]. ZEMP 1978.

Harry Partch's friend and supporter, my teacher Ben Johnston, visited the Ligeti class in early summer 1981. He stayed with me and my family, and loved pickled rolled herring, «rollmops»: «I could commit suicide on them». At that time Johnston wrote extremely complex microtonal string quartets; it took a while, until 2016, for these later quartets to be recorded, by the Kepler Quartet[8].

These years when a new way of thinking broke through, away from the worn-out paths of the old avant-garde, were as thrilling for us as for Ligeti. Suddenly possibilities showed up, saving us from 'neo' ways — not only from Neo-Romanticism, but also from the neo-avant-garde, though a composer like Brian Ferneyhough loved and used Ars subtilior concepts just as we did. He had also been my teacher in Freiburg, when he was an assistant to Klaus Huber.

In 1988, Ligeti's farewell from the Hamburger Musikhochschule arrived. Together with Louise Duchesneau, I organized an International Ligeti Congress at the Hochschule, a present from us and the class for his retirement. It was financed by the Deutsche Forschungsgemeinschaft, so we could invite speakers from many countries. To begin with Ars subtilior, the most prominent scholar in this field, Ursula Günther[9], came, as well as other top-class musicologists like my teacher in musicology Constantin Floros[10], and others[11]. The French-Israeli ethnomusicologist Simha Arom[12] came, together with a band of African musicians, as did the Austrian specialist on African music Gerhard Kubik[13], the pioneer of fractal pictures Peter Richter (1945-2015)[14], the scientist and Nobel prizewinner Manfred Eigen (1927-2019)[15], and the two outstanding computer music specialists John Chowning[16] and Jean-Claude Risset (1938-2016)[17]. For the later publication *Für Ligeti*[18], Kubik even wrote a kind of textbook for us on East African music of Buganda, mostly dealing with pattern techniques. Arom wrote about his use of the microtonal Yamaha DX7-II synthesizer in the bush, where he offered the musicians the possibility of tuning the synthesizer themselves according to their own pitch preferences in order to find out the interval intentions behind their xylophone tuning. John Chowning had been the inventor of this first digital synthesizer, and was also the computer music teacher of two Ligeti students, Wolfgang von Schweinitz and me, from 1978 to 1980. Jean-Claude Risset was a composer and

---

[8]. Kepler quartet 2016.
[9]. Günther 1991.
[10]. Floros 1991, pp. 11-20 and 335-348.
[11]. See the essays by Schneider, Reiche and Petersen in Petersen 1991.
[12]. Arom 1991.
[13]. Kubik 1991.
[14]. Live lecture.
[15]. Live lecture.
[16]. Chowning 1991.
[17]. Risset 1991.
[18]. Petersen 1991.

the programmer of the auditory illusion of a never-ending downwards glissando (in *Computer Suite from Little Boy* (1968); 'Little Boy' was the military nickname of the first atomic bomb in action), which can be compared with Ligeti's ninth étude, 'Vertige', with its impression of never-ending descending lines.

The president of the Hochschule, Hermann Rauhe, was extremely helpful for getting the money for the congress. The vice president, Werner Krützfeldt (1928-2008), presented Ligeti with Willi Apel's famous book, *The Notation of Polyphonic Music, 900-1600*[19], with its focus on Ars subtilior notation. Krützfeldt had been the mastermind behind getting Ligeti to Hamburg in 1973.

Ligeti's never-ending and meandering way of searching, which infected all of us, included more and more far-reaching fields of thinking. Like him, some of us were interested in the visual arts, in natural sciences, in mathematics, or in computers, which in the 80s started to be cheap enough for us to buy — the Japanese student Kiyoshi Furukawa started with a simple Atari computer to create his «cellular automatons». Ligeti thought about a Partch-style organ in forty-three uneven just-intonation steps per octave for himself to use, but this project never came into being. I myself tried out a hybrid duo for harp and synthesizer, where the harp was tuned in just intonation and the synthesizer equidistantly, being almost in just intonation for 5/4 thirds and 7/4 natural sevenths, in the twelfth root of 1.9560685 (a wrong 'octave'). The harp tuning of *Partch Harp* (1987) looks like this[20].

Ex. 1: Harp tuning of *Partch Harp*.

On our DX7 machines we also tested equidistant pentatonic or heptatonic systems found worldwide, such as in Indonesia. For me, 'Galamb borong' seems to be Ligeti's comment on these experiments. Ligeti had no such systems at hand for the piano, of course, but, going further than Debussy's whole-tone scale, he imitated exotic equidistance by interlacing the two whole-tone scales possible on the piano. Ligeti wrote:

> The music itself is composed in an oblique equidistant tonal system. The usual tuning of the piano permits twelve-tone and six-tone equidistance, but not

---

[19]. Apel 1942.
[20]. Soundfile at <https://www.youtube.com/watch?v=rI3yFCy9TSo>, accessed May 2022.

the five-tone one (as in the Javanese *slendro*), whose intervals cannot be found in the well-tempered tuning. But I now have invented another kind of *slendro*-like tone system, which is neither chromatic nor diatonic, but also not whole-tone: it is covertly present in the usual tempered tuning of the piano, but has not been performed before "Galamb borong"[21].

To look in more detail at 'Galamb borong', we have to include the wider fields of thought previously briefly mentioned. In the center of Ligeti's graphic interests were Maurits Escher's forms, which repeat until any movement comes to a standstill — also a basic concept for Ligeti in many of his Études. He was also influenced by Ernst Gombrich's book *Art and Illusion* (called, in the new German version, *Kunst und Illusion*)[22] about the techniques of the old masters. Gombrich argues that the intended signal or content arises in the eye of the viewer, a very Ligetian approach to art. From mathematics and cognitive sciences came more fields for developing our thinking, like the book *Gödel, Escher, Bach: An Eternal Golden Braid* by Douglas R. Hofstadter (1979)[23], which connected music, mathematics, and the arts. In 1986 the book *The Beauty of Fractals*[24] appeared, another dive into a maelstrom. Ligeti, ever interested in mathematics, collected information about the Bourbaki group[25], about the Koch snowflake[26] (he loved its fractal aspect), and about mathematical tessellation akin to Escher.

As for Balinese music, the endless submersion of the layers of pulsation must have fascinated Ligeti, as would its construction of timeless loops. This music does not begin or end since it has no 'aim'. Any 'aim' (only imaginable for us because of a gong at an illusory 'end' of a phrase) leads to a new commencement. The gong also indicates a new beginning, comparable to Machaut's endless canon *Ma fin est mon commencement*.

All this gave Ligeti a new and fresh structural thinking far away from his style in the 60s, often called 'micropolyphony', as well as from his work in the 70s and his polystylistic tendencies related to pop art, such as the opera *Le Grand Macabre* (the first version of which premiered in 1978). In his class, Ligeti liked to refer to the pop artist Richard Hamilton and his collage *Just what is it that makes today's homes so different, so appealing?* (1956). A Herculean male stretches his penis, formed as bellows with 'POP' written on it, towards a pin-up girl who, in retaliation, stretches her breasts towards him, holding one of them in her hand. It is quite clear to me that we can relate this to Ligeti's year-long discussions about pop art with his student Hans-Christian von Dadelsen. In the first movement of the Horn Trio, I recognize the dispute about

---

[21]. Floros 2014, p. 167.
[22]. Gombrich 2002.
[23]. Hofstadter 1979.
[24]. Peitgen – Richter 1986.
[25]. Ligeti mentions Bourbaki in Stahnke 2017, p. 163.
[26]. Koch 1906.

Neo-Romanticism within his class, as I experienced it from 1974 to 1979. This movement may be a lament on the death of Ligeti's mother, who apart from himself was the only survivor of the Holocaust in his family.

In Ligeti's early Hamburg years, the discussions circled not only around pop (the group Supertramp with 'Breakfast in America' was an example)[27] and Neo-Romanticism, but also around jazz. Ligeti's cembalo «pastiche» (a term Ligeti used for it) *Hungarian Rock* (1978) is related to jazz or pop.

Let us now come even closer to the Études and 'Galamb borong' with its additive rhythms. Finally, let us consider its closeness to the Ars subtilior, which so far has not been seen. The extended technique of hemiolas within Ars subtilior has been related by Hannes Schütz to the second étude 'Cordes Vides'[28]. Additive rhythmic procedures, away from simple 'bars', clearly came to the young Ligeti via popular music from the Balkans. Ligeti loved to talk about his encounters with Romanian folk and street music. He was born in a little town called Diciosânmartin, at that time governed by Romania, and the singing of the Romanian policemen impressed the small boy very much. Ligeti mentioned that the Romanian fast *aksak* rhythms[29] had a much bigger impact on him than the Hungarian music influenced by the *kaiserliches und königliches* monarchy and Vienna. Later he was confronted with the research of Bartók and Brăiloiu, and later still with that of Arom, Kubik, and Simon in Africa.

In a recorded talk I held with Ligeti in 2001[30], he said that his rhythmic research restarted in 1982 after encountering Arom's recording of the Banda Linda:

> Ligeti: First, by accident, I found this book of Artur Simon on Africa: *Musik in Afrika*[31]. A collection of many articles. Here I found an article about elementary pulsation, timeline structure, by [Gerhard] Kubik and Alfons Dauer. I don't know him personally, but you invited Kubik to Hamburg.
>
> Stahnke: In 1988 to the Ligeti Congress. [Regarding elementary pulsation:] Was this a predisposition in you? I think of Bartók. Bartók researched this in the Balkans and elsewhere...
>
> L.: Yes, but it is a little different. There was the outstanding Romanian ethnomusicologist Constantin Brăiloiu, whom I did not know. I knew very many recordings of his from the Folklore Institute in Bucharest. He was the chairman of this archive. Then he fled from the communists to Geneva. When I came to Bucharest from Budapest, autumn and winter '49-'50, I stayed there for three months listening to the vinyls, but mainly to wax rolls, from Bartók, with Romanian folk music, and

---

[27]. DADELSEN 2013, p. 60.
[28]. SCHÜTZ 1997.
[29]. BRĂILOIU 1984, pp. 133-167.
[30]. Private audio archive, CD 2001.
[31]. SIMON 1983.

partly from Brăiloiu. It was a big institute with six to ten researchers. They did a wonderful job. Bartók and Brăiloiu knew each other, Brăiloiu was younger...

Ligeti, from 1956 onwards living in the West, undertook a kind of exorcism of his early research and work, and only came closer to pulsation-based compositions in the 60s, to some degree in a kind of Fluxus Happening in 1962, where he, in tails, conducted one hundred metronomes in his *Poème symphonique*, with one hundred arbitrarily and chaotically organized pulses, which he soon after reduced to forty. The pulsating machine became more and more important for him, in the third pizzicato movement of the Second String Quartet or in *Continuum*, both from 1968. *Continuum* mainly previews Ligeti's future, using in-built rhythmic patterns and melodic superpositions[32]. Akin to Bach, the cembalo creates hidden metrical layers, suggesting inherent figures for the listener.

After that point, Ligeti never really abandoned pulses. One of his pieces, *Clocks and Clouds* (1973), became important, where micropolyphonic aspects are confronted with a clicking, mechanistic world. *Clocks and Clouds* seems to be a work of transition. In California, Ligeti experienced deeply the minimalism of Steve Reich, La Monte Young, and Terry Riley, who somehow enter *Clocks and Clouds*[33]. In the 70s, minimalism was a big topic in the Ligeti class, e.g. Riley's *In C*, Young's *The Well-Tuned Piano*, or later Reich's *Tehillim*.

The title *Clocks and Clouds* came to Ligeti from philosopher Karl Popper and his lecture of 1965, 'Of Clouds and Clocks'. Ligeti wrote: «I liked Popper's title and it awakened in me musical associations of a kind of form in which rhythmically and harmonically precise shapes gradually change into diffuse sound textures and vice-versa, whereby then, the musical happening consists primarily of processes of the dissolution of the "clocks" to "clouds" and the condensation and materialization of "clouds" to "clocks"»[34]. In comparison, Popper wrote: «My clouds are intended to represent physical systems which [...] are highly irregular, disorderly, and more or less unpredictable [...] On the other extreme [...] we may [consider] a very reliable pendulum clock, a precision clock, intended to represent physical systems which are regular, orderly, and highly predictable in their behaviour»[35].

The precise and the diffuse also stayed with Ligeti in the Études. This essay argues, furthermore, that there is a connection between the highly 'infinitesimal' Ars subtilior of around 1400 and the seventh étude 'Galamb borong'. I have chosen an extreme example from that time, the ballade *Angelorum psalat*. I brought this piece to the class in the early 80s, and Ligeti was aware of its specialness. We talked about Ars subtilior in 1993[36]:

---

[32]. Ligeti called this a «Supersignal» in German. This is a term from physics which Ligeti often used.
[33]. LOBANOVA 2002, p. 198.
[34]. See LACOSTE, n.d.
[35]. POPPER 1972.
[36]. STAHNKE 2017, pp. 179-180.

Stahnke: The overall building is constructed by the composer. As a musician you fly through it, hoping that you find the proper exit. I heard a very good ensemble from Basel, Project Ars nova, which commented on it [Ars subtilior] like that.

Ligeti: Which composer do you think of? Before my eyes, Rodericus is floating by. You once brought him to the class.

S.: Yes, *Angelorum psalat*, but here a voice is missing, which does not appear in the manuscript. Yes, Rodericus could be an example for the way the local harmony is not directed.

L.: Ah, an incomplete work. It is so crazy what happens there. Stravinsky later did quite similar things artificially. The consciously wrong chorales in *Histoire du soldat*.

S.: The singularity of this medieval music is that one accepts what happens harmonically in the progression. Not every detail is led. This may be a reflection on Perotin.

L.: Only the junctures are important. There you must have octaves and fifths.

S.: Quite similar to gothic arches, where you can fill in in between with a quasi-chaotic ornament.

L.: Such half-chaotic music. After all, you can find it in avant-garde music, in a completely different way.

***

Let us now delve into the chanson attributed to «S. Uciredor» («Rodericus» backwards), *Angelorum psalat*, a ballade in two voices, or two written voices with a potentially improvised contratenor. Around 1400 the intellectuals' scent spread out and led to all kinds of deformations, such as *Fumeux fume* by Solage, a companion of Rodericus. Rodericus's chanson *Angelorum psalat* is soft and flowing, similar to *La harpe* by his other colleague Jacob de Senleches. It uses the same language of symbols, and it is extremely polyvalent in its meaning. The music of Rodericus begins as a hymn for a harp player sitting amid angelic musicians, and it ends as a curse against a biting beast. Is this perhaps the pope in Rome, dividing the Church? Or does it curse Death for having taken away a friend[37]? The tenor of *Angelorum*, with its retrograde elements, points to a dead friend to be lamented, closely related to the retrograde tenor *Amicum querit* («he deplores a friend») of an anonymous motet in the same codex (Codex Chantilly), *Alpha vibrans – Coetus venit – Amicum querit*, which appears shortly after *Angelorum*.

But here I will concentrate on the superius. The whole metrical system of *Angelorum* is quite extraordinary because of the polymetric 9:8 proportion, recurring twice between superius and tenor. To analyze this would be another essay examining another similarity between Ars subtilior and Ligeti, away from additive rhythms.

---

[37]. STAHNKE 2020.

The angel's music («Angelorum [...] musicorum») provides the «embracing» textual structure for the performing musician, who sings and plays a subtle rhythmic figure among the angels, revealing the proportion 8:9 at «psa-[lat]», which is important for the whole chanson. Eight dotted sixteenth notes fit into the same time as nine triplet eighth notes.

The superius — the melody line — expresses a triple-time structure at «[An]gelorum», colored in alternating red and black. The composer creates a chain of syncopations.

Ex. 2: Rodericus, *Angelorum psalat*, «Angelorum psalat», manuscript and transcription.

Senleches and those around him also developed color combinations for the semibreve, and Rodericus is very much at the center of these innovators. To achieve a note length of seven thirty-second notes (as transcribed by Josephson)[38], Rodericus uses a rhombus that is half solid red and half empty at «[tri-]pudium musico[rum]». The symbol appears four times in this sequence, and a fifth time at «ut faus Innocui» at the end of the chanson. In the passage «tripudium musicorum» this special symbol is followed by a double-stemmed black rhombus with an upper hook, indicating a length of three thirty-second notes. The red rhombus gives eight thirty-second notes, the rest sign four. This gives an additive rhythmic pattern of 7 – 3 – 8 – 4.

Ex. 3: Rodericus, *Angelorum psalat*, «[tri-]pudium musico[rum]», manuscript and transcription.

[38]. JOSEPHSON 1971, p. 121ff. See also STOESSEL 2013, p. 61: «The second behavior of arithmetic notes occurs where part of the body of a note is not drawn in order to indicate a corresponding reduction of the duration of the normal note».

We use thirty-second notes as the smallest unit, with rests in brackets:

(4) 4 8 12 **4 7 3 8** (4) 12
        7 3 8 (4)
        4 7 3 8 (4) 12 7 4 4 3 8 (a variation of the sequence follows)

The repetition is evident, as is the permutation 7 4 4 3 8. It is clear that Rodericus was absolutely aware of the effect of these numbers, though the smallest unit, an «infinitesimal» thirty-second note in the transcription, must have been only a number for the composer, not a musical unit. All these musically incomprehensible numbers add up to a perfect mensuration for the whole passage.

Another metrically complex passage with a long suspension (until «blandis») can be seen at «[pessi]ma ante blandis …»:

Ex. 4: Rodericus, *Angelorum psalat*, «[pessi]ma ante blandis ut», transcription.

The proportional note lengths are:

(3) 3 4 3 **(2) 4 3 3** (4) 3 3 4 6
       (2) 4 3 3 (4) 3 4 4 12 3 3 3 3 4 4 …

again with a repetition, aside from 4 3 3 in the permutations.

Dealing with 'infinity' was a new way of thinking in the late fourteenth century, derived from William Ockham's philosophy or the mathematics of Nicole Oresme, who worked with Philippe de Vitry[39]. We confront a mirror, where we see Ockham and Oresme on one side in

---

[39]. TANAY 1999, pp. 211-245; see also RIMPLE 2003, pp. 15-17.

the fourteenth century and Mandelbrot on our side in the twentieth. Let us now compare this with Ligeti's world.

***

It must be taken with a pinch of salt when we find a similarity between Rodericus's melody formations in *Angelorum psalat* and Ligeti's consideration of additive rhythm in 'Galamb borong', composed in 1988 and 1989, as both composers seem to have improvisatory aspects. Very often Ligeti goes back to simple additive patterns, like «5 3» in the first étude, 'Désordre'. It seems logical that Tobias Kunze, from the Center for Computer Research in Music and Acoustics at Stanford University, built a computer algorithm representing its structure[40]. But this program cannot reduce the constant variability of the pattern development to a formula; it has to be transferred as a whole into the program. Ligeti's Études are a dance between cold calculations and lively spontaneity, and even more so in 'Galamb borong'.

Let us first collect some general information about the étude. The title words *galamb* and *borong* are both a pun. 'Galamb' in Hungarian means 'dove' or 'pigeon', 'borok' means 'crying'. «In Hungarian, says Ligeti, they happen to mean "melancholic pigeon"»[41]. Since the words also sound «Indonesian» for Ligeti, as he often said in the class, there will be other meanings in it. Constantin Floros, a close friend of Ligeti, mentions a non-existent island Ligeti thought of[42]. Ligeti read a lot about non-European music, including gamelan. We discussed Jaap Kunst and his musings on the *pélog* and *slendro* scales[43]. 'Galamb borong' is very close to 'gamelan barong'; 'barong' is a Balinese dance, while 'galamb' could be a play on 'gamelan'. The Balinese dancer and cultural scientist I Made Bandem wrote about the «barong dance»: «Barong probably derives its name from the Sanskrit word bahrwang, which literally means bear [...] Nowadays, because of its function as a protector, the Barong is considered as a manifestation of good forces which always fight evil forces, the latter usually taking the form of Rangda, a wild female demon [...] If a village is infected by a serious epidemic, a priest soaks the beard of the Barong in a bowl of clean water; the water thus filled with white magic power is afterwards used to save the lives of the people»[44].

---

[40]. In TAUBE 2006, chapter 22.
[41]. STEINITZ 2003, p. 300. Steinitz visited Ligeti in Hamburg for his book.
[42]. FLOROS 2014, p. 166: «In a comment on the seventh étude of 1988/89, Ligeti remarked that its title, *Galamb borong*, was meant to evoke an imaginary gamelan-like music "at home on an island not found on any map". "For those who understand Hungarian", he continues, "the title will also have an altogether different meaning — Galamb in Hungarian means as much as dove, darling or sweetheart — but that is irrelevant to the character of the music: what matters is solely the verbal sound of the title"».
[43]. KUNST 1973.
[44]. BANDEM 1976, p. 48.

Bandem also writes about the instruments which play the different rhythmic layers:

> Barong is accompanied by Gamelan Bebarongan, an orchestra accompanying only the Barong dance, which is set to a five-tone Semarpagulingan (Legong Music) [...] The complete instrumentation of the Gamelan Barong is the following:
> Two gender rambat (metallophones): 13-15 keys, struck by two hammers are suspended above some tuned bamboo resonators and produce a hard metallic or a sustained musical sound.
> Six to eight gangsa, four pemade, and four kantil: the keys rest above a wooden resonator box and produce a hard metallic sound.
> Two jegogan and two jublag: gender-s of different sizes with five keys for the main tones [...]
> One kendang, or two-headed drum: slightly conical, this instrument is held crosswise on the lap and played on each end with the hand or a stick.

The gong is important for the time structure: «One gong gede: the largest hanging gong, which punctuates the longest melodic phrase on the last note of the phrase»[45].

Ligeti takes the idea of the gong into his étude. It shows up at cue points in phrases 1 to 2, 2 to 3, and 3 to 4 (see below). This is supported by Floros's hint towards a previous title for this étude: «Les gongs de l'île Kondortombol»[46]. This is Ligeti's name for a fantasy island, for which he drew maps and invented a language with its own grammar.

All recordings I have heard from the orchestra Bebarongan are tuned in *pélog*, which means a pentatonic scale with five steps from a quasi-equidistant heptatony. Mathematically this would mean 171-cent steps, in a selection close to C5, low B4, G4, high F4, low E4, and low B3 in relative pitch classes, C4 being middle C. At least, this is the scale I have mostly heard in 'gamelan barong'. In 'Pagodes' from *Estampes*[47] or 'Cloches à travers les feuilles' from *Images*[48], for example, Debussy used whole-tone scales, seemingly as equivalent to equally spaced pentatony (240c, *slendro*).

Ligeti mostly makes his five phrases polymetric. The slowest layer, aside from the «gong», is a melody line, corresponding to the top line of «gamelan barong» which is often supported by bamboo flutes. Underneath we find a multiple arrangement down to the fastest layer, played by *gender* instruments.

How does Ligeti build his phrases? In the first phrase he uses constant sixteenth-note trills, from which a melody with metrical lengths grows, from bar 3 onwards (in sixteenth notes): 12 12 12 12 6 6 5 5, then *p tenuto*, always with the same length of 4 sixteenth notes.

---

[45]. *Ibidem*, p. 51.
[46]. FLOROS 2014, p. 166.
[47]. Mentioned in *ibidem*, p. 166.
[48]. STEINITZ 2003 sees a proximity to 'Galamb borong', p. 299.

The Dove and the Bear

The following example outlines this development: Unfolding trill → melody → medium layer, added figures from the fastest layer:

Ex. 5: Ligeti, 'Galamb borong', bars 1-11, rhythmic and melodic development.

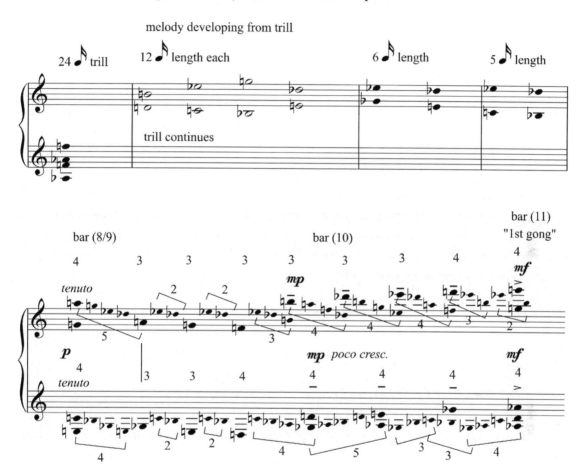

In Phrase 1, bars 8/9, a medium layer of tone groupings develops, the upper group in 4 3 3 3, the lower group in 4 3 3 4, then from *mp tenuto* the upper 3 3 3 4, the lower 4 4 4. This new medium layer continues in Phrase 2, *mf* accent bar (11), supposedly the «first gong» (see description of Phrase 2). The fastest layer, developing from the previous trill, then contains unidirectional sixteenth-note groupings of 2-5, not counting leaps of more than a third.

This is followed in Phrase 2, bars 11-26: (*mf* accent), with *sub. **pp**, **p** dolce*, polymetric without *cresc.* until bar 16, *sub. **ppp**, **mp** tenuto dim.* bar 17. In this bar we have *mp tenuto dim.* ***ppp***. Middle of bar 19: ***p*** *tenuto molto cantabile*, polymetric, *cresc. until **fff*** bar 26: second gong. In Phrase 2 the medium layer continues, from the ***mf*** accent, bar 11:

10 6
3 3 2 3 4
3 3 2 3 4
3 3 2 3 4 11 (*sub.* ***ppp***).

Ligeti gives the upper line a repetitive pattern of 3 3 2 3 4 (4 always with an accent). The lower staves have:

10 (subdivided as 3+7) **6**
3 3 3 3 2
3 3 3 3 2
3 3 3 3 2 14

The bold numbers indicate synchronous events between upper and lower staves.

The bigger part of this phrase is polymetric, the upper staves with 3x15 units, the lower with 3x14 units. Then we have a melody bar again (17), made from four- to five-tone chords, with the following durations, after a «prelude» in bar 16 of eleven sixteenth notes and quite similar to the very beginning of Phrase 1:

11 9 7 14

Then from bar 19 there is a *molto cantabile*, polymetric upper component:

7 7 7 14 7 7 7 7 7 3 3 3 3 2 **2**, then bar 26 «second gong», ***fff sf***.

In bar 19, *molto cantabile*, we have a split. The lower component shows 5 4, except the end in 3 3:

5 4 5 4 5 4 5 4 5 4 5 4 5 4 5 4 3 **3**.

Then in bar 26 there follows the «second gong», almost synchronously with the upper stave only one sixteenth note later, as A♭1 plus a ninth, B♭2. The upper stave has a metric grouping of 7, the lower of 5+4=9 units. Bold numbers again indicate synchronicity.

In Phrase 3, bars 26-45, an enlarged ***ff*** picture occurs, like a sustained «third gong», internally carved out, increasing to ***ffff*** in bar 45. Here for the first time song-like motives occur, in bar 27, durations 2 1 4, then an «answer» 3 3 3 6. The use of the smallest value, the sixteenth note, is striking in the motive 2 1 4. A prefiguring of this lies in bars 23/24 in the medium-layer figures of 1 2 2 2 or 2 2 2 1.

Ex. 6: Ligeti, 'Galamb borong', phrase 3, Song-like motives, from bar 27.

In phrase 4, bars 46-73, (*ffff*) ***ppp*** *subito misterioso, molto cantabile*, added melody ***pp*** *in rilievo*, the building of motives is continued from bar 27, sometimes internally carved from sixteenth notes.

Ex. 7: Ligeti, 'Galamb borong', phrase 4, motives from bar 46.

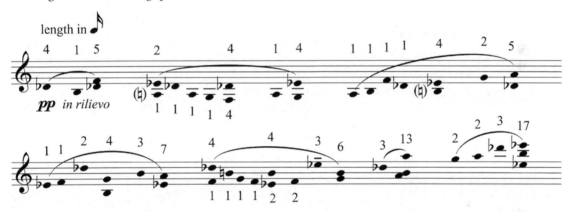

In Phrase 4, from bar 56, there follows *sub.* ***ppp*** *sempre legato* with mushrooming motives of sixteenth notes, followed by a longer note:

1 1 1 1 1 1 1 6

Followed by:

1 1 1 1 1 1 1 6

Then the motive interlaced:

1 1 1 2 and 1 1 1 1 1 1 1 4

With further mushrooming, which finally leads to similar sixteenth note groupings as in Phrase 1, also evoking the trill idea of the beginning. From bar 59, *cresc. molto* until *fffff* in bar 70, these groupings are held until bar 73, like a much prolonged «fourth gong».

Next comes phrase 5, bar 73: *sub. pp*, an added *p* D♭1, the new «double bass» line, soon in the lowest staves, followed by C1, then B♭0 and at the very end A0 instead of A♭0 (Ligeti's joke), again combining the two whole-tone scales. The whole Phrase 5 is like the fading of a gong sound: *diminuendo... al niente*. The lines move down three times in superimposed layers.

Multiple lines follow from bar 73 on. «Effective distances» mean the durations in sixteenth notes from note to note in the same layer; I do not refer to the lengths as they are written here. Ligeti apparently took these effective distances from a table, sometimes shifting the values. The following chart shows the layers one after the other; «(x)» means a free decay.

Ex. 8: Ligeti, 'Galamb borong', phrase 5, motives from bar 73.

In the score this can be located as follows:

Layer 1, beginning on the upper staves, bar 74, until 77.

Layer 2, beginning on the second lowest staves, bar 74 with E4+C5. Split in *2* and *2 a)* in bar 80.

Layer 3, beginning on the second upper staves, bar 73: bass line with D♭1, continued in the lowest staves.

The Dove and the Bear

Table 1
Ligeti, 'Galamb borong', Layers Bars 73-77.

Layers	*1*	*2 a)* see below *2*	*2* continued	*3* Bass
notated	12 7 5 3 4 3 (x)	30 9 27 10 5 <u>1+6+2</u> 14 6	4 7 16 7 4 4 12 (x)	24 47 25 (x)
normalized	12 6 6 3 3 3	30 10 25 10 5 10 15 5	4 8 16 8 4 4 12	24 48 24
proportional factor	4:2:2: 1:1:1 **3**	6: 2: 5: 2: 1: 2: 3: 1 **5**	1: 2: 4:2: 1:1:3 **4**	4: 8: 4 **6**
layer, split		*2 a)*	*2 a)* continued	
notated		8 8 8 24	5 20 5	
normalized		8 8 8 24	5 20 5	
proportional factor		2: 2: 2: 6 **4**	1: 4: 1 **5**	

Proportions close to these ideas can be found in the overall form of the étude:

Table 2
Ligeti, 'Galamb borong', Proportions between the Sections

Phrase	1	2	3	4	5	
number of sixteenth notes	120	188	236	317	ending	
normalized, in bars	120 10	180 15	240 until *"in rilievo"* 20	300 25		
proportional factor	2 **5**	: 3	: 4	: 5		

Numbers 2:3:4:5 are the form proportions as well as the basic proportions in the realm of microrhythm. Ligeti writes in the preface of 'Galamb borong', «The emerging development of the lines of melody and rhythm (within two independent rhythmic layers for the right and the left hand) lies in whole number multiples of a sixteenth»[49].

Ars nova in its essence and the later development of Ars subtilior can be characterized by proportional thinking. Ligeti was fascinated by the talea idea of the isorhythmic motet of that

---

[49]. Ligeti 1988-1989, p. 4.

time, up to Guillaume Dufay and the proportions 6:4:2:3 in his motet *Nuper rosarum flores* of 1436. In 'Galamb borong', bells ring from medieval times in concert with Balinese gongs, and a Hungarian dove, *galamb*, dances with the Sanskrit bear from Bali: *b(a)orong*.

***

La Coda by Ursula Günther. I cite from her lecture held at the Ligeti Congress in 1988, with wonderful music from her beloved Ars subtilior[50]:

> This highly intellectual art of the most complicated fabric, created for a thin stratum within the elitist society of the late medieval era, could never reach popularity. After some decades, this art was completely forgotten. We can easily comprehend the fascination of contemporary composers for this art of the highest level, just recently rediscovered in our century. For they also create works that are rhythmically daring and contrapuntally densely woven, in a stylistically diverse, highly individual fabric. To reach a true understanding of today's music, an intellectual elite is needed.

BIBLIOGRAPHY

APEL 1942
APEL, Willi. *The Notation of Polyphonic Music, 900-1600*, Cambridge (MA), Mediaeval Academy of America, 1942.

AROM 1991
AROM, Simha. 'A Synthesizer in the Central African Bush: A Method of Interactive Exploration of Musical Scales', in: PETERSEN 1991, pp. 163-178.

AROM – DOURNON-TAURELLE 1971
AROM, Simha – DOURNON-TAURELLE, G. *Musiques Banda – république centrafricaine*, (LP), Paris, Vogue, 1971 (Collection Musée de l'homme).

BANDEM 1976
BANDEM, I Made. 'Barong Dance', in: *The World of Music*, XVIII/3 (1976), pp. 45-52.

BAUMANN 1982
BAUMANN, Max Peter. *Musik im Andenhochland (Bolivien)* (2 LPs), Berlin, Museum für Völkerkunde, Abteilung Musikethnologie, 1982.

---

[50]. GÜNTHER 1991, p. 285.

BRĂILOIU 1984
BRĂILOIU, Constantin. *Problems of Ethnomusicology*, English translation by Albert Lancaster Lloyd, Cambridge-New York, Cambridge University Press, 1984.

CHOWNING 1991
CHOWNING, John M. 'Music from Machines: Perceptual Fusion & Auditory Perspectives – for Ligeti', in: PETERSEN 1991, pp. 231-244.

DADELSEN 2013
DADELSEN, Hans-Christian von. 'György Ligeti, Die «NEUROMANTIK» und der Pop: Erinnerungen an einen Unangepassten', in: *Neue Zeitschrift für Musik*, CLXXIV/4 (2013), pp. 60-63.

FLOROS 1991
FLOROS, Constantin. 'Versuch über Ligetis jüngste Werke', in: PETERSEN 1991, pp. 335-348.

FLOROS 2014
ID. *György Ligeti: Beyond Avant-garde and Postmodernism*, translated by Ernest Bernhardt-Kabisch, Frankfurt am Main, Peter Lang, 2014.

GOMBRICH 2002
GOMBRICH, Ernst H. *Kunst und Illusion. Zur Psychologie der bildlichen Darstellung*, Berlin, Phaidon, 2002.

GREENE 1982
GREENE, Gordon K. *Polyphonic Music of the Fourteenth Century. 2*, Monaco, Les Remparts, 1982.

GÜNTHER 1963
GÜNTHER, Ursula. 'Das Ende der ars nova', in: *Die Musikforschung*, XVI/2 (1963), pp. 105-120.

GÜNTHER 1991
EAD. 'Die Ars subtilior des späten 14. Jahrhunderts', in: PETERSEN 1991, pp. 277-288.

HOFSTADTER 1979
HOFSTADTER, Douglas. *Gödel, Escher, Bach: An Eternal Golden Braid*, New York, Basic Books, 1979.

JOSEPHSON 1971
JOSEPHSON, Nors S. 'Rodericus: Angelorum Psalat', in: *Musica Disciplina*, XXV (1971), pp. 113-126.

KEPLER QUARTET 2016
KEPLER QUARTET. Ben Johnston. String Quartets Nos. 6, 7, & 8, (CD), New York, New World Records 80730-2, 2016.

Koch 1906
Koch, Helge von. 'Une méthode géométrique élémentaire pour l'étude de certaines questions de la théorie des courbes planes', in: *Acta Mathematica*, XXX (1906), pp. 145-174.

Kubik 1991
Kubik, Gerhard. 'Theorie, Aufführungspraxis und Kompositionstechniken der Hofmusik von Buganda', in: Petersen 1991, pp. 23-162.

Kunst 1973
Kunst, Jaap. *Music in Java: Its History, Its Theory and Its Technique*, edited by Ethel L. Heins, Den Haag, Nijhoff, 1973.

Lacoste n.d.
Lacoste, Steve. 'Clocks and Clouds: György Ligeti', <https://www.laphil.com/musicdb/pieces/1313/clocks-and-clouds>, accessed May 2022.

Ligeti 1988-1989
Ligeti, György. 'Galamb borong', in: *Études pour piano, deuxième livre*, Mainz, Schott Music, 1988-1989.

Lobanova 2002
Lobanova, Marina. *György Ligeti: Style, Ideas, Poetics*, Berlin, Ernst Kuhn, 2002.

Miller 1976
Miller, Robert (piano). *Sound Forms for Piano*, (LP), New York, New World Records LP NW 203, 1976.

Peitgen – Richter 1986
Peitgen, Heinz-Otto – Richter, Peter H. *The Beauty of Fractals: Images of Complex Dynamical Systems*, Berlin, Springer, 1986.

Petersen 1991
Für György Ligeti. Die Referate des Ligeti-Kongresses Hamburg 1988: "Bilder einer Musik" vom 12. bis 14. November 1988, edited by Peter Petersen, Laaber, Laaber-Verlag, 1991.

Popper 1972
Popper, Karl R. *Objective Knowledge. An Evolutionary Approach*, Oxford, Oxford University Press, 1972.

Rimple 2003
Rimple, Mark T. 'Boethius, Mathematics, and the Mensural Experimentation of the «Ars Subtilior»', in: *Carmina Philosophiae*, XII (2003), pp. 1-47.

Risset 1991
Risset, Jean-Claude. 'Computer – Synthesis – Perception – Paradoxes', in: Petersen 1991, pp. 245-258.

SCHÜTZ 1997
SCHÜTZ, Hannes S. 'Wiedergeburt der Ars subtilior? Eine Analyse von György Ligetis Klavieretüde Nr. 2', in: *Die Musikforschung*, L/2 (1997), pp. 205-214.

SIMON 1983
SIMON, Artur. *Musik in Afrika*, Berlin, Museum für Völkerkunde, 1983.

STAHNKE 2017
STAHNKE, Manfred. *Mein Blick auf Ligeti, Partch & Compagnons*, Norderstedt, BoD, 2017.

STAHNKE 2020
ID. 'Ars subtilior: Angelorum psalat, the Infinitesimal Chanson', 2020, <https://www.academia.edu/41975261/Ars_subtilior_Angelorum_psalat_the_Infinitesimal_Chanson>, accessed May 2022.

STEINITZ 2003
STEINITZ, Richard. *György Ligeti: Music of the Imagination*, London, Faber & Faber, 2003.

STOESSEL 2013
STOESSEL, Jason. 'Scribes at Work, Scribes at Play: Challenges for Editors of the Ars Subtilior', in: *Early Music Editing: Principles, Historiography, Future Directions*, edited by Theodor Dumitrescu, Karl Kügle, and Marnix van Berchum, Turnhout, Brepols, 2013 (Épitome Musical), pp. 49-75.

TANAY 1999
TANAY, Dorit. *Noting Music, Marking Culture: The Intellectual Context of Rhythmic Notation, 1250-1400*, Holzgerlingen, American Institute of Musicology, 1999.

TAUBE 2006
TAUBE, Heinrich K. *Notes from the Metalevel: An Introduction to Computer Composition*, London, Taylor & Francis, 2006.

ZEMP 1978
ZEMP, Hugo, *et al.* *'Aré'aré. Un Peuple Mélanésien et sa Musique*, (LP), Paris, Editions Du Seuil, 1978.

Analysing the Concerto for Violin and Orchestra: Apparitions of the Past and Future

Peter Edwards
(University of Oslo)

As György Ligeti's centenary year approaches, so too does the thirtieth anniversary of one of his most celebrated works, the Concerto for Violin and Orchestra. Since the premiere of the revised version in October 1992, it has rapidly become one of the most recorded large-scale works composed in recent decades and a paragon of the concerto repertoire. While its influence on a range of music — and recent violin concertos in particular — is tangible[1], the Violin Concerto itself indicates the debt it owes to previous music in the rich fabric of its composition. An abundance of allusions to the past can be found in the Concerto, including Ligeti's own music. This chapter will analyse examples from the Concerto and suggest how past musical ideas, techniques and modes of thought are absorbed and transformed in the work. The main purpose of this chapter is not to account for or catalogue all of these references but to gain a better understanding of Ligeti's creative disposition towards tradition as a means to new creative ends. The Concerto unfolds as though it were a remembering vision; an outlook on the past in a contemporaneous present. Analyses in this chapter will give cause to speculate on ways in which such an idea might be manifest in the compositional process and how it is analogous to — and brings new understanding to — a notion of the listening experience as the constitution of the past in the present.

A vast array of expressions, from the virtuosic to the simplistic, the spectral to the folky, are woven together as if the imaginings of a cosmopolitan mind as it draws on a rich pallette of past experience. The Concerto is almost like a chain of thought in the process of reconstituting

---

[1]. While striking works in their own right, the violin concertos of Thomas Adés (2005) and Ligeti's former pupil Unsuk Chin (2001), for example, display thematic and expressive affinities.

memories in its present. While we might not always be able to identify the source of these memories, we can attune to the sense of narrative in the form of this remembering vision and the trajectory that it offers. The musical form gives the impression of having been conceived as a response to ways in which our aggregate previous experiences of many different musics are brought to bear on new listening experiences. The Concerto self-cognizantly draws on an understanding of how we listen, recall, associate and prognosticise as a creative starting point in its conception.

This critical compositional approach in the Violin Concerto not only comprises explicit and concealed allusions to past techniques, styles and expressions, but also emphasises the significance of the reception history of specific compositional and performance techniques. The most prominent of these can be heard from the outset with the glissando violin harmonics which present the expressive and harmonic thematic material underlying the Concerto. This technique can be traced back to composers such as Nikolay Rimsky-Korsakov, who used harmonic glissandi — gliding between the nodes of an open string — sparingly as an effect, the earliest instance of which can be heard in 'Demonic Carol' from the suite *Christmas Eve* (1895), performed in the cellos. In Ligeti's Violin Concerto the technique is not only used as an expressive effect but as an orientating coordinate and recurring motif. The Violin Concerto incorporates the intervallic characteristics of the overtones of the harmonics into the core fabric of the music. The compositional reception of the technique reaches its culmination in the orchestral tradition in Ligeti's concerto, as it is absorbed and transformed, with its aesthetic and compositional implications at the foreground.

Other notable appearances of this technique from the past century can be found in Maurice Ravel's *Rapsodie espagnole* (1908), and subsequently Igor Stravinsky's *The Firebird* (1910) (over two bars before Figure [1])[2]. From an impressionistic effect in Ravel it becomes a structuring feature in Ligeti's Concerto. Following the gradual development of this technique over time, its latent aesthetic potential is brought to bear in the Concerto. The analyses in this chapter include examples of how the overtones of the open solo violin strings and the scordatura (altered) tunings of the solo violin and viola from the orchestra provide the harmonic and melodic foundation of the Concerto. The fusion of just and equal temperaments, the scalar patterns and harmonic foundations drawn from these systems, and the polyphonic rhythms developed from unfolding melodic patterns and inspired by music from around the world, all point to broader philosophical questions of the systems and traditions upon which music is contingent, and the implications of these for how we listen to and experience music.

The first version of the Violin Concerto was completed in 1990 and dedicated to violinist Saschko Gawriloff who premiered the work with the Cologne Radio Symphony Orchestra in Cologne on 3 November 1990 under the direction of Gary Bertini. Ligeti subsequently added

---

[2]. Taruskin 1996, p. 311.

two movements and replaced the first movement for the premiere of the revised version on 8 October 1992 in Cologne with Gawriloff and Ensemble Modern conducted by Peter Eötvös. The third and fourth movements were later reorchestrated in advance of a performance on the 9 June 1993 with Gawriloff and the Ensemble intercontemporain under the direction of Pierre Boulez[3]. Ligeti had initially rejected Gawriloff's suggestion that he compose a Violin Concerto for lack of time. Gawriloff recalls that Ligeti called back a few days later to say that he had reconsidered and found the idea stimulating, while cautioning that it would take several years to complete[4].

Gawriloff had collaborated with Ligeti previously, having premiered Ligeti's Trio for Violin, Horn and Piano (1982), a work that would prove of particular significance in the composition of the Violin Concerto. It was Pianist Eckart Besch, a member of the trio, who approached Ligeti with the request for a horn trio. Reduced to performing Johannes Brahms's trio for lack of other repertoire for this instrumentation, the newly formed trio were in search of new works. Ligeti recalls that «as soon as he pronounced the word horn, somewhere inside my head I heard the sound of a horn as if coming from a distant forest in a fairy tale, just as in a poem by Eichendorff»[5]. This source of inspiration and the subtitle «Hommage à Brahms» did little to dispel critics who cited retrospective, nostalgic or even regressive expressive and formal tendencies in the music. Ligeti was criticised for becoming «an enemy of progressive ideals» by those who saw only the classical-romantic influences in the trio[6]. However, as Richard Steinitz describes, this newfound consonant turn in Ligeti's music features «a rarified sonority» largely owing to the use of natural horn harmonics in the work[7]. As such, the Trio cannot simply be dismissed as a regressive turn to the past. The strange sonorous amalgamation of the equal tempered piano, the natural tempered horn and the violin tuned in natural fifths mediating between the two, distorts the surface allusions to Brahms, Ludwig van Beethoven and Robert Schumann, which appear familiar while simultaneously inferring a tangible absence of the original[8]. It is as though the Trio absorbs into its fabric the classical-romantic Trio tradition perceived from across the gulf of time; the music illustrates that the recollections of this past are only as true as how they are constituted in the present[9].

Composition with natural temperament in the Horn Trio proved fundamental for future works, as Ligeti describes: «in fact, without the Horn Trio there wouldn't have been a Violin Concerto»[10]. Natural temperament in the horns is called upon in the Violin Concerto,

---

[3]. STEINITZ 2003, pp. 333-334.
[4]. GAWRILOFF 1993, p. 16.
[5]. LIGETI 1983, p. 22.
[6]. STEINITZ 2003, p. 251.
[7]. *Ibidem*, p. 253.
[8]. See BAUER 2011, pp. 160-174.
[9]. EDWARDS 2015, pp. 197-198.
[10]. DUCHESNEAU 1992, p. 1.

with uncorrected notes throughout the second and third movements. But also from the outset in the first movement, the 'Praeludium', altered tunings based on open harmonics in the strings contribute to the shimmering expressive character of the work. Ligeti is specific as to how this expression should be achieved: «if the harmonies do not sound properly, artificial harmonics should not be used, as the glassy, shimmering quality of the movement is based on natural harmonics, and the "not always correctly-sounding" notes create the impression of fragility and danger»[11]. The intention behind this direction is reinforced by a remark in the performance notes at the beginning of the score: «To reduce deviations in intonation, both scordatura soloists play non vibrato throughout, and are careful not to adjust stopped notes to the rest of the orchestra. The two scordatura instruments are notated in the score as they sound. In the individual parts, they are notated transposed, as they are played». The timbral character and stability of open harmonics provide consistent intonation and expression, as well as the harmonic foundation for the work, as Ligeti explains, «[b]y combining these "out of tune" notes and harmonics with those of the normally tuned strings, I can build a number of harmonic and non-harmonic spectra»[12].

The solo violin and the solo viola of the orchestra are composed with altered tunings based on overtones, while the main solo violin is tuned as standard. The scordatura of the violin and the viola is to be tuned with the help of a contrabass. The E string of the violin is tuned to the seventh natural harmonic of the contrabass G string (an F): «The violinist tunes the E-string up to the solo double bass player's F, which sounds 45 cents lower than normal, and then tunes the other strings to the sharp E-string in perfect fifths»[13], (100 cents = 1 semi-tone) (Ex. 1):

Ex. 1: Violin Concerto, violin scordatura.

The first string which is closest to an F corresponds to the 7th natural harmonic on the contrabass G string.

A similar procedure is applied to the viola: «The solo double bass player — whose instrument is tuned normally — plays the fifth natural harmonic on the A-string [a C♯] [...] The viola player tunes the D-string down to the solo double bass player's C♯, which sounds 14 cents lower than normal, and then tunes the other strings to the flat D-string in perfect fifths»[14]. (Ex. 2):

---

[11]. LIGETI 2002A, p. 1.
[12]. LIGETI 2002B.
[13]. LIGETI 2002A.
[14]. *Ibidem*.

Ex. 2: Violin Concerto, Viola scordatura.

«The C♯ corresponds with the 5th natural harmonic on the double bass A-string»[15].

In the score in C, the violin scordatura part is notated a semitone higher than played, and a downward arrow attached to the clef indicates the 45-cent intonation deviation. The viola scordatura is notated a semitone lower than played, and the additional 14 cent deviation is again indicated by a downward arrow attached to the clef. The individual parts for the violin scordatura and viola scordatura are transposed to correspond with how they are played.

The lead solo violin commences the movement alone, playing rapidly alternating A and D open string harmonics on the A and D strings (strings 2 and 3). The semiquaver pattern on a single interval is reminiscent of previous works. In the Cello Concerto (1966), the cello begins with a single note superseded by a minor second. *Lontano* (1967) also commences in a similar fashion with an A flat, to which a G is added to give a minor second, and then B flat, before the increasing intervallic complexity smears the texture. The minor third at the beginning of *Continuum* (1968) is another example of this kind of gradual intervallic expansion, where «[t]he initial minor third is slowly blurred by the appearance of other intervals, then this complexity clears away and gradually a major second comes to dominate»[16]. Ligeti describes this progression from simplicity to complexity, both rhythmically and with intervals, as a compositional device used in place of thematic development[17]. This tendency to shift from lucid perfect intervals to dense weaves and back — most noticeably a feature of Ligeti's works from the 1960's — is also present in the Violin Concerto. The opening perfect fifth in the solo violin gradually evolves into an intricate textural weave with increasingly extended phrases as intervals are added.

In bar 7 the open G string is also heard but this time not as a harmonic. The E string is introduced in the same bar in the form of an open E harmonic. The scordatura violin and scordatura viola then join in bars 4 and 7 respectively, similarly playing the open harmonics of the open strings apart from the 4th string which, in likeness with the violin, is played as an open string without harmonics. The first 9 bars consist of these 12 different notes, 3 harmonics, one on each of the first 3 strings and the open 4th string. The tunings thereby provide the pitch material for the first 9 bars (Ex. 3):

---

[15]. *Ibidem.*
[16]. LIGETI 1983, p. 60.
[17]. *Ibidem.*

Ex. 3: Violin Concerto, tunings/pitch classes, first 9 bars of Mov. 1.

The A flat in the violin scordatura and the G sharp in the viola are the pitches in closest proximity (not taking into consideration octave transpositions); however, there is a difference of 31 cents between these notes as the scordatura violin is tuned up 55 cents from its original tuning, i.e. 45 cents lower than the semitone above (F, B flat, E flat, and A flat are notated as these notes are closest to how the notes actually sound). The viola is tuned down 114 cents from its standard tuning (just over a semitone). The G sharp, C sharp, F sharp, and B are notated as such because they are closest to the actual sounding pitches; sounding 14 cents lower than written.

The tessitura expands from bar 9, following which open harmonics in various left-hand positions now begin to dominate. The majority of these harmonics are played rapidly on a single string. The violinists and viola players move dexterously through the nodes, producing notes from the harmonic series. The phrasing also specifies that several notes at a time are played in a single bow and *ad libitum*. This phrasing generally contains an ascending and descending sequence of notes on a single string. The natural harmonics on each of the instruments and the scordatura tunings provide the following harmonic spectra in the opening (Ex. 4). Harmonics on the lower strings are used more frequently and utilise higher nodes of the harmonic series, with an additional seventh node included on the fourth string. Open harmonics on lower strings give greater timbral resonance.

Ex. 4: Violin Concerto, normal and scordatura tunings for the violins and violas.

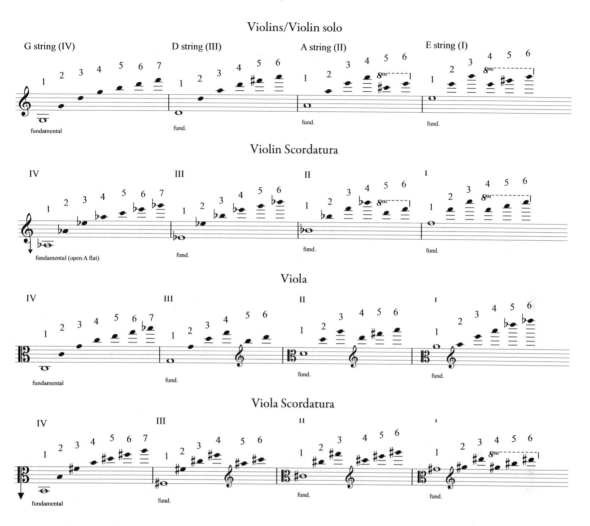

The strings join with semiquaver flurries, largely in an ascending-descending pattern similar to the soloists, and separated by short rests, resulting in a more complex weave of sound. The entry of the marimba in bar 14, rehearsal mark B, marks the beginning of a transition from this spectral weave, with the gradual emergence of a horizontal melodic pattern (Ex. 5), doubled by accented notes in the solo violin taken from the open harmonic flurries. These accented pitches cut through the texture gradually more frequently up to bar 34 (rehearsal mark F) where the textures shifts and a revitalised continuum involving all the parts performing staccato or pizzicato ensues.

The marimba melodic sequence accented by the doubled notes in the solo violin stands out from the polyphonic texture and provides a horizontal focal point. As the melodic sequence in the marimba and solo violin (accented notes) unfolds from bars 14-33, the violin plays gradually fewer open harmonics (expanded on from the initial A and D). The melodic sequence is increasingly braided into the glissando harmonics and eventually replaces them entirely. The only two pitch classes not featured as part of this melodic sequence are A and D, the opening notes of the movement, the exclusion of which signals the completion of the transition from the open harmonic spectra to the scalar melodic sequence.

Ex. 5: Violin Concerto, marimba/solo violin accented notes, bars 14-33.

A rising motion is followed by the same pitches in descent, with additional notes tagged on the end of each ascent or descent, resulting in the gradual expansion of the tessitura. The melody can be notated in ascending order as derived from a scale, unfolding from a pivot note in the middle. The lowest note of this series is also the lowest note on the violin, a G (Ex. 6):

Ex. 6: Violin Concerto, unravelling of marimba/solo violin accented notes, bars 14-33.

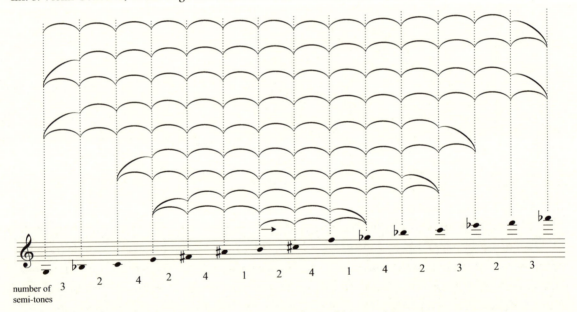

The rising and falling motion from a central pivotal pitch, with the unravelling of vertical harmonies, resembles similar patterns in many of Ligeti's works, collectively known as 'net-structure' technique.

This and other terms coined by Ligeti, including 'meccanico', and 'pattern-meccanico', describe various ways by which horizontal rhythmic patterns unfold from the intervallic structures in many his works[18]. Outer notes are added or removed as a sequence rises and falls, resulting in a gradually longer or shorter series.

Similar patterns are present in the beginning of movements 8 and 9 of the *Ten Pieces for Wind Quintet* (1968). The 8th movement resembles the fast repetitive patterns also found in *Continuum* while the 9th movement is more static in nature, the notes are long and held and change gradually one at a time. The latter bears similarities with the more densely saturated orchestral clusters of *Atmosphères* (1961).

The melodic sequence is representative of the kind of unravelling associated with net-structure technique, with intervals drawn from the overtones providing a horizontal focus as the texture thickens. An increasing number of upper harmonics on the strings result in clustered intervals and harmonic complexity. Symmetrical intervals can be identified in the scale from the C♯ in the middle, as illustrated in Ex. 7. Brackets indicate the mirrored intervals, with the exception of the B to C sharp and the C sharp to F in the middle, and the major and minor third that are indicated. The brackets below the notes show reoccurrences of the same notes:

Ex. 7: Violin Concerto, symmetrical relationships in the melodic sequence.

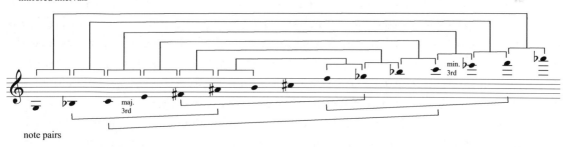

Rising and falling scales from a central pivot pitch, with a similar kind of symmetrical mirroring of intervals, are found in the music of another composer of great influence on Ligeti — in particular for his use of just intonation — Harry Partch. Partch is referred to in a number of places throughout the sketches for the Violin Concerto. While Ligeti voiced his admiration for the sonic attributes and approach to natural temperament in Partch's music, he was less enthusiastic about Partch's musical forms: «His actual compositions are not particularly

---

[18]. ROIG-FRANCOLI 1995. Roig-Francoli offers clarification of often confused analytical references to these terms. He refers to meccanico as the «pitch-repetitive style», found in works featuring the «quick mechanical reiteration of only one pitch per instrument». *Poème Symphonique* (1962) for one hundred metronomes is the purest example of this style. The metronomes are sat in motion and gradually wind down one by one, revealing evolving rhythmic patterns until only one remains. *Continuum* and *Coulée* (1969) (Étude no. 2 for organ), also have very similar origins although the pitch patterns are more closely related to Roig-Francoli's definition of the term 'net-structure' style.

interesting, but harmonically speaking they are very exciting»[19]. Partch advocates an approach to scales harmonically more pleasing and in correspondence with the constitution of the human ear[20]. Both composers share the view that the inconsequentiality of horizontal and vertical pitch relationships that has arisen with the dawn of dodecaphony must be addressed. Their solutions lie in the intervallic characteristics of clustered harmonies of the upper overtones and open string harmonics, which offer a means to establish consequentiality between the vertical harmonic structure and unfolding horizontal melodic sequences.

In Part One of *Genesis of a Music*, Partch critiques the emphasis in Western musical tradition on technical competence on an instrument and good compositional «technique». He cites a failure to delve deeper into the philosophy behind the established traditions that form a vital part of musical creation and experience, and questions the blind acceptance of equal temperament in Western music[21]. In this «age of specialisation»[22] he questions why the philosophy behind the traditions in Western music has ceased to develop, and rhetorically asks whether stagnant philosophy can house new thought. Partch considers the use of equal temperament and systems of dodecaphony as largely incommensurable, resulting in the discontinuous and angular collision of harmonies. In a chapter on equal temperament he writes: «it has long been evident that composers have been taxing both the system and their instruments beyond their capacities, and that the continued tyranny of Equal Temperament is leading to the degeneration of tonality»[23]. For Partch, tonality is a product of equal temperament, and the evolution into atonality or twelve-note systems represents a burden on the existing traditional Western temperament. In order to remedy the situation, he advocates the development of new temperaments to suit new ideas and instruments designed accordingly.

In Part Two, Partch outlines his system of temperament based on just intonation, «a system in which interval — and scale-building is based on the criterion of the ear and consequently a system and procedure limited to small number ratios»[24]. Partch describes how subdivisions of a string lead to gradually smaller ratios, and smaller intervals: a string that vibrates at 100 cycles will vibrate at 200 cycles if a bridge is placed half-way along it, hence the ratio 2/1 (an octave). If the bridge is placed a third of the way along this string and this third is set in vibration the tone will make 300 cycles, hence 300 to 200 or 3/2 etc[25]. Using the first 11 ratios of the harmonic series beginning on a G (392hz), Partch inverts this series, resulting in a series of intervals ascending and descending from the G fundamental. The ascending pitches are

---

[19]. LIGETI 1983, p. 54.
[20]. PARTCH 1974, p. 86.
[21]. *Ibidem*, p. 4.
[22]. *Ibidem*, p. 5.
[23]. *Ibidem*, p. 419.
[24]. *Ibidem*, p. 71.
[25]. *Ibidem*, p 80.

termed «otonality» (overtonality) and the notes descending from the fundamental are termed «utonality» (undertonality)[26]. From each note of the utonality a new otonality is created. This also results in the creation of utonalities for each of the notes of the original otonality sequence. Partch configured these ratios into his table diagram called the «tonality diamond». When these notes are placed in sequence, 29 different pitches emerge to form a just intonation scale. Partch added 14 extra notes to fill in some of the larger intervals in the scale to create his renowned 43-note scale.

There are then some broad conceptual similarities in the unfolding net-structures in Ligeti's scalar material from a central pivotal pitch, and Partch's scales based on just intonation. In the Violin Concerto, however, Ligeti's approach is more flexible, the work as a whole achieving a unique fusion of just and equal temperament and compositionally featuring a vast range of expressive means. The technical possibilities of individual instruments in the orchestra are extremely varied, and the intervals of the overtone series are not as easily achieved on all instruments. But the intervals of the scales on which the melodies are based do have affinities with overtones in the third and fourth octaves above a fundamental. This results in a series of intervals juxtaposed from the overtones, with characteristics closer to the overtone series than any of the modes, with the exception perhaps of the Lydian mode, which contains consecutive intervals from the fourth octave above a fundamental (see Ex. 8). In Ligeti's scale, the semitone from the fourth octave of the overtone series adds a Lydian quality. These intervallic similarities between the scale and the harmonic series help to accommodate the fusion of equal and just temperament in the Violin Concerto. The unfolding scale of the solo violin and marimba melodic sequence continues to be implemented through shifts in texture through the movement, in combination with open strings, double-stopped in the solo violin, and intervals from the overtone series. The glissando harmonics again return towards the end of the movement.

Ex. 8: Violin Concerto, the overtone series, the Lydian scale and intervallic correspondences with the melodic sequence.

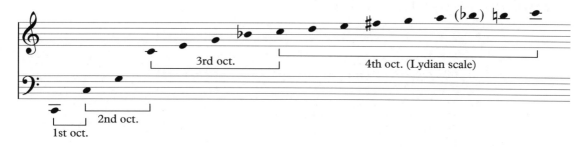

In likeness with Partch, the inspiration for Ligeti's harmonic experimentation came from microtonal structures found in far-eastern music. Many other twentieth-century composers

---

[26]. *Ibidem*, pp. 88-89.

in Europe and North America have shared a similar interest in developing microtonal music inspired by encounters with non-Western music, from Charles Ives and Henry Cowell, to Karlheinz Stockhausen. Claude Vivier in particular made a profound impression on Ligeti, with his fusion of Western and non-Western instruments and tunings systems inspired by trips made to Japan, Bali and Iran[27]. In common with Vivier, Ligeti did not seek to replicate the music of any particular culture, but through his complex system, guided by ear, devised an imagined musical language[28], which both embraces new timbral possibilites in the combinations of overtones and harmonic deviances in different instruments, and addresses underlying philosophical issues of the kind with which Partch was preoccupied. Other expressive affinities with Partch, and in particular the percussive rhythms performed by marimba instruments invented by Partch, can be found in the fluid rhythmic layers and Gamelan-like rhythms in the Violin Concerto. In the first movement, the «net-structuring» entails the gradual lengthening of the scalar patterns and passages of semiquavers. The complex time signatures, the subdivided bars, and the relentless use of various accentuations are a product of the complex subdivision of rhythm that lies beneath the fluid surface. This rhythmic continuity is reminiscent of gamelan music, or African drumming. Polyrhythmic patterns come to dominate as the first movement progresses.

Ligeti's sketches give reference to a number of sources of inspiration, African polyrhythms in particular. References to «cameroun», «Zimbabwe», and even «Afrojazz Bebop», indicate allusions to various approaches to polyrhythmic subdivisions in different instruments and instrument groups marked with accents. Mention of Carlo Gesualdo in addition perhaps gives indication of similarities Ligeti identifies in the African rhythms and the contrapuntal voice entries and note durations in the polyphonic style of the composer. Diagrams of various rhythmic subdivisions of varying complexity, many of which are semi-quaver subdivisions of 24, are found among the sketches. Ex. 9 features on several sketch pages.

Ex. 9: Violin Concerto, «Periódus – structure AFRIQ».

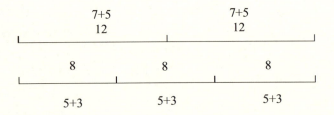

---

[27]. STEINITZ 2003, p. 331.
[28]. *Ibidem*, pp. 331-333.

Analysing the Concerto for Violin and Orchestra

The 'Aria Cantus Firmus'

The second movement is equally as rich with allusion and reference to past music as the first. The opening 'Aria Cantus Firmus' in the solo violin is adapted from the flute melody of the third of Ligeti's *Bagatelles for Wind Quintet*, which in turn is derived from *Musica ricercata* (1951-53) for piano (Ex. 10)[29]. The Lydian character of the aria melody again reinforces the impression of affinity with natural temperament. The theme appears first on the violin and is played exclusively on the G string for the first seventy-four bars. This writing for a single string is also explored at length in his Viola Sonata (1991-1994), with the viola's lowest string, the C string, very much in focus. The first movement, 'Hora lungă', is played entirely on the C string and bears expressive affinities with the opening aria melody of the second movement of the Violin Concerto. As in the Violin Concerto, intervals from the overtone series provide a harmonic foundation in the 'Hora Lungă'.

Ex. 10: Violin Concerto, bars 1-12 of the Second Movement. LIGETI 2002A.

The opening aria provides the theme for the variations that follow. The horns are instructed to play «throughout in the manner of a natural horn»[30], preparing the way for the natural intonation of the ocarinas in bar 75, which provide a sharp timbral contrast to the solo violin. These shifts in timbre and texture, and the combination of equal and natural intonation in different instruments are nevertheless complementary. Again the influence of Partch is apparent, with the theme performed in the ocarinas bearing uncanny melodic and timbral resemblance with the Bolivian flute in Partch's 'The Quiet Hobo Meal' (Act II of *Delusion of the Fury: A Ritual of Dream and Delusion*)[31], one of the few instruments on the recording which is not a Partch invention. The texture in the orchestra, and the melodic contours and just intonation and the choral-like homophony of the four ocarinas ostensibly allude to Partch.

The variations that follow draw on a variety of past compositional techniques, including extensive use of hocketing from rehearsal 85 — the alternation of notes and rests between

---

[29]. LIGETI 2000, sleeve note, p. 4.
[30]. LIGETI 2002A.
[31]. PARTCH 1971.

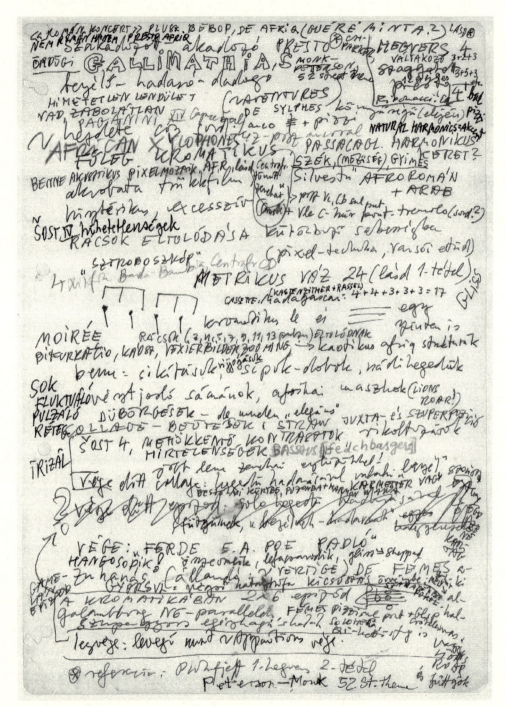

Ill. 1: Verbal sketch page 4th movement. Reproduced by kind permission of the Paul Sacher Foundation, Basel – György Ligeti Collection.

two or more parts, one rests while the other plays, and the fragmentation of melody into smaller phrases separated by rests. The tuplet subdivisions recall the hocketed rhythms of medieval music, while the rapidly alternating patterns and imitation are reminiscent of Bebop. Again, the whole-tone qualities of the Lydian mode dominate throughout, accommodating the assimilation of open harmonies and natural intervals and equal temperament.

The solo violin melody of the third movement, the 'Intermezzo', continues in the character of the Lydian mode, while fleeting, chromatically descending passages in the strings form a dense polyphonic weave. Natural harmonics in the horns and trombones provide pedal points, or a slowly evolving countermelody. The fourth movement, by contrast, entitled 'Passacaglia', recalls previous micropolyphonic works by Ligeti, opening with two clarinets gradually shifting pitch before these are joined by the solo violin. The continuum created, with horizontal movements of semi-tones and tones in each instrument continue unabated. Individual instruments join, their entries imperceptible, as the canon gradually grows. The Passacaglia is true to its name; a continuous variation over a theme or ground bass. Every few bars another instrument enters in a canonic fashion and the harmony becomes more complex. The tessitura expands, also into the lower registers, before the accented string melody enters and the solo violin melody expands its tessitura gradually as the note groupings become longer, building on melodic patterns with the same Lydian qualities as the first movements.

A verbal sketch page (Ill. 1) indicates the wealth of references and ideas that underlie the movement. The sketch pertains to the fourth movement of the Concerto, as specified at the top of the page («Hegvers 4»). On the page there are references to «Paganini», «gamelan», and the «moirée» effect (the superimposition of repetitive patterns not exactly aligned to create a blurred effect), and even the «Peterson — Monk 52nd Street Theme». Verbal sketches for the work by far outnumber notated sketches and give expressive and structural outline to the imagined forms and musical ideas; a means of recalling initial conceptual ideas in order to transform these into a draft score.

The fifth movement, 'Appassionato', begins similarly to the first movement. The scordatura violin and scordatura viola perform rapidly alternating harmonics between two notes. An oboe and piccolo enter, with a version of the ocarina lento motif of the second movement, this time in sixths. The solo violin soon joins, becoming increasingly unsettled. The movement develops through expressive and textual recapitulations of sections of the Concerto before arriving at the cadenza. A note in the score invites the soloist to compose the cadenza, with the specification that it should be between one and two minutes in length. Gawriloff made use of draft material left over from the revisions carried out for the second version of the concerto for his cadenza, which is reproduced in the score. This material stems from the first version of the first movement[32]. The cadenza is characterised by double-

---

[32]. GAWRILOFF 1993, p. 18.

stopping, rapidly ascending and descending sequences, and open harmonics[33]. At bar 93 the orchestra again enters, interrupting the ascending harmonics of the cadenza. Individual pitches ring from different instruments in sequence, before resting on a flute and alto flute E, accompanied by an accented pizzicato in the strings, creating a bell-like effect, an effect that Ligeti attributes to Dmitry Shostakovich's Symphony no. 4[34].

At every turn, there is indication of intensive critical reflection and the distillation of any number of musical references across numerous genres and styles. This awareness of and engagement with past techniques, expressions and questions of the systems from which musical tradition has evolved are embedded in the fabric of the Concerto in manifold ways. The fusion of natural and equal temperament arises from a critical approach to the past music of others who have similarly questioned through expressive means the systems upon which tradition rests. The techniques of open harmonic glissandi, the overtone series and the scalar patterns derived from these, which also contain affinities with the Lydian mode and the polyphonic style of early music, represent a culmination of the past, and point in new directions. The more attentive we are to the rich layers of allusion in the music and the techniques involved, the more we become aware of the extent to which the innovations of the present are reliant on the past. This is made apparent in the Violin Concerto. The same might be said of the listening experience: the more we listen, the richer the possibilities become in future listening experiences. The potential for prognosis and association, involuntary and inherent to any listening experience, increase exponentially, intensifying and enriching future experiences. The Violin Concerto mediates a vision of the future fashioned from the recollections and reinvention of the expressions and techniques of the past. As might be said of the best of new music, the Violin Concerto opens our ears to new ways of hearing music of the past and expands the horizons of future listening experiences.

BIBLIOGRAPHY

BAUER 2011
BAUER, Amy. *Ligeti's Laments: Nostalgia, Exoticism and the Absolute*, Farnham, Ashgate, 2011.

DUCHESNEAU 1992
DUCHESNEAU, Louise. 'György Ligeti on his Violin Concerto', in: *Ligeti Letter*, no. 2 (1992), p. 1-8.

---

[33]. This cadenza is featured on the Deutsche Grammophon recording (LIGETI 1994). The influence of the original is heard in versions by other soloists. Frank Peter Zimmermann's cadenza is relatively true to the score until halfway. He then proceeds to juxtapose and embellish on some ideas already present and omits others, shortening the cadenza and increasing the flow towards the climax (LIGETI 2002c). Christina Åstrand chooses to follow the score with even greater precision (LIGETI 2000).

[34]. DUCHESNEAU 1992, p. 7.

EDWARDS 2015
EDWARDS, Peter. 'Remembrance and Prognosis in the Music of György Ligeti', in: *Transformations of Musical Modernism*, edited by Erling E. Guldbrandsen and Julian Johnson, Cambridge, Cambridge University Press, 2015, pp. 190-200.

GAWRILOFF 1993
GAWRILOFF, Saschko. 'Ein Meisterwerk von Ligeti', in: *Neue Zeitschrift für Musik*, CLIV/1 (1993), pp. 16-18.

LIGETI 1983
György Ligeti in Conversation with Péter Várnai, Josef Häusler, Claude Samuel, and Himself, translated by Gabor J. Schabert, Sarah E. Soulsby, Terence Kilmartin and Geoffrey Skelton, London, Eulenburg, 1983 (Eulenburg Music Series).

LIGETI 1994
ID. *Boulez Conducts Ligeti: Concertos for Cello, Violin, Piano*, Deutsche Grammophon 439 808-2, 1994.

LIGETI 2000
ID. *Ligeti/Nørgård: Violin Concerto, Helle Nacht Sonata ('The Secret Melody')*, Chandos 9830, 2000.

LIGETI 2002A
ID. *Konzert für Violine und Orchester*, Ed9170, Mainz, Schott, 2002.

LIGETI 2002B
ID. *The Ligeti Project III, Violin Concerto*, Teldec 8573-87631-2, 2002.

LIGETI 2002C
ID. *The Ligeti Project III: Cello Concerto, Clocks and Clouds, Violin Concerto, Síppal, Dobbal, Nádihegedüvel*, Teldec 8573-88261-2, 2002C.

PARTCH 1971
PARTCH, Harry *Delusions of the Fury*, Innova Records B000035X6C, 1971.

PARTCH 1974
ID. *Genesis of a Music*, New York, Da Capo Press, 1974.

ROIG-FRANCOLI 1995
ROIG-FRANCOLI, Miguel. 'Harmonic and Formal Processes in Ligeti's Net-Structure Compositions', in: *Music Theory Spectrum*, XVII/2 (1995), pp. 242-267.

STEINITZ 2003
STEINITZ, Richard. *György Ligeti: Music of the Imagination*, Boston, Northeastern University Press, 2003.

TARUSKIN 1996
TARUSKIN, Richard. *Stravinsky and the Russian Traditions: A Biography of the Works Through «Mavra». Volume 1*, Berkeley (CA)-Los Angeles, University of California Press, 1996.

Context and Reception

Listening (to) Ligeti:
Tracing Sound Memories and Sound Images in the Composer's Writings

Ewa Schreiber
(Adam Mickiewicz University, Poznań)

Do you dream in colour, or in black-and-white? [...] *My dreams are 'overcoloured', as in Technicolor*[1]. That is how Ligeti describes his special gift in a conversation with Eckhard Roelcke. He also mentions his synaesthetic tendencies which enabled him to link images, colours and forms with movement and music since he was a child[2]. Ligeti's colourful, metaphorical discourse often directs us towards spatial reveries and suggestive images: spider's web, fabrics, clouds, labyrinths and mirror reflections. As a result his works are often interpreted in these very material and spatial categories.

And yet in the same interview, published a few years before his death, the composer makes the point that it is the sound imaginings (*klangliche Vorstellungen*) that most often provide the creative stimulus[3]. Louise Duchesneau recalls that in his apartment in Hamburg Ligeti did not have a TV set, fearing that it would distract him from creative work. On the other hand, he did have an expensive hi-fi set and an enormous, continuously expanding record collection to which he listened with passion[4]. Ligeti, undoubtedly aware of the organising and explanatory power of material and spatial metaphors passionately uses them not only in his compositional sketches (with their extensive visual layer), but also in the later verbal descriptions of his works. However, it seems significant that when he tries to describe the inner states that release his

---

[1]. «Träumen Sie in Farbe oder Schwarzweiß? [...] Bei mir gibt es "überfarbliche" Träume, so wie Technicolor». Ligeti – Roelcke 2003, p. 19.
[2]. *Ibidem*, pp. 16-17.
[3]. *Ibidem*, p. 167.
[4]. Duchesneau 2011, p. 125.

creative inspiration, he uses musical metaphors, talking about the «ringing of the inner bell»[5], «resonance»[6] or «echo»[7]. In any case this is not a subject that comes up in conversation on the composer's initiative; usually it is his interlocutors who ask about inspiration.

Looking back, beginning with the 1970s, Ligeti reveals an increasing number of facts in his complex and difficult biography, and his reflections demonstrate his sensitivity to environmental sounds, including music, and a concern to present a detailed reconstruction of the soundscape of his childhood and youth. Monika Lichtenfeld regards especially these self-reflective and retrospective texts as the most multifaceted and attractive literary works among Ligeti's collected writings[8].

In the knowledge that the sphere of sound memories is inextricably linked to compositional imagination, I would like to examine more closely their role in Ligeti's discourse, and to identify and characterise their most important contexts. Further on I will also try to answer the difficult question of how the sound memories could influence the composer's musical imagination.

Sound Memories

For Ligeti, memories are the key element in his narration about music, and at different stages of his creative journey he used different strategies in this respect[9]. Initially he distanced himself from his Hungarian roots, and his story about the past took on a stylised literary form of fantasy associated with dreaming or childish reveries. To quote Beckles Willson, the composer «transformed memory into play»[10], keeping his private emotions to himself. However, beginning with the 1970s, texts and statements based on memories increase in number, and the concert repertoire begins to include Ligeti's works written before 1956. The composer takes meticulous care to link these memories with the images constructed earlier, but at many points his story takes on the tone of strikingly detailed and realistic historical account. Monika Lichtenfeld emphasises that in Ligeti's autobiographical writings all the traumatic events of the last century come together: «Discrimination, persecution, genocide, war, destruction, displacement, escape and a new beginning»[11].

---

[5]. Ligeti 1983, p. 22. Ligeti 2007a, p. 71.
[6]. Ligeti 1983, p. 23.
[7]. *Ibidem*.
[8]. Lichtenfeld 2007, p. 26.
[9]. See Schreiber 2019.
[10]. Beckles Willson 2007, p. 118.
[11]. «Diskriminierung, Verfolgung, Völkermord, Krieg, Zerstörung, Vertreibung, Flucht und Neubeginn». Lichtenfeld 2007, p. 25.

Listening (to) Ligeti

Further on I will identify a number of contexts which accompany sound memories most frequently. These are: the local soundscape, languages and identities, limitations linked to musical education, changing sound carriers and elapsing time as well as endangered sounds and existential fear. In my research I will refer to the basic terminology of soundscape studies.

Local Soundscape

In his texts Ligeti talks about sounds in a manner similar to the understanding of soundscape[12]. This is not about abstracted sound objects, but, rather, about sounds intertwined with the local landscape, characterising the local community, constituting «a field of interactions, even when particularized into its component sound events»[13], competing among each other and creating their own inner hierarchies. Sounds are also carriers of specific meanings, emotions, and interhuman relations. When in his biographical film Ligeti visits his birthplace he is surprised to find that the sound of church bells, clearly distinguishable from its surroundings as a «soundmark», has stayed the same for years[14]. In a text from the early 1970s Ligeti recalls Dicsőszentmárton, a little town where he lived until the age of six, which was full of Gypsy music[15]. However, his description is accompanied by ambivalent emotions, and the sense of threat goes hand in hand with comicality and a tendency to aestheticise. Gypsy music accompanied funerals that frightened the small child, but at the same time created a deep impression through their majestic, ceremonial mood. Describing the decorations on the larger black coffins Ligeti also mentions little children's coffins and adds: «to me they meant that my own death was within the sphere of possibilities»[16]. The threatening aura accompanies in his memories also the «shamanic performances» of New Year maskers, i.e., the «wild» Romanian musicians «They played fiddles and pipes ("cimpoi"). One of them had a mask and a goatskin cloak. The mask had horns and looked like a satanic goat, but instead of the mouth there was something that looked like a beak»[17]. What is striking here is that in all the recalled descriptions the sound appears as something alien and hostile. It may be a sign of death or a «whining», deformed invasive signal surrounded by the aura of the night. In conclusion Ligeti says that he did not like Gypsy music, and liked the «Magyar note» of the popular Hungarian

---

[12]. Using the concept of soundscape I refer to the acoustic ecology of Raymond Murray Schafer: SCHAFER 1994, p. 205.
[13]. *Ibidem*, p. 131.
[14]. *György Ligeti – Portrait* 1993.
[15]. LIGETI 2007E, p. 11
[16]. «[...] sie bedeuteten für mich, daß der Tod, mein eigene, im Bereich des Möglichen lag». *Ibidem*, pp. 11-12.
[17]. «Sie spielten Geige und Dudelsack ("cimpoi"). Einer von ihnen war maskiert, er trug einen Umhang aus Ziegenfell. Die Maske hatte Hörner und sah aus wie eine teuflische Ziege, statt des Mauls aber sah man eine Art Schnabel». LIGETI 2007H, p. 151.

melodies or songs from operettas even less, even though his mother used to sing the latter to him at bedtime[18].

At the same time in these descriptions sounds function as a synthesis of different layers of time, and memories take on the form of a palimpsest. Ligeti remains faithful to his «insect» images, for which he reached in the well-known commentaries to *Apparitions* (1958-1959)[19]. In turn, the comparison of the Romanian musicians to African shamanic rituals, made from the perspective of 2000s is a reference to his later fascination with African rhythms.

The composer devoted much space to a description of local musical life. By then the description is more realistic, focused on social and historical problems. Ligeti first describes the musical opportunities offered by Cluj, the main centre of Transylvania, where he settled with his family at the age of six. Life there developed along two tracks, within the Hungarian and Romanian cultures. Concerts of the Romanian symphony orchestra, which Ligeti could hear live, focussed mainly on French repertoire (including works by Léo Delibes, Camille Saint-Saëns and Paul Dukas)[20]. Ligeti's childhood was also shaped by visits to the Romanian opera house, where Italian and French repertoires were dominant. From his first contact with live opera Ligeti carried away above all the memory of visual splendour (the brilliance of the coronation scene in *Boris Godunov*) and social interactions (the crush caused by «fat ladies» and the taste of nougat that his cousin fed to him surreptitiously).

When in 1940 Cluj was reabsorbed into Hungary, musical culture became more vibrant, but at the same time it also provided an arena for nationalist politics. Eminent musicians from Budapest would visit the city. Yet another important place emerges from the reminiscences of Cluj from the 1940s. It is a botanical garden, full of birdsong, large, rich with exotic plants, beautifully situated on a hillside; Ligeti assures us that it is more splendid than the botanical gardens in Vienna and Budapest. This is the place where, by then a student of composition, he would work on exercises in harmony and where he experienced a youthful nervous breakdown[21]. When Ligeti gets to Budapest he meets such musical personages as Sándor Végh, Otto Klemperer, Erich Kleiber and Leonard Bernstein.

Through the rituals of concert life Ligeti shows the local audiences, their divisions and repertoire preferences, often conditioned nationally and politically. Assessing the value of that musical range from a wider perspective, acquired through his later experiences, Ligeti oscillates between provincialism and cosmopolitanism, between the centre and the periphery. However, his judgment is always made in the context of everyday living conditions. The enlivening of concert life may be the result of political tensions, while the other side of Budapest's wonderful cultural offering turns out to be poverty and the gathering communist enslavement.

---

[18]. LIGETI 2007E, p. 12.
[19]. LIGETI 1993.
[20]. LIGETI – ROELCKE 2003, p. 32.
[21]. *Ibidem*, pp. 39-40.

Listening (to) Ligeti

Languages and Identities

In Ligeti's reminiscences musical development goes hand in hand with his linguistic development[22]. In the multi-ethnic Transylvanian society the composer came across the sound of diverse languages. It is there that his sense of what is native and what is alien came to be shaped, and the boundaries of native and alien were always moving. About his native language, he writes, «Hungarian is a very isolated language. So, we used to learn at school and I wonder whether it is still so now»[23]. For Ligeti, who spoke the «isolated» Hungarian language, it was the Romanian language that initially sounded alien[24]. Originally it was that language that served as a model of the exotic for the boy, and fascinated him by its mysterious nature[25]. Ligeti did not become fluent in it until he went to the lyceum, aged ten[26]. At a mature age Ligeti is supposed to have claimed that he is doubly rooted in the Hungarian and Romanian cultures[27]. In fact, one can find traces of the composer's bilinguality in his post-war works[28]. The French language, which Ligeti also used as an adult, entered his education at the same time as Romanian[29]. At the age of four the composer mastered yet another language: from his nanny, who came from Vienna, he learned German and then largely forgot it, even though he continued to be able to read it[30]. It was that language, after the traumatic war experiences and escape from Hungary, that was to become for Ligeti the main tool for communicating with the audiences, while Hungarian remained his «private language». Even though Ligeti's native tongue was Hungarian, his family had Jewish roots. The composer reconstructs in detail the family genealogy and the history of his name. He explains that Jewish surnames would be changed to a Hungarian version, and his paternal surname Auer was translated, «not quite correctly»[31] and «not very felicitously»[32] as Ligeti[33]. In the case of Ligeti, being multilingual brought with it being open to other cultures and

---

[22]. *Ibidem*, p. 18.
[23]. Ligeti 2001, p. 233.
[24]. Ligeti – Roelcke 2003, p. 20; Ligeti 2001, p. 233.
[25]. Ligeti 2007h, p. 151.
[26]. Ligeti 2001, p. 237. Ligeti – Roelcke 2003, p. 20. In a conversation with Niculescu he provides the more detailed information that he did not speak it until the age of eight. See Țiplea Temeș 2018, p. 133.
[27]. Țiplea Temeș 2018, p. 120.
[28]. In 1950 Ligeti composed *Román népdalok és táncok* (*Romanian Folk Songs and Dances*, a work available only in manuscript), a suite of ten compositions in which, according to Țiplea Temeș, some titles «combine the Romanian titles with agogic terms in Hungarian or even with the Hungarian translation of the Romanian original». *Ibidem*, p. 136, fn. 11.
[29]. In a biographical film about him, it is the French language that the composer uses.
[30]. Ligeti – Roelcke 2003, p. 18.
[31]. *Ibidem*, p. 13.
[32]. Ligeti 2007c, p. 20.
[33]. «Wort Liget bedeutet Hain nicht Au [the word Liget means a grove, not a meadow]». *Ibidem*.

their history, literature and art. Looking back, he talks of the seven years spent at the Romanian gymnasium and the escape from Hungary in terms of being enriched[34]. He was also to master some other languages — Swedish, English, and a working knowledge of Italian[35].

Commenting on the concept of *Nationalität* in 2000 Ligeti tries to be maximally inclusive, displaying that cosmopolitan imagination that Amy Bauer has written so much about[36]. He includes in his complex identity the music of Germany, the traditions of France, his native Hungarian language, as well as Jewish intellectual attitude and English irony[37]. Yet at the very beginning he says «Obviously, there is the Russian intonation»[38] thus admitting that in its intonational, sound dimension, each language remains untranslatable and individual in its own way.

Musical Education: The Limitations

Ligeti's many sound memories are marked by the limitations resulting from defective technologies, but also from lack of access to specific sources or information. In the context of the years of childhood and early youth the stress is mainly on the limited access to wider repertoire or instruments, and the background is the political situation in Transylvania. On the other hand, in the postwar years there is a strong emphasis on the context of the Cold War, and the perspective of the inability to catch up[39].

Exploring the past, Ligeti notes the imperfections of the media at his disposal at that time. While the gramophone (together with the collection of bakelite discs) compensated for the absence of instruments at home[40], one of the records that the composer listened to at the early age of five could only play three minutes of Beethoven's Symphony No. 5. The exposition of the first movement thus had to be sufficient to provide an idea of the whole work[41]. Even so, music heard on the radio initially could not compete with the gramophone because of the atmospheric interference and «the equipment's frequent bouts of howling»[42].

Telling the story of his family Ligeti emphasises that artistic talents had already appeared in it earlier[43]. He mentions that his mother used to sing and his father loved music, in particular

---

[34]. LIGETI – ROELCKE 2003, p. 20.

[35]. STEINITZ 2003, p. 12. ȚĂRANU 2020, p. 96.

[36]. BAUER 2012.

[37]. LIGETI 2007A, pp. 70-71.

[38]. «Selbstverständlich gibt es einen russischen Tonfall». *Ibidem*, p. 70.

[39]. Rachel Beckles Willson undertook an analysis of the official discourse relating to Hungarian music after World War II. She has demonstrated how, in the context of changed postwar institutions, Ligeti had to learn the art of making public statements and self-censorship, as well as of being silent. See BECKLES WILLSON 2007, pp. 34-73.

[40]. LIGETI 2001, p. 231.

[41]. LIGETI 2007E, p. 12. LIGETI – ROELCKE 2003, p. 16.

[42]. «[...] das häufige Aufjaulen des Gerätes». LIGETI 2007E, p. 13.

[43]. These were the violinist Leopold Auer and the painter Soma Auer. See LIGETI 2007C, p. 20.

Listening (to) Ligeti

Ludwig van Beethoven and Franz Schubert. In this way he highlights his membership of the intelligentsia, but regards his professional music education as being made difficult, and the environment as «extremely unfavorable to a career as a musician»[44]. His father was against him playing an instrument, since he saw his son's future more as a scientist. It was only when György's younger brother, Gábor, who had perfect pitch, began to play the violin, that Ligeti was sent for piano lessons. By then he was already 14 years old[45]. Initially he practises away from home, at «auntie Marcsi's» on a good but badly tuned piano. As a teenager Ligeti develops his knowledge of instruments by playing in an amateur orchestra whose repertoire consists mainly of popular symphonic pieces. The composer explains in detail the limitations caused by the makeup of the orchestra: «Of Beethoven, only those pieces that had two horns. Two horns and two trumpets was the maximum. That is: symphonies 1, 2, 4 and 7, 'Eroica' and Symphony No. 5 were out of the question. There was no trombone»[46].

Although when applying to become a student he already can boast a sizeable number of compositions, he judges his knowledge to be incomplete for a very specific reason: «I had no idea about instrumentation nor about orchestration. I only owned the second volume of the well-known instrumentation book by Albert Siklós, so I had some idea about how an orchestra worked, but no idea about the basic ingredients, that is, about the instruments themselves»[47].

The greater the constraints turn out to be, the more eager Ligeti is to collect his musical experiences. Music often reaches him in fragments or in difficult acoustic conditions. He hears modern music relatively late, *Also sprach Zarathustra* by Richard Strauss at the age of 15, the music of Béla Bartók even later, at eighteen[48]. In postwar Budapest, records become a luxury item[49], which is why he does not hear the foreign recordings of Arnold Schoenberg and Anton Webern's string quartets until 1956[50], and he plays the music of Stravinsky (*Symphony in Three Movements* and *Symphony in C*) very quietly on the American disc bought on the black market. The only record player available to him is the «Pseudoplattenspieler»[51] and the branch of acacia

---

[44]. Ligeti 2001, p. 231.

[45]. *Ibidem*, p. 235, Ligeti – Roelcke 2003, p. 28.

[46]. «Von Beethoven nur die Stücke, die zwei Hörner hatten. Zwei Hörner und zwei Trompeten waren das Maximum. Das heißt: 1., 2.,4. Und 8. Sinfonie. Die "Eroica" und die 5. Sinfonie gingen nicht. Posaune gab es nicht». Ligeti – Roelcke 2003, p. 34.

[47]. Ligeti 2001, p. 251. In a number of statements Ligeti makes the point that it was not possible to obtain the second volume either in his town, or in the town were his uncle and aunt lived. Ligeti – Roelcke 2003, pp. 35-36. Ligeti 2007e, p. 17.

[48]. Ligeti – Roelcke 2003, p. 34.

[49]. *Ibidem*, p. 73.

[50]. *Ibidem*, p. 74.

[51]. *Ibidem*.

used as a stylus. In those years the radio also offered some limited access to information, but the music turned out to be much more demanding technically: «the reception of music was only fragmentary. I could hear the piccolo and xylophone, but none of the lower instruments because of interference»[52]. It is from the radio that Ligeti learns about the existence of electronic music in 1953 and, as he admits in his conversation with Várnai, «I did not hear the music, I only heard *about it*»[53]. He would listen on the medium wave to the weekly broadcasts from Cologne and Munich[54]. He manages to listen to Stockhausen's *Gesang der Jünglinge* and *Kontrapunkte* without radio interference, although in 1956 the «interference» is being caused by shooting in the streets[55].

In later years Ligeti makes an intensive effort to catch up. He sees his experiences on arrival in Cologne in 1957 as an enormous leap, and now assesses what he has learned up to this point as «nothing»[56]. Throughout his life he keeps buying many recordings and is a regular customer of record shops in the cities he visits. He listens to a much greater range of music than is mentioned in his statements[57].

Changing Sound Carriers – Elapsing Time

In Ligeti's reminiscences the irreversibility of transience manifests itself in two contrasting ways. The civilisation's forward rush contributes to the development of the media during his childhood and youth. On the other hand, war and totalitarianism bring about the twentieth-century disasters and devastation. Both the ephemeral and elusive sound and its changing, decaying carriers turn out to be the perfect embodiment of elapsing time. Remembrance of the omnipresent and evolving media also provides an opportunity to reflect on the technology of recording and emission of sound in spite of its elusiveness and particularity.

The descriptions of the media are accompanied by childhood fascination and curiosity. Ligeti's passion was the only «musical instrument» in the house, a crank gramophone (*Kurbelgrammophon*), modern for those times[58]. Ligeti regarded it as an instrument, with all that this entails, and so he was intrigued by the absence of «the sonorous body»: «Of course I was looking for a little man in the gramophone box, I imagined him with an enormous head

---

[52]. «Musik allerdings nur bruchstückhaft. Piccolo und Xylophonkonnte konnte ich hören, alle tieferen Instrumente wegen der Störungen nicht». *Ibidem*, p. 75.
[53]. Ligeti 1983, p. 35.
[54]. Duchesneau 2011, p. 129.
[55]. Ligeti – Roelcke 2003, p. 75.
[56]. Ligeti 2007d, p. 31.
[57]. Duchesneau 2011, p. 125.
[58]. Ligeti 2007e, p. 12.

filling the box and a vanishingly tiny body that could barely fit in it (the box), folded like an accordion, but could achieve full voice tone only through the fully developed head»[59].

This fairytale description brings to mind Peter Szendy's comment about the «radical dislocation» of sound typical of the era of electricity and the separation of sound from its source for «potentially infinite» distances[60]. «Never will we have pursued the materiality of sonorous bodies as much as during the era of their dislocation [...]. It would seem that the more we look for it by hypostatizing it, the more "the body" goes missing»[61] stresses Szendy, and Ligeti's reminiscences provide a humorous illustration of this thesis.

For Ligeti, the radio appears in 1927, when his uncle becomes the owner of the first radio receiver in town. After that this medium quickly becomes popular and shortly appears also in Ligeti's home[62]. The radio makes it possible to expand the known repertoire and listen to concerts from metropolises such as Budapest and Bucharest.

The material carriers of sound, admired so much by the composer in his childhood, turn out to be fragile when after the war «78 RPM records had cracked as did all the window panes in the besieged Budapest»[63]. In 1949, while carrying out ethnomusicological research in Romania, Ligeti also comes across exceptionally fragile recordings of sound on wax cylinders used in collecting folk music. Not only the quickly wearing out sound carriers, but also the necessity of faithful notating of the recorded music. As documented by Ligeti, transcriptions were helped by contact with live instruments. Ligeti's own works show that he himself attached attention to careful description of tuning or articulation, as well as conveying the instruments' original names[64]. In time even the cylinders turn out to be a luxury. From January 1950[65] they are in short supply, which means that ethnomusicologists have to notate the music by ear. Still in 1950 the composer returns to working with cylinders in Hungary: «since I had destroyed a few wax cylinders at the museum, I felt that I was not qualified for this type of work»[66]. Memory turned out to be much more durable than sound

---

[59]. «Selbstverständlich suchte ich nach dem winzigen Menschen, der im Grammophonkasten steckt, ich stellte ihn mir mit großem, den Kasten ausfüllendem Kopf und mit verschwindend kleinem Körper vor, der ziehharmonikaartig zusammengefaltet gerade noch Platz findet, konnte doch der volle Gesangton nur von einem entsprechend voll ausgewachsenen Kopf hervorgebracht werden». *Ibidem*.

[60]. SZENDY 2016, p. 141.

[61]. *Ibidem*, p. 152.

[62]. LIGETI – ROELCKE 2003, p. 29. LIGETI 2007E, p. 13.

[63]. «Die 78-er Platten sind in der belagerten Stadt Budapest wie alle Fenster-Scheiben kaputt gegangen. Einige Leute hatten noch welche zu Hause». LIGETI – ROELCKE 2003, pp. 73-74

[64]. LIGETI 2007B, pp. 69-70.

[65]. LIGETI 2001, p. 257.

[66]. *Ibidem*, p. 259.

carriers. In his mature years Ligeti listened to Romanian music and expanded his knowledge of it, strengthening memories through studies[67].

Endangered Sounds – Existential Fear

Reminiscing about the people he encountered on his life's journey, the teachers and the artists, Ligeti often comments on their political choices and later fate. He is sensitive both to Ferenc Farkas's «weak character» and political opportunism[68], and to the broken careers of uncompromising artists, such as Victor Vaszy[69]. Politics, even though it happens in the background of the composer's story, determines everything; it also carries a direct existential threat. In Ligeti's statements it manifests itself, among other things, in the description of the competition between sounds, in particular in the sounds bursting in from the public into the private sphere, and the disturbance of the rituals of everyday. The composer's reminiscences carry many elements typical of a soundscape of war that underwent quick changes and resulted in a sense of alienation. Among them are the sounds of Nazi propaganda which in the countries of Central-Eastern Europe were to turn into Communist propaganda within a few years, get also the disappearance of familiar sounds, including those associated with particular persons, the sound of the media bringing bad news, and noise colliding with sound[70].

It seems significant that it was the sound of the demonstrating crowds that convinced Ligeti's father of the inevitability of the situation and the unleashing of extreme emotions: «in January 1938, my father came back from a trip to Berlin with the conviction that very soon Hitler would attack the whole of Europe. He saw demonstrations of the Nazi mob in the streets, listened to the march songs and slogans and was sure that there was no way back»[71]. Many years later, watching the recordings of the old parades with the participation of the General Secretary of the Hungarian Workers' Party, Mátyás Rákosi, Ligeti himself mentions in his biographical film that the rhythmic clapping brings to his mind terrorism and this association stays with him even during the applause at concerts[72]. Shortly before the outbreak of the Second World War the disturbances of the external world were still being balanced by the routine of everyday life, peaceful life at home and communal music-making[73]. At that time Ligeti sees his father gradually

---

[67]. Țiplea Temeș 2018, p. 130.

[68]. Ligeti – Roelcke 2003, p. 42.

[69]. Vaszy was the director of the Conservatory in Cluj when Ligeti was a student and would not respect the numerus clausus. After the war he was professionally sidelined by the communists. See *ibidem*, p. 38.

[70]. See Tańczuk – Wieczorek 2018, p. 8. The publication discusses examples of European cities such as Warsaw, Wrocław, Lviv, Amsterdam and the Ruhr area.

[71]. Ligeti 2001, p. 245.

[72]. *György Ligeti – Portrait* 1993.

[73]. Ligeti 2001, p. 245.

giving up his ambitious plans for producing sociological and philosophical works[74]. «Previously I would almost always fall asleep to the calming sound of the clatter of his typewriter in another room»[75] reminisces Ligeti, and he compares the sound of the typewriter heard throughout the night in childhood to a lullaby sending him to sleep[76]. In the Ligeti household the sound of the typewriter became an endangered sound, auguring the death of his father in 1945. Another sound that was to disappear forever from the composer's home was that of the playing of the viola. Ligeti writes about his brother, Gábor, killed by the Nazis in 1945: «I admired his skill on the violin and when he changed to the viola later on — in the hope of getting a chance to play in a string quartet — he made even more progress»[77].

In the reminiscences of the war time, silence appears in many configurations, and its meanings change, from the dying out of the noises of normal life, through waiting and listening out, to the silence that comes from trauma. Ligeti remarks that at the time when the country was not yet at war, the city lights would already be turned off and along the unlit street at night: «there were no cars [...] driving, there were only pedestrians moving. There was total silence. It had a peculiar charm. Those nights of war [...] were spellbindingly beautiful»[78]. Such remarks are typical of Ligeti's subtle aesthetisation of memories, perhaps a way of neutralising moments of terror.

On the question of the events of war the composer remained silent throughout most of his life, and in later years he remained restrained in describing the scenes of his most dramatic experiences. From Ligeti's narrative there emerges the noise of alarms, mechanical commands, shots and explosions. The tone of his story varies from instinctive reactions, such as evaluating a threat («When you hear missiles, you are not in danger. Those that hit are not audible»[79]), to escaping into the world of literature (when Ligeti recalls reading a book in an abandoned Jewish house as more realistic than the shouts outside the window[80]). Reverberations of war return in his story when he talks of the uprising in Hungary when, together with the students, he takes part in crowd protests[81]. «In the street there was shooting from tanks and cannons all the time. I did not take the danger too seriously. During the revolution and afterwards nobody ever knew

---

[74]. LIGETI 2007c, p. 25

[75]. «[...] früher schlief ich fast immer mit dem beruhigendem Klappen seiner Schreibmaschine aus einem entfernten Zimmer ein». LIGETI 2007e, p. 15.

[76]. LIGETI 2007c, p. 25.

[77]. LIGETI 2001, p. 245.

[78]. «[...] fuhren [...] keine Autos, in der Dunkelheit waren nur Fußgänger unterwegs. Es war total still. Das hatte ein eneigenartigen Reiz. Diese Kriegsnächte [...] waren bezaubernd schön». LIGETI – ROELCKE 2003, p. 48.

[79]. «Wenn man die Geschosse hört, ist man nicht in Gefahr. Die einschlagenden Geschosse kann man nicht hören». *Ibidem*, p. 58.

[80]. The book was Aldous Huxley's *Eyeless in Gaza*. See *ibidem*, pp. 57-58.

[81]. LIGETI 2001, p. 261.

who shot from where»[82]. Ligeti also hears shots above his head when he finally makes his escape from his country by train, and crawls on his stomach through the snow close to the border with Austria[83].

Sound Images and Creative Transformations

Protocompositions

«Imagination» became one of the keywords associated with Ligeti's works, also used in the title of his famous biography[84], and for this reason for Ligeti sound images are a complement to sound memories. The composer often talks about his «protocompositions», melodies created only in his head in order to survive daily rituals[85]. Ligeti supplies details about the duration of these compositions (related to a shorter or longer walk), their scoring (even including a full symphony orchestra), genre (symphony, concerto, overture) and even stylistic models taken from concerts and life. We learn that the imaginings arose when he is on the move, because «sitting without moving reduced my musical fantasy»[86]. For the purposes of his childhood utopia Ligeti also invented a language very similar to the mysterious Romanian language[87], which could not include any elements of the «normal» Hungarian language.

The question of how Ligeti approached his sound memories and how he creatively transformed his sound environment can only be answered piecemeal and hypothetically. In what follows I will, however, point to a number of tropes which may be helpful in this context. Yet again we find in them the key contexts of memories characterised earlier, such as local soundscape, language and elapsing time.

The Aura of Creativity

Bernard documents the fact that in Ligeti's sketches from at least the 1980s there appear «many, sometimes great many handwritten lists for each work, often on tiny pieces of paper, which indicate the intended character of individual movement but do not break them down

---

[82]. «Auf der Straße wurde aus Panzern und Kanonen die ganze Zeit geschossen. Um die Gefahr habe ich mich nicht sehr gekümmert. Während der Revolution und nachher wußte man überhaupt nicht wer von wo schießt». Ligeti – Roelcke 2003, p. 75.

[83]. *Ibidem*, p. 79.

[84]. Steinitz 2003.

[85]. Ligeti – Roelcke 2003, p. 18.

[86]. Ligeti 2001, p. 243.

[87]. Ligeti – Roelcke 2003, p. 20.

further than that»[88]. These lists, made up of short entries, include references to the most diverse, often incompatible, kinds of music, both artistic and ethnic. Ligeti himself claimed that inspiration for composing may resemble an elusive smell or taste which «evokes a whole world»[89]. The multiplicity and diversity of the associations jotted down by the composer, and the fact that he never developed them in later notes, lead Bernard to conclude that these were «preliminary exercises»[90]. In addition, these jottings were almost always written in the composer's native, «private» language. It is in these jottings that we find memories of the local soundscape from childhood and youth, the «blurred autobiographical echoes»[91] of Romanian or Hungarian folk music that interpenetrate Ligeti's works particularly in his last two creative decades. Márton Kerékfy comments that «Folkloristic allusions in Ligeti's late works are sometimes self-referential, where they refer to his own youthful compositions»[92]; moreover, they often have a deeply transformed, syncretic-synthetic form and serve a variety of aesthetic aims[93].

Transformations of Nature and Musical Space

Evidence showing that Ligeti was not indifferent to the influence of sound memories and transformations of the music of the environment is provided by his descriptions of the works of the composers whom he included in his artistic genealogy. They include Béla Bartók, Anton Webern, Gustav Mahler and Charles Ives. Working on Romanian folk melodies at the Folklore Institute in Bucharest, Ligeti largely made use of methods devised by Bartók[94]. Ligeti stresses: «It becomes increasingly clear how little speculation there is in Bartók's use of dissonances and how much his regularities rely on living folk music»[95]. Opposing speculation to «living music» may also testify to Ligeti's view that music is not only an abstract «structure» (let us add, which he also eagerly explored), but a sound creation difficult to capture in its particularity and ephemerality. This way of thinking is apparent both in his criticism of serialism, and in his later turning towards the «imprecise», «out of tune» microtonality.

At the turn of the 1950s and 60s Anton Webern becomes one of the key figures described by Ligeti. The composer sees a link between this music and that of Claude Debussy, manifesting

---

[88]. BERNARD 2011, p. 152.
[89]. «[...] evoziert eine ganze Welt». LIGETI – ROELCKE 2003, p. 167.
[90]. BERNARD 2011, p. 152.
[91]. ȚIPLEA TEMEȘ 2018, p. 128.
[92]. KERÉKFY 2016, p. 252.
[93]. *Ibidem*, pp. 251-252.
[94]. LIGETI 2007I, p. 63.
[95]. «Immer deutlicher zeichnet sich ab, wie wenig spekulativ die Verwendung von Dissonanzen bei Bartók ist und wie sehr ihre Gesetzmäßigkeiten auf lebendiger Volksmusik basieren». LIGETI 2007B, p. 76.

itself in, among other things, a sensitivity to musical images of nature[96]. In the descriptions of Webern's music one can discern Ligeti's nuanced attitude to imitating sounds of nature in music. In *Sechs Stücke für Orchester* Op. 6 the composer traces «associative moments» in the form of a tremolo of the timpani resembling the sounds of distant gale or the sound of a bell in a «funeral march music of Mahlerian character»[97]. However, he warns against suspecting Webern of naturalism: «The sounds of nature are totally absorbed by the compositions and transcended into the unreal space of pure music»[98]. By the *Fünf Stücke für Orchester* Op. 10 there is already a fuller «internalisation of the sounding outside world»[99]. When the quoted fragments talk of the autonomy of music, this certainly does not mean an abstract, structural view, but thinking about music in the categories of «delicate and strange poetry» or «non-real space of pure music»[100], rooted in romanticism. Considering that Ligeti regarded Webern as the precursor of the instrumental colour series we might even arrive at the far-reaching conclusion that at the source of the abstract ordering of «sound relationships» we find precisely those auditory experiences of the environment and discover that which is present in nature: «Nature here also has become music»[101].

Ligeti also devotes much attention to the effects of space (*Raumwirkung*) in the music of Gustav Mahler[102]. He is above all fascinated by the creation of the illusion of space without recourse to space-related sound but by «purely compositional» means: skilful orchestration, colour achieved by muffling the sound, appropriate juxtapositions of timbres etc. This achieves effects of distancing, getting closer, emptiness, filling or change of perspective, and timbre appears as «independent musical parameter»[103]. Ligeti writes suggestively about space being «totally uninhabited»[104] or populating empty space with sound signals in *Symphony No. 1*[105]. In the use of the image of empty space, i.e., silence which becomes populated by live sound organisms, this is close to the metaphors of John Cage and Raymond Murray Schafer. Ingrid Pustijanac emphasises that references to Mahler's music helped Ligeti to work out his own

---

[96]. LIGETI 2007J, p. 345.

[97]. «[...] konduktartige Trauermusik Mahlerscher Prägung». *Ibidem*.

[98]. «Die Klänge der Natur werden von der Komposition völlig aufgesogen und in die nichtrealen Bereiche reiner Musik transzendiert». *Ibidem*.

[99]. «Verinnerlichung der tönenden Außenwelt». *Ibidem*.

[100]. «[...] zarte und eigentümliche Poesie», «nichtreale Bereiche reiner Musik». *Ibidem*.

[101]. «Die Natur ist hier ebenso zu Musik geworden». *Ibidem*.

[102]. Ingrid Pustijanac, who describes Ligeti himself as «Il maestro dello spazio immaginario» emphasises that Mahler was not one of the composers of interest to the then contemporary representatives of the avant-garde. See PUSTIJANAC 2013, p. 262.

[103]. «[...] selbständige musikalische Dimension». LIGETI 2007F, p. 280.

[104]. «[...] vollkommen unbevölkert». *Ibidem*, p. 279.

[105]. *Ibidem*, p. 280.

solutions, for example when composing the Requiem[106]. It is no accident that the metaphor of music as striding across a landscape as well as the metaphor of the sound event, developed above all in the note to *Apparitions*, were close to Ligeti's heart[107].

The perception of a composition as a soundscape becomes even more apparent when the composer discusses the collage technique. After clarifying this «terminus technicus» with reference to the visual arts, Ligeti stipulates that, in his opinion, Ives and Mahler did not know this term at all: «it is more concerned with acoustic events that one can gather during a fair or Oktoberfest»[108]. The ease with which Ligeti himself points to the sources of collages in these composers' reminiscences indicates he was no stranger to that kind of identification[109]. Perhaps the subtlety of musical arrangement protected the composers in question in each case from the charge of «naturalism», since on this occasion Ligeti did not formulate it at all, and perhaps towards the end of the 1970s the charge was not as serious as it had been two decades previously. However, the composer does not take the opportunity to present his own works in a similar way. It is significant that in his description of *San Francisco Polyphony* (1974) Ligeti employs a purely «mute» the spatial-architectonic description, that takes into account the map of the city, its transport, ethnic diversity of its inhabitants or the picture of the misty landscape seen from on high[110]. Here sounds are present only implicitly and there is no trace of them even in the documentation of the creative process. Bernard regards the first sketch for this composition as a typical example of drawings[111], although in the notes we also find references to the «tumult» or to the «Mahlerian» tempo[112], and thus indirectly to the associations with the soundscape evoked by Mahler's music.

Memory and Measuring Time

In Ligeti's descriptions of Mahler's music distance is not only a spatial but also a temporal category, since the hazy sounds of the orchestra bring to mind «old-fashioned industry»[113], and the materials used in the musical collages have in them «something obsessively outdated» and

---

[106]. PUSTIJANAC 2013, p. 262.

[107]. Amy Bauer analyses it in the context of the cognitive theory of metaphor and what is known as conceptual metaphors. See BAUER 2011, p. 37.

[108]. «Eher handelt sich um akustische Erlebnisse, die man auf einem Jahrmarkt oder auf dem Oktoberfest sammeln kann». LIGETI 2007K, p. 286.

[109]. LIGETI 1983, p. 25.

[110]. *Ibidem*, p. 66.

[111]. BERNARD 2011, p. 153.

[112]. STEINITZ 2011, p. 175.

[113]. «[...] altmodische Industrie». LIGETI 2007F, p. 279.

bring associations with «a gramophone with a bent tube»[114]. This aspect of linking distance in space with a memory seems all the more significant when we consider how strongly Ligeti identified with the Central European identity he shared with Mahler[115].

Importantly, it is precisely because of the «old-fashioned industry» and the idea of mechanical movement that measuring time acquires its sound representation in Ligeti's music. In the context of such works as *Poème Symphonique* (1962), *Continuum* (1968), or *Coulée* (1969) the composer most often recalls the Gyula Krúdy's story about a widow living in a house full of ticking clocks, but in a late interview he replaces this literary source with his father's typewriter: «It sounded like irregular percussion. It produced in me many specific rhythmic ideas»[116].

The aesthetic effect achieved by the use of mechanical rhythms[117] is not obvious yet deeply thought-provoking. As Benjamin Levy notes, in *Poème Symphonique* the mechanical metronomes, abandoned by the people who set them in motion «are surprisingly musical», and the initial chaos with time gives way to order[118]. In turn Johnson claims that the counted time is only a pretext to show with all the greater power, in the poetic silence that crowns the whole composition, the present moment and human presence, veiled by the clicking of the mechanical timekeepers[119]. The regular sound thus not only represents the passing time, but also embodies it.

The Overcoming of Language

The problem of language, argues Beckles Willson, permeated Ligeti's artistic biography from his earliest works. He retained sensitivity to «the music inherent to language»[120], evidenced both by his interest in synthetic speech production in *Artikulation* (1958), on which Ligeti worked in the electronic studio, and the imitation of language in the vocal parts stripped of semantics and combined with theatrical expression in *Aventures* (1962) and *Nouvelles Aventures* (1962-1965). Natural language also became for Ligeti the most accurate metaphor for music as a system. He saw it in categories of «semi-consistency of the grammar of natural

---

[114]. «[…] etwas penetrant Antiquitiertes», «Grammophonen mit verschnörkelten Schalltrichtern». LIGETI 2007K, p. 287.

[115]. Lóránt Péteri writes penetratingly about the links between Ligeti's identity and that of Mahler, as well as about the allusions to his Symphony No. 9 in Horn Trio. See PÉTERI 2019.

[116]. «Es klang wie ein unregelmäßiges Schlagzeug. Das hat bei mir viele konkrete rhythmische Vorstellungen ausgelöst». LIGETI – ROELCKE 2003, p. 166.

[117]. As Levy reminds us, the regular clicking of the metronome had already been used previously by other artists linked to Fluxus, such as Toshi Ichiyanagi and George Maciunas. See LEVY 2017, p. 141.

[118]. *Ibidem*, p. 142.

[119]. JOHNSON 2015, p. 91.

[120]. BECKLES WILLSON 2007, pp. 96-98.

languages»[121], but at the same time doubted the possibility of returning to a universal language, such as tonal music, and even regarded this vision as utopian[122]. Amy Bauer argues that in opera, the traditional battlefield for supremacy between music and language, as an example, Ligeti demonstrates «the failure of language». In *Le Grand Macabre* (1974-1977), where language, stripped of its meanings and collapsing into nonsense, surrenders to music, and music itself achieves freedom through, among other things, revealing its arbitrary mechanisms and conventions, «the collapse of the representational function of the word can only be overcome, or affectively illustrated, by resorting to music and the sonic dimension of language»[123]. During the final decades of his creative life Ligeti returns to his private, not widely understood Hungarian language, focussing on the experimental and constructivist potential of language, also because of a return to the «untranslatable» poetry of Sándor Weöres at the beginning of the 1980s.

Conclusion

The fact that in the reconstruction of Ligeti's biography sounds play an important part may have partly resulted from the public demand for his musical reminiscences. The repeatability of selected themes, but also the multiplicity and variety of contexts (often previously unknown) imply that the composer could not imagine depicting reality without that sphere. It seems perfectly comprehensible if we take into account that the relation to music defined Ligeti's entire professional life, and thus also shaped his identity.

Music, but also all the sound memories turn out to be an excellent tool for constructing the concept of the self, and as a consequence also for building one's self-identity[124]. They serve «as a device for ordering the self as an agent, and as an object known and accountable to oneself and others»[125]. In Ligeti's case the identity-shaping and performative role of his «musically composed identities» seems evident. «A subject divided by geography, language, history and culture»[126], as Bauer describes Ligeti, is painstakingly, with great attention to detail, put together into one story in spite of all its ruptures and discontinuities. It is a story being created by a mature composer from the perspective of the second half of his life. Western audiences learn from it about the prenatal[127] or even «prehistoric Ligeti», who is supposed to have

---

[121]. LIGETI 2001, p. 247.
[122]. LIGETI 2007G, p. 133.
[123]. BAUER 2019, p. 429.
[124]. SPYCHIGER 2017, p. 281.
[125]. DENORA 2000, p. 73.
[126]. BAUER 2011, p. 5.
[127]. LIGETI 1983, p. 33.

preceded the life of «the real Ligeti», and yet remains closely linked to him. These terms only go to confirm what an enormous caesura in the public and private life of Ligeti was his escape from Hungary, but the «prehistoric» fragment of his life will be emphasised as particularly important for its formation until the end.

Sound memories may have served as the carrier of longing for the past, mourning and nostalgia that left such a powerful mark on Ligeti's works[128]. However, as Bauer stresses, the conservative understanding of nostalgia was alien to the composer[129], and his reminiscences themselves show a tendency to aesthetise and self-create. Making memories present and transforming them through music may thus also have been an attempt to find oneself in the present[130].

Memories not only play an identifying role, but also enable a fuller characterisation of the medium of sound itself. This means that the image of sound, including musical sound, that emerges from the reminiscences, is richer not only than the one which we have become used to through the discourse of the post-war avant-garde, but also richer than the recurring tropes found in Ligeti's commentaries to his own compositions. Sound placed in context, dependent on its unstable and imperfect carriers, loses its abstract and autonomous quality but at the same time gains in power. One cannot tame it by way of compositional technique. It is not limited to «thought structures communicated with acoustic signals», to «pure» music, for which Ligeti otherwise longed, or perhaps, rather, mourned its loss[131], or even to the «semi-consistency» of natural language. In the composer's narrative sound generates complex and changing meanings, associations and emotions, imposes its presence, materiality, immediacy and particularity, it has its own «smell and taste» and the power to conjure up unintended sound imaginings, to «evoke the whole world». This brings it closer to the rich experiences that Ligeti's compositions themselves leave in their interpreters and listeners. Quoting the composer's own words, you might say that in his music an «internalisation of the sounding outside world» takes place. And that is why his reminiscences, in spite of all their ephemerality and particularity, will continue to reverberate long after his death.

Translated by Zofia Weaver

---

[128]. See Bauer 2011. It is worth noting that lament is also present in the works of other composers at the turn of the twenty-first century. See Metzer 2009, pp. 144-174.

[129]. Bauer 2011, p. 17.

[130]. This is the way Johnson interprets memory in music and regards it as the opposite of nostalgia, Johnson 2015, p. 36.

[131]. Bauer 2011, p. 17.

Bibliography

Bauer 2011
Bauer, Amy. *Ligeti's Laments: Nostalgia, Exoticism, and the Absolute*, Aldershot, Ashgate, 2011.

Bauer 2012
Ead. 'The Cosmopolitan Absurdity of Ligeti's Late Works', in: *Contemporary Music Review*, XXXI/2-3 (2012), pp. 163-176.

Bauer 2019
Ead. 'Contemporary Opera and the Failure of Language', in: *The Routledge Research Companion to Modernism in Music*, edited by Björn Heile and Charles Wilson, Abingdon-New York, Routledge, 2019, pp. 427-453.

Beckles Willson 2007
Beckles Willson, Rachel. *Ligeti, Kurtág, and Hungarian Music during the Cold War*, Cambridge, Cambridge University Press, 2007.

Bernard 2011
Bernard, Jonathan W. 'Rules and Regulation: Lessons from Ligeti's Compositional Sketches', in: *György Ligeti: Of Foreign Lands and Strange Sounds*, edited by Louise Duchesneau and Wolfgang Marx, Woodbridge, The Boydell Press, 2011, pp. 149-167.

DeNora 2000
DeNora, Tia. *Music in Everyday Life*, Cambridge, Cambridge University Press, 2000.

Duchesneau 2011
Duchesneau, Louise. '"Play it like Bill Evans": György Ligeti and Recorded Music', in: *György Ligeti: Of Foreign Lands and Strange Sounds*, op. cit., pp. 125-147.

György Ligeti – Portrait 1993
György Ligeti – Portrait, film by Michel Follin, Judit Kele and Arnaud de Mezamat. Produced by Artline Films, Abacaris Films, Centre Pompidou, Les Productions du Sablier, La Sept ARTE, RTBF-Radio Télévision Belge Francophone, Magyar TV (Budapest), 64 minutes, 1993.

Johnson 2015
Johnson, Julian. *Out of Time: Music and the Making of Modernity*, Oxford, Oxford University Press, 2015.

Kerékfy 2016
Kerékfy, Márton. 'Folkloristic Inspirations in the Music of György Ligeti: Problems of Identification and Interpretation', in: *Musicologica Istropolitana XII: Paths of Musicology in Central Europe*, edited by Marcus Zagorski and Vladimír Zvara, Bratislava, Vydavateľstvo Univerzity Komenského v Bratislave, 2016, pp. 243-265.

Levy 2017
Levy, Benjamin R. *Metamorphosis in Music: The Compositions of György Ligeti in the 1950s and 1960s*, Oxford, Oxford University Press, 2017.

LICHTENFELD 2007
LICHTENFELD, Monika. 'Komposition und Kommentar. György Ligetis Kunst des Schreibens', in: LIGETI, György. *Gesammelte Schriften. 1*, edited by Monika Lichtenfeld, Mainz, Schott, 2007 (Veröffentlichungen der Paul Sacher Stiftung, 10), pp. 9-38.

LIGETI 1983
György Ligeti in Conversation with Péter Várnai, Josef Häusler, Claude Samuel, and Himself, translated by Gabor J. Schabert, Sarah E. Soulsby, Terence Kilmartin and Geoffrey Skelton, London, Eulenburg, 1983 (Eulenburg Music Series).

LIGETI 1993
LIGETI, György. 'States, Events, Transformations', translated by Jonathan W. Bernard, in: *Perspectives of New Music*, XXXI/1 (1993), pp. 164-171.

LIGETI 2001
ID. 'Between Science, Music and Politics', in: *The Inamori Foundation: Kyoto Prizes & Inamori Grants 17*, Kyoto, The Inamori Foundation, 2001, pp. 230-268, <https://www.kyotoprize.org/wp-content/uploads/2019/07/2001_C-1.pdf>, accessed 16.08.2021.

LIGETI 2007A
ID. 'Bagatellen', in: ID. *Gesammelte Schriften. 2*, edited by Monika Lichtenfeld, Mainz, Schott, 2007 (Veröffentlichungen der Paul Sacher Stiftung, 10), pp. 68-71.

LIGETI 2007B
ID. 'Ein rumänisches Ensemble aus dem Komitat Arad', translated by Éva Pintér, in: ID. *Gesammelte Schriften. 1, op. cit.*, pp. 69-76.

LIGETI 2007C
ID. 'Mein Judentum', in: ID. *Gesammelte Schriften. 2, op. cit.*, pp. 20-28.

LIGETI 2007D
ID. 'Mein Kölner Jahr 1957', in: ID. *Gesammelte Schriften. 2, op. cit.*, pp. 29-32.

LIGETI 2007E
ID. 'Musikalische Erinnerungen aus Kindheit und Jugend', in: ID. *Gesammelte Schriften. 2, op. cit.*, pp. 11-19.

LIGETI 2007F
ID. 'Raumwirkungen in der Musik Gustav Mahlers', in: ID. *Gesammelte Schriften. 1, op. cit.*, pp. 279-284.

LIGETI 2007G
ID. 'Rhapsodische Gedanken über Musik, besonders über meine eigenen Kompositionen', in: ID. *Gesammelte Schriften. 2, op. cit.*, pp. 123-135.

LIGETI 2007H
ID. 'Über mein *Concert Românesc* und andere Frühwerke aus Ungarn', in: ID. *Gesammelte Schriften. 2, op. cit.*, pp. 151-153.

LIGETI 2007I
ID. 'Volksmusikforschung in Rumänien', translated by Éva Pintér, in: ID. *Gesammelte Schriften. 1, op. cit.*, pp. 61-68.

LIGETI 2007J
ID. 'Webern und die Romantik', in: ID. *Gesammelte Schriften. 1, op. cit.*, pp. 343-346.

LIGETI 2007K
ID. 'Zur Collagetechnik bei Mahler und Ives', in: ID. *Gesammelte Schriften. 1, op. cit.*, pp. 285-290.

LIGETI – ROELCKE 2003
ID. – ROELCKE, Eckhard. *«Träumen Sie in Farbe?». György Ligeti im Gespräch mit Eckhard Roelcke*, Vienna, Zsolnay Verlag, 2003.

METZER 2009
METZER, David. *Musical Modernism at the Turn of the Twenty-First Century*, Cambridge, Cambridge University Press, 2009.

PÉTERI 2019
PÉTERI, Lóránt. 'Whose Farewell? Ligeti's *Horn Trio* and Mahler's *Ninth Symphony*', in: *Musical Analysis. History – Theory – Praxis. 5*, edited by Anna Granat-Janki, Wrocław, Akademia Muzyczna im. Karola Lipińskiego we Wrocławiu, 2019, pp. 345-355.

PUSTIJANAC 2013
PUSTIJANAC, Ingrid. *György Ligeti. Il maestro dello spazio immaginario*, Lucca, LIM, 2013 (Quaderni di Musica/Realtà. Supplemento, 3).

SCHAFER 1994
SCHAFER, Raymond Murray. *The Soundscape: Our Sonic Environment and the Tuning of the World*, Rochester, Vermont, Destiny Books, 1994.

SCHREIBER 2019
SCHREIBER, Ewa. 'Childhood Memories and Musical Constructions. Autobiographical Threads in György Ligeti's Notes on His Works', in: *Musical Analysis. History – Theory – Praxis. 5, op. cit.*, pp. 169-181.

SPYCHIGER 2017
SPYCHIGER, Maria B. 'From Musical Experience to Musical Identity: Musical Self-Concept as a Mediating Psychological Structure', in: *Handbook of Musical Identities*, edited by Raymond MacDonald, David J. Hargreaves and Dorothy Miell, Oxford, Oxford University Press, 2017, pp. 267-287.

STEINITZ 2003
STEINITZ, Richard. *György Ligeti: Music of the Imagination*, Boston, Northeastern University Press, 2003.

STEINITZ 2011
ID. 'À qui un hommage? Genesis of the Piano Concerto and the Horn Trio', in: *György Ligeti: Of Foreign Lands and Strange Sounds, op. cit.*, pp. 169-212.

SZENDY 2016
SZENDY, Peter. *Phantom Limbs: On Musical Bodies*, translated by Will Bishop, New York, Fordham University Press, 2016.

TAŃCZUK – WIECZOREK 2018
Sounds of War and Peace: Soundscapes of European Cities in 1945, edited by Renata Tańczuk and Sławomir Wieczorek, Berlin, Peter Lang, 2018 (Eastern European Studies in Musicology, 10).

ȚĂRANU 2020
ȚĂRANU, Cornel. 'Meeting Ligeti', in: *A Tribute to György Ligeti in His Native Transylvania: Nos. 1-2*, edited by Bianca Țiplea Temeș and Kofi Agawu, Cluj-Napoca, Media Musica, 2020, pp. 95-100.

ȚIPLEA TEMEȘ 2018
ȚIPLEA TEMEȘ, Bianca. 'Ligeti and Romanian Folk Music. An Insight from the Paul Sacher Foundation', in: *György Ligeti's Cultural Identities*, edited by Amy Bauer and Márton Kerékfy, Abingdon-New York, Routledge, 2018, pp. 120-138.

'Functional Music' and *Cantata for the Festival of Youth*: New Data on Ligeti's Works from His Budapest Years

Márton Kerékfy
(Bartók Archives, Institute for Musicology,
Research Centre for the Humanities, Budapest)

Perhaps the most formative period in György Ligeti's professional career were those eleven years during which he was active at the Liszt Academy in Budapest. He studied there from September 1945 to summer 1949, and from September 1950 until the October 1956 revolution he was Assistant Professor. The first ground-breaking study devoted to this period of the composer's life and work, written by Friedemann Sallis, was published in 1996[1]. Relying on a large body of archival sources but also on existing work lists by Ove Nordwall and Pierre Michel, Sallis compiled a catalogue of Ligeti's composed works and published writings up to 1956, analysed several key works from this period, and also made an attempt to set out their historical context. Ligeti's relation to Hungarian musical life was investigated further, based on newly accessible archival sources and using a comparative method within a broader time scope, by Rachel Beckles Willson in her 2007 book[2]. Since then a number of articles have been published that discuss particular events of and works from Ligeti's early years from a historical perspective[3], but no comprehensive study on this period has appeared.

Since the publication of Sallis' book, a significant body of compositional sources from Ligeti's early years (including manuscripts of works formerly considered lost) has become available for research in the PSS SGL, and in 2016 even an inventory of all musical manuscripts preserved in the Ligeti Collection was published[4]. Yet a considerable part of Ligeti's juvenilia

---

[1]. Sallis 1996.
[2]. Beckles Willson 2007.
[3]. See, for example, Kerékfy 2012, Țiplea Temeș 2018 and Zimmermann 2018. See also Kerékfy 2018, pp. 27-42 and 57ff.
[4]. Sammlung György Ligeti 2016. On the history of the PSS SGL, see pp. 5-6.

and early biography is still under-researched or unexplored, with several works remaining unpublished or being missing. It is owing to this that most of the information on this period in even more current literature stems from the composer's recollections rather than from facts supported by historical sources.

In the present chapter I aim at providing factual information on the perhaps least noted part of Ligeti's early output: his 'functional music' and his *Cantata for the Festival of Youth*. Focusing on both the external circumstances of their genesis (such as commissions, competitions and censorship) and also their reception (concert performances, radio broadcasts, publications and reviews), I make an attempt to put these works in the historical and social contexts of Hungary's musical life.

Sources and Methods

Sallis relied upon three contemporary and three retrospective work lists when compiling his catalogue of Ligeti's early works[5]. The most detailed of these contemporary lists is Ligeti's personal catalogue maintained on yellow slips of paper[6]. These slips provide detailed information on 72 works written between 1943 and 1952, including title and scoring, the place and date (mostly year and month) of the composition, the commissioning institution and data on the first and subsequent performances and radio broadcasts (providing the venue or radio channel, the date and the performers), as well as on printed editions (the publisher's name and place plus the date of publication). Sallis incorporated many of these data into his own catalogue, but he quoted and translated some of them inaccurately (mostly names, but occasionally work titles, too), and he excluded the commissioning institutions and subsequent performances. Therefore, Ligeti's catalogue has been indispensable for my survey of his juvenilia. Further sources for the present survey include radio programmes (primarily from the weekly *Magyar Rádió* [Hungarian Radio], the official radio programme at that time, but occasionally also from newspapers), the records of the Hungarian Radio's Sound Archives, as well as concert and radio reviews and reports on musical subjects in the daily press. Regarding biographical details I have profited from archival sources in the Hungarian National Archives and the records of the Liszt Academy.

According to Sallis' catalogue, Ligeti composed 84 works (nos. 31-114) in his Budapest period, that is, between September 1945 and December 1956. This number includes arrangements

---

[5]. Sallis 1996, p. 263. For the catalogue, see pp. 262-291.

[6]. See work list no. 1 in *ibidem*, p. 263. According to Sallis, these slips are remnants of two separate catalogues; they were recovered by Ove Nordwall in Ligeti's Vienna apartment in 1969 and were then taken to Stockholm. They are now housed in PSS SGL and are available on microfilm under shelf marks MF 109.1 1464-1555. In the following, I will simply call it Ligeti's catalogue.

'Functional Music' and *Cantata for the Festival of Youth*

and transcriptions of the same works as well as unfinished and missing compositions. In terms of functionality, Ligeti's juvenilia can be divided into two broad categories: 'autonomous works' and 'functional music'. Although it is not always easy to draw a line between these two categories, and there are indeed a few border-line cases, the criteria for this categorisation can be set up quite clearly. I consider all pieces of music functional that were intended to accompany a staged performance or social event, as well as arrangements that do not go beyond the level of harmonisation or scoring. In this sense, more than a third of Ligeti's output composed in his Budapest period can be regarded as functional music. Produced from 1947 to 1953 (mostly in 1948 and 1949), this repertoire basically falls into four genres (see TABLE 1).

On the following pages, I will focus on Ligeti's functional music and his *Cantata for the Festival of Youth* from two perspectives:

1. Which opportunities, requirements and political-cultural framework did determine the genesis of these works?

2. What was the position of these works and what role did they play in Hungary's musical life of the time?

TABLE 1: LIGETI'S FUNCTIONAL MUSIC BY GENRE (SEPTEMBER 1945 TO DECEMBER 1956)[7]

Marches, dances and marching songs
57.* *8 kis induló* [8 Little Marches] for one and two voices (Sep 1948)
58.* *Zúgva árad* [Wildly Flowing] for four-part men's choir (Sep 1948)
59.* *Zúgva árad* [Wildly Flowing] for two-part men's choir and piano (Sep 1948)
61.* *Tánc* [Dance] for orchestra (1948)
62.* *Menetdalok* [Marching Songs] for one and two voices, partly with accompaniment (Jan 1949)
63.* *Induló* [March] for orchestra (Jan-Mar 1949)
64.* *Katonatánc* [Soldier's Dance] for two voices and piano (Feb 1949)
65.* *Katonatánc* [Soldier's Dance] for orchestra (Mar 1949)
69.* *Festival-trombitajel* [Festival Trumpet Call] for trumpet (11 Aug 1949)

Folk song arrangements for voices and instruments
60. *Bölcsőtől a sírig* [From Cradle to Grave] for two voices and chamber ensemble (Nov 1948)
67.* *Népdalharmonizálás* [Folk Song Harmonisation] for voice and string quartet (May 1949)
72. *Népdalfeldolgozás* [Folk Song Arrangement] for voice and piano (Dec 1949)
77. *Román népdalok és táncok* [Romanian Folk Songs and Dances] for two voices and gypsy orchestra (Sep 1950)
84. *Négy lakodalmi tánc* [Four Wedding Dances] for three female voices (or female choir) and piano (22 Nov - 6 Dec 1950)
96. *Középlokon esik az eső* [It's Raining in Középlok] for voice and piano (1951)
100a. *Menyasszony, vőlegény* [Bride, Bridegroom] for voice and piano (Aug 1952)

---

[7]. The numbers in front of work titles are the catalogue numbers in *ibidem*. Titles, scoring and dates of composition are given according to Ligeti's catalogue and other primary sources; in cases of works not included in Ligeti's catalogue these data are quoted from *ibidem*. Missing works are marked with an asterisk. All English translations are mine.

100b. *Aki dudás akar lenni* [Whoever Wants to Become a Piper] for voice and piano (2 Dec 1949; 2nd version: Aug 1952)
107. *Hat inaktelki népdal* [Six Folk Songs from Inaktelke] for three female voices and folk orchestra (1953)

Arrangements for instruments
44.* *Székely tánc* [Székely Dance] for piano (Apr 1947)
45.* *Ballada* [Ballad] for piano (Apr 1947)
52. *Dansuri* [Dances] for piano (10 Apr 1948)
53. *Dans* [Dance] for piano (Apr 1948?)
54. *El kéne indulni* [One Should Go] for piano (Apr 1948)
66. *Régi magyar társastáncok* [Old Hungarian Ballroom Dances] for string quartet or string orchestra with *ad libitum* flute and clarinet (May 1949)
71. *Három tánc cigányzenekarra* [Three Dances for Gypsy Orchestra] (Dec 1949)
86. *Három lakodalmi tánc* [Three Wedding Dances] for piano duet (30 Dec 1950)
89.* *Induló és három tánc* [March and Three Dances] for gypsy orchestra (10-11 Jan 1951)
91.* *Három tánc* [Three Dances] for piano (12 Apr 1951)

Incidental music
43. *Tornyos Péter* [Peter Tornyos] for voice and piano [text by János Illei?] (Mar 1947)
70. *Tavaszi Virág* [Spring Flower] for seven voices and chamber ensemble [text by Dr. László Körmöczi after S. Preobrazhensky] (Sep 1949, revised Feb 1951)
95.* *Kínai bábjáték suite* [Chinese Puppet Play Suite] for two voices and chamber ensemble [text by Dr. László Körmöczi after S. Preobrazhensky] (Oct-Nov 1951)

Institutional Background

Ligeti's juvenilia were obviously basically determined, both in their volume and content, by the requirements and opportunities of Hungary's musical life for the simple reason that Ligeti composed a significant part of his works to commission. Exactly the years of Ligeti's emergence as a professional composer (that is, the late 1940s and early 1950s) saw an increasing demand for new compositions in Hungary, owing to the consolidation of state socialism and the total centralisation of musical life. Cultural politics demanded both representative 'serious' works and 'music for the masses', which resulted in generous state commissions and an exaggerated circulation of works that were deemed politically correct[8]. This led to an increasing importance of composers. In the Magyar Zeneművészek Szövetsége [Association of Hungarian Musicians], which supervised and controlled the country's musical life since 1949, composers (and also musicologists) became dominant, although they were much fewer in number than some other groups of musical life, for example performers or music educators.

Before surveying Ligeti's juvenilia it is essential to briefly set out the institutional framework of his activity as a composer. In April 1949, Ligeti, still a final-year student at the Liszt Ferenc Zeneművészeti Főiskola [Franz Liszt Academy of Music], had entered the Zeneművészek

---
[8]. See TALLIÁN 1991, p. 106.

'Functional Music' and *Cantata for the Festival of Youth*

Szakszervezete[9] [Labour Union of Musicians], a predecessor of the Association of Hungarian Musicians, which was soon incorporated into the Művészeti Dolgozók Szakszervezete [Labour Union of Artistic Workers]. Within the latter, Ligeti was member of the union of composers. He held no function in the Association, nor did he seem to play an active role in its activity[10]. From February 1953 on, he was also a member of the Magyar Népköztársaság Zenei Alapja[11] [Musical Fund of the Hungarian People's Republic]. The recently established Musical Fund managed state commissions, made advance payments for composers and payed their royalties. The commissioned works were judged by a so-called consultancy committee [konzultációs bizottság], whose members were delegated by the Association of Hungarian Musicians[12]. In addition, the Musical Fund supported its member composers and musicologists through social allowances, grants, scholarly benefits and by maintaining resorts available (almost) free for members.

Marches, Dances and Marching Songs

Written over one year between September 1948 and August 1949, all of Ligeti's marches, dances and marching songs are considered lost. The earliest of them, *8 kis induló* [8 Little Marches] (no. 57[13]), was written to the commission of the Magyar Ifjúság Népi Szövetsége [Folk Association of Hungarian Youth] (abbreviated MINSZ). MINSZ was a communist-controlled youth organisation established in early 1948 with the aim to supervise all youth organisations in the country. Ligeti entered the Magyar Egyetemisták és Főiskolások Egységes Szervezete [United Organisation of Hungarian Undergraduates] (abbreviated MEFESZ) in September 1948 and became President of its union at the Liszt Academy[14]. Originally called Magyar Egyetemi és Főiskolai Egyesületek Szövetsége [Association of Hungarian Unions of Undergraduates], MEFESZ was established after World War II as a democratic umbrella organisation of Hungary's autonomous unions of undergraduates, but it gradually went under the control of communists, and practically lost its autonomy in May 1948, when it was taken under the supervision of MINSZ, and the autonomy of the faculty unions were also ceased. The Association was renamed at that time[15], and in September (that is, approximately the same time when Ligeti entered it) MEFESZ was downgraded to the undergraduate division of MINSZ[16]. By the beginning of 1949, MEFESZ had *de facto* become an executive body of the state power.

---

[9]. See Ligeti 1950.
[10]. See the minutes of meetings quoted in Beckles Willson 2007.
[11]. See Ligeti's membership card (in personal collection, photo in the author's possession).
[12]. Péteri 2013, pp. 170-171.
[13]. For easy reference I always give the numbering of each work in Sallis' catalogue at first mention.
[14]. Ligeti 1950, curriculum vitae.
[15]. Micheller 1990, pp. 141-142.
[16]. *Ibidem*, p. 143.

With more than 15,000 members, equalling two thirds of the 23,000 undergraduates in the country, it exerted a massive influence on young people all over the country[17]. During the autumn semester in 1948, elections were held at each faculty, and, according to an anonymous internal report, «the masses unanimously elected the faculty directorates proposed by [the Communists]»[18]. Ligeti was obviously elected President of the MEFESZ union at the Academy at that time. It is not known why he was nominated and why he accepted this position. Twenty-five years later he told Imre Fábián: «one took me for a kind of left-wing useful idiot» and «I was still naïve»[19].

Thus the commission from MINSZ was most probably related to Ligeti's MEFESZ membership. In the background of *8 kis induló* there seems to have been the 'exclusive competition' for composers reported by the daily *Népszava* on 2 September 1948:

> In the framework of an exclusive competition, the music committee of the Folk Association of Hungarian Youth commissioned composers Ferenc Szabó, Endre Székely, Sándor Veres[s], István Raics, György Ligeti, András Mihály, [and] Béla Tardos to compose the representative march of the Hungarian youth. The works will be judged by a four-member committee, whose members are composers Pál Kadosa, Endre Szervánszky, Pál Járdányi and Lajos Kiss, Director of the Béla Bartók Folk College[20].

It is remarkable that Ligeti was not only by far the youngest of the six composers commissioned (he was 25, while the others were aged between 31 and 46) but the only one not being member of the state communist party, the Magyar Dolgozók Pártja [Hungarian Workers' Party]. (Ligeti never entered any political party in Hungary.) Although the results of the competition are not known it is certain that Ligeti was not rewarded, because *8 kis induló* did not appear in print and are not documented to have ever been performed. According to Sallis, it was written for piano, which is obviously a misunderstanding. Ligeti's catalogue writes

---

[17]. It is to be noted, however, that the proportion of MEFESZ members was significantly lower at the Liszt Academy; even a year later, in December 1949, it was only 38.4%.

[18]. «[...] a tömegek mindenütt egyhangúan választották meg az általunk javasolt kari vezetőségeket». Anonymous and undated typescript in Magyar Nemzeti Levéltár Országos Levéltára [Hungarian National Archives], Budapest, XXVIII-M-16-11. őrzési egység (MEFESZ-anyagok, 1949).

[19]. «[...] olyan baloldali hasznos idiótának tartottak» «[...] még naiv voltam [...]». Quoted in MIKUSI 2019, pp. 278-279.

[20]. «A Magyar Ifjúság Népi Szövetségének zenei bizottsága zártkörű pályázat keretében Szabó Ferenc, Székely Endre, Veres[s] Sándor, Raics István, Ligeti György, Mihály András, Tardos Béla zeneszerzőket kérte fel a magyar ifjúság reprezentatív indulójának megkomponálására. A műveket négytagú bizottság bírálja el, melynek tagjai Kadosa Pál, Szervánszky Endre, Járdányi Pál zeneszerzők és Kiss Lajos, a Bartók Béla Népikollégium igazgatója». Untitled news in *Népszava*, 2 September 1948, p. 5. Note that István Raics — a communist poet, author and lyricist — is probably mistakenly called a composer in the article; it is more likely that he was commissioned to write the lyrics of the march.

«1-2 szólamú, MINSZ-nek» [for 1 and 2 voices, for MINSZ], which means most probably that the eight marches are for one or and two voices, presumably without accompaniment. On their texts there is no data available.

Ligeti set another march, *Zúgva árad* [Wildly Flowing[21]], on words by one of the most successful lyricists for mass songs of the time, István Raics, in two versions: for unaccompanied four-part men's choir and for two male voices with piano accompaniment (nos. 58 and 59, respectively). According to Ligeti's catalogue, it was written for a competition announced by the miners' labour union and was awarded the second prize on 12 February 1949[22]. I was not able to track down its text. Furthermore, according to Ligeti's catalogue, István Sárközy and György Kurtág revised the work in February 1949, and Tibor Papp transcribed it for wind band; the parts of this version were even published by the Béla Bartók Association in 1950. For the time being, however, no copy of this publication is available[23].

Nothing is known about *Tánc* [Dance] for orchestra (no. 61); it is not included in Ligeti's catalogue. On the next four works, however, the composer's catalogue does provide information. All of them were written to the commission of the Honvédelmi Minisztérium [Ministry of Defence]. *Menetdalok* [Marching Songs] (no. 62) is for one and two voices, «partly with accompaniment»[24]. In Ligeti's catalogue, two surnames appear in parentheses next to that of the Ministry of Defence, «Benjámin» and «Mátyás»; these two persons, whom I have not been able to identify, might have mediated the commission to the composer.

Both *Induló* [March] and *Katonatánc* [Soldier's Dance] for full orchestra (nos. 63 and 65, respectively) — the latter being a transcription of *Katonatánc* for two voices and piano accompaniment (no. 64) — were first performed on 29 April 1949 at the festive debut of Honvéd Központi Művészegyüttes [The Army's Central Art Ensemble] at the Városi Színház [Municipal Theatre] in Budapest. Following the model of the Soviet Red Army's renowned Alexandrov Ensemble, the Hungarian ensemble consisted of a dance company, a male choir and an orchestra; the dance company was led by Iván Szabó, the choir by Zoltán Vásárhelyi and the orchestra by Gyula Dávid. While *Induló* was most probably played by the orchestra alone, *Katonatánc* was performed together by the orchestra and the dance company with choreography by Szabó, with the title «Gyakorlat után» [After Drill]. The latter item is mentioned by author Gábor Devecseri in an enthusiastic review published in the festive issue of 1 May of the official party newspaper *Szabad Nép* [Free Folk], but he does not name any of the composers[25].

---

[21]. «Wildly Flowing» is Sallis' translation. Note that *Zúgva árad* is obviously the incipit of the words, which might be translated in other ways as well, depending on the continuation.

[22]. «A bányász szakszervezet pályázatára. [...] II. díjat nyert».

[23]. Sallis relates this work to a manuscript for wind band titled «Induló» [March] and signed by Kurtág, which is now found in PSS SGK.

[24]. «részint kísérettel». See Ligeti's catalogue.

[25]. Devecseri 1949.

While no further performance of *Induló* is documented (there is a question mark after «Further performances» in Ligeti's catalogue), *Katonatánc* obviously became a popular item of The Army's Central Art Ensemble; according to the composer's catalogue, they performed it «many times» in 1949 and 1950 in Budapest and «all over in the country», and in May 1950 it was even «recorded by the newsreel». On 29 September 1951, it was revived in the National Theatre with new choreography by Sándor László-Bencsik, who had taken over the dance company in 1950. The revival was also followed by «many further performances»[26]. One of these might have been the performance in late July 1952 that the ensemble (which had meanwhile been renamed Magyar Néphadsereg Táncegyüttese [Dance Company of the Hungarian Folk Army]) gave in the Municipal Theatre «for professional audiences». This show was reviewed in some detail in the daily *Magyar Nemzet* [Hungarian Nation]. According to the review, the performance started with three Soviet dance pieces, followed by some Hungarian items, among which there were «two scenes from "Katonaképek" [Military Tableaux] (conscription and reception of recruits)» with music by György Ligeti and György Vetési[27]. Since it is not known that Ligeti composed any music for this ensemble other than the aforementioned, it is presumed that the Ligeti item mentioned in this review was *Katonatánc*.

Dated 11 August 1949, *Festival-trombitajel* [Festival Trumpet Call] (no. 69) was also composed to commission by MINSZ. It might have been an occasional fanfare, written obviously for the 2nd World Festival of Youth and Students that took place in Budapest from 14 to 28 August 1949. Since Ligeti was also commissioned to compose a cantata for this festival, he must have been an obvious choice for writing the festival's trumpet call as well. (I will discuss both the festival and the cantata in detail below.)

Arrangements

The major part of Ligeti's functional music consists of arrangements (harmonization or scoring) of folk music and art music, produced between 1947 and 1953[28].

Both *Székely tánc* [Székely Dance] and *Ballada* [Ballad] for piano (nos. 44 and 45, respectively) were written in April 1947 to a commission by Olga Szentpál's dance company, which premiered them in the same month in Budapest. None of them has survived. According to Ligeti's catalogue, *Székely tánc* was performed «several» times. The composer's cousin, Mária

---

[26]. There is a partly illegible note in Ligeti's catalogue on this revival: «új tánc, zene [...]ssal». The illegible word is most probably «kórussal», in which case the note would mean «new dance, music with choir». This suggests that Ligeti probably made a version of *Katonatánc* for choir and orchestra as well.

[27]. «két jelenet» «a 'Katonaképek'-ből [...] (bevonulás és újoncfogadás)» (Sz. I. 1952).

[28]. Ligeti's folk music arrangements are discussed in more detail in Kerékfy 2018, pp. 57ff.

Ligeti (called Mary by family members) was a member of this dance company; presumably it was she who mediated the commission to Ligeti. A year later he produced the cycle *El kéne indulni* [One Should Go] for piano (no. 54), again «for choreographic purposes for Mary Ligeti»[29]. According to Sallis, it is a reworking of *Ballada*. Ligeti's catalogue does not include *Ballada* but gives 'Ballada' as an alternative title for *El kéne indulni*. Choreographer Mária Ligeti graduated in 1948 from the Országos Magyar Színművészeti Főiskola [National Hungarian Academy of Theatre] in Budapest, where she had to make an individual choreography as part of her final-year project. She had the idea to dramatize the Hungarian folk song *El kéne indulni* in such a way that its content is performed by dancers only, without singing or spoken text. Although she was aware of Kodály's arrangement of the same folk song for voice and piano[30], she wanted to have a version of her own; therefore she commissioned Ligeti to look up and arrange this and other folk songs and to compose the music. The solo dancer of this piece is a young man; his marriage plans («Whom should one marry?») are represented by the solos of various girls, some of whom even dance duets with the lad. For the girls' solos Ligeti also used folk songs other than *El kéne indulni*[31]. Both Sallis and Simon Gallot[32] have considered this work lost, but its piano draft preserved by the choreographer has recently surfaced[33]. It was performed in an orchestrated version by György Tornyos in April 1949 by the company of the Szegedi Tájszínház [Szeged Country Theatre], with choreography by Mária Ligeti and Gábor Zakariás conducting. This was followed by «ca 15 performances» during that year[34]. One of these was a free performance on May Day (1 May) at the National Theatre of Szeged[35]. According to Ligeti's catalogue, *El kéne indulni* was also performed by the company of the Debrecen County Theatre in the town's Csokonai Színház [Csokonai Theatre] in 1950, but the number of performances is not given. Still in April 1948, Ligeti reused the music of *El kéne indulni* in a piano piece with the Romanian title *Dansuri* [Dances] (no. 52). Another piano piece consisting of three folk song settings, *Dans* [Dance] (no. 53), was probably written at the same time and presumably also for Mary[36].

---

[29]. Ligeti's catalogue.

[30]. See Kodály's *Hungarian Folk Music*, vol. I, no. 4. Kodály also arranged this folk song for male choir with the title *Kit kéne elvenni?* [Whom Should One Marry?], and included in his *Spinning Room*, too.

[31]. See Vera Ligeti's letter to Heidy Zimmermann, 8 June 2008, attached to the work's manuscript in PSS SGL: El kéne indulni.

[32]. See 'Catalogue des œuvres', in GALLOT 2010, pp. 233ff.

[33]. See PSS SGL: El kéne indulni. Because the piano draft bears no title, it is impossible to ascertain whether the music belongs to *El kéne indulni* or *Ballada*. It cannot be determined either whether or not these two titles really cover two different versions.

[34]. See Ligeti's catalogue.

[35]. See *SZÍNHÁZI HÍREK* 1949.

[36]. For the drafts of both pieces (written in pencil) see PSS SGL: Dansuri and Dans.

In November 1948, Ligeti composed a large-scale cycle consisting of 19 movements and lasting about 25 minutes for soprano and baritone and chamber ensemble (oboe, clarinet and string quartet) for the Hungarian Radio. In this work, titled *Bölcsőtől a sírig* [From Cradle to Grave] (no. 60), he reused music from *El kéne indulni*, *Dansuri*, *Dans* and the choral work *Magos kősziklának* [From a High Mountain Rock] (no. 39). According to Gallot, Ligeti received this commission on the recommendation of his composition professor Ferenc Farkas[37]. According to the available data, it was performed only once, on 22 February 1949 at 7 p.m., broadcast on the Petőfi channel (the second channel of Radio Budapest), sung by Olga Kotlári and György Melis, and played by Ferenc Kiss, Ferenc Meizl, Péter Hidi, Vera Kármán, Zoltán Sümegi and Ágnes Gerő. If *Bölcsőtől a sírig* was really not performed anymore, this does surely not owe to its compositional quality. It might simply have been considered too long for broadcast. Another reason for its having been set aside might be the fact that *Bölcsőtől a sírig* ends, corresponding with its narrative from birth to death, with a plaintive melody on the oboe and a dying postlude on the muted strings, rather than with a merry and fast dance song, as generally expected in that genre. The work was not published in Ligeti's lifetime[38].

The most important commissioner and disseminator of such simple arrangements like the ones discussed above was the Hungarian Radio. It was thanks to the Radio that *Régi magyar társastáncok* [Old Hungarian Ballroom Dances] (no. 66), a four-movement suite consisting of national dances written by four 18th-century composers (János Bihari, Antal Csermák, János Lavotta and Márk Rózsavölgyi), compiled and scored for chamber ensemble (string quartet or string orchestra with *ad libitum* flute and clarinet) by Ligeti, became something of a hit. Ligeti produced this arrangement in May 1949 on the commission of the Közoktatási Minisztérium [Ministry of Education]. The first performance, given by the Radio Orchestra conducted by György Lehel, took place in February 1950 in the radio, where it was also recorded[39]. According to Ligeti's records in his catalogue, the recording was broadcast regularly: an average of twice a month in 1950, 1951 and 1952, eight times in 1953 and nine times in 1954. In November 1950, Hungary's state-owned Zeneműkiadó Vállalat [Music Publishing Company] produced the parts and made photocopies of the score, and in March 1952 it even brought out the score in a regular printed edition[40]. According to the composer's catalogue, the first public performance of *Régi magyar társastáncok* was given by the orchestra of the Államvédelmi Hatóság [State Security Authority] under the baton of a conductor with the surname Sebestyén in September 1951; this orchestra played the work several times both in public and radio broadcast.

---

[37]. GALLOT 2010, p. 58. Gallot does not cite the source of this information.

[38]. An autograph full score and a fair copy in foreign hand survive in PSS SGL: *Bölcsőtől a sírig*. The work was published by Schott Music, Mainz, in 2018.

[39]. See Ligeti's catalogue. The recording is not available in the Sound Archives of the Hungarian Radio.

[40]. See Ligeti's catalogue. Schott brought out the work in a new edition in 2003.

'Functional Music' and *Cantata for the Festival of Youth*

Also in May 1949, Ligeti wrote *Népdalharmonizálás* [Folk Song Harmonisation] for voice and string quartet (no. 67). According to his catalogue, he produced it «for the Music Academy students», and it was recorded by the Radio in the same month[41]. Neither the performers' names nor any data on broadcasts or public performances are known. The work is considered lost.

Thanks to a state grant, Ligeti stayed from mid-December 1949 to the end of June 1950 again in Cluj, Romania, where he was on the staff of the local «collecting centre» of the Institutul de Folclor [Institute for Folklore] of Bucharest, directed by music folklorist János Jagamas[42]. Ligeti had produced two folk song arrangements for voice and piano in December 1949 to the commission of this institution: *Népdalfeldolgozás* [Folk Song Arrangement] and *Aki dudás akar lenni* [Whoever Wants to Become a Piper] (nos. 72 and 100b, respectively). Both were performed on the 21st in Cluj (the venue and the performers' names are not known). *Három tánc cigányzenekarra* [Three Dances for Gypsy Orchestra] (no. 71) was also written in the same month, presumably also to a commission, and was first performed by the gypsy orchestra of the Kolozsvári Színház [Cluj Theatre] and Dénes Elekes's dance company on 20 December[43]. Upon returning to Budapest, Ligeti recycled all of these five arrangements: he reused the music of *Népdalfeldolgozás* and *Három tánc cigányzenekarra* in *Induló és három tánc* [March and Three Dances] for gypsy orchestra (no. 89) in January 1951, and he revised *Aki dudás akar lenni* in August 1952. Only the revised version of the latter piece survives in fair copy[44]. The original version, just as all of the other arrangements discussed in this paragraph, has been considered lost by both Sallis and Gallot. In reality, however, pencilled drafts for all arrangements made in December 1949 survive in a sketchbook titled «Ellenpont 1947/48 5.» [Counterpoint 1947/48, no. 5][45], and only *Induló és három tánc* is missing. The reasons why Ligeti reworked these arrangements are not known. It is conceivable that the revised version of *Aki dudás akar lenni* was intended for Ligeti's and Veronika Spitz's wedding on 8 August 1952, just as the folk song setting *Menyasszony, vőlegény* [Bride, Bridegroom] for voice and piano (no. 100a), also composed that month. (Ligeti had already arranged this latter folk song for mixed choir two years earlier with the title *Lakodalmas* [Wedding Dance], see no. 85.)

Ligeti's folkloristic experience in Romania also found way to four works based on Romanian folklore: *Baladă și joc* [Ballad and Dance] for two violins (no. 73) as well as for so-called pioneer orchestra[46] [úttörőzenekar] (no. 78), *Concert românesc* [Romanian Concerto]

---

[41]. See Ligeti's catalogue. The recording is not available in the Sound Archives of the Hungarian Radio.

[42]. For details on Ligeti's folk music study in Romania, see KERÉKFY 2012.

[43]. See Ligeti's catalogue.

[44]. See PSS SGL: [*Drei Lieder*]. In Ligeti's catalogue, this version is dated to July 1952, but the fair copy is dated August.

[45]. See PSS SGL: Skizzenheft [24].

[46]. Pioneer orchestras were school orchestras or youth orchestras consisting of schoolchildren who were members of the Communist youth movement, the so-called pioneer movement.

for orchestra (no. 94), and *Román népdalok és táncok* [Romanian Folk Songs and Dances] for two voices and gypsy orchestra (no. 77). Of these only the latter can be considered as functional music. Regarding its dimensions, *Román népdalok és táncok*, consisting of ten movements, is similar to *Bölcsőtől a sírig*, but here the female and male singers are accompanied by an authentic gypsy orchestra rather than an ensemble of instruments of art music. The orchestra's role in this work is emphasised by a structure in which every second movement is purely instrumental. Ligeti notated the fair copy in two staves (melody and bass) with letters referring to the chords between; in addition, he gave the type of the accompaniment in the manuscript (like «gyors» [fast] and «lépést» [in walking pace]). A full score written in a foreign hand also survives; according to its title page, the orchestration was made by József Rácz[47]. Neither these manuscripts nor Ligeti's catalogue provides information on whether the work was written to a commission, but the fact that the stamp of the sheet music collection of the Hungarian Radio appears on the full score suggests that there might have been a radio commission in the background. *Román népdalok és táncok* was first broadcast on 16 October 1950 at 7.10 p.m. on the Petőfi channel (performed by Mária Berei and Sándor Tekeres and the Radio Gypsy Orchestra led by Sándor Lakatos). It was programmed on the radio once more in 1950, once in 1951 and twice in 1952; and no public performance is documented. This suggests that it did not become a popular item, which is hardly surprising in the light of the fact that its words are in Romanian.

Nothing certain is known about the function of *Négy lakodalmi tánc* [Four Wedding Dances] (no. 84), a cycle of arrangements of four Hungarian folk songs, but its scoring for three female voices with piano accompaniment suggests that it was composed likely for the vocal group Menyecskék [Young Wives] (Mária Berei, Olga Kotlári and Jolán Máthé[48]), who sang the premiere with Pál Arató at the piano, broadcast on the Petőfi channel on 29 June 1951 at 3 p.m. Menyecskék often appeared on the radio programme in the first half of the 1950s. They performed *Négy lakodalmi tánc*, broadcast on radio, two more times in 1951. According to Ligeti's catalogue, on 25 May (or February) 1956, the women's choir of the Munkáslíceum [Workers' Lyceum] in Cluj conducted by Loránd Péter also performed the work, and this was followed by broadcasts on Radio Cluj. Interestingly, Ligeti has also noted that *Négy lakodalmi tánc* «was broadcast on radio even after [his] emigration»[49] in December 1956. It must have been one of Ligeti's most popular arrangements, since it was published by Zeneműkiadó as early as February 1952[50]. In late 1950, Ligeti transcribed movements 2 to 4 for piano duet, which appeared in an album containing works for piano duet by Hungarian composers in March

---

[47]. Both the autograph and the manuscript full score see in PSS SGL: Román népdalok és táncok.

[48]. Note that each of these three singers participated in other Ligeti premieres as well: Kotlári sang in *Bölcsőtől a sírig*, Berei in *Román népdalok és táncok* and Máthé in *Öt Arany-dal* [Five Songs on Poems by János Arany] (no. 101).

[49]. «távozásom után is játszották a rádióban». Ligeti's catalogue.

[50]. Schott brought out the work in a new edition in 2007.

'Functional Music' and *Cantata for the Festival of Youth*

1952[51] with the title *Három lakodalmi tánc* [Three Wedding Dances] (no. 86). It seems likely that Ligeti produced this transcription specifically to be included in this album. According to his catalogue, it was premiered on 6 April 1954 by students of Ernő Szegedi, broadcast on radio. This first performance must have taken place in the programme *Hangverseny gyermekeknek: Magyar szerzők gyermekdarabjai* [Concert for Children: Pieces for Children by Hungarian Composers], aired at 2.20 p.m. on the Kossuth channel (the first channel of Radio Budapest). Pianist and pedagogue Ernő Szegedi was running a series on the radio (under various titles), in which he presented new Hungarian music for children. Within that, he also presented Ligeti pieces at least two times in 1955[52]. No further performance or broadcast of *Három lakodalmi tánc* is documented.

It is not known on which occasion Ligeti set the Hungarian folk song *Középlokon esik az eső* [It's Raining in Középlok] recorded by Jagamas in Transylvania's Gyimesek region (Zona Ghimeșului in Romanian) for voice and piano (no. 96) in 1951. It might have originated from Ligeti's friendship with Jagamas[53] or even from a request from Zeneműkiadó. At any rate, it was published in the publishers' new-year album in late 1952[54].

According to his catalogue, Ligeti composed folk song arrangements with the title *Három tánc* [Three Dances] for piano on 12 April 1951 to a commission by the Népművészeti Intézet [Institute for Folklore] for the famous Soviet Moiseyev Dance Company, but no performance is documented, and the work does not survive either.

Ligeti's last piece of functional music was *Hat inaktelki népdal* [Six Folk Songs from Inaktelke] (no. 107), a cycle consisting of settings of folk songs recorded by the composer himself in 1950 in Inaktelke (Inucu in Romanian), Transylvania, for three female voices and folk orchestra. According to Sallis, it was written in 1953. Since Ligeti seems to have stopped maintaining his own catalogue of works in autumn 1952[55], *Hat inaktelki népdal* is not included in it. Both Sallis and Gallot have considered the work lost, and they do not give the date of its first performance either. In reality, a short score draft in pencil (similar to the autograph manuscript of *Román népdalok és táncok*) does survive for five of the six arrangements[56]. It is conceivable

---

[51]. See SZELÉNYI 1952. For a new edition of *Három lakodalmi tánc*, see LIGETI 1999.

[52]. No. 9 and no. 1 from *Musica ricercata* were programmed on 22 February and 7 May 1955, respectively. See records in the Sound Archives of the Hungarian Radio.

[53]. Ligeti became friends with the music folklorist ten years his senior during his stay in Cluj, and they kept in touch via correspondence after Ligeti's return to Budapest. The surviving letters and postcards are now housed in the holdings of the Hungarian Heritage House, Budapest.

[54]. See ZENEMŰKIADÓ 1952.

[55]. The last items in his catalogue are *Menyasszony, vőlegény* and *Aki dudás akar lenni* from August 1952. Ligeti nevertheless continued to enter data on performances, broadcasts and publication on the existing slips up until 1956.

[56]. See PSS SGL: [*Hat inaktelki népdal*].

that the orchestration was again done by someone else. This cycle, too, was written presumably for Menyecskék, who seem to have recorded it with the accompaniment of the Radio Folk Orchestra (the successor of the Radio Gypsy Orchestra) led by Lakatos. This is suggested by the fact that four numbers of *Hat inaktelki népdal* were broadcast on the Kossuth channel on 14 May 1955 at 7 p.m. in the programme *Bemutatjuk legújabb népzenei felvételeinket!* [We Present Our Newest Folk Music Recordings][57]. No other airing or performance of this work is documented, however.

Incidental Music

During his Budapest years Ligeti composed incidental music on just two occasions.

Dated to March 1947, *Tornyos Péter* [Peter Tornyos] for voice and piano (no. 43) is not included in Ligeti's catalogue. Sallis has considered it lost, but its 11-page fair copy with the inscription «Finale» does survive[58]. Although the text of *Tornyos Péter* is attributed in all work lists as well as in the inventory of the PSS SGL to an anonymous author, it is most probably based on János Illei's (1725-1794) «fársángi játék» [carnival play], first published in 1789 in Komárom and Pozsony and reissued in 1914[59]. For the moment, however, there is no data available on any performance to which Ligeti composed this piece of music.

The circumstances of the other piece of incidental music, *Tavaszi Virág* [Spring Flower] (no. 70) are much better documented. It was written in September 1949 for the debut of the Állami Bábszínház [State Puppet Theater] in Budapest, established in the course of the nationalisation of the capital's theatres. The 8 October 1949 premiere included three puppet plays; Ligeti composed music for the first one, *Tavaszi Virág*, a tale with a Chinese subject matter written by Soviet author S. Preobrazhensky. The music is scored for voices, recorder, viola, piano and percussion. The libretto was translated to Hungarian by János Zsombor and revised by Dr. László Körmöczi, who directed the performance. In the performance, *Tavaszi Virág* was followed by two animal fables, *A kalács* [The Loaf] by Sándor Derzsi and *Macskalak* [Cat's House] by Samuil Marshak. This show was given 70 times[60]. Several newspapers published reviews of the premiere. *Népszava* [People's Word] has written on *Tavaszi Virág*:

> The characters are the heroic Chinese girl Spring Flower, the valiant swain Faithful Heart, the 500-year old Turtle, the Wise Dragon and, in addition, mason, poor people, court sycophants and the Chinese emperor himself.
> "Help others and you help yourself as well", teaches the Wise Dragon, and the suppressed Chinese people understand these mysterious words. Shoulder to

---

[57]. The recording is not available in the Sound Archives of the Hungarian Radio.
[58]. See PSS SGL: *Tornyos Péter*.
[59]. Illei 1914.
[60]. See Óhidy 1959.

> shoulder they depose the people-oppressing emperor, and by the time the morning star rises the liberated people are tinklingly singing the song of liberty.
>
> Beyond being fabulous and spectacular, Preobrazhensky's tale play is a serious, socialistic production for children with an educative message[61].

As suggested by the above quote, this Soviet tale play with a Chinese subject matter was politically topical at that time, regarding the Chinese civil war that was in full swing during 1949, and especially the proclamation of the Chinese People's Republic on 1 October. According to the unknown reviewer, «György Ligeti's music, which is rich in timbres and melodies and excellently dubs in the tale play, deserves special mentioning»[62]. *Tavaszi Virág* must have been a considerable success, because it was soon revived, in contrast with the two other plays premiered on 8 October 1949. First performed on 1 March 1951, the revival (in a revised version by Dr. László Körmöczi and Miklós Mészöly, directed by Géza Nagy) was played 138 times[63]. For the revival Ligeti revised the music in February 1951. This version survives in manuscript[64].

According to his catalogue, Ligeti also compiled a six-movement suite from the music for *Tavaszi Virág* in October and November 1951 for a female and a male voice, piano, recorders, violas (or violins) and percussion with the title *Kínai bábjáték suite* [Chinese Puppet Play Suite] (no. 95). The titles of the movements are: «Előzene» [Prelude], «…dala» [Song of …][65], «A kertész dala» [Song of the Gardener], «Trombitajel és a teknős dala» [Trumpet Call and the Song of the Turtle], «Fonódal» [Spinning Song] and «A császári udvarban» [In the Court of the Emperor]. Ligeti had arranged the last number for pioneer orchestra already in September 1950 with the title *Kínai ünnepi muzsika* [Chinese Festive Music] (no. 79). Neither the suite nor *Kínai ünnepi muzsika* has survived. Although it is very likely that both were composed to a commission or at least in the hope of a performance, there is no available data on their function or performance.

A strange moment in the afterlife of the music for *Tavaszi Virág* is that in 1982 Ligeti produced an occasional transcription of the turtle's song for trumpet solo for Martin Nordwall, son of his biographer Ove Nordwall, who was learning to play the trumpet[66].

---

[61]. «Szereplői a hőslelkű kínai leány, Tavaszi Virág, a bátor pásztorlegény, Hűséges Szív, az 500 éves öreg Teknős, a Bölcs Sárkány — ezenkívül kőművesek, szegény népség, udvari talpnyalók és maga a kínai császár. / 'Segíts másokon és segítsz magadon is' — tanítja a Bölcs Sárkány és az elnyomott kínai nép megérti a rejtélyes szavakat. Egyesült erővel elűzi a népsanyargató császárt s mire feljő a hajnali csillag az égre, a felszabadult nép ajkáról csengőn száll a szabadságról szóló ének. / Preobrazsenszkij mesejátéka a meseszerűségen, a látványosságon felül komoly, nevelő mondanivalóval rendelkező, szocialista gyermekdarab». M. M. 1949.

[62]. *Ibidem*.

[63]. See ÓHIDY 1959.

[64]. See PSS SGL: *Tavaszi Virág*.

[65]. «…» marks an illegible name.

[66]. See *The Big Turtle Fanfare from the South Chinese Sea* in FANFARES n.d.; for a recording see THE LIGETI PROJECT V 2004. Note that this piece is generally dated to 1985; the correct date is quoted from SAMMLUNG GYÖRGY LIGETI 2016, p. 58.

Márton Kerékfy

Cantata for the Festival of Youth

Ligeti's largest-scale work composed in Hungary is *Kantáta az ifjúság ünnepére* [Cantata for the Festival of Youth] (no. 68) in three movements, scored for four solo voices (SATB), mixed choir and symphony orchestra, with an estimated duration of over 15 minutes. According to the composer's catalogue, it was written to the commission of MINSZ, which organised the Second World Festival of Youth and Students (henceforth abbreviated WFYS) that took place in Budapest between 14 and 28 August 1949.

The First WFYS was held in summer 1947 in Prague. Up until 1957, the festivals were held biannually in the capital of an East Bloc country. The festivals were organised by the World Federation of Democratic Youth, an international organisation established in 1948 on the Soviet Union's initiative; its members included not only the national youth organisations of socialistic countries but also Communist youth movements from Western Europe. The public aim of the WFYS was to integrate the so-called 'peace camp' (that is, Soviet Union and other socialistic countries as well as Western Communist parties) against the Western 'imperialistic camp'. At the same time, however, these meetings served as power demonstrations against the 'imperialistic camp' and to showcase the achievements and the superiority of socialistic social system and — above all — the Soviet Union, for both foreign participants and the whole domestic society. Thus the festivals also served the agenda of increasing the acceptance and the influence of local Communist parties within the society.

The Budapest WFYS was the biggest international mass programme of the period in Hungary. 10,371 foreign participants came from 70 countries; it is remarkable that 60% of them were from capitalist or colonial countries. The festival had been preceded by a powerful propaganda campaign already months before its opening, which, as Sarolta Klenjánszky writes, sought to «present [the festival] as a 'bottom-up' initiative»[67]. In reality, everything was planned and organised «from above», including even the number of participants from each country[68]. The festival's lavish programme included sports tournaments and artistic competitions (each won by the Soviets), dance parties, opera performances, concerts, film screenings, theatrical performances, visiting factories, open-air campfires and torch-lit processions, among others. Many of Hungary's most prominent state and party leaders took part at the opening ceremony held in the stadium of Újpest (near Budapest), where the participants were greeted by President of the Republic Árpád Szakasits. At the closing ceremony at Heroes' Square in Budapest, Prime Minister and Secretary General of the Hungarian Workers' Party Mátyás Rákosi (the much feared dictator) addressed the participants. According to Klenjánszky, «[t]he highlight of the festival was the evening ceremony at [river] Danube on 20 August [a national holiday].

---

[67]. «[...] 'alulról jövő' kezdeményezésnek tüntette fel». Klenjánszky 2016, p. 216.
[68]. *Ibidem.*

'FUNCTIONAL MUSIC' AND *CANTATA FOR THE FESTIVAL OF YOUTH*

Hundreds of thousands of spectators were delighted by the unsurpassably beautiful scenery offered by 13 illuminated ships and the fireworks displaying the portraits of Stalin and Rákosi reflected on the water»[69].

Kantáta az ifjúság ünnepére is documented to have been performed three times during the festival: at the Opera House on the 18th and the 19th (the latter was a gala, at which Kodály's *Spinning Room* was also programmed), and at the Municipal Theatre on the 21st. The vocal soloists were Magda Seress, Anna Farkas, Zoltán Kenderessi and Lajos Keveházi, and the Csenki Choir of Debrecen and the chorus and orchestra of the Liszt Academy's MEFESZ circle was conducted by Ligeti's friend Károly Melles, a conducting student at the Academy. According to the composer's catalogue, the Hungarian Radio recorded the gala performance at the Opera House and aired the cantata's first movement on the next day and the whole work on the 27th. The latter airing was part of an hour-long programme reviewing the musical events of the WFYS. Ligeti's cantata was announced in a ridiculously bombastic way:

> The ghost of fascism spites again from the West: American money-mad millionaires and manufacturers want to instigate again the well-known monster against the world: they have not had enough of blood; they don't care about the welfare and the happiness of millions [of people]. They want to see hills of corpses, which overlook new territories for earning money. As the peoples' self-awareness increase, their markets shrink: after Europe, not even Asia needs their costly bazaar trucks and coloured pearls. The world wants peace, [but] they speculate on war. The people stand against them everywhere, and it is such a power that cannot be expressed with dollars. The World Festival of Youth was also a huge demonstration for peace: young people showed that they are united and strong, and, if necessary, they are willing to fight for defending peace. This huge, overwhelming will is expressed in the Peace Cantata by György Ligeti, which you are about to hear now[70].

---

[69]. «A fesztivál fénypontja az augusztus 20-án este a Dunánál rendezett ünnepély volt, a partokon több százezer néző gyönyörködhetett a felülmúlhatatlan szépségű látványban, melyet 13 kivilágított hajó s a Rákosi és Sztálin óriásportréit az égbolton megmintázó, a vízfelületen tükröződő tűzijáték nyújtott». *Ibidem*, p. 224.

[70]. «Nyugatról ismét acsarkodik a fasizmus szelleme: Amerika pénzőrületben tobzódó milliomosai és árugyárosai ismét rá akarják szabadítani a világra ezt a jól ismert fenevadat: nekik még nem volt elég a vérből, számukra nem lényeges kérdés milliók jóléte és boldogsága. Hullahegyeket akarnak látni, melyeknek tetejéről újabb pénzterületekre nyílik kilátás. A népek öntudatra ébredésével egyidőben fogynak piacaik: Európa után, már Ázsiának sem kellenek a drágán mért bazári holmik, színes gyöngyök és kábeldobok. A világ békét akar, ők háborúra spekulálnak. A nép mindenütt szembeáll velük, és ez akkora erő, amelyet dollárokkal nem lehet kifejezni. A Világifjúsági Találkozó is egy hatalmas békedemonstráció volt: a fiatalság megmutatta, hogy egységes és erős, s ha kell, kész harcba menni a béke védelmében. Ennek a hatalmas, mindent elsöprő akaratnak kifejezője Ligeti György Béke-kantátája, melyet most hallanak majd kedves hallgatóink». *A világ ifjúsága együtt énekel*, broadcast on 27 August 1949 at 10.15 p.m. on the Kossuth channel; quoted from the transcript surviving in the Sound Archives of the Hungarian Radio. Ligeti's own catalogue dates the airing of the *Cantata* to 26 August, which seems to be an error.

There is no available data on the afterlife of the cantata. According to a newspaper report on 17 August, the Csenki Choir planned to perform it in Debrecen as well[71], but it is not known whether this materialised. No further airing is documented either. In his catalogue, Ligeti has written: «the Radio's record has been destroyed at my request»[72]. The recording is indeed unavailable in the Radio's Sound Archives, but this does not necessarily mean that it was deleted on the composer's request, and it is not known either when Ligeti asked the Radio to destroy the recording. Only the vocal score of the cantata was printed (according to Ligeti's catalogue, this had happened on 23 July, that is, already before he finished the orchestration), but probably even this was not commercially distributed, but served as performing material only[73].

As to the reasons why it was Ligeti who got the only commission for a work of classical music to be performed at the WFYS, there are no documents available. An obvious reason might be that he was regarded one of the most gifted (if not the most gifted) composition student at the Academy, but it is also likely that his position in MEFESZ played a role as well[74]. According to Ligeti's recollection, he started to write the cantata naively in summer 1948 as part of his final year project at the Academy, not suspecting which political agenda the WFYS would be to serve[75]. Richard Steinitz describes the genesis of the cantata pronouncedly as if the possibility of a performance at the festival emerged only later, and Ligeti was encouraged to submit the work by his professor Ferenc Farkas[76]. This is, however, unrealistic for two reasons. First, Ligeti's catalogue gives exact dates for both the beginning and the completion of composition: accordingly, he composed the work in June and July 1949 and did not finish the orchestration until 10 August. Second, the cantata's words are obviously occasional. But even if one hypothesised that the text was written independently of the WFYS, it would be inconceivable that Ligeti chose such a libretto of his own free will. Consequently, both the libretto and the music of the cantata were in all likelihood written from the beginning as an occasional work for the WFYS. (See the libretto in TABLE 2.)

---

[71]. See – J. R. – 1949.

[72]. «rádió lemezét kérésemre megsemmisítették» (Ligeti's catalogue).

[73]. The autograph full score survives in PSS SGL: Kantáta az ifjúság ünnepére.

[74]. Note, however, that Ligeti told Imre Fábián in 1973 that he had been asked to be President of the MEFESZ union at the Academy because he had been regarded as the «state composer» [díszzeneszerző]. Quoted in MIKUSI 2019, pp. 278-279.

[75]. See GRIFFITHS 1983, p. 20, and LIGETI 2000, p. 3.

[76]. STEINITZ 2013, pp. 26-27 and 46-47.

'Functional Music' and *Cantata for the Festival of Youth*

Table 2: Libretto of *Kantáta az ifjúság ünnepére*[77]

Movement I

||: Fel! Előre ifjuság! :||
Előre hát!
Zengjen a dal!
||: Harsanjon ének!
Egységbe ifjuság! :||
Zengjen a dal!
Harsanjon ének! Fel!
Egységbe ifjuság! Fel!
Békéért zengjen ma száz nemzet száz dala.
Zengjen a dal!
Harsanjon ének!
Zengjen a dal! Fel! Fel!

||: Up! Forward, youth! :||
Forward now!
Sing the tune!
||: Sound the song!
In unity, youth! :||
Sing the tune!
Sound the song! Up!
In unity, youth! Up!
For peace sing today the hundred tunes of hundred nations.
Sing the tune!
Sound the song!
Sing the tune! Up! Up!

Movement II

Jöttünk szivünkben a nyár melegével,
küldtek a gyárak, a messzi mezők,
lengyel a Búgtól, délről a néger, a
hősi csatákból a kínai nők,
küldött a béke hazája, a Szovjet!
Éljen a harcunk vezére, a Szovjet!

We've come with the warmth of summer in our hearts,
the factories have sent us, the far fields,
the Pole from Bug, from the South the black,
from the heroic battles the Chinese women,
the fatherland of peace has sent us, the Soviet!
Long live the leader of our battles, the Soviet!

Mit tegyünk, mi, gyarmati népek,
mit tegyünk, mi, elnyomottak?
Küzdjetek a szabadságért!
Jobb jövőért, elnyomottak!

What should we do, we, the colonial peoples,
what should we do, we, the oppressed?
Fight for freedom!
For a better future, oppressed!

Mit tesztek értünk, szabad népek?
Segítitek harcainkat?
Védjük a békét, gyarmati népek.
Nem! nem lesztek soká, nem lesztek elnyomottak!

What do you do for us, free peoples?
Do you help our battles?
We defend peace, colonial peoples.
No! You'll not much longer, you'll not be oppressed!

Harcolunk érted! Dolgozunk érted! Szabadság! Béke!
Mert a béke magvakat s az arcokon mosolyt érlel,
ont a földre aranyat, tornyosul a buzakéve,
ugy tekint ránk, mint a nap, és mint anyánk, szép szemével.

We fight for you! We work for you! Freedom! Peace!
Because peace lets seeds and smiles on faces ripen,
it pours gold on fields, it piles the sheaves of wheat,
looks on us as the sun and as our mother, with her beautiful eyes.

---

[77]. English translation quoted from Sallis 1996, pp. 221-222, slightly amended by myself.

Movement III

‖: Fel! Előre ifjuság! :‖		‖: Up! Forward, youth! :‖
Előre hát!		Forward now!
Zengjen a dal!		Sing the tune!
‖: Harsanjon ének!		‖: Sound the song!
Egységbe ifjuság! :‖		In unity, youth! :‖
Zengjen a dal!		Sing the tune!
Harsanjon ének! Fel!		Sound the song! Up!
Egységbe ifjuság! Fel!		In unity, youth! Up!

Légy erősebb a zúgó vizeknél,   Be stronger than rushing water,
szilárdabb, mint a kő, a fém.   harder than stone, than metal.
Élesebb acél fegyvereknél,   Sharper than steel weapons,
s mint igaz gondolat, kemény.   and as hard as true thoughts.

Béke lesz, mert békét akar a nép!   Peace will be because the people want peace!
Mert a béke úgy tekint ránk, mint a nap!   Because peace looks on us as the sun!
Béke lesz, mert békét akarunk!   Peace will be because we want peace!
Béke lesz, mert békét akar a nép!   Peace will be because the people want peace!
‖: Mert a béke úgy tekint ránk, mint a nap,   ‖: Because peace looks on us as the sun,
ont a földre aranyat, :‖   it pours gold on fields, :‖
hisz béke lesz, mert békét akar a nép!   for peace will be because the people want peace!

Péter Kuczka (1923-1999), a successful young Communist poet and a loyal party member coeval with Ligeti, was commissioned to write the libretto. The text was fully adequate for the occasion. The first movement (much of which is recapitulated in movement III) consists exclusively of slogans; one of them, «Egységbe ifjuság!» [In unity, youth!] is in fact a short version of the festival's official slogan «Egységbe ifjúság! Előre a tartós békéért!» [In unity, youth! Forward for lasting peace!] (see the banner in Ill. 1). The second movement focuses on subjects of «fight for peace», the Soviet Union as «the fatherland of peace» and the liberation of colonial peoples, and it also refers to the national and social affiliations of the festival's participants («the factories have sent us, the far fields», «the Pole», «the black», «the Chinese women»). The final movement ends with slogans calling upon the «fight for peace».

In various interviews, Ligeti always said that at the time of composition he still naively believed in these slogans and the ideology behind them, but by the time of the premiere he had been disillusioned, and he would have withdrawn the work had he been in the position to do that:

> In [...] 1949, a World Youth Festival was planned "for freedom, against imperial oppression" where the work was to be performed. I actually believed in these socialist slogans and began to compose the cantata in the summer of 1948 together with my friend Peter Kuczka, who wrote a text on freedom for all people. When I began the work, I was completely sincere and honest; I believed in the cause. But when I finished the work in the spring of 1949, it made me sick to my stomach.

Ill. 1: The award ceremony of the musical competition of the Budapest World Festival of Youth and Students in the Grand Hall of the Liszt Academy on 25 August 1949. The emblems of the International Federation of Students and the World Federation of Democratic Youth and the festival's slogan in Russian and Hungarian are on the prospect. Downstage is the first prize, a huge silver bowl offered by the Central Directorate of the Hungarian Workers' Party with the inscription «For peace and democracy», which was won by the Soviets.

> I was nauseated by the degree to which these socialist ideas were used for a filthy
> purpose in the worst possible police regime, with mass arrests and executions[78].

---

[78]. Ligeti 2000, p. 3. See also Griffiths 1983, p. 20, Oehlschlägel 1989, p. 94, and Steinitz 2013, p. 27.

Márton Kerékfy

Vera Ligeti, who had been in a close contact with the composer since 1948 (Ligeti rented a room in the apartment of Vera's mother in Alkotmány Street at that time), confirmed that Ligeti got gastric catarrh during the composition of the cantata, and remembered that Kuczka had sat at their place, and Ligeti had tried to cut the politically delicate passages from the libretto, but by the time it had been completed, the two men had completely fallen out[79].

In the absence of sources it is not possible to document exactly what role Ligeti played in shaping the final version of the libretto. Neither is there any document available on why he undertook the commission to write the cantata and what he thought about it during or after the composition. Ligeti's statements, according to which the work was criticised by the Association of Hungarian Musicians because the third movement's fugue was considered «clerical» and «reactionary», and he was then asked to write a new cantata praising Rákosi[80], cannot be verified either. It is a fact, however, that following *Kantáta az ifjúság ünnepére* Ligeti did not set any text that could be considered directly political or to be charged with political ideology of any kind — in contrast with many Hungarian fellow composers (not just young ones but established ones as well) who did write works praising Stalin, Rákosi, the state party and its politics.

In Lieu of a Conclusion

In this chapter I made a first attempt to put the least known part of Ligeti's juvenilia in context on the basis of historical sources. Further research is needed, however, to re-evaluate his activity as a composer and his entire output in this period, as well as to study his compositional evolution and to document his early biography in more detail. On the one hand, the background and the reception of Ligeti's 'autonomous' works should also be uncovered, and, on the other, serious attempts should be made to discover missing works.

Abbreviations

PSS SGL   Paul Sacher Foundation, György Ligeti Collection, Basel
PSS SGK   Paul Sacher Foundation, György Kurtág Collection, Basel

Bibliography

Beckles Willson 2007
    Beckles Willson, Rachel. *Ligeti, Kurtág, and Hungarian Music during the Cold War*, Cambridge, Cambridge University Press, 2007.

---

[79]. Personal communication with Vera Ligeti, 25 April 2009.
[80]. Ligeti 2000, p. 4.

'Functional Music' and *Cantata for the Festival of Youth*

DEVECSERI 1949
DEVECSERI, Gábor. 'Harcos és vidám táncokkal, zengő kórusszámokkal bemutatkozott a Honvéd Művészegyüttes', in: *Szabad Nép*, 1 May 1949, p. 2.

FANFARES n.d.
Fanfares: Contemporary Trumpet Pieces for Young Players, Vienna, Universal Edition UE 19060, n.d.

GALLOT 2010
GALLOT, Simon. *György Ligeti et la musique populaire*, Lyon, Symétrie, 2010.

GRIFFITHS 1983
GRIFFITHS, Paul. *György Ligeti*, London, Robson Books, 1983.

ILLEI 1914
ILLEI, János. *Tornyos Péter: Farsangi játék, 1789*, edited and preface by Zsolt Alszeghy, Budapest, Magyar Tudományos Akadémia, 1914 (Régi magyar könyvtár 33).

– J. R. – 1949
– J. R. –. 'Debreceniek, akik a VIT-en szerepelnek', in: *Tiszántúli Néplap*, 17 August 1949, p. 4.

KERÉKFY 2012
KERÉKFY, Márton. 'Ligeti György 1949-50-es népzenei tanulmányútja', in: *Zenetudományi Dolgozatok 2011*, edited by Gábor Kiss, Budapest, MTA BTK Zenetudományi Intézet, 2012, pp. 323-346.

KERÉKFY 2018
ID. *Népzene és nosztalgia Ligeti György művészetében*, Budapest, Rózsavölgyi és Társa, 2018.

KLENJÁNSZKY 2016
KLENJÁNSZKY, Sarolta. '«Világ fiataljai, egyesüljetek!»: Az 1949-es budapesti Világifjúsági Találkozó és a francia fiatalok részvétele a fesztiválon történeti kontextusban', in: *Múltunk*, no. 1 (2016), pp. 207-232.

LIGETI 1950
LIGETI, György. Files in the records of the Liszt Academy, Budapest, call number 6261. Includes 'Szolgálati lap' [Official sheet], 'Nyilvántartási lap' [Records sheet], 'Kérdőív' [Questionnaire] and 'Életrajz' [Curriculum vitae], all filled in by Ligeti's own hand and dated 9 December 1950, and stamped by the Személyzeti Nyilvántartó [Personnel Record Office] of the Népművelési Minisztérium [Ministry of Culture].

LIGETI 1999
ID. *Fünf Stücke für Klavier zu vier Händen*, Mainz, Schott Music, 1999.

LIGETI 2000
ID. 'An Art Without Ideology', in: BEYER, Anders. *The Voice of Music: Conversations with Composers of Our Time*, Aldershot, Ashgate, 2000, pp. 1-15.

M. M. 1949
M. M. 'Bemutató új gyermekszínházunkban', in: *Népszava*, 9 October 1949, p. 6.

MICHELLER 1990
MICHELLER, Magdolna. 'A MEFESZ szervezeti élete és politikai tevékenysége (1945-1950)', in: *Múltunk*, XXXV/4 (1990), pp. 131-148.

MIKUSI 2019
MIKUSI, Balázs. '«Olyan baloldali hasznos idiótának tartottak»: Ligeti György és az '56-os forradalom', in: *1956 és a zenei élet: Előzmények, történések, következmények*, edited by György Gyarmati and Lóránt Péteri, Budapest-Pécs, Liszt Ferenc Zeneművészeti Egyetem-Állambiztonsági Szolgálatok Történeti Levéltára-Kronosz Kiadó, 2019, pp. 277-286.

OEHLSCHLÄGEL 1989
OEHLSCHLÄGEL, Reinhard. '«Ja, ich war ein utopischer Sozialist»: György Ligeti im Gespräch', in: *MusikTexte. Zeitschrift für neue Musik*, nos. 28-29 (1989), pp. 85-102.

ÓHIDY 1959
ÓHIDY, Lehel. *Az Állami Bábszínház tíz éves műsora: 1949-1959 (Adattár)*, Budapest, Színháztudományi és Filmtudományi Intézet-Országos Színháztörténeti Múzeum, 1959 (Színháztörténeti füzetek, 28).

PÉTERI 2013
PÉTERI, Lóránt. 'Magyar zenészek az 1950-es évek második felében – emigráció és jövedelmi viszonyok', in: *Korall*, XIV/51 (2013), pp. 161-185.

SALLIS 1996
SALLIS, Friedemann. *An Introduction to the Early Works of György Ligeti*, Berlin, Studio, 1996.

SAMMLUNG GYÖRGY LIGETI 2016
Sammlung György Ligeti: Musikmanuskripte, Mainz, Schott Music, 2016 (Inventare der Paul Sacher Stiftung, 34).

STEINITZ 2013
STEINITZ, Richard. *György Ligeti: Music of the Imagination*, London, Faber & Faber, ²2013.

SZ. I. 1952
SZ. I. 'A Néphadsereg táncegyüttese', in: *Magyar Nemzet*, 31 July 1952, p. 5.

SZELÉNYI 1952
Magyar szerzők négykezes zongoradarabjai, edited by István Szelényi, Budapest, Zeneműkiadó, 1952.

SZÍNHÁZI HÍREK 1949
'Színházi hírek', in: *Világ*, 30 April 1949, p. 4.

TALLIÁN 1991
TALLIÁN, Tibor. *Magyarországi hangversenyélet 1945-1958*, Budapest, MTA Zenetudományi Intézet, 1991.

THE LIGETI PROJECT V 2004
The Ligeti Project V, Teldec 8573-88262-2, 2004.

ȚIPLEA TEMEȘ 2018
ȚIPLEA TEMEȘ, Bianca. 'Ligeti and Romanian Folk Music: An Insight from the Paul Sacher Foundation', in: *György Ligeti's Cultural Identities*, edited by Amy Bauer and Márton Kerékfy, Abingdon-New York, Routledge, 2018, pp. 120-138.

ZENEMŰKIADÓ 1952
A Zeneműkiadó Vállalat 1953. újévi albuma, Budapest, Zeneműkiadó, 1952.

ZIMMERMANN 2018
ZIMMERMANN, Heidy. 'Reflections on Ligeti's Jewish Identity: Unknown Documents from His Cluj Years', in: *György Ligeti's Cultural Identities, op. cit.*, pp. 103-119.

Mourning in Folk Style:
Ligeti's Reliance on Romanian Laments[*]

Bianca Țiplea Temeș
(Gheorghe Dima National Music Academy, Cluj-Napoca)

In Ligeti's oeuvre, multiple sources of inspiration are blended as if in a multicolored kaleidoscope, providing his music with a uniquely rich sonority. Apart from influences of the established repertoire, dating from the Renaissance to his own period, and intersecting the world of jazz in a most original way, traditional musics from across the globe coexist, filtered through the composer's refined lens.

Born in Transylvania, Ligeti witnessed in the years leading up to 1945, before moving to Budapest, a model of cultural exchange among Romanians, Hungarians, Germans, Jews, and other ethnic groups. He therefore became familiar with the folk music of the region becoming, from a very young age, a polyglot in terms of musical idioms. Yet, rather than exploring the multi-layered sources of his inspiration, the present paper focuses upon the Romanian funeral repertoire, generically named *bocete* (dirges) that inspired his music. As a nostalgic look back on his youth, and encripting a sense of mourning both for his personal losses and for the many victims of historical events in the first half of the twentieth century, these funeral songs symbolically unify a number of pieces written by Ligeti during the 1980s and 90s.

According to the composer's own words, death was always in his proximity («it was something that was very close to me»[1]) and the fear of it haunted him from an early age, as a witness of the horrors of the holocaust: («I have been steeped in the fear of death from a very young age»[2]). Therefore, the integration of these funeral melodies in his music had a profound psychological basis and was a response to the atrocities of the troubled times in which he lived.

---

[*]. This publication was supported financially by the Research Fund of the Gheorghe Dima Music Academy Cluj-Napoca, awarded by the Education Ministry in Romania.

[1]. Follin 1993: «C'était quelque chose qui était très proche de moi».

[2]. *Ibidem*: «J'ai été imprégné par la peur de la mort depuis quand j'étais très jeune».

The impact of Romanian folk traditions on Ligeti was very strong even from his childhood spent in Transylvania (Diciosânmartin, today Târnăveni, and later in Cluj, the city where he started to study music). In his writings, György Kurtág is a key witness to the direct contact that Ligeti had with Romanian music since his childhood. In his book *Entretiens, textes, dessins*, he provides the following description: «Ligeti's knowledge on folk music was not just the result of his readings. Since the age of three, the Hungarian and Romanian folk music that surrounded him was a living truth»[3].

Later on, in 1949-1950, Ligeti had the chance to study this heritage in depth when he returned to Romania and spent a few months in Bucharest and in Cluj. In Bucharest, at the Folklore Institute, Ligeti studied and transcribed folk music from across the whole Romanian territory, which had palpable consequences for his career as a composer.

Apart from listening to such melodies while he lived in Transylvania, Ligeti also had the opportunity to hear a rich Romanian folk funeral repertoire in Bucharest (1949-1950), during his research at the archives of the Folklore Institute. He reminisces about his stay and describes the atmosphere in 1950: «For a musician, the Institute in Bucharest seems paradisiac and exceeds anything one can imagine»[4], adding that «the Institute makes great efforts to disseminate the collected music. Its extremely rich sound archive (over 1500 discs comprising about 3500 melodies) is very useful for this purpose. The recordings cover all genres of Romanian folk traditional music: ritual songs, burial melodies, wedding and harvest songs, *colinde*, songs unrelated to any ceremony (ballads, *doinas*, etc.), as well as vocal and instrumental dances»[5].

Clearly, the wax cylinders in Bucharest afforded him the opportunity to listen to a large number of funeral melodies from across the whole country. One of the folk genres which impressed him the most was the Romanian «bocet» (dirge), a folk lament also collected by Bartók in his ethnomusicological journeys in Transylvania, most of these melodies published in the second volume of the series *Rumanian Folk Music*[6]. The bocet becomes a vehicle for the expression of grief, and the fabric of many of his works. A fertile seed for Ligeti's music of the

---

[3]. KURTÁG 2009, p. 172: «Les connaissances de Ligeti en matière de musique populaire n'étaient pas seulement le résultat de ses lectures. Dès l'âge de trois ans, les folklores hongrois et roumain l'entouraient comme une réalité vivante».

[4]. LIGETI 2014, p. 35: «Pour un musicien, l'Institut de Bucarest semble paradisiaque et dépasse tout ce que l'on peut imaginer». The original text, in Hungarian was published under the title 'Népzenekutatás Romániában', in: *Zénei Szemle*, I/3 (1950), pp. 18-22.

[5]. LIGETI 2014, p. 40: «l'Institut entreprend de grands efforts pour la diffusion de la musique collectée. Sa très riche phonotèque (plus de 1500 disques comptant environ 3500 mélodies) est très utile dans ce but. Les enregistrements couvrent tous les genres de la musique populaire roumaine: chants de conjuration, mélodies pour les rites d'enterrement, de mariage et de récolte, *colinde*, chansons sans liens avec une coutume (ballades, *doine*, etc.) ainsi que danses chantées et instrumentales».

[6]. BARTÓK 1967, pp. 647-693.

80s and 90s, this melodic kernel, masterfully fused with the Baroque Lament, permeates many of his works of this period, within a variety of settings.

In Ligeti's case, pieces such as the Piano Études 'Automne à Varsovie' and 'Arc-en-ciel' rely on this melodic source, as well as his Piano Concerto, the Violin Concerto, the Horn Trio, the Viola Sonata, and the *Hamburg Concerto*[7]. The melodic funeral thread functions as a symbolic catalyst of these pieces, generating a group which, speaking about his own oeuvre from a structural point of view, Aurel Stroe entitles «unit of compositions» (clase de compoziții[8]). The bocet motif which runs through the aforementioned pieces has in fact multiple anchors (as compellingly demonstrated by Amy Bauer[9] and Richard Steinitz[10], among others), yet we will bring into focus its grounding in folk heritage. Constantin Floros also emphasizes the fact that

> Lament themes play a surprisingly large role in Ligeti's later work. Laments occur in the Horn Trio as well as in the Piano and the Violin Concerto, and the Sixth Etude here under discussion is labeled "great lament" (*nagy lamento*) in the drafts. The theme, which is modified time and again, consists primarily of descending half- and whole-tone intervals, but occasionally also exhibits ascending intervals, which are frequently furnished with a sforzato mark. The sorrowful character of the music is unmistakable — not surprisingly the sketches contain the characterizing notes *dolente* and *molto dolente*[11].

In the second volume of the Romanian Folk Music Collection, Bartók provides in the Introduction the following explanation:

> Mourning song melodies (Class *G*). – The most important of their four subclasses is Subclass α), containing the proper songs of mourning, which are called *bocet*(e) in literary Rumanian. Their designation in Bihor (and in Valcani, county Torontal) is *Vaiet* (*ul după morți*)[12]; in Mureș and Cerbăl, *D'e glăsit* — designations from other areas are missing. The melodies are sung by female relatives at any time during which the corpse is laid out in the house of mourning. In addition, they may be sung in the cemetery by the female relatives any time at the tomb thereafter (for example, on the anniversary of the death, and so forth). The texts are improvisations using certain traditional patterns; the metrical structure is the well-known acatalectic or catalectic quaternary, with a a, b b rhymes[13].

---

[7]. In this piece Ligeti only presents the melody once, 'camouflaged' in the spectral form of the untempered intonation.

[8]. A concept or pattern admitting a certain number of new materializations. See Octavian Nemescu's explanation in NEMESCU 2017, p. 29. He points out the piece 'Grădina structurilor', which had 7-8 versions.

[9]. BAUER 2011.

[10]. STEINITZ 2003, pp. 293-299.

[11]. FLOROS 2014, p. 165.

[12]. The term, a regionalism, could be translated as «wheeping» (for the dead).

[13]. BARTÓK 1967, pp. 25-26.

Ex. 1a: Bocete 'La privedji'[14], Bartók 1967, p. 690.

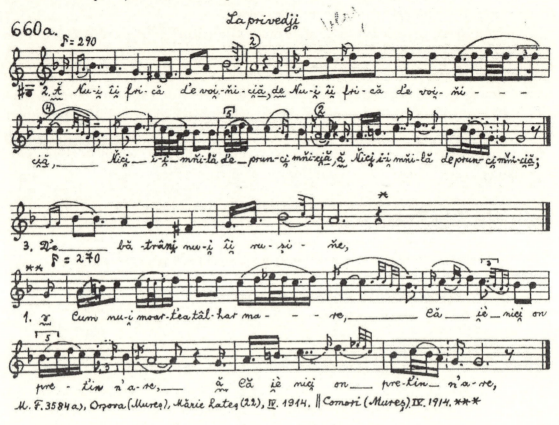

Ex. 1b: Incipit scale.

---

[14]. Bartók transcribes in the title the regional pronunciation of the Romanian noun «priveghi».

'Functional Music' and *Cantata for the Festival of Youth*

After outlining the characteristics of these songs, Bartók emphasizes that «these mourning song melodies may perhaps have originated from some chanting or psalmodizing music of the Orthodox Church»[15].

For their complex symbolism and archaic roots, the funeral rituals of Romanian rural culture have been the subject of detailed study by notable musicians and ethnomusicologists, among them Constantin Brăiloiu (who considers the dirges «a melodic outburst of sorrow and grief»[16]), George Breazul, Ioan R. Nicola, Traian Mârza, Tiberiu Alexandru[17], Gail Kligman[18], Mariana Kahane together with Lucilia Georgescu-Stănculeanu[19], and Lucia Iștoc[20], among others.

The modal scale segment, a chain of descending tones and semitones, is in evidence in the Romanian dirges. More often than not, in practice, these scales turn into a vocal *glissando*, as in a semitonal descent, sometimes even microtonal. In those pieces by Ligeti that rely on the bocet pattern, various melodic hypostases of the tones-semitones combinations are presented, sometimes attaining, through chromatic saturation, the character of a *passus duriusculus*. Merging the bocet with the *lamento* bass, the composer fuses in his music the ancestral folk tradition with most refined aspects of the established repertoire.

Bartók came across the tone-semitone pattern of the Romanian dirges while acquiring his folk collections in the region of Transylvania (Bihor, Arad, Mureș areas). Heard many times at the beginning of the melody, it features the scale pattern of the melodies below. The two selected dirges (Exs. 1a, 1b, 2a, 2b) serve as a sonic proof; they are sung only by women during the wake, while the deceased is still in his/her home.

In Ligeti's pieces employing this motif (such as the Piano Concerto, Exs. 3a-c), the descending motion is sometimes balanced out by an upward or downward stepwise motion of a tetrachord, made of major seconds. This segment is also present in the Romanian dirges, in the same context of balancing the descendant tone-semitone contour (Exs. 4a, 4b). Bartók referred to such resultant a scale that chains together a diminshed and an augmented tetrachord, as an 'acoustic mode'.

---

[15]. *Ibidem*, p. 27.
[16]. Brăiloiu 1981, p. 109 («o revărsare melodică a părerii de rău»).
[17]. Alexandru 1979.
[18]. Kligman 1988.
[19]. Kahane – Georgescu-Stănculeanu 1988.
[20]. Iștoc 1991, pp. 197-222.

Ex. 2a: Bocet 'La privedji', reproduced from BARTÓK 1967, p. 668.

Ex. 2b: Bocet scale.

'Functional Music' and *Cantata for the Festival of Youth*

Ex. 3a: György Ligeti, Piano Concerto, 2nd mvt., bb. 33-35, Facsimile score LIGETI 1986A. © 1986 by Schott Music, Mainz. Reproduced by permission. All rights reserved.

Ex. 3b: Melodic motif (piano, right hand), b. 33.

Ex. 3c: Melodic motif (clarinet), bb. 34-35.

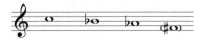

Ex. 4a: Bocet 'La privedji', Bartók 1967, p. 690.

Ex. 4b: Bocet scale (acoustic mode).

One of the first arrangements of the bocet melody merged with the Baroque lament in Ligeti's music can be found in the Horn Trio (1982); labeled more than once as a transition piece in his stylistic evolution, it marks the boundary between the composer's adherence to the Darmstadt avant-garde and his third stage of creative activity, when he revisited the folklore of both Romania and Hungary, also absorbing the influence of extra-European musical cultures.

As observed by Amy Bauer, «The Horn Trio's "Lamento" directed most of its melodic and rhythmic energy at an entropic dissolution of the Baroque *basso ostinato* lament. Although the "Lamento" drew on folk influences, it functioned as a kind of genre parody, with clearly-marked emblems of the form and a postlude that, in spirit, recalled the celebrated coda to Dido's lament»[21]. Exs. 5a-5f show different occurrences of the *lamento* motif in the score and separately.

Romanian composers also had recourse to funeral folk music, and one might draw attention to the case of Myriam Marbe, who employed a strikingly similar melody in her Requiem entitled *Fra Angelico – Chagall – Voroneț*. The second movement of Marbe's work replicates a Dawn Song (*Cântecul zorilor*) with a very simlar intervallic design (compare, for instance, the descending melodic line of the text «Morgenröte», bb. 121-124 [Ex. 6] with Ex. 5b).

Commissioned by the festival *Komponistinnen: gestern – heute* in Heidelberg, whose 'motto' was 'Blau – Farbe der Ferne' (Blue – the Colour of Distance), Marbe's Requiem was completed in 1990. Taking the form of an extended lament, the piece presents the dawn song in German translation («Morgenröte, Morgenröte, ihr Schwestern, eilet nicht zu uns herab»[22]), placing it in the middle section, subtitled Lacrimosa. Of pre-Christian origin, the Dawn song is performed by women in rural Romania on the very morning of burial, facing East, when the deceased is still in his home. The song entreats the natural elements (the Dawn) to slow its pace, so that the deceased can properly be prepared for burial, postponing the moment of final departure.

---

[21]. Bauer 2011, p. 181.
[22]. In Romanian: «Zorilor, Zorilor, voi surorilor, să nu vă grăbiți...» («Dawns, dawns, you sisters, slow down your pace, do not rush...»).

'Functional Music' and *Cantata for the Festival of Youth*

Ex. 5a: György Ligeti, Horn Trio, 4th mvt. «Lamento», bb. 1-21, Facsimile edition Ligeti 1984. © 1984 by Schott Music, Mainz. Reproduced by permission. All rights reserved.

Ex. 5b: Violin motif, bb. 1-5.

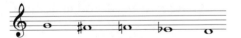

Ex. 5c: Piano motif, bb. 6-10.

Ex. 5d: Piano motif, bb. 7-11.

Ex. 5e: Violin motif, bb. 14-17, upper melodic line.

Ex. 5f: Violin motif, bb. 17-20, lower melodic line.

Ex. 6: Myriam Marbe, Requiem, 2nd movement, Lacrimosa, bb. 119-124, Autograph score, 'Sophie Drinker' Institute, Bremen.

Although the first enunciation of the folk funeral song in Ligeti's Horn Trio is almost identical with that which Marbe employs in her Requiem later on, Ligeti chains together the entries of the polyphonic/hererophonic texture at intervals of minor and major seconds, thus reproducing vertically the scale pattern of a traditional bocet.

Fostering a cluster of significations (*Hommage à Brahms*, also referencing Beethoven's Piano Sonata 'Les Adieux'), the Horn Trio captures the *bocet* motif in a more complex web of allusions and aesthetic associations.

The bocet motif surfaces within a richer timbric garb in both the Piano Concerto (1985-1988) and the Violin Concerto (1989-1993). The Piano Concerto builds two movements departing from the bocet melodic motif, displaying its versatility and expressive power within a hauntingly sorrowful «Lento e deserto» 2nd movement (enhanced with microtonal *glissando* sighs of the slide whistle, Ex. 7a-7c) and a fast 3rd movement.

Ligeti's favourite settings of the formal structure for the *bocet* motif are those provided by the Baroque period. Even in his concertos, he leans towards this historical and aesthetic space. Amy Bauer considers the second movement («Lento e deserto») «a kind of theme and variations, as forms of the *lamento* topos (identified by expression or style) are introduced, juxtaposed, and played off against one another in variants that cite trademark Ligeti textures and forms»[23].

---

[23]. BAUER 2011, pp. 181, 183.

Ex. 7a: György Ligeti, Piano Concerto, 2nd mvt. «Lento e deserto», bb. 1-20, Facsimile Score Ligeti 1986a. © 1986 by Schott Music, Mainz. Reproduced by permission. All rights reserved.

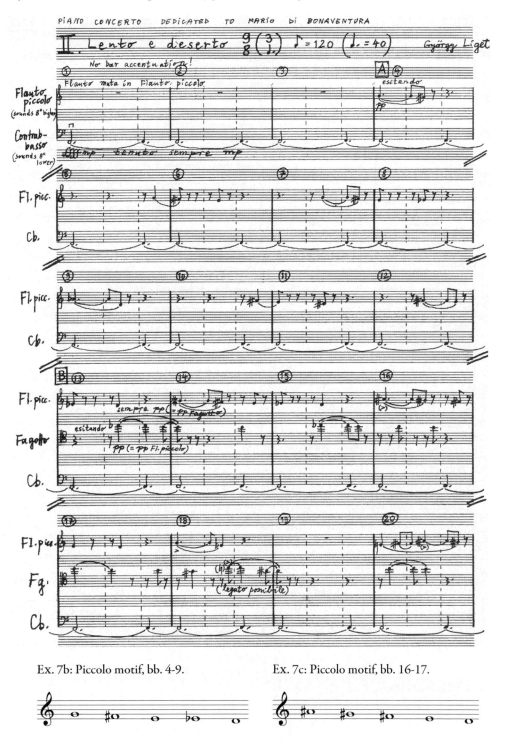

Ex. 7b: Piccolo motif, bb. 4-9.   Ex. 7c: Piccolo motif, bb. 16-17.

The Violin Concerto opens a new symbolic space for the presence of the *bocet* motif; quoted in the last movement («Appassionato»); together with the pastoral Romanian melodic motif[24] that opens the 2nd movement («Aria, Hoquetus, Choral»), it allows for a new decoding of Ligeti's encrypted message. In Romanian culture the most iconic myth is that of the folk ballad *Miorița*, placed within a rural pastoral atmosphere, in which one shepherd is killed by his two peers out of envy — could Ligeti have envisaged this myth, which he knew very well, as a metaphor for the extermination of the Jews in Second World War? In the folk ballad, death is accepted and viewed as a cosmic wedding. Its significance is in a reconciliation with death by re-entering the cycle of nature and reintegrating into the cosmos, a philosophical aspect also addressed by Mircea Eliade in his book *The Myth of the Eternal Return or, Cosmos and History*[25]. The two motifs presented in the same movement work at a symbolic level as two sides of the same ontological coin.

Discussing the case of the Viola Sonata (1991-1994), Amy Bauer acknowledges the kernel of the Transylvanian dirges (Exs. 8a-8c): «Although more wide-ranging than any folk model, the "Lamento" could be said to expand on those Transylvanian laments, or *bocete*, analyzed by Bartók»[26].

Ex. 8a: György Ligeti, Viola Sonata, «Lamento», bb. 43-45, Ligeti 2001.

Ex. 8b: Viola motif, lower line, bb. 43-45.   Ex. 8c: Viola motif, top line, bb. 43-45.

---

[24]. See Țiplea Temeș 2018a.
[25]. Eliade 1971.
[26]. Bauer 2011, p. 199.

Ligeti himself, explains that «[o]ne can take the sixth movement literally as a chaconne left over from the Baroque period, complete with *lamento* bass, but this interpretation is misleading»[27].

Viewed within the context of the entire Viola Sonata, the «Lamento» and the last movement — «Chaconne chromatique» — both quoting the folk funeral melodic motif, should not be regarded only in relation to one another, but also in connection with the first movement, which is also based on a Romanian folk genre (*Hora lungă*). This conveys a deep feeling of yearning and resonates with the concluding fifth movement: an archetypal folk lament kept as if a fossil in the amber of a 'chaconne left-over' form, enriched with the sonorous brightness of the glassy overtones.

Indisputably an especially intense expression of the bocet is to be found in one of the most intricate pieces in the entire piano repertoire: the Étude 'Automne à Varsovie' (1st book, 1985), described by Richard Steinitz as «more chromatically saturated than anything else in his music»[28]. Characterizing the piece as a «melancholic Chopinesque study»[29], Steinitz shows the lineage of the *lament* motif in this Étude: «Deeper still it has an ancestor in the funeral laments of traditional folklore, including the Romanian bocet which Ligeti heard as a child»[30]. A brilliant blending of various sources (the African polyrhythm, the music for mechanical piano by Nancarrow, intersection with the paradoxical graphics of Escher and the universe of the fractals), 'Automne à Varsovie' stands out as a gem.

Described as an extended hemiola, and by Ligeti himself as a fugue[31] (again, a Baroque form), this piano piece displays nested bocete, layered in various tempi and repeated obsessively across 122 bars, as a musical *mantra*. It echoes perfectly the practice of the singing during the wake and burial ceremonies in rural Romania, where the groups of women weeping for the deceased (*bocitoare*) do not sing in synchrony, but rather start at different times in their own pitch and tempo. Beyond the composer's technical mastery of «choreographing» the multi-layered discourse (an aspect outlined in a detailed analysis by Alessandra Morresi[32], among others), the focal point are the *bocet* motifs chained together as in an *ostinato*. They surface from different strata of the texture, in different registers, thus providing spatiality, as if being a genuinely four-dimensional object.

In the *Dimensionist Manifesto*, written back in 1936, Charles Sirató showed how «literature left the line and entered the plane»[33], similarly, «painting abandoned the plane

---

[27]. LIGETI 1998, CD booklet, p. 17.
[28]. STEINITZ 2003, p. 293.
[29]. *Ibidem*.
[30]. *Ibidem*, p. 295.
[31]. GOJOWY 1991, p. 362.
[32]. MORESI 2002, pp. 120-145.
[33]. SIRATÓ 1936.

and entered space»[34], adding that «sculpture stepped out of closed, immobile forms». Finally, he pointed towards «the artistic conquest of four-dimensional space»[35] and reaching a cosmic form of art. In music, Ligeti was the composer who artfully achieved this effect, 'Automne à Varsovie' providing the best possible sonic evidence (Exs. 9a and 9b).

Perceived as a musical tesseract, one could interpret 'Automne à Varsovie' as Ligeti's *Corpus hypercubicus* (to reference Dalí's painting), a four-dimensional cross on which his Polish friends (the dedicatees of the piece) symbolically remain. The parallel to be drawn is inspired by Ligeti himself, when speaking about his Requiem (a piece in which he says he included the only vocal form of the Romanian folk laments, as «a heterophony of bocete»[36]): «I have often been asked how it is that coming from a Hungarian family of Jewish ancestry, I took a text of the Catholic mass, without being a believer (I am not a believer, but neither am I an atheist; there are other possibilities»[37]). His music is indeed a continuous quest for those «other possibilities» and his religion is, above all, that of profound humanism.

Richard Steinitz, referring both to the 2nd movement of the Piano Concerto and to the Horn Trio, acknowledges «a primacy of feeling over technique»[38]. One could take the idea still further by highlighting in Ligeti's music the primacy of significance over feeling, mostly in those pieces containing the lament motif.

By addressing the subject of death in his music, Ligeti described a refined and complex topography of grief, passing through into the realm of the transcendental. In it, he blurred the boundaries between ancestral folk traditions (bocete) and established cultural values (the Baroque heritage), embracing in an alchemical way even jazz, in the case of ‚Arc-en-ciel'[39]. He also removed the demarcation between sacred and secular, and erased the line between the tragic and the grotesque, turning «in-betweenness» into his favourite artistic space. Mined from the ancestral layer of his native land's purest rural culture, these melodic motifs were melded together and set into the most refined Baroque elements («Lamento, Chaconne, Fugue» forms and polyphonic techniques). Transplanted into this new soundworld and stylistic mix, they realised their full expressive potential and imparted a novel postmodern sensibility to his music.

---

[34]. *Ibidem.*

[35]. *Ibidem.*

[36]. Ligeti's words, in a discussion with Constantin Rîpă, conductor of the Antifonia Choir (Gh. Dima Music Academy, Cluj-Napoca), during the Festival Musique d'Aujourd'hui, Strasbourg, 1994. The Romanian choir presented Ligeti's Requiem. See Țiplea Temeș 2018b, p. 323, and Țiplea Temeș 1999, p. 157.

[37]. Follin 1993: «On m'a beaucoup demandé, moi qui viens d'une famille hongroise d'origine juive, comment est-il possible que je prends un texte de la liturgie catholique, sans être croyant (je ne suis pas croyant mais je ne suis pas athée; il y a d'autres possibilités)».

[38]. Steinitz 2011, p. 212.

[39]. See Callender 2007, pp. 41-77.

'Functional Music' and *Cantata for the Festival of Youth*

Ex. 9a: György Ligeti, 'Automne à Varsovie', bb. 1-7, Ligeti 1986b. © 1986 by Schott Music, Mainz. Reproduced by permission. All rights reserved.

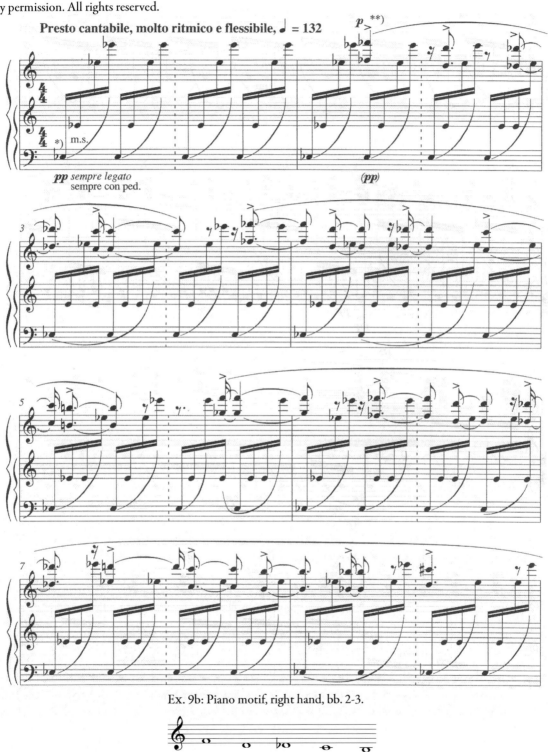

Ex. 9b: Piano motif, right hand, bb. 2-3.

Relying heavily on Romanian bocete in the works of his final creative decades, not only does Ligeti mourn in folk style, with an unprecedented artistic sophistication, but also marks an eternal, yet metaphorical return, to his native Transylvania.

BIBLIOGRAPHY

ALEXANDRU 1979
ALEXANDRU, Tiberiu. 'Rumänien, B. Die Volkmusik', in: *Die Musik in Geschichte und Gegenwart: Allgemeine Enzyklopädie der Musik. Personenteil, 16 (Supplement)*, edited by Friedrich Blume, Kassel, Bärenreiter, 1979.

BARTÓK 1967
BARTÓK, Béla. *Rumanian Folk Music. 2: Vocal Melodies*, edited by Benjamin Schuhoff, The Hague, Martinus Nijhoff, 1967.

BAUER 2011
BAUER, Amy. *Ligeti's Laments: Nostalgia, Exoticism, and the Absolute*, Farnham, Ashgate, 2011.

BRĂILOIU 1981
BRĂILOIU, Constantin. *Opere. 5*, Bucharest, Editura muzicală, 1981.

CALLENDER 2007
CALLENDER, Clifton. 'Interactions of the Lamento Motif and Jazz Harmonies in György Ligeti's 'Arc-en-ciel'', in: *Intégral*, XXI (2007), pp. 41-77.

ELIADE 1971
ELIADE, Mircea. *The Myth of the Eternal Return, or Cosmos and History*, Princeton (NJ), Princeton University Press, 1971.

FLOROS 2014
FLOROS, Constantin. *György Ligeti: Beyond Avant-garde and Postmodernism*, translated by Ernest Bernhardt-Kabisch, Frankfurt am Main, Peter Lang, 2014.

FOLLIN 1993
FOLLIN, Michel. *György Ligeti : Portrait*, documentary on an idea by Judith Kele and Arnaud de Mezamat, La Sept. Artline Films, Les Productions du Sablier (coproduction with Le Centre Georges Pompidou, La RTBF, Magyar Televizió), 1993.

GOJOWY 1991
GOJOWY, Detlef. 'György Ligeti über eigene Werke: Ein Gespräch mit Detlef Gojowy aus dem Jahre 1988', in: *Für György Ligeti: Die Referate des Ligeti-Kongresses Hamburg 1988*, edited by Constantin Floros, Hans Joachim Marx and Peter Petersen, Laaber, Laaber-Verlag, 1991, pp. 349-363.

'Functional Music' and *Cantata for the Festival of Youth*

Iștoc 1991
Iștoc, Lucia. 'Tipuri melodice de bocet din Transilvania', in: *Anuarul de Folclor VIII-IX (1987-1990)*, Cluj-Napoca, Editura Academiei Române, 1991, pp. 197-222.

Kahane – Georgescu-Stănculeanu 1988
Kahane, Mariana – Georgescu-Stănculeanu, Lucilia. *Cîntecul zorilor și bradului: tipologie muzicală (Colecția națională de folclor)*, Bucharest, Editura muzicală, 1988.

Kligman 1988
Kligman, Gail. *The Wedding of the Dead: Ritual, Poetics and Popular Culture in Transylvania*, Berkeley (CA), University of California Press, 1988.

Kurtág 2009
Kurtág, György. *Entretiens, textes, dessins* (Trois entretiens avec Bálint András Varga. Deux hommages à György Ligeti. Autres textes), Geneva, Contrechamps Editions, 2009.

Ligeti 1984
Ligeti, György. *Horn Trio*, Facsimile edition, Mainz, Schott, 1984.

Ligeti 1986a
Id. *Concerto for Piano and Orchestra*, Facsimile score, Mainz, Schott, 1986.

Ligeti 1986b
Id. *Études pour Piano, premier livre*, Mainz, Schott, 1986.

Ligeti 1998
Id. *György Ligeti Edition, 7 – Chamber Music*, Sony Classical SK 62309, 1998.

Ligeti 2001
Id. *Viola Sonata*, Mainz, Schott, 2001.

Ligeti 2014
Id. 'La recherche sur la musique populaire roumaine', in: Id. *Écrits sur la musique et les musiciens*, translated by Catherine Fourcassié, Geneva, Contrechamps Éditions, 2014, pp. 35-44.

Moresi 2002
Moresi, Alessandra. *György Ligeti: 'Études pour piano premier livre'. Le fonti e i procedimenti compositivi*, Turin, De Sono Associazione per la Musica, 2002.

Nemescu 2017
Nemescu, Octavian. 'Aurel Stroe – originalul', in: *Muzica*, no. 6 (2017), pp. 27-37.

Sirató 1936
Sirató, Charles. 'The Dimensionist Manifesto', in: *Le Revue N+1*, 1936.

STEINITZ 2003
STEINITZ Richard. *György Ligeti: Music of the Imagination*, London, Faber and Faber, 2003.

STEINITZ 2011
ID. 'Genesis of the Piano Concerto and the Horn Trio', in: *György Ligeti: Of Foreign Lands and Strange Sounds*, edited by Louise Duchesneau and Wolfgang Marx, Woodbridge, The Boydell Press, 2011, pp. 169-212.

ȚIPLEA TEMEȘ 1999
ȚIPLEA TEMEȘ, Bianca. *Antifonia in extenso*, Cluj-Napoca, MediaMusica, 1999.

ȚIPLEA TEMEȘ 2018A
EAD. 'Ligeti and Romanian Folk Music: an Insight from the Paul Sacher Foundation', in: *György Ligeti's Cultural Identities*, edited by Amy Bauer and Márton Kerékfy, Abingdon-New York, Routledge, 2018, pp. 120-138.

ȚIPLEA TEMEȘ 2018B
EAD. 'Haunting Soundscapes of Transylvania', in: *Studia U.B.B. Musica*, no. 2 (2018), pp. 318-323.

György Ligeti's Film Music
beyond Stanley Kubrick

Julia Heimerdinger
(Universität für Musik und darstellende Kunst Wien)

It is well known and has been widely examined how filmmaker Stanley Kubrick (1928-1999) has successfully used a handful of György Ligeti's works in three of his films. The first was the immediately famous, epic *2001: A Space Odyssey* from 1968, extensively featuring *Atmosphères* (1961), the Kyrie from the Requiem (1964-1965), *Lux Aeterna* (1966) as well as bits of *Aventures* (1962-1965), at that time truly contemporary music, acting as literal atmospheres, or ambiences, of different spaces or objects. A decade later, one more work for orchestra, *Lontano* (1967), accompanied iconic moments of the horror film *The Shining* (1980) as the sound of metaphysical appearances like ghosts from the past or telepathy. In Kubrick's last film, *Eyes Wide Shut* from 1999, the «Mesto, rigido e cerimoniale» from the *Musica ricercata* (1953) — the only piece from a decade further back in time — is employed as a recurring musical theme (or even leitmotif) of dismay.

The way Kubrick and his staff searched for, chose, and arranged the music, was sophisticated, very effective, and, as it turns out, exceedingly influential[1]. It popularized Ligeti's music — and Ligeti's music amplified Kubrick's film artistically[2]. Occupationally, filmmakers or their staff aren't particularly interested in pre-existing music's originally intended place of performance, but instead in what it offers, in its potential effects and possibilities. They not only choose pieces but also pick suitable excerpts, ranging from short motifs to longer passages, hardly ever the whole. The task is to select *effective* parts.

Uses as successful as like Kubrick's have ensured that Ligeti's music was added to (unwritten) cinema libraries, and that specific compositions or techniques have become

---

[1]. Regarding the music selection process for *2001* see McQuiston 2011.
[2]. Heimerdinger 2018.

established for certain contexts. It is also a fact that if works are used in a very ostensible way, they are specifically connoted, and further uses will refer to this — like the Kyrie from the Requiem in *2001*, where it lends the mysterious monolith a powerful, quasi-religious meaning. The monolith's 'leit-music' apparently lingered in the memory and reappeared in later films like *Charlie and the Chocolate Factory* (USA 2005) where the monolith is replaced by a chocolate bar shown on a futuristic TV, or in the context of an exaggeratedly pregnant theatrical scene in the Finnish satire *Suuri Performansi* (FI 2008). The famous excerpt is seriously re-used for the first time in the sci-fi monster film *Godzilla* (USA/Japan 2014) during an epic scene of a military parachute jump. Though the film's original music by Alexandre Desplat (with its orchestration that at some points even includes a choir) is similarly voluminous, Ligeti's Kyrie is still clearly set apart from Desplat's score and so underlines the mission's importance.

So, what about the use of Ligeti's works in films after and besides Kubrick's *2001*, *The Shining* and *Eyes Wide Shut*? To what extent is this influence noticeable and where does the use of music go beyond it? A glance on the list of titles (see TABLE 1) shows short films, series episodes, and documentaries, besides a whole range of feature films, most of them covering one or more genres including sci-fi, horror, mystery, thriller, and drama. Among the titles there is a considerable proportion of arthouse films or works with a certain claim to art, as well as documentaries about artists.

Over the following pages I will reflect on the film-musical qualities of Ligeti's music in specific films, but will not, as musicologists have often claimed in the past[3], assume that filmmakers have not understood the music (*per se*) or have understood it incorrectly when used in a film, but will instead concentrate on how they obviously understood and used it.

In contrast to the Kyrie's rather one-sided use, *Atmosphères* has made the biggest career of all the *2001*-pieces (see TABLE 1). It might be assumed that the comparatively neutral or even film-music-like nature of the work, its varied texture, and its partly dramatic dynamics have contributed to this.

Its first — and maybe most striking — reappearance occurs in a movie in which one might not have expected to find this kind of material, namely the martial arts film *Fist of Fury* (Hong Kong 1972) starring Bruce Lee as Chen Zhen, the avenger of his revered master. The soundtrack by Joseph Koo is an astonishing mix of Jazz, Western-style music, traditional (Chinese and Japanese) and avant-garde elements, and a very short excerpt from Ligeti's *Atmosphères*, namely 20 seconds from section F with its shrill piccolo texture — so short that one wonders why nothing was just written in that style for the two situations in which they were used: In the first scene the drilling sound starts when Chen spies on two men talking about the murder plot and continues until he attacks them. The second time the excerpt is used during one of the final fights, this time mixed with the sound of Chen's battle cry. The piccolos only gradually emerge

---

[3]. See the discussion in HEIMERDINGER 2007, pp. 77-89.

György Ligeti's Film Music beyond Stanley Kubrick

Table 1: List of Films Featuring Music by Ligeti

This list was mainly compiled based on a search for the term 'György Ligeti' in the *International Movie Database* (<imdb.com>), which in many cases provides detailed information on the music used. Enquiries with Ligeti's publishers have not yielded any significant further results. The compilation shown here contains only films that could be accessed without disproportionate effort. All were checked to see whether music by Ligeti was used and if so, which pieces. In particular, short films and student films were omitted from the full list which would contain approximately 50 titles.

Title	Type of film & Genre(s)	Piece(s) used
2001: A Space Odyssey (UK/USA 1968, Stanley Kubrick)	Feature (Sci-Fi)	*Atmosphères*, *Aventures*, *Lux Aeterna*, *Requiem* (Kyrie)
Fist of Fury (HK 1972, Lo Wei)	Feature (Action, Martial Arts)	*Atmosphères*
Ghost Story for Christmas (BBC series, Episode 'A Warning to the Curious', UK 1972, Lawrence Gordon Clark)	TV Movie (Mystery, Horror)	*Atmosphères*, Cello Concerto (first movement), String Quartet No. 2 (fourth movement: «Presto furioso, brutale, tumultuoso»)
The Silent Witness (UK 1978, David W. Rolfe)	Documentary	*Atmosphères*
Schalcken the Painter (UK 1979, Leslie Megahey)	TV Movie (Mystery, Horror)	*Continuum*
The Shining (UK/USA 1980, Stanley Kubrick)	Feature (Horror)	*Lontano*
2010: The Year We Make Contact (USA 1984, Peter Hyams)	Feature (Sci-Fi)	*Lux Aeterna*
Merci la vie (FR 1991, Bertrand Blier)	Feature (Drama)	*Musica ricercata* (IV «Tempo di valse»)
Heat (USA 1995, Michael Mann)	Feature (Action, Crime)	Cello Concerto (first movement)
Eyes Wide Shut (UK/USA 1999, Stanley Kubrick)	Feature (Drama, Thriller)	*Musica ricercata* (II «Mesto, rigido e ceremoniale»)
Lemming (FR 2005, Dominik Moll)	Feature (Mystery, Thriller)	*Continuum*
Charlie and the Chocolate Factory (USA 2005, Tim Burton)	Feature (Comedy, Fantasy)	*Requiem* (Kyrie)
Bang Bang Orangutang (SE/DK 2005, Simon Staho)	Feature (Drama)	*Musica ricercata* (I «Sostenuto»)
Miss Gulag (USA 2007, Maria Ibrahimova)	Documentary	*Musica ricercata* (VII «Cantabile, molto legato»)
Suuri performanssi (FI 2008, Tapio Piirainen)	TV Movie (Drama, Satire)	*Requiem* (Kyrie)
For the End of Time (SI 2009, Ema Kugler)	Feature (Experimental, Fantasy)	*Atmosphères*, Cello Concerto (Movement unclear), *Lontano*, *Lux Aeterna*, Two Etudes for Organ (Movement unclear), *Ramifications*
Shutter Island (USA 2010, Martin Scorsese)	Feature (Mystery, Thriller)	*Lontano*, Two Etudes for Organ (1 «Harmonies»)
Hjernevask (Episode 'Likestillingsparadokset') (NO 2010, Terje Lervik)	Documentary	*Artikulation*
Over Your Cities Grass Will Grow (FR/NL/UK 2010, Sophie Fiennes)	Documentary	*Atmosphères*, Cello Concerto (1 Movement), *Lontano*
Viagem a Portugal (PT 2011, Sérgio Tréfaur)	Feature (Biography, Drama)	Etude No. 5 'Arc-en-Ciel', Etude No. 11 'En Suspens', *Musica ricercata* (IX [«Béla Bartók in memoriam»] «Adagio. Mesto - Allegro maestoso»)
The Pervert's Guide to Ideology (UK/IE 2012, Sophie Fiennes)	Documentary	*Clocks and Clouds*
Godzilla (USA/JP 2014, Gareth Edwards)	Feature (Sci-Fi)	*Requiem* (Kyrie)
As Above, So Below (USA 2014, John Erick Dowdle)	Feature (Horror)	*Drei Phantasien nach Friedrich Hölderlin* («Abendphantasie»)
The Whole Town's Sleeping (USA 2014, Lynn Lowry)	Short	*Ramifications*
Embers (ES 2015, Claire Carré)	Feature (Drama, Sci-Fi)	Sonata for Cello solo (I «Dialogo»)
Mais Do Que Eu Possa Me Reconhecer (BR 2015, Allan Ribeiro)	Documentary	String Quartets No. 1 and No. 2 (Movements unclear), Two Etudes for Organ (I «Harmonies»), Sonata for Cello solo (Movement unclear), *Ramifications*
Cartas da Guerra (PT 2016, Ivo M. Ferreira)	Feature (Drama)	String Quartet No. 1 («Lento»; «[…] Molto sostenuto - Andante tranquillo»)
The Killing of a Sacred Deer (IE/UK 2017, Yorgos Lanthimos)	Feature (Drama, Mystery, Thriller)	Cello Concerto (1 Movement), Piano Concerto («Lento e deserto»)
La Douleur (FR 2017, Emmanuel Finkiel)	Feature (Drama)	Piano Concerto («Lento e deserto»)
Homecoming (Season 1, Episode 'Pineapple', USA 2018, Sam Esmail)	TV Series (Mystery, Thriller)	*Atmosphères*
Homecoming (Season 1, Episode 'Redwood', USA 2018, Sam Esmail)	TV Series (Mystery, Thriller)	Piano Concerto («Lento e deserto»)
Other Worlds (CH 2020, Ivan Maria Friedman)	Short	*Atmosphères*, *Lontano*

from the surrounding sounds and end with the beaten opponent hitting the ground with the caesura — the onset of low strings from section G, which immediately give way to a whirling sound resolving into harmonic chords as Chen smilingly realizes that the enemy is finished. In both scenes, *Atmosphères*' most outstanding section virtually represents the whistling of Chen's inner boiling kettle.

A similar example can be found almost 50 years later, in an episode of the series *Homecoming* ('Pineapple', USA 2018). *Atmosphères*' swelling in section B (which is at first mixed with other sounds before emerging clearly) corresponds here with the growing aggressiveness of an angry young man.

Other films still lean more towards the *2001* model and relate the music to cosmic, mythical or religious subjects and images. For example, the short film *Other Worlds*, «An ode to the infinity of worlds»[4], (Switzerland 2020) combines footage shot in the Atacama Desert in Northern Chile and NASA photographic material with passages of Joep Franssens's *Harmony of the Spheres* (first movement), Ligeti's *Lontano*, and *Atmosphères*. In similar fashion, the experimental film *For the End of Time* (2009) by Slovenian filmmaker Ema Kugler focuses the fundamental conflicts and questions of body and mind, life and death — essentially on the basis of Christian symbolism and fantastic, partly computer-generated images, which are combined with an almost incessant flow of text (the English version is spoken by performer Lydia Lunch with a powerful dark voice) and music. The soundtrack is composed of works by György Ligeti, George Crumb, Sofia Gubaidulina, and Krzysztof Penderecki and could be described as a concentrate of their most poignant pieces, which are assembled into a constant flow and make a corresponding impression. Some vocal pieces from a quasi-liturgical context — for example Gubaidulina's *Alleluia*, or Ligeti's *Lux Aeterna* — color the surrounding music in terms of meaning but don't come into full effect as individual pieces.

Compared to these, *Fist of Fury* and *Homecoming* use the music in a more direct, profane way, but the piece works effectively for either.

Further titles belong to the series of *Atmosphères*' uses in film, and in two of them more music of György Ligeti plays an important role: 'A Warning to the Curious' (UK 1972) and the documentary *Over Your Cities Grass Will Grow* (FR/NL/UK 2010), which will be considered in more detail later. The episode 'A Warning to the Curious' from the BBC series *A Ghost Story for Christmas* has an interesting history. As Adam Scovell notes, «the early [ghost stories] adaptations make use of what were then new, avant-garde classical works found in the BBC's gramophone library at Egton House»[5]. In 1967, the BBC had broadcast some of Ligeti's music in a radio program on «Hungarian music after Bartók» as well as the Requiem in the series

---

[4]. FRIEDMAN s.d.
[5]. SCOVELL 2014.

Music in Our Time. As has been revealed by Paul Merkley and Kate McQuiston[6], Kubrick's wife Christine listened to the latter and told her husband that it would be «marvellous for the film»[7]. That is, the BBC had Ligeti's music on its radar, and practically in its library. As a matter of fact, all of Ligeti's works used for 'A Warning' had been broadcast on BBC radio before 1972. Besides *Atmosphères*, these are the Cello Concerto (with Siegfried Palm) and the String Quartet No. 2 (LaSalle Quartet). The TV film, an adaptation of a ghost story by M. R. James, plays in the 1930s and is about a hobby archaeologist who, after finding one of the lost crowns of Anglia, is haunted by the crown's ghostly guard. The opening titles and a view on the empty Norfolk beach are accompanied by the opening 80 seconds of *Atmosphères*. When the first adventurer is digging in the hill the famous piccolo passage from section F can be heard creating tension that 'erupts' with the basses from section G when the guard appears on that hill and tells the man to stop. After that introduction, section F is repeatedly heard during the film, when the ghost is near, or his name is mentioned, seen, or only heard (quasi as something 'in the air'), sometimes it is running through to G that is also occasionally synched with his sudden appearances. The F-G passage is used in such a strong leitmotivic way that it also closes the film, with the G-basses consequently concluding the end titles.

In addition to *Atmosphères*, a longer and at some points trimmed section of the Cello Concerto is used twice at important points of the plot: firstly when the archaeologist digs out the crown, and the second time when he puts it back to appease the guardian ghost. The very calm and slow beginning of the Concerto's first movement with its unfolding to more tension and excitement is well applied along the developing digging scene, the quasi-screaming tones synchronised to the moment, when the man finds the crown. In the final scene, when he is chased by the guardian ghost on the beach and through the woods, a mixture of *Atmosphères* (the first sections from the beginning) and snippets from the String Quartet No. 2, the beginning of the fourth movement («Presto furioso, brutale, tumultuoso») are played. They are partly superimposed on top of each other, adding more agile — and 'brutal' — dynamics to the action, whereas the more eerie and menacing mood of the unfolding, dialogue-poor story prior to that is musically underlined with the static, atmospheric pieces. In summary, this score is following the Kubrickian method in that it completely consists of pre-existing recordings, whereby the music is also used in a more descriptive way.

Still more BBC productions used Ligeti's music, including a horror film from 1979, *Schalken the Painter*. The narrative is set in the golden age of Dutch painting and mixes period music, especially for Harpsichord and a couple of avant-garde bits for the spook. The choice of Ligeti's *Continuum* for Harpsichord seems consistent concerning the timbre, but the effect is that of a sharp alarm, fitting a scene in which a young woman is fleeing from her creepy devilish

---

[6]. MERKLEY 2007, MCQUISTON 2011.
[7]. HEIMERDINGER 2011, p. 128.

husband, who eventually drives her to her death. A similar employment of *Continuum* can be found in the French mystery thriller *Lemming* by Dominik Moll from 2005 in which a young couple, an aspiring engineer, Alain, and his wife Bénédicte (Charlotte Gainsbourg) have very bizarre encounters with Alain's boss, Richard, and his wife Alice. A series of strange events ultimately leads to Alain murdering Richard. The first minute of *Continuum* (a transcription for two player pianos, performed by Jürgen Hocker) is played when Alain, sitting in the dark of his living room, decides to take action and drives to his boss's house. It starts again with the piece's last 100 seconds, that is the more excited part, matching the action as Alain suffocates Richard in his bed, the dripping-out part being played after he's dead.

What Ligeti wrote about the piece's texture apparently applies to the employment of *Continuum* in *Schalcken the Painter* and *Lemming*, namely that through the instrument's lightness of attacks it has something of a «ghostly humming» («gespenstisch Summendes»[8]). Besides that, the continuous and unforeseeably changing ringing reminds the listener of an uncontrollable and fast machine which has been set off to fulfil some weird task — in both cases murders, after which the playing consequently stops.

Another French film starring Charlotte Gainsbourg, *Merci la vie* from 1991, contains music by Ligeti, namely the fourth movement «Tempo di valse» from *Musica ricercata* — eight years before Kubrick's more prominent use of the «Mesto» in *Eyes Wide Shut* from 1999 —, underlining absurd comedy. The film is about two young women, Camille (Charlotte Gainsbourg) and Joëlle (Anouk Grinberg), on a — particularly sexual — discovery tour, during which the elder and bolder Joëlle is intentionally infected by a medical doctor, Marc Antoine Worms (Gérard Depardieu), with a sexually transmitted disease as part of an experiment. A strongly accelerated excerpt of the valse, that is the first 33 bars including repetition and stopping with the rest in bar 34, is played to a surreal and itself partly accelerated scene where Dr. Worms, dressed in a pyjama, is filmed carrying the freshly cut-out eye of Camille's father through a corridor and finally plugs it into the vagina of Joëlle, who is laying on a bed surrounded by a group of people, including the film team. As one observes the film team's work, the illusion is at the same time created and exposed. The music's superficiality and exaggerated tempo are supporting this, on top of it being reminiscent of the techniques of silent film. Several movements of *Musica ricercata* have been used as film music since then (see TABLE 1), and it is striking that all these corresponding films have a poetic touch and a basic and apparent consciousness about aesthetic perception.

For example, the aggressive initial tremolos (bars 1-3) of the «Sostenuto...» open the Swedish film *Bang Bang Orangutang* from 2005. They immediately create suspense, much the same as Benjamin Levy states in his analysis[9], and are reverberating on the following silent images of the tragicomic protagonist, sitting wounded in a car with an idle glance.

---

[8]. LIGETI 2007, vol. II, p. 250.
[9]. LEVY 2017, p. 13.

A strong stylization is also effected with bits of *Musica*'s ninth movement (together with excerpts from Étude No. 5 'Arc-en-Ciel', and Étude No. 11 'En Suspens') in the chamber play-like, black-and-white film *Viagem a Portugal* (*Journey to Portugal*, Portugal 2011) about the cruelty of immigration controls at European airports. Apart from creating an atmosphere of bad premonition and melancholically toned hope, the music shares the reductive style with the film's sparse image aesthetics and dynamics of the narrative.

A different contextualisation occurs in the documentary *Miss Gulag* (USA 2007) about women in a Siberian prison camp and their annual beauty competition. The perhaps most outstanding piece of *Musica ricercata*, the seventh movement «Cantabile, molto legato», is underscoring a former inmate's recount of the crime that led to her imprisonment. The piece's combination of the very fast and incessant flow of a repeated pentatonic pattern (in the left hand) with a folk-like, calm and searching melody (in the right hand) on a completely different plane, has something of a sounding contradiction — kind of mirroring the apparent disconnection between the woman's sympathetic, reflective manner and the brutality of the attempted manslaughter she describes. Solitude, remoteness, and concentrated (musical) thoughts and ideas seem to be some of the general aspects of the *ricercata* movements and their uses — including the «Mesto» in Kubrick's *Eyes Wide Shut*, for that matter.

Staying with Ligeti's early solo and chamber music, it is again noticeable and plausible that they appear in rather poetic or dialogic movies. For example, the first movement («Dialogo») of the Sonata for Cello solo (1948/1953) is used as diegetic music in the postapocalyptic sci-fi drama *Embers* (Spain 2015). The survivors have lost their ability to remember. A father and his adolescent daughter are living in a bunker and have apparently not been affected by the amnesic virus. The cello is introduced early in the film in the frame of the original film score as a repeated subject of conversation between father and daughter, so the sonata picks up and condenses this specific sound. The first two minutes of the «Dialogo» (up to the first double bar, before the *Poco più mosso*-part) are finally performed by the girl for her father as her own composition. It repeats and varies a simple theme introduced and demarcated by pizzicati and does really sound like a dialogue when the melody is changing registers. This impression is supported by the images of the daughter and her father alternately glancing at each other — and because the subject of their conversation is on repetition mode anyway. The minor-like, Phrygian mode melody (starting prominently with the pitches g – a – b flat – a) seems sad and thus fits the situation as well.

More of Ligeti's early chamber music appears in two Portuguese-language films, the documentary *Mais Do Que Eu Possa Me Reconhecer* (BR 2015) about the Brazilian artist Darel Valença Lins, who has used Ligeti's music in his experimental videos (besides music of other modern and avant-garde composers), and the poetic black-and-white movie *Cartas da Guerra* (*Letters from War*, PT 2016), based on letters by novelist António Lobo Antunes written to his wife while serving as a military doctor in Angola in the early 1970s. Two excerpts from *Métamorphoses nocturnes* (String Quartet No.1) (1953/54) are assembled together to accompany a nightly scene, changing into a day shot showing a naked soldier running into the forest with a gun. The «Lento»'s nocturne character is first matching the nightly atmosphere, whereas the following motive from the «molto sostenuto» gives the ambiguous impression that the forest scene could also be a dream.

Before panning to the movies which used Ligeti's more famous works for orchestra in a comparatively prominent fashion, two rather curious cases of Ligeti as creepy music should be mentioned, the short film *The Whole Town's Sleeping* (USA 2014) and the horror film *As Above, So Below* (USA 2014). In *The Whole Town's Sleeping*, actress Lynn Lowry dramatically recites the eponymous horror story by Ray Bradbury standing in front of a fireplace. The background sounds are directed by the narrator in the course of her recitation, as well as the music, namely *Ramifications*. As long as the music is described in the story as being heard by a hounded woman, it continues with its steady and slowly shifting pulse while underlining her flight, and also broadly conforming to its description in the text.

It is an interesting coincidence that Ligeti's verbal sketches of *Ramifications* actually «include references to the idea of an accelerating chase, the film directors René Clair and Charlie Chaplin, and scenes from Kafka's *Amerika* [...]»[10]. If this is what he intended to conjure up, he has certainly succeeded.

An even creepier effect is aimed at with the «Abendphantasie» from *Drei Phantasien nach Friedrich Hölderlin* for 16-part mixed choir in *As Above, So Below* (USA 2014). A young archaeologist and a small group of people are going on an expedition in the catacombs of Paris where they find materializations of their worst traumas. The «Abendphantasie» is performed by a cult-like group of women they pass in the catacombs. One guy, who has been detected and stared at by the choir leader, gets stuck in a tunnel and seems to go crazy over the singing («God, why are they singing? Why are they singing this fucking song? Just tell them to shut the fuck up!») — and will eventually be killed by the very same woman later in the film. The music primarily seems to reflect the strangeness, complexity, and unpredictability of the place, and virtually gives a musical introduction to what is to come. The rest of the film contains almost no music yet elaborate sound design, as is common practice in today's horror movies.

Only a selection of Ligeti's works for orchestra is employed in movies, and it seems that certain pieces and even snippets have become favoured. In addition to the works already discussed, these are the Cello Concerto (1966), *Lontano* for large Orchestra (1967), and the Piano Concerto (1985-1988). Of these, the Cello Concerto, respectively its first, not exceedingly orchestral, but 'static' movement, can be said to have the longest, though not continuous, career, being first used in the BBC-film 'A Warning to the Curious' (UK 1972) and again, in a similar way, in the 1995 blockbuster *Heat*, a crime thriller with Robert De Niro

---

[10]. *Ibidem*, p. 259.

as criminal mastermind Neal McCauley and Al Pacino as police lieutenant Vincent Hanna trying to hunt him down. In one scene, the police crew is observing a burglary by McCauley and a colleague at a metal's depository, but McCauley breaks off the operation due to a noise, accidentally made by an imprudent policeman. The scene's suspense is strongly supported by a montage of several excerpts from the movement that are welded rather discreetly; partly the music disappears behind the scenes' diegetic noises such as the sound of a drilling machine. A particularly thrilling moment is when McCauley looks directly into the surveillance camera on whose monitor Hanna is staring so that they quasi glance at each other. The tension of this situation is heightened by the tones rising ever higher until the music literally snaps (bar 54, section M), as Ligeti himself describes it in one introductory text[11]. This rupture is coupled with the moment when McCauley turns away and decides to stop the burglary — and Hanna realizes that he won't get hold of him this time and lets him go.

The Concerto's first movement has been used in other films, for example in the documentary *Over Your Cities Grass Will Grow* and in the mystery thriller *The Killing of a Sacred Deer* (IE/UK 2017), which will be discussed later. Generally, the films take advantage of the pieces' essential qualities. In the Cello Concerto movement, its diversified states of tension in particular make it attractive for soundtracks. The same applies to *Lontano*, which is furthermore appreciated for its associative character, alluded to in the title — and observable in the music. With manifold, constantly changing, sometimes superimposed intervallic constellations («eine allmähliche Metamorphose von intervallischen Konstellationen»[12]) Ligeti purposely created impressions of spatial and temporal distance, which are also brought to bear in the neo-noir psychological thriller *Shutter Island* (USA 2010)[13]. Like in *The Shining*, excerpts from *Lontano* accompany appearances of «ghosts from the past», partly even the same sections as in Kubrick's film are used. That Scorsese's film begins with *Lontano* played during the title sequence can be interpreted as a literal foreshadowing and gives a hint on the films' subject, the shadows of memory behind — and sometimes passing — «the shutter» or the lid of the protagonist's repressed memory. While on the surface U.S. Marshal Teddy Daniels (Leonardo DiCaprio) investigates the disappearance of a mentally abnormal murderess from a hospital island that is supposed to be escape-proof, the real story is about his own past, his traumas, and crimes. The doctors' plan to bring his memories back with a complex role game eventually fails, apparently

---

[11]. LIGETI 2007, vol. II, p. 244. «Der erste Satz besteht aus einem einzigen Spannungsbogen mit einem deutlichen Höhepunkt an der Stelle, an der das Solocello plötzlich zu hohen Flageolettönen übergeht. Diese Stelle wirkt wie ein Riß: Der Bogen wird weiter und weiter gespannt, bis er die Spannung nicht mehr aushält. Hier stellt die abstrakte musikalische Form einen fast konkreten Materialzustand dar».

[12]. *Ibidem*, p. 245.

[13]. Unlike *Lontano*, I couldn't locate *Harmonies* from the Two Etudes for Organ, which is also credited in the film's end titles. Regarding the question of associations of distance in the reception of *Lontano* see BULLERJAHN 1989.

because these memories are just too cruel — in his function as marshal he was taking part in the liberation of the Dachau concentration camp and in private life his manic-depressive wife has killed their three children (see *The Shining*!). The use of *Lontano* can be understood as a reference to Kubrick's film[14]. Martin Scorsese's long-time collaborator Robbie Robertson, who acted as a music supervisor for *Shutter Island* compiled the soundtrack exclusively from existing, mostly «modern classical music»[15] by, among others, John Cage, Krzysztof Penderecki, Morton Feldman, Alfred Schnittke, Gustav Mahler, and György Ligeti, stating that «[t]his may be the most outrageous and beautiful soundtrack I've ever heard»[16]. What Robertson is not talking about here, yet has been addressed in literature on film music, is the self-referentiality of (Hollywood) cinema that is noticeable in *Shutter Island*[17].

Yet another psychological thriller with a compiled soundtrack containing music by Ligeti is Yorgos Lanthimos's *The Killing of a Sacred Deer* from 2017. The first movement of the Cello Concerto and the «Lento e deserto», that is the second movement of the Piano Concerto (1985-88) are combined with other avant-garde works by Sofia Gubaidulina and Jani Christou, as well as choral works by Franz Schubert (Stabat Mater D 383, 'Jesus Christus schwebt am Kreuze') and Johann Sebastian Bach ('Herr, unser Herrscher' from the St. John Passion, BWV 245), among others. Due to the way the pieces are employed they give an impression fraught with meaning, some even portentous, though some 'over the top' couplings create a cynical distance, too. The film, set in present-day Cincinnati (USA), is not only based on Euripides's tragedy *Iphigenia at Aulis* but is also an exceedingly metaphorical film. 16-year-old half-orphan Martin is invited to the family of the wealthy heart surgeon Steven who sometimes takes care of him to help him with his grief about his father. As it turns out later in the film, Steven was responsible for the father's death on the operating table, because he had been drinking alcohol before the surgery. After Martin has met Steven's family he sets in motion a perfidious plan of revenge, in which Steven is instructed to kill one of his family members as redemption. Otherwise, Martin threatens to kill the family one by one slowly through a curse. The density of the music increases more and more as the plot thickens (a principle that can be observed in *The Shining*, too); it is mostly tuned quite loudly and therefore from the beginning very present on the surface. At times diegetic sounds are even absent when the music plays. While the massive choral works by Schubert and Bach frame the film and contribute to the 'sacred' aspect, at least amplifying the message that one is always subject to more powerful and mystical forces, the avant-garde pieces chime in at different points. For example, Gubaidulina's *De profundis* for accordion, which is

---

[14]. The musical reference to *The Shining* is not the only one, but references are also made on other levels, such as the image, see WITTMANN 2013.

[15]. KRAWEN 2011.

[16]. Quoted after ROSS 2010.

[17]. See KUPFER 2012.

used repeatedly in the film's first half, gives the impression of a strange breathing, especially the high frequencies seeming very unsettled. In the film's second half only orchestral pieces are used, and the passages featuring music become considerably longer. Moreover, the excerpts and textures that have been selected from the works are similar, like parts of Ligeti's Piano Concerto. They all underpin suspenseful scenes on the way from peripeteia to catastrophe — and are arranged accordingly. Most relevant is the slowly growing tension, reaching its peak (with section M, just like in *Heat*) during the final shooting.

While the Cello Concerto excerpts, though manipulated, stand by themselves, the first excerpt from the Piano Concerto (second movement, «Lento e deserto») is accompanying a brutal scene in which Steven threatens to shoot Martin. The excerpt starts with the strongly attacked, descending chords of sections S-T (bar 75, *fffff*) and continues until the movement's end, the chromatic descent played by a chromonica, giving the moment a bizarre touch. The other excerpt from the «Lento»-movement is not identical with the former. Bars 4-19 (from section A and B), a very thin texture with a sustained double bass tone at the base and short, mostly chromatic motifs of the piccolo flute and the bassoon are repeated one time (unlike in the original piece) and create a curious though not very tense or aggressive atmosphere in a scene in which Steven's wife Anna takes care of Martin's wounds.

A similar compilation from the «Lento»-movement is used in the series *Homeland* (episode 4, 'Redwood'). The cue is compiled from bars 4-19 (that are repeated) and section F (bars 32-35), in which the piano plays descending chromatic lines in *ppp*, then accompanied by dizzy chords in the high strings. In the given narrative context — a former soldier tells that he can't leave his traumatic memories — the motifs, especially those of the woodwinds, really appear like sighs. Even a short flashback is interjected to illustrate his haunting images, interestingly a harmonica laying on a dusty ground.

One more film containing the «Lento»-movement is *La Douleur* (FR 2017), which is based on autobiographical texts by Marguerite Duras about her waiting and desperate fight for the return of her husband, who has been arrested and deported by the Nazis for his activities in the Résistance. On the auditory level, which 'hovers' over the action, there are voice-overs of Duras's text as well as passages from the «Lento» and from Luigi Nono's *'Hay que caminar' soñando* (1989). Music is used sparingly (eleven cues in all) and both pieces basically alternate. The six excerpts of the «Lento e deserto», which are spread throughout the film, all start with the deep sustained cello tone from the movement's beginning, always continue well into section B or until the slide whistle and ocarina come in, the longest cue running through to section F (solo piano). They underpin — but also seem to slow down — Marguerite's agonizing restlessness during her lonesome struggle, though the exact placements seem a bit random.

Finally, I would like to look at Sophie Fiennes's documentary *Over Your Cities Grass Will Grow* (F/NL/UK 2010) about the eponymous work by the German artist Anselm Kiefer. On the one hand the film concentrates on the creative processes and follows Kiefer and his assistants at work, on the other hand it offers the viewer a slow uncommented tour of the site — a former silk factory in southern France, where Kiefer created an artistic synthesis of architecture, painting, installation, and landscape, including a labyrinth of tunnels, buildings, bridges, lakes, and towers. Kiefer's mostly big and heavy, material-intensive, and achromatic works are explorations of themes such as mythology, mysticism, or biblical language. For the long passages presenting the artworks a piece by Jörg Widmann, the tenth of his *Free Pieces for Ensemble*, and three by Ligeti have been selected: *Lontano*, the Cello Concerto's first movement, and *Atmosphères*. *Lontano* is played completely during a tour of a tunnel system and along buildings, above and below ground, in dusky and bright light showing different rooms and objects, without it becoming clear how they relate to each other. As it were, the spatial confusion and changes of light are amplified by the music, adding constantly changing shapes and shadings on a musical level. After a long section showing production processes and the interview, the first movement of the Cello Concerto is played in its entirety to images of austere, artificial interiors furnished with strange objects and artefacts. The music seems to dock onto the relative monotony of the place, with the objects shown being reminiscent of their possible former 'lives'. Finally, *Atmosphères* accompanies a tour of the concrete towers, ending at dawn. Here, the focus seems to be on the materiality, as the concrete architectural sculptures are shown in different landscapes and states, including a lot of construction waste. The famous orchestral piece has not been shortened either and is continuing into the film's end titles. Its placement seems to correspond to Ligeti's compositional idea of initial states transforming into new and different ones[18].

According to her own statement[19], Sophie Fiennes came across Ligeti's music via Alex Ross's book *The Rest is Noise: Listening to the Twentieth Century* and initially had inhibitions to employ music that had been famously used by Stanley Kubrick before (obviously not realizing that she was not at all the first to reuse it[20]). During the production process of the film — which is in fact based on an initiative by Kiefer and his Roman gallerist Lorcan O'Neill (!) —, Fiennes showed Kiefer her material with Ligeti's music, probably *Atmosphères*, who reportedly reacted to the music «as sound»[21], and asked whether there was more music of Ligeti that could be added[22].

---

[18]. LIGETI 2007, vol. II, p. 181.

[19]. Audio commentary, in FIENNES 2010.

[20]. «I thought, god, this is a bit cheeky of me to reuse this music in another way, but then I thought, no, it's maybe time to get away from those plastic rooms and hallucinogenic sequences and do something completely different with the music». *Ibidem*, audio commentary.

[21]. «Er reagierte auf sie als Klang». *Ibidem*, booklet, p. 8.

[22]. In the film's audio commentary, Fiennes talks about the reasons for her choice in more detail: «I wanted some music that would relate to the spiritual emotional theme as in the work and when I came across this musique statique of Ligeti it's also formally fascinating, [...] because it's not made with the kind of melodies that you would

György Ligeti's Film Music beyond Stanley Kubrick

Although Fiennes's description of the relation of Ligeti's music to Kiefer's work as a «dialogue» can be considered inaccurate, she still relates them to each other in various ways, giving the impression that Ligeti's pieces are literally employed here as *art to inflate art*.

The filmmaker used Ligeti's music again in her documentary *The Pervert's Guide to Ideology*, featuring Slovenian philosopher Slavoj Žižek. Here, Ligeti's *Clocks and Clouds* is employed alongside Beethoven's Ninth Symphony and a couple of (mostly Russian) revolutionary songs. Ligeti's piece is clearly set apart from the other selected pieces in terms of content. It is also used in a different function, accompanying pictures of revolutionary scenes in the film's concluding section where Žižek talks about the «depressing lesson of the last decades». The music — a fast swirling instrumental pattern combined with wafting female voices — seems to correspond with the swarming masses of people shown in the montage and in this respect moves on the cinematic meta-level.

Looking at the films in which Ligeti's music has been featured since it first appeared in Kubrick's space epic more than half a century ago, it becomes clear that certain standards were set by *2001*. One of the most influential 'innovations' certainly was the use of pre-existing recordings as compositional material of a film score, another the accompanying plurality and heterogeneity of the music, which nowadays is rarely from the same mould. In all the films considered here (except for a few short films) Ligeti's music was always used alongside that of other composers. Contextualisation (which can of course also result in contrast) thus takes place not only through a connection with cinematic sequences or plots, but also on the musical level — in any event, Ligeti is never alone. Recordings of his works are often compiled with other works by composers of (more or less) his generation, like John Cage (*Shutter Island*), Jani Christou (*Killing of a Sacred Deer*), George Crumb (*For the End of Time*), Morton Feldman (*Shutter Island*), Philip Glass (*Merci la vie, Miss Gulag*), Sofia Gubaidulina (*Killing of a Sacred Deer, For the End of Time*), Luigi Nono (*La Douleur*), Krzysztof Penderecki (*The Shining, Bang Bang Orangutang, For the End of Time*), Arvo Pärt (*Bang Bang Orangutang*), Steve Reich (*Miss Gulag*), or Edgard Varèse ('A Warning to the Curious'). They have been inserted in between period music (as in *Schalcken the Painter*), beside older art music and popular music, but remarkably rarely in the context of original film scores (as in *Fist of Fury* and *Godzilla*).

---

have in classical pieces of orchestration. The first piece and the last piece are both full orchestral pieces, but they don't have bombastic musical closures. Everything is suspended, in a sense open ended. There is not the [...] feeling of 'Here we are, great anthemic collective certainty'. And it's this lack of certainty the music creates. The suspension that I think has a dialogue with Kiefer's work. It's also the layering of chords and the harmonics that come through literally layering sound in a way that he's layering texture [...]. It was a project of Ligeti to create music that would [...] make time stand still or create an object of time. So, in that sense it's like a sculpture [...] using time and to turn it into a sculpture and so that idea of monumentality that is inherent to what Ligeti is doing with his musique statique [...]. I was very happy when I discovered this could work». *Ibidem*, audio commentary. Fiennes de facto talks more about the music and about Ligeti, though some of her statements are uninformed. This, however, is not the subject of this article.

This range of uses is broad and, in some cases, surprising, starting with *Atmosphères*' most striking snippet-appearance as «the boiling of Bruce Lee» in *Fist of Fury* from 1972 to the inclusion of three pieces in full length in Sophie Fiennes's documentary about Anselm Kiefer's *Over Your City Grass Will Grow* from 2010. The music fulfils very different functions, reaching from the 'profane' reflection of a character's mood (*Fist of Fury*, *Homeland*) and the generation of tension[23] (*Heat*, *Shutter Island*, *The Killing of a Sacred Deer*, etc.) over spine-chilling effects (*As Above, So Below*; *The Whole Town's Sleeping*, etc.), absurd and comic moments (*Merci la vie*, *Suuri performanssi*), nocturnal and poetic colorings (*Cartas da Guerra*, *Viagem a Portugal*), the amplification of discrepancy (*Miss Gulag*) to a quasi-religious charge of meaning (*Godzilla*, *For the End of Time*) and the creation of ambience or atmosphere (*2001*, 'A Warning to the Curious', *Over Your Cities Grass Will Grow*, *Other Worlds*).

Whether the music is manipulated, shortened, cut[24], reassembled, faded in or out, or adjusted in terms of dynamics, it always remains identifiably Ligeti — even though most of the audience will probably not perceive Ligeti's music in films as quoted concert music, but rather as genuine film music.

Some of Ligeti's music seems virtually predestined for films, and a couple of '*favourite parts*', like the aforementioned section from the Cello Concerto's first movement, have crystallized as such. It is indeed remarkable how frequently ideas and imaginations which Ligeti often figuratively delineated in commentaries on his compositions appear concretized in films, as if the filmmakers had first read his texts. Apparently, they understood Ligeti's music perfectly well, even if this understanding usually refers to specific aspects and not necessarily to the whole, which, of course, means that structural aspects recede (often completely) into the background and internal references hardly play a role. Though, in my opinion, it is by no means certain whether the use of complete pieces in Fiennes's film on Kiefer's work is indeed more congenial than the uninhibited use of that *Atmosphères* snippet in *Fist of Fury*.

Nevertheless, the category of 'pure music', as which the pieces used in the films discussed were originally intended, still hovers over the scenery like a signpost. In an interview with Josef Häusler in 1967, Ligeti declared:

---

[23]. On its website Schott advertises the licensing of *Lontano*'s synch-rights as follows: «Lontano has not only established itself in the concert repertoire, but has also found its way as film music into Hollywood blockbusters. This is no surprise as the work is ideal for the generation of an almost unbearable tension as Stanley Kubrick realised during the production of *The Shining* in 1980. Now Martin Scorsese is also exploiting Ligeti's "harmonic crystallisation": in his new film *Shutter Island* (2010), Leonardo DiCaprio stalks through Block C of the psychiatric hospital to the strains of Lontano». In: <https://en.schott-music.com/shop/lontano-no175056.html>, accessed May 2022.

[24]. Interestingly, excerpts are very often taken from pieces' beginnings or climaxes (*Atmosphères* section F-G, Cello Concerto, mvt. 1, beginning etc.).

> Whenever I listen to music, I see colours and shapes. But that does not signify that it is literary or illustrative music in the sense of programme music. If I say, for example, that *Lontano* is a work in which colours and space are very significant, these colours and this space exist only in the music. *Lontano*, distance, remoteness, as an aura of feeling that surrounds this music, is to be understood as a purely musical category. It has nothing to do with programme music as in Liszt, Berlioz or Strauss, for example. If I were to mention Debussy and Mahler, two composers whom I especially love, I would say that their music brings in its wake, as a comet in its train, a whole wide area of associations from every level of human experience. In this way, music or the artificial product, "a work of art", is truly bound for me with every stratum of imagination and of actual life. But everything is transposed into music! So I would say: Programme music without a programme, music that is developed extensively in its associations, yet pure music. Everything that is direct and unambiguous is alien to me. I love allusions, equivocal utterances, things that have many interpretations, uncertainties, background meanings. And the various figurative associations in my music are also ambiguous, as I see them, think them or feel them while I imagine music[25].

Of course, one can find obvious, unambiguous couplings unappealing, but one can also enjoy that a music fits a scene, which, according to Ligeti's own account, he eventually did himself, as in the cases of *2001* or *Eyes Wide Shut*[26]. After all, the interplay of film, or of various filmic elements with music generates new — and unique — kinds of meanings, associations, and (aesthetic) experiences.

Bibliography

BULLERJAHN 1989
BULLERJAHN, Claudia. 'Assoziationen für Kenner? Zu Ligetis außermusikalischen Anspielungen, erläutert am Beispiel des Orchesterstücks *Lontano* (1967)', in: *Zeitschrift für Musikpädagogik*, XIV/51 (1989), pp. 9-23.

FIENNES 2010
FIENNES, Sophie. *Over Your Cities Grass Will Grow*, DVD, Mindjazz Pictures, 738329080525, 2010.

FRIEDMAN s.d.
FRIEDMAN, Ivan Maria. 'Other Worlds', plot summary, *Internet Movie Database*, s.d., <https://www.imdb.com/title/tt13183542/plotsummary?ref_=tt_ov_pl>, accessed May 2022.

---

[25]. LIGETI 1983, p. 102.

[26]. See LIGETI 2001 and Ligeti's statement in Jan Harlan's documentary *Stanley Kubrick: A Life in Pictures* (USA 2001).

HEIMERDINGER 2007
HEIMERDINGER, Julia. *Neue Musik im Spielfilm*, Saarbrücken, Pfau, 2007.

HEIMERDINGER 2011
EAD. '«I Have Been Compromised. I Am now Fighting against It»: Ligeti vs. Kubrick and the Music for *2001: A Space Odyssey*', in: *The Journal of Film Music*, III/2 (2011), pp. 127-143.

HEIMERDINGER 2018
EAD. 'Populäre Adaptionen. György Ligetis Musik in Stanley Kubricks Film *2001: A Space Odyssey*', in: *RE-SET. Rückgriffe und Fortschreibungen in der Musik seit 1900*, edited by Simon Obert and Heidy Zimmermann, Mainz, Schott, 2018, pp. 302-309.

KREWEN 2011
KREWEN, Nick. 'Robbie Robertson. Finding Good Medicine by Fearlessly Facing His Past', in: *M Music & Musicians*, May 2011, <https://mmusicmag.com/m/2011/08/robbie-robertson/>, accessed May 2022.

KUPFER 2012
KUPFER, Diana. 'Neue Musik und Neo-Noir: Martin Scorseses *Shutter Island*', in: *Kieler Beiträge zur Filmmusikforschung*, no. 8 (2012), pp. 200-230, <http://www.filmmusik.uni-kiel.de/KB8/KB8-Kupfer.pdf>, accessed May 2022.

LEVY 2017
LEVY, Benjamin R. *Metamorphosis in Music: The Compositions of György Ligeti in the 1950s and 1960s*, Oxford-New York, Oxford University Press, 2017.

LIGETI 1983
LIGETI, György. 'György Ligeti – Josef Häusler', in: *György Ligeti in Conversation with Péter Várnai, Josef Häusler, Claude Samuel, and Himself*, translated by Gabor J. Schabert, Sarah E. Soulsby, Terence Kilmartin and Geoffrey Skelton, London, Eulenburg, 1983 (Eulenburg Music Series), pp. 83-110.

LIGETI 2001
ID. 'Ligeti im Streit mit Kubrick: für 3000 Dollar *2001* – Atmosphäre – Interview mit György Ligeti', in: *Die Welt*, 1 March 2001, <https://www.welt.de/print-welt/article436785/Ligeti-im-Streit-mit-Kubrick.html>, accessed May 2022.

LIGETI 2007
ID. *Gesammelte Schriften*, edited by Monika Lichtenfeld, 2 vols., Mainz, Schott, 2007 (Veröffentlichungen der Paul Sacher Stiftung, 10).

MCQUISTON 2011
MCQUISTON, Kate. '«An Effort to Decide»: More Research into Kubrick's Music Choices for *2001: A Space Odyssey*', in: *The Journal of Film Music*, III/2 (2011), pp. 145-154.

Merkley 2007
Merkley, Paul. '«Stanley Hates this but I Like It!» North vs. Kubrick on the Music for *2001: A Space Odyssey*', in: *The Journal of Film Music*, II/1 (2007), pp. 1-34.

Ross 2010
Ross, Alex. 'Lo and Behold!', in: *The New Yorker*, 3 February 2010, <https://www.newyorker.com/culture/alex-ross/lo-and-behold>, accessed May 2022.

Scovell 2014
Scovell, Adam. 'The Aural Aesthetics of Ghosts in BBC Ghost Stories', 2014 (unpublished).

Wittmann 2013
Wittmann, Matthias. 'Mnemozid auf *Shutter Island* (2010). Scorseses Traumatologie des 20. Jahrhunderts', in: *Österreichische Zeitschrift für Geschichtswissenschaften*, XXIV/3 (2013), pp. 79-102.

Reading Ligeti

Letters from Stanford:
György Ligeti to Aliutė Mečys

Vita Gruodytė
(Lithuanian Academy of Music and Theatre, Vilnius)

Introduction

Aliutė Mečys (Metschies, Meczies) was born in Koblenz (Germany), in 1943. From 1959-1962 she attended Walter-Leister drawing and painting school in Trier. For a year (1963-1964) she was taking up lessons in the studio of painter Erich Wessel in Hamburg and, in addition also worked as a scenography and costume design assistant. From 1964-1968 she studied at the Munich Academy of Fine Arts under Professor Rudolph Heinrich, went on study tours to France and Italy. From 1968-1979 she was occupied with stage and costume design at various theatres and on TV (Schiller Theatre in Berlin, Hamburg Opera, Stockholm Royal Opera, Royal Opera House Covent Garden in London. She was also engaged in organizing stage design and costume exhibitions. Her most famous theatrical work became the opera *Le Grand Macabre* (1974-1977), created together with György Ligeti[1].

Little is known about the friendship and artistic collaboration between György Ligeti and Aliutė Mečys (1943-2013), a scenographer, costume designer, and painter of Lithuanian descent who lived in Hamburg (Germany). Aliutė hinted at their bond in merely two of her interviews, published in German and Lithuanian[2], while Ligeti never mentioned it in any written source[3]. Thus, the only documentary material about their twenty-two-year-long

---

[1]. Andriušytė-Žukienė 2014, p. 134.
[2]. Herms-Bohnhoff 1995a and Mečys 1998.
[3]. Many thanks to the Paul Sacher Foundation in Basel for providing access to the Ligeti archive.

relationship[4] that began in Darmstadt[5] shortly after Ligeti's arrival in the West consists of the letters exchanged between them[6] while Ligeti was composer-in-residence for the first semester of 1972 at Stanford University. They were preserved by Aliutė together with her surviving drawings and paintings depicting Ligeti[7].

This correspondence is valuable primarily because the Stanford period coincided with a very intense and important time of Ligeti's career and with the genesis of his opera *Le Grand Macabre*. In early 1972, Oedipus was scheduled to be the plot of the future opera; it was to be staged by Göran Gentele, the then director of the Metropolitan Opera in New York. Ligeti described his conversation with Gentele in a letter to Aliutė on 15 February:

> Gentele wants from me, quasi as a replacement for his Stockholm plans, an operatic piece for New York — and he insists on it being Oidipus, but a shorter one (about 1 hour or 45 minutes), and for a chamber stage — not for the Metropolitan as they don't play modern pieces there at all, but there is a good chamber theatre in the Lincoln Center, part of the Metropolitan (something like an experimental stage); he wants to do *Aventures* there in 1973 and then Oidipus in 74 or 75. [...] So I have to write two operatic pieces, but that is quite good.

A month after Ligeti's last letter from Stanford, on July 18, Gentele was killed in a car accident. «In search of a new style, the project team for a representation in Stockholm met towards the end of 1972 in Berlin-Wilmersdorf: it consisted of Michael Meschke, stage director and director of the Stockholm Puppet Theatre, Aliutė Mečys, stage designer, and musicologist Ove Nordwall. [...] Aliutė Mečys suddenly remembered that there was indeed such a play, and she brought us *La Balade du Grand Macabre* of Ghelderode»[8]. Thus, Aliutė, who at that time collaborated with the Schiller Theatre in Berlin, both suggested the plot for the opera and was also the set and costume designer of its first production at the Royal Swedish Opera (Kungliga Operan) in Stockholm (1978).

Aliutė's letters to Ligeti testify to her active involvement in the search for the plot at the beginning of 1972. She wrote: «So far I have read a lot of texts, still hoping to find THE 'ideal' material for an opera for you without success»[9]. In return, Ligeti thanked her: «Thank you

---

[4]. Herms-Bohnhoff 1995b, p. 172.
[5]. According to a letter from Ligeti to Aliutė, 18 May 1972 (NČDM archive in Kaunas, Lithuania).
[6]. Many thanks to the M. K. Čiurlionis National Museum of Art (Kaunas, Lithuania), for providing access to the Aliutė Mečys archive and for permission to publish the extracts of letters. I also thank Vera Ligeti for permission to publish them.
[7]. Some of them have been used for Ligeti's vinyl record covers: Ligeti 2021 and Ligeti 1986.
[8]. Ligeti 2013, pp. 268-269.
[9]. Letter from Aliutė to Ligeti, 8 February 1972, NČDM archive in Kaunas.

Letters from Stanford: György Ligeti to Aliutė Mečys

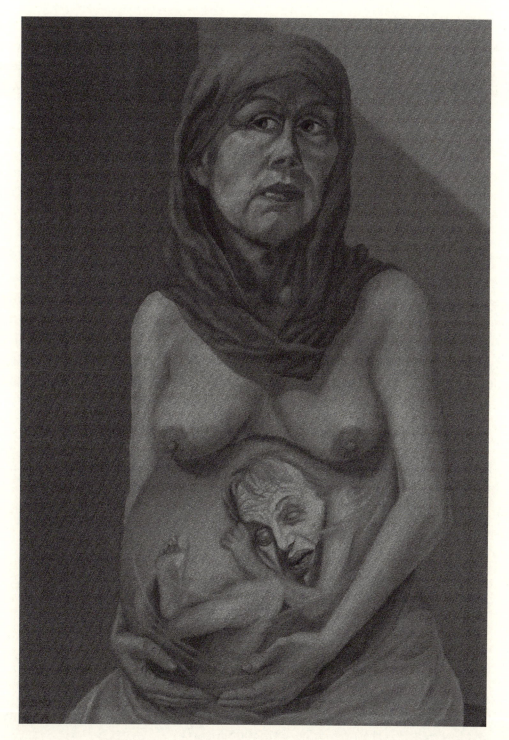

Ill. 1: Aliutė Mečys, *Mother* (1982), oil/fibreboard, 59.5 x 41.5 cm © 2021, Photo: Forum für Künstlernachlässe (FKN) Hamburg.

for reading and looking around so much»[10]. Aliutė confirmed the fact in her interview with Raminta Lampsatis: «We set up the project of the opera *Le Grand Macabre* together with Ligeti. [...] I chose the subject and persuaded Ligeti to use it. I created the costumes and set design. [...] I proposed that the chief of the police would be a bird on roller skates, and the king, on stilts»[11].

Ghelderode's *Ballad* corresponded to Ligeti's «musico-dramatic concepts» at the time: «an end of the world that doesn't really take place; as hero, death, which is perhaps only a small mountebank»[12]. However, there is a possibility that Ghelderode's work, directly inspired by Breughel's *The Triumph of Death*, also resonated with the tragic death of Gentele. There is also another possibility of the visual aesthetics of the opera having been influenced by Aliutė's eschatological vision of the world, glaucous and secret, in the tradition of Hieronymus Bosch or Pieter Breughel: «In the paintings of Aliutė, Death appears in person — in her pictures, hands and eyes disappear, she even removes Death's eye itself. Death rages, and only the act of painting can fight against it», wrote art historian Dietrich Diederichs Gottschalk[13]. «In her paintings, she herself plays different roles behind different masks [...]. Aliutė has only one goal — capture the evil spirits, lock them in the space of the painting, and thus continue to live with them»[14], noted gallerist Gerd Wolfgang Essen. The opera's characters are also made as masks or puppets: they do not undergo changes or develop, have no temporal direction. Hence their archetypal appearance. These symbol-objects represent a wide range of emotional and psychological affects, from the lowest (e.g. the alcoholic Piet, the shrew Mescalina) to the highest (e.g. the goddess Venus or the couple in love).

Painting came to Aliutė's life quite late. Around 1979[15], she ended her successful career as a scenographer and stage designer[16] to devote herself entirely to painting[17]. Up to her death she remained a freelance artist, living in her favourite (albeit poor) Schanzen quarter in Hamburg. She began to actively participate in exhibitions; some of her works were acquired by Vladimir Karbusický and his wife[18].

---

[10]. Ligeti's undated answer to Aliutė's letter of 8 February 1972, NČDM archive in Kaunas.

[11]. Mečys 1998, p. 65.

[12]. Ligeti 2013, p. 269.

[13]. Mečys 1998, p. 66.

[14]. *Ibidem*.

[15]. After the premiere of the opera in Stockholm Ligeti and Aliutė went their separate ways. Maybe her decision has something to do with this split.

[16]. Unfortunately, most of her work for stage has nor survived.

[17]. 24 May 1992, letter to Jonas Jurašas, NČDM archive in Kaunas.

[18]. Mečys 1998, p. 64. Vladimir Karbusický (1925-2002) was Chair of Systematic Musicology at the University of Hamburg.

Letters from Stanford: György Ligeti to Aliutė Mečys

In her early thirties, Aliutė established contacts with the Lithuanian community in Hamburg. She was extremely interested in the processes related to Lithuanian independence, and always signed her paintings using a Lithuanian form of her name (Mečys). To Raminta Lampsatis she said: «Lithuania has been my homeland for decades. I have created for myself visionary country from paintings, literature, narratives. This is my "private" Lithuania [...]. When I dream about Lithuania, I imagine cities, especially Vilnius and Kaunas [...]. Witches are for me part of Lithuanian countryside — in alle kinds of combinations. Lithuanian music is part of my visual world-folk music [...]».

An autobiographical background expressly permeates Aliutė's creation, so Ligeti, as an important part of her life, naturally became one of the figures in her imagery. Elke Herms-Bohnhoff wrote:

> Ligeti often features in her paintings. Sometimes as a protective, paternal figure that holds a woman in his lap/womb like a child. The woman is much smaller than the man, pale, and bleeding from the mouth. Sometimes as a human being who wears his own face as a mask. On one portrait he is presented from many angles at the same time, just like a character that can only be understood when looked at from different perspectives while remaining strangely beyond reach. Yet always the canvas speaks of a person with whom the painter has a difficult relationship. On a self-portrait Ligeti features as an embryo in the womb of the painter who is wearing a headscarf[19]. "As a Turkish mum with a headscarf I offered him a nice place to be. It was an offer of reconciliation". Whether he can accept it? "I never imagined that one day he would be displayed in an exhibition a dozen times, and that there are, of course, many people who will know him". That was rather naïve and made the rumor mill work overtime. Because few people are able to separate the person from the picture and take the picture as a statement that also has meaning with regard to other human beings. Today she wouldn't do something like that anymore. With the exhibition this part of her life was complete and no longer on her mind[20].

Aliutė and Ligeti were probably brought closer together not only by their artistic sensitivity, but also by a similar perception of the epoch and possibly by some individual traumatic experiences[21]. Both already shared certain experiences before they met: they felt uprooted, foreigners in the countries in which they lived, and they were strongly marked by war. Ligeti had written about it in the biography of his Jewishness[22], a typewritten copy of

---

[19]. This painting is *Mother* (1982), reproduced here as Ill. 1. Ill. 2 shows *Self-Portrait with Ligeti* (1982). The painting on the cover of this book is also by Mečys (untitled, 1985). All are reproduced with kind permission by the Forum für Künstlernachlässe in Hamburg.

[20]. Herms-Bohnhoff 1995b, p. 173.

[21]. For more information, see Gruodytė 2018.

[22]. Ligeti 2007.

which Aliutė kept together with his letters. Meanwhile, Aliutė was marked by the Nazi past of her father, who was a member of the SS troops during the war[23]. She, too, felt a foreigner in Germany even though she was born there. In an interview, she said: «I am different from the majority of Germans, despite the fact that I am a hybrid and have half German blood»[24], and then again: «We were always the Others, the Foreigners, during the war and the postwar period. I always felt an outsider, extraneous, a queer bird»[25].

It may be for this reason that we can find in both artists a common attraction to psychological processes and emotional states, which form the basis of Aliutė's work:

> I am interested in processes [...], in interior development. I do not belong either to the surrealists or the hyperrealists. I have created the word that suits me: unrealism. What does not exist in reality, yet is real. I paint in a very realistic way, but it is impossible to find these things in the real world. The content is not real, and at the same time it is real, since these states, these processes, these directions exist — I find them when I am painting and thinking. Why are the characters of my paintings crippled, blind, decadent, broken, aged? Because there is no normal human being on this earth, at least, I've never met one. That is why there is a reality that is an unreality[26].

When viewing Ligeti's opera through the prism of both the epoch and of his personal experiences, we can see it not only as an original and exclusive opus (in the context of his other compositions), but also as a product of the relationship, collaboration, and intellectual compatibility between two creative personalities. Perhaps some aspects of the said opera, containing multiple clues for its understanding, will only become apparent through the awareness of these reciprocal influences. Because without understanding the closeness of the artists at the time, it would be difficult to understand these letters as well.

Ligeti's letters survived only thanks to professor Raminta Lampsatis, a pianist and musicologist living and working in Hamburg[27]. She was a long-time friend of Aliutė's and a colleague of Ligeti at the Hamburg Music and Theatre Academy [Hochschule für Musik und Theater Hamburg]. After Aliutė's death (2013), Raminta Lampsatis and her students saved as many of her works and belongings as possible. Eventually Aliutė's drawings and personal documents (including her correspondence with Ligeti) found their way into the archives of the Mikalojus Konstantinas Čiurlionis Museum in Kaunas, Lithuania. In 2014, an exhibition of a

---

[23]. Aliutė grew up in the family of a Lithuanian father, Werner by name, and a German mother (her name is unknown).
[24]. Mečys 1998, p. 65.
[25]. Herms-Bohnhoff 1995b, p. 169.
[26]. Mečys 1998, p. 65.
[27]. Interview with Raminta Lampsatis (December 2015).

Letters from Stanford: György Ligeti to Aliutė Mečys

Ill. 2: Aliutė Mečys, *Self-Portrait with Ligeti* (1982) oil on canvas, 70 x 50 cm © 2021, Photo: Forum für Künstlernachlässe (FKN) Hamburg.

small part of Aliutė's art was held in the M. Žilinskas Art Gallery (Kaunas), and a comprehensive catalogue was published[28]. After the exhibition, her paintings returned to the Forum of Artists' Legacies [*Forum für Künstlernachlässe*] in Hamburg, where they are presently kept.

Aliutė preserved not only Ligeti's letters, but also the duplicates of her own typed or handwritten answers. This very short epistolary period is primarily interesting in its fullness. It reflects not only a very intimate but also a professionally interesting relationship. Maybe someday all of her letters will be published in full, along with postcards, telegrams, and other minor documents.

The correspondence consists of eight letters from Ligeti (29 January to 18 May, 1972) and twelve letters from Aliutė (21 January to 24 May, 1972). For this chapter key extracts from Ligeti's letters were selected, interspersed with a handful of quotations from Aliutė's side that help understanding what Ligeti refers to. The letters are quite long, and therefore they are both informative and also reveal the style of thinking and writing of these two creative minds, which reflects a very specific atmosphere of the relationship between them. The writing style of both is reminiscent of an uninterrupted conversation, almost a stream of consciousness, jumping directly from one topic to another: from everyday details to work, from common acquaintances to feelings, from health problems to future plans, or from professional problems to new commissions. Punctuation does not matter in the letters, they seem to have neither a beginning nor an end; sometimes a letter is interrupted and then continued the next day. Both of them mention from time to time that this correspondence and the mutual support it provides are important to them, and thus it reflects a very strong mutual trust — both personal and professional. One can sense that Ligeti appreciated Aliutė's opinion, while Ligeti's personality and his advice helped Aliutė in her work as a theatre scenographer at the time, when she was working on Goethe's *Urfaust* at the Schiller Theatre in Berlin in early 1972. In his letters, Ligeti reveals himself not only as a creatively active and observant contextualist, but also as a sensitive epistolary partner. In his last letter on May 18 we can read:

> It is so strange: I just wanted to write to you quickly that I need you, and before I got down to writing your letter arrived, and you wrote to me EXACTLY the words I wanted to send to you. [...] my feeling (and opinion) has increased that you are the most wonderful woman. I knew that from the first day, but it got more and more obvious over time, [...] in the past we didn't write letters that long to each other, that is you wrote wonderful letters to me, but I didn't as I'm lazy about writing; but now the long absence led to us writing long letters, not so much I, but you wrote me the most wonderful letters, as we were talking to each other, and that opened up to me another aspect of you, I can't explain it very well, you will understand. [...] This feeling is a kind of trust. I had this trust in you all along

---

[28]. ANDRIUŠYTĖ-ŽUKIENĖ 2014.

Letters from Stanford: György Ligeti to Aliutė Mečys

(otherwise we wouldn't have been together the way we were and are), yet this trust has increased during the time of separation. I was deeply moved somehow that you have such a deep trust in me [...]. You have been good to me, in the way you wrote to me. You have, as a "person" or "personality" a high element of integrity, and that is important both for your potential as an artist, as well as my relationship to you, as I'm feeling a higher and higher "esteem" for you — please, Aliutė, darling, don't laugh about this word, you know how I mean it.

***

Nowadays, Aliutė Mečys is attributable to the group of Western modernist artists who have experienced the existential crisis in the second half of the twentieth century. Her creation is an authentic commentary on personal experiences and public events. Art filled with anxiety, fear, mental conflicts, loneliness, images of personal degradation sprang up not yesterday. Such characteristics are frequent in European painting from Hieronymus Bosch to Lucian Freud. Therefore, paintings by a modest artist from Hamburg should be remembered when trying to perceive a Western citizen of the mid-20th century who had survived war, felt a collective guilt and was disturbed by love and freedom[29].

---

[29]. *Ibidem*, p. 140.

Vita Gruodytė

Ligeti's Letters to Aliutė Mečys (Extracts)

Published with kind permission by Vera Ligeti and the M. K. Čiurlionis National Museum of Art, Kaunas

Letter 1

Stanford 29th Jan. 72

Aliutė, darling,

All VERY STRANGE (starting with this typewriter from the age of dinosaurs). Until now I was sort of paralysed (only o and u on this typewriter, no ö or ü). MUCH different from Europe. The language itself isn't causing TOO MANY problems, even though I speak English much worse than expected. (The people here simply can't understand that someone doesn't speak English or know the habits over here.) Of course, an American in Europe would be even more lost than I am over here, yet they don't understand that someone doesn't know his way around here. Everything here is regarded as self-evident. For now being foreign actually suits me (and in principle it isn't more foreign than Sweden). Of course, the first five days were the most complicated ones. By now I am starting to understand most people as they speak (they all speak like Cage), and my courses are not at all difficult with regard to language (I speak atrociously, but every day it gets a little bit better). During the first days I felt like being on the moon. [...]

Now let me report about the journey: the flight was long but interesting (in a Jumbo Jet) and I initially didn't take any medication and had no anxiety attack, even though there was the occasional turbulence, just once, already over America, roughly above Kansas, as I calculated based on the time, a massive tornado appeared, and then I got anxious and took some sleeping pills, yet when they started to kick in we had already left the storm behind. Apart from this one bad hour everything was fine and also pleasantly exciting. No flight across the polar region since it had emerged (when the plane was already in the air just beyond London) that there is a strike in Canada, and no plane is allowed to cross its airspace since radar doesn't operate there, so the jumbo jet didn't fly London/Las Angeles via the polar cap and Canada but instead across the Atlantic, South of Canada, past New York, yet nothing was visible as New York was completely covered by clouds, and then the plane had to land in Washington, probably because due to the detour it didn't have enough fuel to get to Los Angeles in one go. Everything was undramatic and easy, just that the flight was some six hours longer, instead of 14 hours London/San Francisco (with a normal stop in Los Angeles) it took 20 hours London/Washington/Los Angeles/San Franc., and nobody could leave the plane in Washington, but one could walk up and down the aisle inside the plane since it is VERY big, and during the flight one could also walk while it was quiet (although it was rarely quiet, albeit not uncomfortably so). It is odd that it is afternoon here when it is night for us, and that when it is night here it is already morning, and my inner clock has not adapted, so everything feels strange to me. But that time-related chaos is small beer by comparison. The strangest thing is the people's mentality. I think one has to come here at a young age in order to be able to full adapt; your brother could do that. To me this is all strange and remains so, for the way of thinking is so different. One can't judge from the Americans whom we meet in Europe, for while many people from New York and the East Coast travel to Europe as tourists etc., only the rich people from the West Coast have been there as it is too expensive. So for the people here New York is a long way away, and Europe is somewhere in a hazy distance, just like Japan, or further away still. The only foreigners here are some university lecturers etc. The so-called "man from the street" has never been outside the US, and most never outside California. Of course, it is the same with us, and a Berliner knows on average nothing but Berlin. A lack of empathy with other people is here

Letters from Stanford: György Ligeti to Aliutė Mečys

FAR more prevalent than with us, as the many small countries in Europe get mixed up; an average Berliner — even if he never travels outside Berlin — has at least an idea of other countries because French, Americans, Czechs and Italians etc. come here, but here in California foreigners only exists as former immigrants who have adapted to the "American way of life". If one adapts to it, it can be very nice. I have mentioned difficulties, but not everything is difficult. The sea air is nice (although I haven't seen the ocean yet, nor have I been to San Francisco — time will resolve that). The university is a city in its own right, with residential areas (I'm staying in a music professor's home, everything is very comfortable, full of useful machines which, however, are all outdated, everything is automatized yet doesn't work, one could say it's like our old toilet), and still very comfortable, one has great privacy and is left to one's own devices. In reality there is no city called "Stanford", there are two cities here, Palo Alto and Menlo Park, and the university is an unstructured conglomerate of houses that grows into both of these cities, with the administration buildings in between, and everything is spacious, like a gigantic Dahlem[30] as Morton Feldman has said, and cycling lanes and then nothing, and somewhere a student residence and then somewhere, in a forest, a building for lectures and so on. They are laughing about me for not driving a car, this is entirely unbelievable here as children learn how to drive in middle school. Yet I can get everywhere by bike, and several students carry me around by car. The distances are so vast that when I want to get from the music building to administration, they have to bring me there by car, or I have to cycle for 15 minutes; walking is not possible. I have been given a strange bicycle, perhaps a French one from the last century, it has only a handbrake, no pedal brake, and no transmission — the pedal is directly connected to the turning of the wheel (via a belt rather than a cogwheel), but I can operate it well, and there is so little car traffic here — or rather, there is a lot of traffic, but everything is so vast that one only sees a car every now and then while there are separate cycle paths everywhere. Cycling is no problem as long as it doesn't rain. The weather is indeed Californian, palm trees everywhere, flowering citrus and orange trees.

    Here it rains very rarely (in San Francisco it supposedly rains every January/February, but here, one and a half car hours away from San Francisco, it is rather dry. We always have a kind of March weather, rather coolish, yet very comfortable, it already gets warmer in February, and apparently never hot, not even in the summer. That the oranges blossom is not due to the heat, as it is slightly chilly, but due to the regular temperature which never falls below 10 degrees. Now we ALWAYS have 11 or 12 degrees (I'm estimating as the thermometers are in Fahrenheit, and I don't understand the Fahrenheit scale, and I haven't seen a thermometer anywhere anyway). The university is like a gigantic boy scout camp, everything looks improvised, everything is old, the chairs in the lecture rooms are breaking down, the windows can either not be opened or not be closed, although that isn't necessary anyway, it doesn't matter whether they are open or closed. One doesn't feel cold as there is automatic heating everywhere, regulated by thermostats.

    The strangest thing is that on the one hand everything is furnished like at the turn of the century (when the university was built) and nothing gets repaired when it breaks down while on the other hand everything works; the necessary things such as water, power, heating all work well. Close to a complete breakdown, but as yet just before the line. (Contradiction to what I said before, that nothing works. Some things work well, even very well. Yet so much is entirely "wild west", almost improvised and OLD[31].) A great contrast to this world comparable to the Zillemarkt[32] is the fact that the university if full of the most modern equipment (not in music, there no equipment is necessary, the pianos can be out of tune and the chairs breaking down, no soap is to be found etc.). All

---

[30].   A leafy suburban quarter of Berlin.
[31].   Handwritten addition by Ligeti on the side of the sheet.
[32].   Today there is only a restaurant bearing that name, but it may once have been a square with a market on certain days of the week. Heinrich Zille lived in the area yet had died in 1929.

the money is spent on scientific projects, they have the largest data centre for research in America, a radio telescope, nuclear research with massive pieces of equipment (linear accelerator) etc. etc. Next to the most modern pieces of equipment one finds buildings that are almost collapsing. A strange world. Despite of all apparent slovenliness there is an incredible discipline at work, even among the students — everything is punctual and precise. Super Germanic precision at work and slovenliness everywhere else. If one lives here knowing these rules of the game life can be very nice here. Just odd to us. The most stupefying thing is the naivety, real American naivety, alongside — and in sharp contrast to — the focus on everything related to the job. The students know (on average) MUCH less than in Germany, know nothing at all about what we call "culture" (many really think that the university's main building is Romanesque in style, the difference to a Romanesque church is completely incomprehensible to them; both are ROMANESQUE, so what does it matter that one was built 800 years ago and the other one 80 years ago?). On the other hand, professional training is much better than in Europe, everyone is extremely well versed in THEIR OWN area of expertise yet have not the slightest understanding of anything falling outside its remit. So far I have not really done anything apart from carefully teaching my course, every step is complicated. An example: There is a post office in the university, one can give them letter, but no one working there knows which stamps have to go on an air mail letter which is above the standard weight. I said there has to be a printed table listing weights and stamp values. Yes, they once had such a table, it has gone missing, I should write several shorter letters to Europe, then the fee is 21 cent to Europe, or I should write aerograms, 15 cent to anywhere abroad. So I say please give me aerograms. They are just not available here, only in the main post office in Palo Alto. However, this is not an abnormal situation, not a developing country like India, quite the opposite, a technological civilization transcending what we are used to in Germany. The postal worker just doesn't KNOW the fees and tariffs, he only does his usual job and isn't interested in doing anything beyond that. The shops — dotted around the forest — are full of goods. You can buy EVERYTHING that is available. I was looking for a clothbrush, it was not available. NOBODY can tell me where one finds one. And this is quite normal. One can buy a computer yet not a clothbrush while a fully automatic electrical clothbrush is available. They want to give me money at the university. I say all right, I gladly accept an advance payment. So he (the administrator in the office) asks for my bank account. I say that I don't have one, I just arrived from Europe. Well, then I first have to establish one, for they are only allowed to transfer the money to a bank account, they don't have cash, right now not even cheques, yet they urgently want to give me money straight away. I say that I have enough money on me for a while. Yes, but they want to give me money. Yes, I say, then I will apply for a bank account, and ask where in this forest I can find a bank. The administrator doesn't know. Well, I ask, you yourself must have a bank account, so he has to know a bank. Yes, he says, of course he has a bank account, but his bank is in San Mateo where he lives, which is ¾ hour away by car and not practical for me. Well, I say, isn't there a bank here in Palo Alto or Stanford? Of course there is, he says, yet he doesn't know where. Couldn't you ask someone where a bank is NEARBY, I say, which I could reach by bicycle? No, nobody can tell me that, everyone in the office uses banks far away. So I go home to ask Professor Crosten who lives there, but he isn't at home. Eventually I find the addresses of 15 banks in the phone directory, but a map of the area is nowhere to be found. There are book shops and the likes, but they don't offer maps of the city, I should ask at a petrol station. There is a petrol station there. I want to buy a map. They have maps, but they are not for sale, you get one for free when buying petrol. Yet I can't buy petrol, I'm there by bike. I offer a tip for a map. That's impossible, it only can be had in conjunction with petrol. Eventually I am allowed to look at a map, although the attendant is indignant, he has to serve cars. You can give tips in restaurants, yet IN PRINCIPLE not at petrol stations. Suddenly the attendant mentions, extremely nicely, that the building opposite on the street is the Bank of America. I enter it and have a bank account within five minutes. Next they want to give me a cheque book and I joyfully say yes, please, I would like a cheque book. A smiling, middle-aged lady shows me a book with about 100 different types of cheques, one can have cheques with a view of San Francisco Bay or with flowers. The cheques may

Letters from Stanford: György Ligeti to Aliutė Mečys

look like our greetings telegrams. She is quite disappointed when I pick just ordinary, grey cheques, without flowers or hearts. At least I should have my initials printed on the cheque book, it costs just one dollar. In general it is a wonderfully kitschy country, the houses either collapsing or ultra-modern, cinemas in fairground style, positioned in the forest, gigantic highways with pop-like neon signs, one urgently has to join this or that sect, a neon sign of a massive, moving hand: one can have one's future read from a palm reader for 3 dollars in a shed, next door a petrol station and a gigantic department store with the most super McIntosh amplifier, yet no clothbrush (I need the clothbrush as I had found chalk, albeit coloured chalk only, which is good, yet my trousers are always coloured from it). I shall buy blue jeans tomorrow or whenever it will be possible. In the end I found a clothbrush in the store, no problem. The people are so easy, not tense, and charmingly naïve. There is the supposedly most perfect surgical clinic in the world here, the researchers in the data centre already plan robots that can speak and listen yet one can't flush the toilet in the university, as it is defect so that water flows all the time, and no plumber will attend to such a bagatelle. And California's ETERNAL SUN, it is there. Everything else is true too, yet is EVEN MORE American. Please, write to me about Urfaust[33] [...]. Exhibitions: very good. [...]

Letter 2

[Stanford 15th Feb. 72]

America is difficult, just like this typewriter. So far I have not yet got round to composing, but now this will happen at high speed. Once one has spent some time here and knows one's way around everything becomes easier than in Europe, just the standards are so incredibly different, thus making it difficult to adapt to them. Apparently in New York and the "East Coast" more generally everything is still closer to the European way of life, yet California and the entire West of the West [sic] is still pioneer country, complete proficiency at work and in business while being completely ignorant in all areas outside of work and business is normal here. A few days ago I met musicians from New York who came to California for the first time; they found everything as incomprehensible as I did. A Scandinavian or Northern German punctuality in everything related to work and earning money, and Spanish unreliability in all other areas. It is still normal here that a human being studies, for example, chemistry, then becomes a costume designer (to pick an obvious example), then works for two years as a beautician, composes some symphonies and eventually concludes his life as a level-headed farmer. There is no difference whatsoever here between a craftsman and an unskilled worker, everybody has a "practical" ability and may work for a week servicing car, then one week in a pharmacy. Consequently the performance is always an amateurish one; everything works just roughly. The gigantic prosperity is down to the efficiency of the large-scale industry; mass production works impeccably. Yet: Whenever REAL precision such as in airplane production or building skyscrapers or medical research etc. is required, real craftsmen are at work, are paid accordingly, and don't adapt their working style. This results in a massive difference between wonderful machinery and laboratories (including the new skyscrapers etc., bridges, roads), this is all precise and good, and on the other hand the everyday things: the smallest things break down immediately, and once they are broken they are not repaired but somehow fixed provisionally and then, if there is no other option, thrown away.

---

[33]. In 1972, Aliutė created the costumes and stage design for *Urfaust* (by Goethe) at the Schiller Theatre in Berlin.

Vita Gruodytė

The people's attitude: EVERYTHING is possible. Then it is being undertaken with an incredible implicitness, yet only half-decently. For example, an experience of my own: At the beginning of March, and thus in two-and-a-half weeks, they will perform my Wind Quintet in concert. There already are four wind players, and the parts are there, too. They don't have the fifth player, the clarinet. So I say that the concert is unlikely to be possible as an established wind quintet requires two or three months to practice the piece. Yet the musicians don't understand at all what I'm worrying about. One will call this or that clarinetist by phone, and all will be fine. I have mixed feelings, yet I see from other experiences that despite an incredible ignorance these things in the end usually somehow DO work out, even if only half-decently. "Take it easy, but take it". For now a lot of work with teaching, rehearsals, etc. etc. etc. my English is getting better, yet I still have serious problems with my teaching, but only I would regard this as a problem, a Californian wouldn't understand it at all. So that is where we stand. The most interesting thing for me (apart from the very different way of life) is that Stanford University currently has the best-equipped and best-working computer music studio which I hadn't known in advance. There are people working there who don't know too much about music, but are real computer experts, and this studio offers fascinating musical opportunities — a very important experience for my work and my compositional technique. [...]

Was it HORRIBLE to have to work so quickly?

> On 8 February 1972 Aliutė had written: «*I am working on Urfaust even more than before and have reduced my sleeping time drastically. This is because I visited the tailors' workshop last week. The 'female' head tailor (looks like the Furzewa[34], is also dressed like her) immediately gave me a "final" deadline for the figurines (14 February — oops!) while the head male tailor appears to be a very nice person and is open to discussion. He didn't give me a specific deadline, although he would like to see the drafts the day before yesterday. You know what it's like*».

For me it will become terrible (I am now starting the SERIOUS work), since I now know the main rules of the American way of life, or more precisely the Californian way of life, and work more seriously as of today. The most terrible thing is actually good news: Gentele has finally contacted me, has even called me at the university from New York with advance notification (New York is already halfway to Europe), and we had a long talk. Thus: green light for Meschke in Stockholm for a piece that is NOT Oidipus. Thus confirming everything we have planned with you, Ove, Meschke (I'll write to Ove straight away). BUT: in addition Gentele — who will stay for quite some time in New York, at the Metropolitan Opera, apparently he was not hampered by the difficulties, despite the pessimism and the warnings of several theatre people — Gentele wants from me, quasi as a replacement for his Stockholm plans, an operatic piece for New York — and he insists on it being Oidipus, but a shorter one (about 1 hour or 45 minutes), and for a chamber stage — not for the Metropolitan as they don't play modern pieces there at all, but there is a good chamber theatre in the Lincoln Center, part of the Metropolitan (something like an experimental stage[35]); he wants to do Aventures there in 1973 and then Oidipus in 74 or 75. I am meant to adapt the libretto for a chamber stage, no choir, no large dance troupe, with simple means etc. The idea is not too bad, and I am in the mood for it. So: don't continue with the stage designs for Oidipus, everything is going to

---

[34]. Yekaterina Alexeyevna Furtseva (German transliteration: Furzewa), 1910-1974, was a politician and the first woman admitted to the Central Committee of the Communist Party of the Soviet Union. At the time of this letter she was Minister for Culture of the USSR.

[35]. «Werkstattbuehne» — a small theatre, often also used as rehearsal stage, for small and experimental pieces.

be a bit different. But, if this gives you time, please do some designs for Aventures (scale doesn't matter, probably Amsterdam first, then New York). But only if you have time, it's not too pressing. So I have to write two operatic pieces, but that is quite good.

> On 19 February 1972 Aliutė would respond: «*I find Gentele's offer wonderful. For Oidipus this is t h e idea and meets your expectations, doesn't it? And even a second opera! I look really forward to it, too. Right now I don't read new texts as I don't even get to visit a book shop due to the amount of work. At least I can finally read Ove's book, in the evening in bed. I'm learning many, many new things about you and your work. Will you keep the Macbett text for me once you get it? I still don't have the poems by Wolfgang Müller (friend of Heis). There is only a small print run, and it is not available in shops, so he has to wait until Müller is back from his trip*».

Thank you for the information regarding Macbett[36]! If the reviews are bad, too, I would be highly interested in it, have asked Scholl to send me the Ionesco piece, so you won't have to take care of it, Scholl will do it. If in the meantime you have an idea tell me about it; Meschke is thinking as well.

> On 8 February 1972, Aliutė had written: «*I have read many plays recently, always hoping to find "the" ideal sujet for your opera, yet so far without success. I always thought Julius Hay [...] might be suitable, as your quasi compatriot and in general. Now I have read three of his plays: "Attila's Nights", "The Horse" and "The Turkey's Shepherd", but what happens there is so bad that it is indescribable. A mix of Gerhard Hauptmann, Max Halbe, Pearl S. Buck, "The Forester of the Silver Forest" and "Rose-Girl Resli", plus a pinch of "Sylvia Woman's Novel"*[37]*, all placed in the Third Reich and embellished with a bit of nineteenth-century views and kitsch from the 1950s, boiled three times, that lukewarm broth would come closest to what I have read. Furthermore I am very hopeful about Ionesco's new play: Macbeth (in French pronunciation); while I haven't read it yet I have read several bad reviews. In addition: Felicien Marceau... quite murky*».
> And later, on 02.03.72: «*Do you already have plans for the (Stockholm) opera? I have listened to a radio drama by Friederike Mayröcker: "Game for 4", I will produce something like that for you every second day for an entire year. But perhaps that doesn't matter, we have already talked about this*».

All not so urgent as I am doing the Double Concerto first anyway. Keeping Ubu or Macbett in mind right now. Ove's idea of a Last Judgement won't work. Thank you for reading so much and looking around! O,

---

[36]. An Ionesco adaptation of Shakespeare that Ligeti considered as a possible source for the opera.

[37]. *Der Förster vom Silberwald* and *Rosenresli* were successful «Heimatfilme» of the 1950s; Austrian and German movie dramas mainly set in nature (here the alps), depicting an unspoiled, rather simplistic world in which good always triumphs over evil. *Silvia* (misspelled by Mečys as «Sylvia») is the title of a series of German dime novels directed at women which were sold in large numbers during this period. Under the headings «Silvia-Gold» and «Silvia-Schicksal» they are being produced to this day.

had I been with you I would have warned you of Julius Hay[38]. I do know pieces by him from Hungary — he is a TERRIBLE writer, completely ungifted (he was important politically since he fought against Stalinism, etc., but as a writer he is just rubbish). And you, darling, have read even several pieces by him. How do people become famous? That Arrabal is also bad. Genet not good either. And the so famous Auduberti[39] also rubbish. But I love Ionescu. It is POSSIBLE, of course, that Macbett is bad, but I have to read it MYSELF first, I don't trust the critics.

> On 2 February 1972 Aliutė would respond: «Jorge Lavelli has been praised a lot for his direction of Arrabal's *"La guerre de mille ans in the Paris"* at the Theatre national popularize in Paris. *An ideal combination of word and music (Lavelli's idea), unique, wonderful, etc.*».

There is a fashionable common critique, emerging from Hamburg (Spiegel etc.), see their music reviews. It is one-sided. I just read a new book by Cage here, also to train my English. Unfortunately — as much as I like Cage — it's COMPLETE rubbish, full of learned quotations. Was very disappointed, just like you on the radio. Felicien Marceau: Hands off, bad, unfortunately Artaud bad too. But somehow it will come together (take it easy, but take it), Ravel's example appears to me on the horizon. Thanks for the Ravel consolation! [...]

> On 8 February 1972 Aliutė had written: «*On the radio I heard about Ravel, I have to tell you this as a consolation: Colette had written the libretto for "L'enfant et les sortilèges": for him within four weeks or so since it was so urgent. Yet then she didn't hear anything further, and despite being initially impatient tried to forget about it. Hence she was extremely surprised when Ravel asked her after... f i v e years for some details about the text [...] then she had to wait a further three years, and even then it only worked out because the impresario (in Nizza, I think) had determined the date of the premiere and insisted on it. Yet during those eight years Ravel is meant to have worked on it continuously. This again confirms to me that you are a 'fast worker'. What do you think?...*».

Don't forward letters to me — just the most important ones, as discussed, official things. Gentele writes to me here anyway — also publishers, they all have the Stanford address. Thank you for the information regarding the radio programming, Night and Morning[40] are two old choral pieces by me, still from Budapest, on texts by a very good poet, Sandor Weores[41]. They are manuscripts, only Ove has them, and were sung by the Swedish choir (also for the Elektrola LP — has it arrived?). Unfortunately not that well sung, I wasn't present at this recording. That Schott doesn't announce it is clear, these choruses don't belong to Schott and are unpublished, my old style. I am happy that you like them anyway. Hashish I want to try just once (according to new American research it is dangerous after all — despite of what Leonhardt says in *Die Zeit* — but once or twice one can try it. I want to try it with you together. Wait for it. [...] (I also do some sport here, long distances on the bike. Perhaps I will learn how to drive here, it is easier here, the roads are very wide, all roads are really highways here in Stanford-Palo Alto,

---

[38]. Originally Gyula Háy.
[39]. Probably Jacques Audiberti.
[40]. *Éjszaka* and *Reggel*.
[41]. Spelled this way in the letter — American typewriters had no 'ö'

Letters from Stanford: György Ligeti to Aliutė Mečys

it's like a spa town in combination with rubbish dumps. However, I won't benefit in Europe from learning how to drive HERE as they use EXCLUSIVELY automatic gearboxes here, so one couldn't learn shifting gears. Hence I will most likely stick to this old bicycle, I got used to it, I even managed to inflate the wheel, and also to brake by hand only. Cycling is not dangerous as there are cycle paths everywhere.

Letter 3

Stanford-Palo Alto 26th Feb. 72
[...]

There is no problem with the food here; of course, the "Hamburgers" etc. are available, just like Weisswurst in Munich, but there is a lot else besides, very normal food, particularly simple for me that one gets nice steaks everywhere, I can also eat sausage everywhere (Frankfurtes, known as "Hot Dogs" as served in white bread) [...]. Generally many things are very easy in "daily life", and prices are not really higher than in Germany if one assumes an exchange rate of about 3 dollars for 1 mark — sorry, the other way round, if one takes 3 marks for 1 dollar, then everything costs more or less the same (there are some deviations, for example food bought in small restaurants or in supermarkets is cheaper than in Germany, yet eating in better restaurants is more expensive, like in very expensive ones in Germany — but one doesn't have to go to the expensive ones). At the university — which is a town in its own right in the city of Palo Alto which in turn is like a large spa town, surrounding the university like a crescent —, at the university there are several easy options to eat, a range of cheap localities, cafes etc., no problem. A problem is rather the mentality of people which is SO DIFFERENT from central Europe, but you know the "typically American" mentality, it is just like that, except here in California even "more American" still. I'm gradually discovering what that mentality is — and starting to understand why Americans often feel lost in Europe. In a letter I can't explain it in more detail as it is very extensive, it will be easier in person. By the way, this is apparently the most pleasant region in America, there are relatively few poor people [...] than in the large cities in the "East" (New York etc.) for that reason the unrest and the racial problems are less obvious here. Thanks be to God, here in Stanford there is no racism at all to be detected, whites, blacks[42], and also Japanese and Chinese sit together at a table, the young people generally reject racism, which results in a much nicer atmosphere. Yet one hears that in the large industrial cities on the "East Cost" everything is indeed as it is described in the "Spiegel", a very explosive situation. Racial hatred between blacks and whites — that is just the same artificially created nonsense as anti-semitism in central Europe. Yet also slightly different, since here it is based on money issues: it is a circulus vitiosus: blacks earn less money, thus their children receive a worse education, with that worse education the next generation then earns less money etc. We know that very well from newspapers. Well, San Francisco and its surroundings are not typical insofar as there are fewer poor people here; the whole city (even though the streets are incredibly dirty) gives an impression of general affluence, just like we in Europe imagine the "golden West". It is not the clean affluence of Switzerland, but very colourful, unsanitary, Southern — a muddle. Now I'm curious about New York. [...] New York is meant to be "the" city — even though one gets mugged in the street (in San Francisco this apparently happens very rarely, so far I don't[43] have any experience of this myself). In the meantime I have seen wonderful areas, San Francisco itself is an experience, then the Golden Gate bridge, in reality much

---

[42]. Ligeti uses the (then less politicised) «Neger» in the original.
[43]. He writes «ein»–«do» —, yet I think he means 'kein'–'don't' — as there is an extra space at the beginning, and it would make more sense this way.

more monumental than in photos, overwhelming like the Eiffel Tower, then the "redwoods", spruce-like trees which grow almost 100m tall, and thus all the Californian things that you see in prospectuses. Music: on the one hand the exciting computer centre, on the other hand nothing else. In this respect we are in the deepest province here, and the local composers yearn for Europe (although once they have made it to Paris or Berlin they are equally disappointed that in Europe, too, "nothing happens"). The technical training is VERY BAD, music can't be studied as a university subject (and neither the fine arts), in this respect the European system of conservatories is much better. What is MUCH better here than in Europe is the scientific training, most young people are totally uneducated with regard to "general knowledge", but very good in their own respective areas. (This comment is about technology and not music, at least not here at Stanford.)

[I] Didn't know that Kaufmann wrote a libretto. Weishappel[44] is a bad composer but a nice human being, and a very good film critique in Vienna, very bright and funny. [...]

> On 19 February 1972. Aliutė had written: «*Did you know that Harald Kaufmann has written an operatic libretto (King Nicolo, after Wedekind), some 15 years ago, and one Herr Weishappel or -apfel has worked on the music ever since, as they said on the radio. Now it is meant to be finished and performed somewhere, yet I don't know where. Herr Mathus's latest operatic work carries the humorous title "Another spoonful of poison, darling?" Text by Peter Hacks. It is now being given in the Komische Oper (director: Götz Friedrich; he is said to be good). The other day several people involved in it have talked about it (on GDR radio), their ideas etc., and what they thought while working on it. Initially I thought they had discovered an illegitimate son of Monteverdi and forced him to speak, so new was all of this to me*».

Incredibly busy. Not the university work, that's 8 hours and nothing more, but the outstanding dealings with Schott regarding corrections, revisions etc., next the Double Concerto etc. etc. then there is the exciting computer studio, and I want to compose a piece in it, then there are many issues related to musicians who come for advice etc. etc. etc., you know what it's like. Even this letter I had to interrupt by now, and it already is 1 March. [...]

Letter 4

4th March 72

Aliutė, Darling,

Just a little interim letter in the shape of this "air letter"[45], thank you for this recording (a really big help!) [...]. I am just like that at work, as you know: always planning, then I need much more time and then I get desperate. Thinking I will have completed it tonight, then this tonight is (in the best case) the evening after tomorrow. Or the day after that. Just now I am startled: There was a press conference in San Francisco (with a meal in a Japanese restaurant, a really Japanese one, you have to sit on the ground and surrender your shoes at the entrance, one can

---

44. Probably Rudolf Weishappel.
45. «air-letter» features in the text in English.

only enter it in socks), and that was all due to my San Francisco commission (orchestral piece for 1974, has to be finished before Dec. 73). That's 8 commissions until 1976. Horrible. But also great. I have to be very focused. Also looking very much forward to working. Am also healthy.

I have now almost finished corrections and start (again from the beginning) the Double Concerto. I can't yet say much about it, not more than in Berlin that is. The San Francisco orchestral piece (commissioned for much later, first come the Meschke opera AND Gentele opera — incredible), anyway the San Franc. piece I have finished in my head already, it will be the real Melodien (yet with another title), in such a way that the melodies will be presented naked, not always served with sauce as in "Melodien". Here they now play quite a bit of my music, the day after tomorrow the Wind Quintet in Stanford (average), on Wednesday the same in Los Angeles with the same ensemble, on Thursday in San Diego (the southernmost city in California, not far from here), I'll come along and do an introductional talk, but then come "Melodien" in April in Los Angeles and also in San Francisco and quite a bit more (*Lux Aeterna* and *Lontano* in Stanford).

Letter 5

Stanford- Palo Alto, 16th Feb. 72

Aliutė, darling,
[...] I have learned a lot here, not just English. About the possibilities of computer music (phantastic prospects), SCIENTIFICALLY everything here is much more developed even than in Germany. Even than in Switzerland, even in Eastern Switzerland. [...]

In the meantime I undertook a short trip to Hollywood (2 ½ days, to Hollywood by plane, yet I didn't see Hollywood but was brought to Pasadena, a garden city nearby (just like Los Angeles, which I only saw from the air, a gigantic chessboard) (it is a combination of hundreds of garden cities), and in Pasadena I was giving a talk, and a wind ensemble from Stanford played my Wind Quintet twice, very well in Pasadena, earlier in Stanford badly, but Pasadena was a massive success. Next by plane to San Diego, the southernmost city of California, at the Mexican border, there both talk and concert were repeated, not quite as well, but passable. There is a university there, full of mad people who meditate and so on, they didn't want to understand me. The whole trip was wonderful from a scenic point of view. In the meantime I have received a telegram form the Akademie der Künste in Berlin informing me that I have been awarded an Arts Prize from the city of Berlin, DM 15,000. That's not too bad, i.e. it's quite good. The day after tomorrow (Saturday, 18th) I'll fly to Mexico City, an invitation from the Goethe Institute, I'll be there for a week, with three talks. Will be back in Stanford, that is Palo Alto, on the 25th. Those are wonderful trips, Los Angeles, San Diego, Mexico City — just my work is suffering, I'm meant to submit the first movement of the Double Concerto for winds in April, but no trace of it yet. Well, I'll do it. NOW FOCUS ALL ENERGIES ON WORK. Just as it is with you. Here at the university I have listened to a lot of music (on LP) that I didn't know, American composers. VERY INTERESTING: Terry Riley and Steve Reich (I'll bring recordings back with me). Then an American [Gerard] Hoffnung, with incredible mystifications: P.D.Q. Bach (1742-1802), a so far unknown son of Joh. Seb. Bach, discovered in the bin of Professor Schickele (photo of Professor Schickele on the cover as he picks the PDQ Bach manuscripts out of the bin, hence their authenticity is proven), wonderful pseudo classical music, a very high level of joking that will astonish Kagel. Everything else I have heard so far: pretty mediocre. Yet CAREFUL: I have adopted the habit over here not to judge prematurely; things are more nuanced, there are wonderful things here in America. I have an invitation to Tanglewood, haven't accepted it yet, would like to go to New York together with you, we'll talk about that. You have to experience all this too. NOW LET'S

WORK. Terrible, I'm starting the Double Concerto from scratch. And Gentele calls regularly, what about the opera FOR NEW YORK. And letters from Meschke, ANDANDAND. Terrible, but also good. I just checked the mail (always looking for a letter from you, I have a mailbox here in the music department with my name on it; nothing from you but Jonesco's Macbeth in Germany[46], sent by Schott. Now reading quickly whether this could be suitable. Will write in more detail after the Mexico trip, from there just briefly because of a very packed programme, and after Mexico immediately writing the Double Concerto. Am under pressure, as always, as you know, it's my own fault.

Letter 6

1st April 72

Then I have received Ionesco's Macbeth from Schott, and I think this piece is of interest to me (a kind of mix of Ionesco, Shakespeare and Jarry), there are some weaker moments in it, but those can be cut, and overall I can apply my "wordless" language ["sprachlose" Sprache], too — I shall write to Ove and Meschke to suggest this. I would like you to read the play soon as well. [...]

I am a guest of the university; they have houses for lecturers (these universities in America are like separate villages or small towns), and there Prof. Crosten lives who works on French opera and is uninteresting, and Prof. Leland Smith whom I don't know as he is in Paris, and I live here in his stead, and everything is comfortable, even though scruffy. I don't have to pay rent as the university is covering it. Daily life here is easy, firstly because the weather is always (ALWAYS) great, then you can buy everything here (not as close as Edeka[47] at Furstenplatz but some 200m away, still very close), and there is a fridge and a gas stove and many appliances that I don't use (all half-corroded yet just about in working order) and eating is no problem since the nearby cafeteria serves simple food, just good enough for me (sandwiches and toasts) and there's a university restaurant, self-service. A laundry and the likes are also here. Don't imagine all that as being American but rather as half-decayed, but all you need is there [...]. Eating is no problem here because one easily (and very quickly) gets steaks which I can eat. [...] I would like to return later to do a computer piece, but now I don't have time, due to the Double Concerto, theatre pieces etc., but I will try to learn something in a computer studio for a while — the musical potential is surprisingly extensive.

At the university itself (which has a separate music building) I have been given an office [...]. It offers a nice view of Stanford (the building sits on a mountain, hence difficult to reach by bicycle — or rather, a hill, as the mountains are much further away, I see from my window the entire university village compound as well as Palo Alto and Menlo Park; both are garden cities and have merged (the house I live in is already "across the border" in Palo Alto), yet those boundaries only exist in theory, in reality it is a gigantic complex consisting of garden cities and motorways, with soft hills and a view of San Francisco bay, a little bit like the Lake Constance, San Francisco is invisible, there is a high mountain in between. Palm trees everywhere, flourishing trees and flowers, comparable to Italy, just that the buildings are mostly quite tasteless in terms of architecture. Los Angeles, then, is a gigantic complex of similar villages, just much much larger, full of palm trees, small buildings and swimming pools, and some 7 million people and 5 million cars. But Stanford is far away from Los Angeles, it belongs to the similarly

---

[46]. Ionesco wrote *Macbett* in 1972, and it premiered at the Théâtre de l'Alliance Française in Berlin on 27 January 1972.

[47]. Edeka is a German supermarket chain.

Letters from Stanford: György Ligeti to Aliutė Mečys

complex San Francisco (an hour's drive away from San Francisco city centre), here only half as many people live around the bay and San Fr. is a wonderfully beautiful city, I have to tell you everything and later you have to see it for yourself (first New York as it is meant to be fascinating with regard to the arts). Cleaning: that isn't done here, yet that's no problem; I get clean bedsheets etc. once a week. No problem at all (beds are very different here due to the heat: no duvet but soft cotton sheets directly from the laundry, more is not necessary); if something is VERY dirty there are powerful hoovers — yet as the air is very clean (many cars, but factories only working with electric power and clean air due to permanent wind) there is little dirt or dust. (Los Angeles is very different, there is little wind there, and always a yellow haze above the city). Doing the dishes etc. is rarely done over here; meals are served like on a plane, in plastic cups and plates with plastic fork etc., everything goes straight into the bin. Not very palatable, but HIGHLY practical. You have no idea how ugly and practical everything is over here (that is America). Not everything, but almost everything. Yet this "almost" makes all the difference to Europe, and I never could feel fully at home in America. Hjalmar Bergmann, a Swedish writer, in the Twenties when one had to go to America by ship, received in invitation to live in Hollywood and asked a fellow writer whether he should really go to America. Response (the colleague was already there): "you should certainly go there by ship, yet never set foot on land". However now one can also set foot on land and it is INTERESTING, yet ALIEN, but more on that in person.

[...]

Letter 7

Gyorgy Ligeti
Music Department
Stanford University
California 94305
USA

[17th April 72]

[...] But then the trouble with the rehearsals in Los Angeles, a very good orchestra, nice players, BUT the conductor Zubin Mehta, a good-looking young Indian, yet super-Karajan-like attitudes, for him it was only important to do the first American performance of the piece, he hadn't studied the piece AT ALL, [...]. It was quite embarrassing, I explained several details to him, which instrument had played wrongly, and he didn't hear it, and the players knew that he didn't hear it, etc. Then strange experiences with the invitation, I was sent a ticket for the one-way flight OUT, and was put up in a VERY posh hotel, something like Tannenhof, just in Los Angeles, this city is INCREDIBLY big, since all people have cars there is no public transport, neither subway nor tram, in some areas there are buses once per hour for the poor people who don't have a car, and there are VERY few taxis, as all people have several cars there is no need for them. In this city which has 7 million inhabitants yet is 20 times the size of Berlin, like a country in its own right, and all roads wide, carparks everywhere, so that all people can get everywhere, I felt totally lost without being able to drive a car. Imagine: The posh Sheraton Hotel was the hotel closest to the concert hall (Music Centre), this meant one hour and 35 minutes walking. The city isn't a city but a collection of suburbs without a centre, with skyscrapers, all very interesting in principle. So I stayed in this posh hotel and walked an hour 35 minutes to the rehearsal and again back (once I got a lift from Leonard Stein, a lovely person, Monika[48] will tell you about him). Then came the dress rehearsal, Mehta had no clue and I was desperate. The concert was meant to take place in the evening. I had not ticket, didn't know when the concert was to begin, 8, 8:30? No idea, no taxi to be found, I called the Music Centre, the man who had invited me couldn't be found, etc. etc., finally I was picked up by someone from administration who asked me whether I was a musician, too — I have to tell you that in detail, there were even more ridiculous details, eventually I arrived, and was led to the dressing room, Mehta welcomes me with a filmstar-smile and asks me where I sit so that he can call me up when the piece is over so that I can take a bow and shake his hand, I said I have no idea where I'll sit, I have no ticket, the concert is sold out, some gentlemen said they will soon arrange a seat for me, then they let me wait for 20 minutes, I had a coat on me, for once it was chilly, I couldn't access the cloakroom, couldn't get a programme booklet, then a man appears and shows me where to sit, by then I was already quite angry, then Mehta appears to ask whether I already have a seat, I say yes, he asks where it is so that I can call my up, yet I am so annoyed from having to wait that I tell him I'm not sure whether I'll come up to take a bow, that will depend on whether he'll deliver an acceptable performance of the piece, now Mehta is (rightly) annoyed and plays the piece like a limp dick, I almost didn't recognise the music, it was worse than in Nuremberg, yes, I was also annoyed because originally my piece was meant to come after the interval yet there was a last-minute change, it came first and drowned in coughing and the noises of people arriving late etc., so I didn't go up to take a bow. Yes, in the meantime my coat has been brought to Mehta's room. Next there was a Bartók violin concerto (Isaac Stern, a wonderful violinist, and THIS piece Mehta knew how to do, it was conducted perfectly. Next there is the interval, and I went for the dressing room in order to a) tell Stern how much I loved his violin playing, b) tell Mehta how wonderful his conducting of Bartók was and say goodbye (without a word about Melodien), c) pick up my coat, d) ask someone to call me a taxi or another mode of transport, I may also possibly stay for the second half of the concert. HOWEVER: when I tried the door separating the audience area from backstage it was locked (earlier it had been open so that I could go up to the stage to take my bow), so I went out to the street to reach it via the stage door (it's a giant building, modern), I want to enter, two black guys in uniform won't let me, I say I have to get to Mehta, they say I should use the door from the audience area, I say that door is unfortunately locked, they say they are very sorry but I can't get in here (even though I had used it before the concert), I should wait until the end of the second half of the concert, then the door from the audience area will be opened for people to congratulate the artists, I asked him to please call someone (he had a telephone like a porter, but in uniform and with a gun, it transpired they are policemen, for good reason, due to high criminality etc.), yet he didn't want to call, I say I want my coat which is in the dressing room, then the timpanist from the orchestra showed up and wanted to take me in yet the policemen wouldn't let him as I'm not a member of the orchestra, the timpanist said nicely that I am a member of the orchestra, then one of the black policemen became annoyed not unlike Pearson in Darmstadt, and we almost got into a fight which the two policemen against the timpanist (who hadn't brought his mallets) and myself would have totally dominated, I was rather brutally removed I shouted they should get hold of Herr Fleischmann (the orchestra's manager who had sent me the ticket — one way only —, had formally invited me and booked me into the luxury hotel (which was generously paid for by the Los Angeles Symphony Orchestra), after much back and forth eventually Fleischmann appeared, I shouted at him that I had never experienced this kind of treatment, and I wanted my coat and a taxi straight away, then Fleischmann started shouting back, eventually we almost got into a fight again, then more orchestral players arrived as well, and audience members from the street (who, like I, could only be in front of the door), then two girls, members of the audience, said they had a car and will bring me to the hotel. I got my coat, left Fleischmann behind, the girls were students at Los Angeles University, a very young singer (18) and a violist (25);

---

[48]. This may be Monika Meynert whom Aliutė mentioned in her letter from 21 January 1972.

Letters from Stanford: György Ligeti to Aliutė Mečys

they drove away with me, laughed and said they would kidnap me, and the police won't search for me given that I am now in their bad books. I was beside myself due to the butchering of the piece, went to dinner with the girls [...].

In the meantime I had to interrupt this letter several times due to work, university, etc., it is already the 19th today. This will be my last long letter, for the MOST URGENT working phase has started and will last a few years — today Gentele called me in the university from New York, I am to call back immediately; I did so, he has grand plans with Oidipus, chamber version, this will become more concrete, it means several flights to New York together with you, terrible and great, I have to work on Graz and Stockholm and San Francisco commission andandandandand — how to cope with all that?

> On 25 April 1972 Aliutė would respond: «*I am so excited about your operatic plans! That we will fly to New York together is already wonderful! Moreover I find it correct and 'proper' that they are so interested in you and your pieces in the US, too, and that Gentele makes such significant plans for Oidipus*».

Today I have pledged to myself that I finish this letter and then launch straight into a MERCILESS PERIOD OF HARD WORK for several years, MERCILESS!!! I WANT to write these pieces and will work like you do when the figurines HAVE to be ready in the morning. Right now work means a very quick focus on the Double Concerto and the many many concerts here that are now lining up one after the other, mainly Melodien in San Francisco (with Ozawa and in better conditions than in Los Angeles). And in Stanford many nights in the computer studio. And many concerts in Stanford. I have become something of a celebrity over here, and a lot of interest in my music is emerging, more and more invitations arrive from all over America, which is nice, yet now I have to focus entirely on composing and also on the performances in California (San Francisco and Stanford and Oakland and also Los Angeles, but not with Mehta, but the Leonard Stein concerts), I am incredibly tired, but I keep going.

About Monika: she has called me, but we have not yet met; I was in Mexico when she arrived in the US, she called me from Los Angeles yet had to fly to the East Coast again, but will probably return to California soon and then I will see her (only if she comes to San Francisco or Stanford, she films in the Stein School in Valencia, near Los Angeles, then she will probably also come here. She was very nice on the phone and then your parcel arrived, she sent it to me by mail since she doesn't yet know when she will get here. [...]

About Mexico: Don't think it is far away from here, since here in the US distances are very different, flying is like taking a train, and Mexico is a four-hour flight away from San Francisco (Stanford is very close to San Fr. airport). I was afraid, but all flights in this region are without turbulences, very smooth, for the weather is continuously good. In Mexico there are meant to be horrific storms in the summer, but at this time of the year everything is (or was) quiet. Although not quite: on the way out I was a bit anxious, for there was some shaking for an hour, and took the usual tablets. Otherwise all flights were quiet. Berlin is difficult to fly to due to the 3,000 metre limit[49], yet here even the short flights (San Francisco-Los Angeles is roughly like Frankfurt-Berlin) go very high, above the cloud cover, which are mostly absent anyway.

[...]

Yours, GG

---

[49]. The Allied air corridors connecting West Berlin to the Federal Republic of Germany did not allow planes to fly higher than 10,000ft (3,048m).

Vita Gruodytė

Letter 8

18th May

Aliutė, darling,

[...] there was a "Ligeti Festival" here in Stanford, half of which worked well (the other half not at all, yet the positive aspects weigh heavier). I gave a long public lecture, there were VERY many people there, including from San Francisco, and then there were performances of: electronic piece (Artikulation) with first-class technology (four speakers), that worked very well; then the metronome piece (they had 117 metronomes instead of 100), that went very well, too, and twice the Wind Quintet, which was equally excellent. *Lux Aeterna* as presented by the university choir was bad. The next day (last Saturday) Volumina was on, unfortunately totally misunderstood by the organist, yet strangely the reviews highlighted just that performance as the best one. (The artistic criteria are a bit provincial here.) And on Sunday the university orchestra played *Lontano*, unfortunately also badly, yet with much effort. More important than this "Fest" (strange to see posters inscribed with "Ligeti Festival") was the rehabilitation of "Melodien" in San Francisco by Ozawa. Today it was performed the second time, I will attend the third one tomorrow as I'm interested in the piece (there will be a fourth performance on Saturday which I will give a pass; serious lack of time). My concerns in Nuremberg were groundless: the piece is one of the best of my works, if not the best one, yet what we heard in Nuremberg wasn't that piece. What I heard in Los Angeles also didn't have anything to do with it. In San Francisco the following happened: the orchestra members had prepared everything very well (that was also the case in Los Angeles, Mehta had just forgotten to study the score). Ozawa, on the other hand, has studied the score carefully, and then a miracle happened just like that: the piece sounded exactly as I imagined it, everything was transparent, and all melodies clearly audible (in Nuremberg and Los Angeles the melodies drowned in the thick sauce of ignorance). The San Francisco orchestra isn't even "first class" (Los Ang. is better), and the practice time was minimal (two rehearsals), as is usual in America. There were two reasons for the good outcome: the commitment of the musicians and the ability of the conductor. With Nuremberg on your mind you wouldn't have recognized this as the same piece; everything was crystal clear and comprehensible. However, it was really necessary for me to be present at the rehearsals. Due to these two rehearsals (and a lot of discussion with Ozawa) as well as the Festival in Stanford I accrued a DELAY with the Double Concerto, which is why I close in telegraphic style[50]. [...] there is still an awful lot to do here, apart from the Double Concerto the unique opportunity to study the methods of computer music, I need to be aware of those, they open up entirely new ways to compose. I now work day and night. This area is VERY remote, and while one gets more quickly to New York or "East Coast" it is much further to California, and I have to use the opportunity to learn something that exists neither in New York nor in Europe. More in person. There are still a few shorter trips to come over here, to Los Angeles (about a project for the future, related to computer music, and the opportunity to develop them at Hamburg University etc. etc.) [...] I have to harvest the "fruits of wisdom" here, it will influence all my composing. Today is the 18th, tomorrow on the 19th the mailbox will be collected, I hope this letter will be with you on the 22nd. You can then still respond to me once; if your letter arrives here in May it will still reach me. As of 1st June (no, as of 2nd or 3rd)[51] I will travel to Los Angeles and probably Seattle so that letters won't reach me here anymore. Then I'll fly back to Europe directly from California (Los Angeles or Seattle), probably to London (it has the best flight connections).

---

[50]. There is a typo leading to a subsequent word play here which is omitted in the translation.
[51]. The parenthesis is a handwritten later addition.

Letters from Stanford: György Ligeti to Aliutė Mečys

You will learn everything, as I will write to you, and call you once I'm in London. I won't write another letter, now it's the final spurt for both the Double Concerto and the computer issues, I will only send you short notices. I will probably really still be here until the beginning of June, 2nd and 3rd. [...] Until then I'll be under an enormous work pressure, just like you know it, like before a premiere, hardly time to pee, hence I'll only write you brief notes from now on. It is possible (I'm exploiting the option now) that I can fly with a plane chartered by the university which would be cheaper than a standard flight (I just have to wait until I learn whether I can fly one way or return; there are several charters, most with return option, yet I probably will get one way. The planes fly from Oakland — that is an airport for charter fights close to San Francisco — to London or Paris around the middle of June). If I am in Seattle prior to that (there is a Nordwall-like Ligeti centre there) it probably won't be the charter flight; if it's Los Angeles I'll fly to Oakland if the charter plan works out. Flying is like taking a bus over here, and there's no reason for anxiety as there is ALWAYS fine weather, the flight across the Atlantic Ocean can be turbulent.

[...]

[...] Urfaust at the Festival with your stage design, that's the thing: Did the Falstaff masks work out?

Double Concerto: I was meant to sent off the first movement by the end of April, everything by the end of May. Now the first movement will be sent off by the end of May, and the whole thing will be completed in Berlin at the end of June. Yet: I can't make any concession regarding quality. That has been proven through Melodien, the piece is incredibly good. Like a very richly knotted carpet, with a lot of gold and other metallic components, something Klimt-like. And no sauce at all, but clearly drawn, colourful.

Double Concerto: flute (Zoller) and Oboe (Koch) feature both equally in it, in both movements, sometimes separately, sometimes together. [...] On the plans regarding Gentele "piccolo Met" and Meschke in Stockholm more personally, there's a lot of work coming up in relation to this for both of us.

Translated from German by Wolfgang Marx

Bibliography

ANDRIUŠYTĖ-ŽUKIENĖ 2014
ANDRIUŠYTĖ-ŽUKIENĖ, Rasa. 'Aliutė Mečys. Person and Creation', in: *Aliutė*, exhibition catalogue, edited by Rasa Andriušytė-Žukienė, Kaunas, M. Žilinskas Art Gallery of the M. K. Čiurlionis National Museum of Art, 2014, pp. 133-140.

GRUODYTĖ 2018
GRUODYTĖ, Vita. 'Le Grand Macabre at the Crossroads of Two Exiles', in: *TheMa*, VII/1-2 (2018), <http://www.thema-journal.eu/index.php/thema/article/view/69/117>, accessed May 2022.

HERMS-BOHNHOFF 1995A
Den Traum erfüll' ich mir. Frauen wagen ein neues Leben, edited by Elke Herms-Bohnhoff, Zürich, Kreuz Verlag, 1995.

HERMS-BOHNHOFF 1995B
HERMS-BOHNHOFF, Elke. 'Grenzgänge in Traum-Welten. Aliutė Mečys, 50 Jahre, Malerin', in: HERMS-BOHNHOFF 1995A, pp. 163-174.

Vita Gruodytė

Ligeti 1986
Ligeti, György. *Trio für Violine, Horn und Klavier / Passacaglia ungherese / Hungarian Rock / Continuum / Monument-Selbstportrait-Bewegung*, Wergo 60100, 1986.

Ligeti 2007
Id. 'Mein Judentum', in: Id. *Gesammelte Schriften. 2*, edited by Monika Lichtenfeld, Mainz, Schott, 2007 (Veröffentlichungen der Paul Sacher Stiftung, 10), pp. 20-28.

Ligeti 2013
Id. *L'Atelier du compositeur. Ecrits autobiographiques. Commentaires sur ses œuvres*, translated by Catherine Fourcassié, Pierre Michel *et al.*, edited by Philippe Albèra, Catherine Fourcassié and Pierre Michel, Geneva, Contrechamps, 2013 (Écrits sur la musique, 2).

Ligeti 2021
Id. *Konzert für Violoncello und Orchester / Lontano / Doppelkonzert / San Francisco Polyphony*, Wergo 286163-2, 2021.

Mečys 1998
Mečys, Aliutė. 'Irealizmas ir fantazijų Lietuva', an Interview with Raminta Lampsatyte [Lampsatis], in: *Kultūros barai*, no. 11 (1998), pp. 63-66.

More than Printing Scores: Ligeti and His Post-1960 Publishers

Heidy Zimmermann
(Paul Sacher Stiftung, Basel)

When György Ligeti submitted his large handwritten orchestral score for *Lontano* to Schott in 1967, his years-long search for a suitable publisher came to an end. His ties to the Mainz firm were now established — ties that would last almost forty years and prove at once fruitful and fraught. He had signed an exclusive contract with the proviso that all his works would be prepared by engravers or professional copyists and would appear in print within a reasonable span of time. For years he had known of the importance of efficient publishers, and he valued the availability of scores both as an author and as a recipient. But his emigration in 1956 had severed his contacts with Hungarian publishers, and in consequence he had to create a new foundation in the West.

The function of publishers and the importance of their relations with composers are a peripheral topic in musicology. Yet in the latter half of the twentieth century publishers were crucial for mediating between the various agents on the music scene. The reproduction, publication, distribution, promotion, exploitation, and copyright protection of New Music resided in their hands, as did the support, advancement, and long-term backing of composers. Although it may be difficult to imagine today, the publication of contemporary music was a highly lucrative business, at least before the wholesale spread of copying machines and other reproduction methods. It was within this context that promising young composers were encouraged by the publishers. Not least of all, publishers play a crucial role in composers' subsequent history, ensuring that their works remain available over time and, ideally, maintaining their own archives or cooperating with institutions devoted to the preservation of composers' estates. The accessibility of sources and documentary material is a *sine qua non* for scholarly editions and for historical and analytical research.

This essay will show how Ligeti found his bearings after arriving in the West, and how his search for a reliable publisher finally reached its goal after ten years. Recently resurfaced archival dossiers from the publishers involved offer a differentiated view of his negotiations and personal reflections. They shed light not only on the importance of the New Music networks in which a composer had to find a foothold, but equally on long-term personal relations in the post-war period, relations to which Ligeti was particularly sensitive. Especially revealing is his voluminous correspondence with publishers, which took up a large part of his communications until well into the 1970s. Not only does it allow us to correct or adjust well-known facts, but a comparison with later oral reminiscences and a critical examination of the sources yield a detailed picture of this chapter in Ligeti's life.

«Starved and Isolated» — Finding New Bearings in Vienna

Ligeti established contacts with his first Western publisher, Universal Edition, from Budapest in summer 1956. It was a period of relative political calm during which contacts and exchanges abroad could proceed unimpeded. In retrospect, he felt the experience was like «air rushing into a vacuum»[1]. He hoped to travel to Vienna for a few days in early September and pay a visit to UE so as to peruse new scores and especially to listen to records and tapes of current music and the works of Webern: «Despite my great and unstinting efforts, I have been unable to make contact with the modern musical world. [...] But I hope you will understand how starved and isolated I am»[2].

His urgent plea was answered by return of post with a friendly invitation from UE's reader Otto Tomek, who would soon move to West German Radio in Cologne. This visit never came about, but UE, at the intercession of Karlheinz Stockhausen and Herbert Eimert, sent him several scores and the special Webern issue of *die reihe* — welcome material for discussions in the Circle for New Music and Private Musical Performances that Ligeti had just founded[3]. As is well known, Hungary's détente did not last long, and on 10 December, after the suppression of the October Uprising, Ligeti fled to the West. As he had already initiated contact with the most renowned publisher of contemporary music, he was quickly able to arrange a meeting and present his abilities and interests. Soon he was entrusted with writing introductions to Bartók's Fifth String Quartet and Webern's Five Movements Op. 5. Paid assignments of this sort, as well as his Boulez analyses for *die reihe*, helped him to somewhat

---

[1]. «[...] das Einströmen von Luft in ein plötzlich geöffnetes Vakuum». Ligeti 2007, vol. ii, p. 75.

[2]. «Trotz meiner grossen und beständigen Anstrengungen war ich nicht in der Lage in Verbindung mit der modernen musikalischen Welt zu sein. [...] Ich hoffe aber, dass Sie verstehen, wie ausgehungert und isoliert ich bin». György Ligeti, letter of 8 September 1956 to UE; Historical Archive of Universal Edition, AG, Vienna (hereinafter UE Archive).

[3]. György Ligeti, [Curriculum vitae, March 1957], manuscript, 1 p. (UE Archive).

lessen the «chronic shortage of money» of his early years in the West[4]. At the same time UE assured the newcomer that they would follow his compositional development «with great interest»[5].

As Rachel Beckles Willson has pointed out, «Ligeti rapidly switched from being an anonymous refugee to a significant and popular teacher», but his «letters to compatriots also suggest a prolonged moment of in-between-ness, a struggle to find the future»[6]. Despite plunging into the avant-garde circles of Cologne and Darmstadt, in 1957 he felt a deep ambivalence toward post-war Germany and could not imagine settling there permanently[7]. When the publishers Suvini Zerboni, through the good offices of his former teacher Sándor Veress, showed interest in his first string quartet, he was honest enough to pass this information to UE, assuring them at the same time that «it would be a great pleasure and honor to be published by UE». He was, he continued, writing «a new piece [*Apparitions*]» and hoped to show it to them «in the near future»[8].

Alfred Schlee (1901-1999), UE's longstanding director, decided to accept *Apparitions* into the UE catalogue with an eye to its scheduled première at the Cologne ISCM Festival in June 1960[9]. While the firm was already courting Ligeti's age-mates, such as Pierre Boulez and Luciano Berio, he had to make do with the role of backup composer. Apart from an electronic piece produced in Cologne, all he had to show was the string quartet he had brought along from Hungary. As a result, it was not until early 1961 that the powerful Heinrich Strobel chose to program the emerging orchestral piece *Atmosphères* at the Donaueschingen Festival, when it seemed doubtful that Berio would complete his commissioned work on time[10]. The acceptance was granted after Ligeti, at Schlee's behest, presented a few pages of the score. Schlee, adopting a quite imperious tone, complained: «My dear friend, hadn't you promised to show Herr Court Councilor Strobel at least part of the score of your new piece by now? And did you do so? Why are you neglecting UE?»[11]. Thus *Atmosphères* was

---

[4]. «[...] chronischen Geldmangel»; Ligeti's letter of 3 March 1958 to Alfred Schlee (UE Archive).

[5]. «[...] mit grosser Aufmerksamkeit»; letter of recommendation from Schlee, 4 March 1957 (UE Archive). The letter was meant to support Ligeti's application for a Rockefeller Scholarship, which he submitted in June 1957 along with his 'Presentation for a new concept of Music Theory' for a book project (see AIGNER 2021).

[6]. BECKLES WILLSON 2011, p. 87.

[7]. *Ibidem*, p. 91; letter of 12 July 1957 from Ligeti to Adolf Weissmann.

[8]. «[...]grosse Freude und Ehre bedeuten, bei der UE zu erscheinen» – «ein neues Stück» – «in nicht allzu langer Zeit einmal»; Ligeti to Schlee, 5 October 1958 (UE Archive).

[9]. See Schlee's letter of 29 June 1959 to Ligeti, and Ligeti's letter of 3 May 1960 to Dr. Hift (UE Archive).

[10]. Strobel to Ligeti, 21 April 1961 (Paul Sacher Foundation, Basel, György Ligeti Collection; hereinafter PSS-GLC), and Schlee to Ligeti, 25 April 1961 (PSS-GLC).

[11]. «Verehrtester, hatten Sie nicht versprochen, Herrn Hofrat Strobel wenigstens eine teilweise Partitur Ihres neuen Stückes um diese Zeit vorzulegen? Taten Sie es? Warum vernachlässigen Sie die UE?»; Schlee to Ligeti, 7 April 1961 (PSS-GLC).

not written on commission, as was normally the case, but was proclaimed *ex post facto* to be a commissioned work[12].

Despite the rousing success of *Atmosphères* at Donaueschingen, UE evidently displayed no particular commitment to the budding refugee from Hungary. Ligeti was upset at not having met Schlee at the premières of his two orchestral works, and toward the end of 1961 he delivered an orchestral piece for Schlee's sixtieth birthday — *Fragment* — that vacillates between self-parody and renunciation in its barebones radicality[13]. The reasons why Ligeti left UE shortly after the première of *Atmosphères* are probably many and varied. The subject is unbroached in his correspondence with the publishers, and it was not until much later that he went on record by recalling that he had sat in Schlee's office and announced that his first commissioned work, *Volumina*, had been premièred in Bremen. Schlee had replied that he would not publish it, adding «Find a different publisher»[14].

Nor did Schlee countenance the prospect of publishing the First String Quartet, already premièred in Vienna on 8 May 1958. The work did not fit stylistically into the UE catalog. «Commercially, a string quartet is of course never a success», he argued. At the same time he advised against giving the piece to Suvini Zerboni, proposing instead that Ligeti could write out the transparencies himself for reproduction at UE[15]. With *Atmosphères*, too, UE merely had the score «facsimiled», whereas most of the scores of Boulez, Stockhausen, and Berio were, as Ligeti indignantly noted, «properly engraved»[16]. On the other hand, his first work to be engraved at UE was the less significant and insubstantial *Fragment* with a birthday dedication to Schlee — a fact that left Ligeti no more reconciled than the long-delayed facsimile print of *Apparitions* in 1964 for his analysis seminar in Darmstadt[17].

---

[12]. LIGETI – ROELCKE 2003, p. 107. Ligeti was sensitive to such matters and never concealed in later years that *Atmosphères* had been turned «into a sort of commission» («zu einer Art Auftrag»); *ibidem*, p. 107. In fact, Strobel's and Schlee's correspondence with Berio and Ligeti reveal that the completion of Berio's *Epifanie* remained uncertain until July 1961, and Ligeti's new piece was initially considered a potential substitute. The fee for *Atmosphères* was two-thirds of the amount promised to Berio. Ligeti was also asked at the last minute to stand in for Hans Heinz Stuckenschmidt's lecture series *Musik im Technischen Zeitalter* (1962-1963); see ZIMMERMANN 2016, pp. 177ff.

[13]. STEINITZ 2003, p. 123; Ligeti, draft letter to Schlee [Februar 1962], on a letter from Vera Ligeti (PSS-GLC).

[14]. LIGETI – ROELCKE 2003, p. 108. Autobiographical memoirs are used several times as source material in this essay. In Ligeti's case their reliability has already been called into question (see e.g. MARX 2016). However, it is worth considering the psychological insight that autobiographical memoirs are less a matter of facts and objective truth than the meaning and subjective interpretation of experiences. In this light, even reconstructed falsifications of memories can be revealing, in that they tell us something about the importance of memories for the writer's momentary self-image (see POHL 2007 and RUBIN 1986).

[15]. Schlee to Ligeti, 8 October 1958 (PSS-GLC).

[16]. «[...] richtig gestochen»; Ligeti to Ove Nordwall, 13 May 1964 (PSS-GLC).

[17]. *Ibidem*. See STEINITZ 2003, p. 123.

More than Printing Scores: Ligeti and His Post-1960 Publishers

What truly interested Schlee about Ligeti was the prospect of a substantial book on Webern. He waited at least ten years for it — to no avail[18]. At the age of ninety Schlee, who had exercised a formative influence on New Music for decades, openly stated his assessment of Ligeti in an interview: «Actually I wanted to steer Ligeti away from composing. [...] I found it unnecessary; there's already lots of that sort of music. I always told him that what I wanted from him was a book on Webern»[19]. Miffed at the lack of support for his compositional career, Ligeti drew the consequences.

«Transit Status»: Peters/Litolff in Frankfurt

In the first half of 1962 Ligeti switched to the publishing firm of Peters. Besides his dissatisfaction with UE, several other factors influenced his decision. First of all Rudolf Lück, a reader at Peters from 1955 to 1964, announced the company's interest[20]. Then Mauricio Kagel, thoroughly taken by Peters's managing director Johannes Petschull (1901-2001), encouraged his friend to make the switch[21]. Both composers thus entered the catalogue of Henry Litolff, the publishing firm that belonged to Peters from 1940 on and served as a platform to expand its contemporary music sector. In the 1960s Peters/Litolff began with noticeable interest to represent not only German modernists but international figures as well[22]. Ligeti fitted the bill. But whereas Kagel continued to cooperate with UE and ultimately entered an exclusive agreement with Peters, Ligeti's ties to the Frankfurt firm amounted to an intermezzo of barely five years' duration.

---

[18]. The project receded into the background from the 1960s as Ligeti increasingly received commissions for new pieces. The basic material for the book — roughly a dozen lectures on Webern — was ultimately published in his collected writings (Ligeti 2007, vol. I, pp. 325-410).

[19]. «Ligeti habe ich eigentlich immer vom Komponieren abhalten wollen [...] Ich fand das nicht notwendig, es gibt schon viel solche Musik. Ich habe ihm immer gesagt: Ich möchte von Ihnen ein Buch über Webern haben». Kapp 1996, p. 198, with the afterthought: «I mean, his music is readily marketable. Commercially, what I did back then was a mistake» («Ich meine — seine Musik ist gut anzubringen; geschäftlich war ein Fehler, was ich da gemacht habe».) Schlee congratulated Ligeti on his seventieth birthday with the double-edged comment, «I have to admit that you were right not to follow my siren song and sacrifice time for the Webern book. Although I still hope that one day you will take a creative break that might prove doubly effective» («[...] ich muss gestehen, dass Sie recht haben, meiner Verführung nicht zu folgen und keine Zeit für das Webernbuch zu opfern. Wenngleich ich noch immer Hoffnung habe, dass sich einmal eine schöpferische Pause ergeben könne, die dann doppelt wirksam wäre»); Schlee to Ligeti, 28 May 1993 (PSS-GLC).

[20]. Ligeti – Roelcke 2003, p. 109. See also Ligeti's letter of 2 June 1962 to Johannes Petschull (Sächsisches Staatsarchiv, Staatsarchiv Leipzig, Bestand 22107 C. F. Peters, Frankfurt).

[21]. Mauricio Kagel to John Cage, 6 October 1961 (Northwestern University, John Cage Collection).

[22]. See Petschull 1965, pp. 45-49: 49.

Once the situation with UE had been clarified and preliminary talks had been held (e.g. at the Bremen première of *Volumina* in May 1962), Ligeti sealed his collaboration with Peters by offering them the organ piece and *Aventures*, then still unfinished[23]. The managing director reaffirmed that he was looking forward to the collaboration and hoped that it would be «good and fruitful»[24]. Although Ligeti now had «far better conditions» with Peters, he encountered «unforeseen difficulties» in the production of his scores[25]. The firm was apparently unprepared for the meticulous demands from the composer of the *Requiem* and the Cello Concerto. Nor was Peters, which lacked a book program, the right place to fulfill his dream of an edition of his writings[26]; it even proved impossible to produce a brochure in good time for *Aventures* and *Nouvelle Aventures*[27]. Thus it happened that Ligeti, in 1966, switched allegiance after publishing only half a dozen pieces. By then he had many performances and major commissions under his belt, was making plans for a full-length opera, and sensed interest from various publishers. Both UE and Peters expressed a firm commitment, and Schlee even tried to fetch the successful composer back into the UE fold[28]. But above all Ligeti discovered that Krzysztof Penderecki wanted to go to Schott, and that Schott wanted to «offer him similar conditions». To be sure, he felt moral qualms, for Peters was «putting forth serious efforts»[29]. But after protesting against the misguided Stuttgart staging of *Aventures* and *Nouvelles Aventures* and sensing Peters's lack of support[30], he felt compelled to change publishers.

«[...] WITH SCHOTT TO THE END OF MY DAYS»

Ligeti had already made initial contacts with Schott as a twenty-five-year-old student in Budapest. In September 1948, at the recommendation of the publisher Miklós Weisz, he had introduced himself as a Hungarian correspondent for their house organ *Melos*[31], which soon carried his reports on contemporary music in Hungary (1949) and dodecaphonic music and

---

[23]. Ligeti to Rudolf Lück, 2 June 1962 (Sächsisches Staatsarchiv, Staatsarchiv Leipzig, Bestand 22107 C. F. Peters, Frankfurt).

[24]. «[...] gut und fruchtbar»; Petschull to Ligeti, 6 June 1962 (PSS-GLC).

[25]. «[...] sehr viel bessere Bedingungen» – «ungeahnte Schwierigkeiten»; LIGETI – ROELCKE 2003, p. 109.

[26]. See Ligeti's letter of 14 August 1965 to Nordwall (PSS-GLC).

[27]. See KAUFMANN 1993, pp. 217-221, *passim*.

[28]. See Ligeti's letter of 5 February 1967 to Heinz Schneider-Schott (PSS-GLC).

[29]. «[...] ähnliche Bedingungen anbieten» – «nun sehr bemüht»; Ligeti to Nordwall, 17 April 1966 (PSS-GLC).

[30]. Ligeti's press release is reproduced in KAUFMANN 1993, pp. 225ff. See his letter of 7 February 1967 to Nordwall (PSS-GLC).

[31]. Ligeti to the editorial office of *Melos*, 18 September 1948 (PSS-GLC)

«new tonality» in Budapest (1950)[32]. His fees were paid in the form of a *Melos* subscription and a series of books and musical editions, which Schott were happy to send to the inquisitive young man from Eastern Europe[33].

Against this backdrop, Ligeti was delighted when, in late 1964, he learned from Ernst Thomas of «Schott's secret interest» in his music. Thomas was head of the Darmstadt International Institute of Music and connected with Schott as editor of the *Darmstädter Beiträge*. Ligeti expressed his thoughts on publishing matters to him with remarkable candor and a clear-cut strategy:

> At the moment I have no particular reason to leave Peters — unless I find better conditions elsewhere for the publication of my music. It was indeed the case, as you rightly noted, that several things at Peters left me dissatisfied. But I frankly informed them of this, and with the best will they are now at pains to fulfill my requests. I must also note that my contractual conditions at Peters (royalties, etc.) are quite favorable and leave me no reason to switch publishers in this respect. My demands were aimed at matters of a technical nature, and at matters of marketing and publicity. But despite Peters's good will, there are certain natural limitations in these matters, a result of the well-known discontinuity in their history. There is no doubt that larger publishers with a tradition of issuing New Music can offer a better home to today's composers, the best examples being Schott and UE. But these larger publishers have well-known gradations in the manner and extent of their dedication to particular composers. It's clear what I'm aiming at: if a larger firm were to see me as belonging to the small circle of composers to whom it offers publicity, material and technical support — whom it actually backs up — I would prefer that solution. [...] There's another essential point, namely, that my work has recently undergone a favorable change: for many years I was intent on increasingly focusing on composition and gradually reducing my teaching activities etc. to a bare minimum. [...] This change has also been made possible by several commissions I've recently received. [...] This beneficial transformation has made it urgent that I need a publisher wholly dedicated to my music[34].

---

[32]. 'Neue Musik in Ungarn' (1949) and 'Neues aus Budapest: Zwölftonmusik oder "Neue Tonalität"'; LIGETI 2007, vol. I, pp. 49-60. Ligeti's deceptive memory made its way into the preface of this new edition. The first article cannot have originated in 1946, for the contact with *Melos* only arose in 1948.

[33]. His wish list included Hindemith's *Unterweisung im Tonsatz*, Stravinsky's *Musikalische Poetik*, and Wörner's *Musik der Gegenwart*, as well as scores by Hindemith, Orff, and Stravinsky. See Ligeti's letters of 22 July 1950 and 6 August 1950 to the editorial offices of *Melos* (PSS-GLC).

[34]. «Im Augenblick besteht für mich kein besonderer Grund von Peters wegzugehen — sei es denn, dass ich anderswo bessere Umstände für die Veröffentlichung meiner Stücke vorfinde. Tatsächlich war es so — Sie haben das richtig bemerkt —, dass ich bei Peters mit Einigem nicht zufrieden war. Dies habe ich aber dem Verlag aufrichtig mitgeteilt und man ist dort nun mit bestem Willen bemüht, meine Wünsche zu erfüllen. Ich muss dazu noch bemerken, dass meine Vertragsbedingungen bei Peters (Tantièmen, etc.) recht günstig sind und

In the fall of 1966 Heinz Schneider-Schott (1906-1988), son-in-law of Ludwig Strecker jr. and a member of the management board, entered negotiations with Ligeti that led to the signing of an exclusive contract in early 1967. By then the composer had received so much international acclaim that he could set conditions himself. He considered it crucial for all his new works to be «issued in print» in customary commercial fashion «within a generally agreed period of time», normally two years[35]. He was thus no longer willing to accept facsimile prints of his music. He also demanded a monthly stipend to free him from the need to accept hackwork for a living. In compensation, Schott would receive the right to keep the manuscripts of his works «in the interest of scholarly research and subsequent textual revisions» on their premises as their own property[36]. This agreement remained in force until 1974, after which the autographs remained the author's property or, in some cases, entered the holdings of their respective patrons.

What Ligeti experienced with Schott, no doubt putting wind in his compositional sails, involved not only personal dealings with the firm's management but also an especially direct way of working with its employees. With UE and Peters, too, he had valued certain employees on whom he could rely in practical matters[37]. At Schott, however, he had at his side an enthusiastic editor (Klaus Schöll) and the head of the production department (Anton Müller). From the very outset, the correspondence that quickly ensued with the signing of the contract reveals a mutual rapport. Ligeti spoke freely of his planned compositions, commissions, and undertakings;

---

diesbezüglich hätte ich keinen Grund, den Verlag zu wechseln. Meine Forderungen zielten auf Fragen technischer Art, ausserdem auf Fragen des Vertriebes und der Propaganda. Trotz bestem Willen bei Peters gibt es dort aber in Hinsicht dieser Fragen — als Ergebnis der bekannten Diskontinuität in der Geschichte des Verlages — bestimmte natürliche Begrenzungen. Es besteht kein Zweifel diesbezüglich, dass grössere Verlage mit einer Tradition auch in der Veröffentlichung neuer Musik, einen günstigeren Heimort für heutige Komponisten bedeuten können — in dieser Hinsicht sind freilich Schott und die UE die besten Orte. Es gibt aber bei den grösseren Verlagen die bekannten Abstufungen in der Art und dem Mass des Einsatzes, die diese Verlage für einzelne Komponisten leisten. Es ist eindeutig, worauf ich hinziele: sollte mich ein grösserer Verlag zum engeren Kreis seiner Komponisten gehörend betrachten, für denen [sic] sich der Verlag propagandistisch, materiell und technisch vor allem einsetzt, denen der Verlag einen tatsächlichen Rückhalt bietet, so würde ich diese Lösung vorziehen. [...] Es kommt noch ein wesentlicher Aspekt dazu, nämlich dass sich in meiner Arbeit in letzter Zeit eine günstige Veränderung abzeichnet: seit mehreren Jahren war ich bestrebt, mich immer mehr auf das Komponieren zu konzentrieren und die Lehrtätigkeit usw. allmählich auf das unbedingt nötige einzuschränken. [...] Diese Umstellung ist auch dadurch ermöglicht worden, dass ich in letzter Zeit mehrere Kompositionsaufträge erhielt [...]. Diese günstige Wandlung macht es aktuell, dass ich einen Verlag brauche, der für meine Stücke sich ganz einsetzt». Ligeti to Ernst Thomas, 1 January 1965. The letter ends with a request to forward the information to Schott. An annotated copy is found in the correspondence of Heinz Schneider-Schott (PSS-GLC).

[35]. «[...] gedruckt publiziert» – «innerhalb einer allgemein gesetzten Frist»; Ligeti to Schneider-Schott, 23 September 1966 (PSS-GLC).

[36]. «[...] im Interesse der Quellenforschung und späteren Textrevision»; contract, Article 6 (PSS-GLC). The contract was signed on 8 February 1967 and went into effect on 1 March 1967.

[37]. Ligeti to Nordwall, 27 May 1964, and Ligeti to Petschull, 5 February 1967 (PSS-GLC).

his editor displayed interest, assured him of support, and reported regularly on promotional activities. Besides the exchange of letters, discussions were increasingly held by telephone and painstakingly set down in memoranda which, like travel reports, served the purpose of inhouse communication. This fairly dense body of documents on Ligeti's collaboration with Schott (nearly 3000 pages) permits nuanced insight into negotiations, production processes, and artistic and economic deliberations. Time and again Ligeti expressed his appreciation for the firm, an extended family business with clear organizational structures, loyal employees, and smooth operations. For his part, he promised maximum commitment while citing his inviolable conditions: artistic freedom and an unwillingness to compromise: «I place great stock [...] on having my first Schott piece [*Lontano*] be especially good. [...] I simply need enough time for this highly poetic piece to mature»[38].

To be sure, it did not take long for difficulties to arise. While the première and production of *Lontano* went off smoothly in 1967[39], *Ramifications* brought points of friction to the fore: the compositional process took much longer than expected, so that Paul Sacher, who «immediately took a shine» to the piece on Schott's recommendation, had to «cancel this new Ligeti with a heavy heart» because of his precept of never programming a work sight unseen[40]. If the publishers had to negotiate several postponements of the première, encouragement came from the reader with increasing regularity: «What's happening with *Ramifications*?»[41] – «Keenly awaiting delivery of "R"»[42]. – «Urgently waiting for rest of *Ramifications*. Special Ligeti copyist twiddling thumbs. Production department disgruntled»[43]. – «Sighs of *Ramifications* relief from Vienna and Mainz»[44].

The years from 1967 to 1972 were extremely productive for Ligeti; *Continuum*, the organ études, String Quartet No. 2, *Ten Pieces for Wind Quintet*, *Ramifications*, the Chamber Concerto, *Melodien*, and the Double Concerto arose in rapid succession, mostly commissioned by renowned performers and institutions. Occasionally the composer felt «pampered» by meticulous

---

[38]. «Es liegt mir [...] sehr viel daran, dass mein erstes Schott-Stück besonders gut sei. [...] ich brauche zu diesem sehr poetischen Stück einfach genügende Reifungszeit». Ligeti to Schneider-Schott, 14 March 1967 (PSS-GLC).

[39]. For example Anton Müller, the head of production, valued Ligeti's «very precise and comprehensive suggestions for producing the material» of *Lontano* («sehr präzise und umfassende Hinweise zur Material-Herstellung»); letter of 21 July 1967 (PSS-GLC).

[40]. «[...] sofort Feuer gefangen» – «schweren Herzens auf diesen neuen Ligeti verzichten»; [Klaus Schöll], memorandum of 6 December 1967, and Schöll's letter of 14 August 1968 to Ligeti (PSS-GLC).

[41]. «Was macht "Ramifications"?»; Schöll to Ligeti, 16 October 1968 (PSS-GLC).

[42]. «In grosser Erwartung der "R"-Lieferung»; Schöll to Ligeti, 6 December 1968 (PSS-GLC).

[43]. «[...] erwarten dringendst ramificationsrest. Ligeti-spezialschreiber unbeschaeftigt. herstellungsabteilung verstimmt»; Schöll to Ligeti, telegram of 7 February 1969. See Müller to Ligeti, 7 February 1969 (PSS-GLC).

[44]. «erloestes ramifications aufatmen in wien und mainz»; Schöll to Ligeti, telegram of 17 March 1969 (PSS-GLC).

editions[45], awarded top marks for the production, and charmingly expressed appreciation for his partners at the publishers. The partners worked in the field of tension between deadline pressure and perfectionism, now supportive, now demanding, at times critical yet good-humored. All the while the reader displayed interest in Ligeti's opera plans, acquired potential textual sources (e.g. Ionesco's *Macbett*), and actively accompanied the seemingly endless creative process of *Grand Macabre* up to the première. People at Schott were aware that Ligeti was to be cultivated as «the best horse in the stall» and his wishes were to be granted, or better yet, anticipated. The composer was delighted at such advertising measures as a catalogue of works (1969), a Ligeti dossier in *Schott aktuell* (1972), and the publication of Nordwall's monograph (1971), and expressed his gratitude for «great Ligeti publicity» in an issue of *Melos*[46]. On the other hand, he never tired of insisting that he did not want to become a «deadline composer» and was «incapable of artistic compromise»[47]. Ligeti was surely not the only composer with high artistic standards and resultant deadline problems. What is extraordinary is the deliberately articulated candor and disarmingly open tone of his communications — features that Ewa Schreiber found characteristic of Ligeti's writings as a whole[48].

Ligeti identified so closely with his publisher that he even intruded in their business dealings and innovation policy without being asked. In the tenth year of their collaboration he dispatched an urgent letter to the entire management board, criticizing the new line of popular music, and expressing deep concern at the publisher's image and continuity. For neither the first nor the last time he threatened to give notice on his contract while avowing that he felt happy with Schott as a composer, given his many experiences, and wanted to «remain with Schott to the end of my days»[49]. Despite all the ups and downs in their collaboration, a balance seems to have been struck, on the whole and lastingly, between material and economic interests, compositional and publishing standards, and mutual gain in prestige.

Dark Histories

Ligeti's letter of February 1967, officially parting ways with Peters and his publisher Petschull, is exquisitely courteous and diplomatic. He explained his new alignment by saying

---

[45]. «[…] verwöhnt»; Ligeti, letter of 10 January 1971 to Schneider-Schott regarding the publication of *Continuum* (PSS-GLC).

[46]. «[…] grosse Ligeti-Propaganda»; see Ligeti's letters to Schöll of 12 December 1969, 17 February 1972, and 28 February 1973 (PSS-GLC).

[47]. «Termin-komponist» – «unfähig zu künstlerischen Kompromissen»; Ligeti's letters to Schöll of 15 June 1972 and 24 February 1974 (PSS-GLC).

[48]. Schreiber 2019, esp. 33.

[49]. «[…] den Wunsch, lebenslang bei Schott»; Ligeti's letter of 24 March 1976 to Schott's managing board (Arno Volk et al.) (PSS-GLC).

that he wanted to shift the focus of his compositional activities to the stage and needed a publisher with a specialization in theater. At the same time he expressed his gratitude and hoped for a continuation of their untroubled and cordial ties[50]. Many years later, however, these relations acquired a bitter aftertaste. «Back then I was never informed that the director, Johannes Petschull, was a Nazi,» Ligeti claimed in an interview with Eckhard Roelcke. «If I had known, I would never have turned to Peters. [...] Schlee, who did know, never told me»[51]. Where Ligeti got his information about Petschull's Nazi past is a matter of guesswork. He may conceivably have heard about it in conversation with insiders in the music publishing scene. The varied repetition of his statement, «When I was with Peters I learned, as I said, that Johannes Petschull had been an active Nazi»[52], suggest that he knew of this state of affairs far earlier. Yet there is nothing to suggest that he had been informed of Petschull's role in the Third Reich in the 1960s. His letters to the publisher are too friendly to imply dissimulation. Nor do his remarks to third parties intimate anything along these lines[53]. On the contrary, nothing was said about such continuities in German or Austrian music life until well into the 1980s. Even the dispossessed owners of the publishing houses, reinstalled after the war, held their peace. Not until the late 1990s did music publishing firms come under historical scrutiny. It was now made public that Petschull, a doctor of musicology, had not only been a member of the Nazi party from 1937, and managing director of «Aryanized» Peters from 1939, but had acquired ownership of UE with the help of the Nazi authorities in 1941. To do this he had evidently made use of inside information previously obtained during his management position at Schott. After 1945 Petschull was able to maintain his position at Peters and, with the restitution of the firm's earlier owners and its relocation from Leipzig to Frankfurt in 1950, even to expand it. Soon he was entrusted with leadership roles on the committees of Germany's publishing scene[54].

---

[50]. Ligeti to Petschull, 3 February 1967, copy enclosed in the letter of 5 February 1967 to Heinz Schneider-Schott, who had advised him to pursue this line of argument (PSS-GLC).

[51]. «Ich habe damals keine Informationen gehabt, dass der Direktor, Johannes Petschull, ein Nazi war. Wenn ich das gewusst hätte, wäre ich nie zu Peters gegangen. [...] Schlee, der es wusste, hatte es mir nicht erzählt». LIGETI – ROELCKE 2003, p. 109. Vera Ligeti, when asked about the switch to Schott, stated that Petschull was a Nazi, but that this information probably only reached her husband in the 1990s (telephone conversation with the author, 5 June 2021). Schlee, when asked about Petschull's party membership, replied nebulously: «I don't know. He must have been. [...] I simply didn't want to know precisely» («Das weiss ich nicht. Er muß es wohl gewesen sein. [...] Ich wollte das einfach nicht genau wissen»); KAPP 1996, p. 186.

[52]. «[...] als ich bei Peters war, habe ich, wie gesagt, erfahren, dass Johannes Petschull ein aktiver Nazi gewesen war»; LIGETI – ROELCKE 2003, p. 109.

[53]. See Ligeti's letter of 19 February 1977 to Petschull and Karl Rarichs (PSS-GLC); Ligeti to Nordwall, 7 February 1967 (PSS-GLC). The «discontinuity» mentioned in the letter to Thomas (see above, n. 34) probably relates to the relocation of the publishers' headquarters from Leipzig to Frankfurt am Main, but hardly to the political aspect.

[54]. Detailed account in FETTHAUER 2007, pp. 178-180 and 200-206. PETSCHULL (1965, pp. 47), in the entry on Peters, gives a wide berth to the Nazi period.

The interviews in Roelcke's book were held between June 2001 and October 2002. In summer 2001 the *Österreichische Musikzeitschrift* published an issue devoted to UE's first centenary. Here, for the first time, Hartmut Krones named the agents involved in UE's «Aryanization» in 1938 and mentioned Petschull's purchase of the firm[55]. It is safe to assume that Ligeti, as a subscriber, took note of the article, which may well have sparked his statement about Petschull[56]. But the same special issue also touched on Schlee, who is said in the preface to have operated «with a rare combination of objective in- and oversight and tactical acumen» during his decades with the company[57]. Indeed, Schlee had managed to leave behind few seriously compromising tracks in the 1930s and 1940s and could position himself after 1945 as a proven champion of New Music. He was viewed as the man who had «rescued things from destruction» and given UE «a new intellectual profile in the decades following the Second World War»[58]. While not exactly false, this was not the whole truth: the Nazis considered Schlee to be Jewish by marital relations. His «non-Aryan» wife Anna Taussig had committed suicide in February 1939[59]. That he was involved in the «Aryanization» of UE, and had negotiated for its postwar relocation to Switzerland, left behind only a faint paper trail[60]. Schlee always relied on silence, declining to mention his memories of 1938 and the years that followed[61]. He succeeded in projecting an image of humble restraint, so that New Music figures such as Pierre Boulez could speak positively of his extraordinary discretion[62].

Ligeti, on the other hand, drily attested that Schlee was «in the know». Sophie Fetthauer, in her study of music publishers, arrived at a «quite ambivalent picture» of UE's director on the basis of solid archival research[63]. In view of everything that has come to light in the meantime, his «tactical acumen» and «discretion» in personal matters take on a different hue, and it is difficult to interpret his silence as humble restraint. That Schlee, in the unpublished parts of

---

[55]. KRONES 2001.

[56]. Whether he also knew of Schlee's remark in the Kapp interview (see n. 51) cannot be determined.

[57]. «[...] in seltener Verbindung von sachlicher Ein- und Übersicht mit taktischem Geschick»; DIEDERICHS-LAFITE 2001.

[58]. «Untergehendes gerettet» – «in den Jahrzehnten nach dem Zeiten Weltkrieg ein neues geistiges Profil»; STEPHAN 1981, p. 643.

[59]. See FETTHAUER 2007, pp. 211-213, and KOWALKE 2001, p. 24.

[60]. See KRONES 2001, p. 22, and FETTHAUER 2007, p. 212. The correspondence between Alfred Schlee and Paul Sacher in 1946 mentions «fundamental decisions» and mutual visits. Schlee wanted to see Sacher «at all costs» («unbedingt sehen») in order to «discuss a great many important things» («sehr viel Wichtiges zu besprechen»); PSS, Paul Sacher Collection.

[61]. His «dedication to the survival» («Einsatz für das Überleben») of UE was lauded in the *Österreichische Musikzeitschrift* beneath the heading '50 Years Later' with an extract from an interview (KNESSL 1988, p. 190).

[62]. See HERBORT 1991.

[63]. «[...] recht ambivalenten Bild»; FETTHAUER 2007, p. 271. Kim Kowalke (2001, p. 32) raised the question of whether Schlee worked as «a double-agent, an apolitical, modernist 'mole' in the enemy camp».

his interview with Lothar Knessl, saw himself as UE's «poster goy» and the death of his wife indirectly as a «chance to remain»[64], seem more like a symptom of the sort of embroidery that allowed many agents of his generation to launch second careers.

Ligeti had no illusions about Germany history, and would not have been greatly astonished to learn that Schott's directors, Ludwig and Willy Strecker, had been interested in taking over UE during the war years. Without being party members, they vainly tried, in competition with Petschull, to exploit their connections with Winifred Wagner. Later they painted their failed takeover of UE as an attempt to rescue the notoriously debt-ridden company[65].

«My Finest Piece»: The Publication of the Second String Quartet

To illustrate Ligeti's collaboration with Schott let me take a specific example. The materials for the Second String Quartet, one of his earliest pieces to enter the Schott catalogue, offer a dense and revealing body of sources. Its genesis and publication can be retraced closely in the conspectus of manuscripts among Ligeti's personal papers, production materials, and accompanying correspondence from the Schott archives.

In spring 1968 Ligeti informed Schott that the quartet was one of his «most difficult and complicated works» and sought their understanding for its delayed completion[66]. As a result, he submitted the finished manuscript one movement at a time. Even so, the première scheduled for autumn 1968 had to be postponed, for the LaSalle Quartet, who initiated the work and likewise received copies of the score one movement at a time, were no less perfectionist than the composer and preferred to postpone the première by one year[67]. After completing the fifth movement in July 1968, Ligeti again stated that «it is my finest piece to date. Very complicated»[68]. Then began a production process as wearisome as it was complex, making it clear that the work's publication was an integral part of the compositional process. Although Ligeti made few changes to the music's skeletal fabric (pitch and rhythm), he sought to codify the no less substantial timbral dimension as precisely as possible. To ensure an adequate performance despite the piece's performative and compositional complexity, he took scrupulous charge of optimizing the notation and graphic design.

---

[64]. «Renommiergoj» – «Möglichkeit zu bleiben»; Lothar Knessl, '1938/1988: Alfred Schlee im Gespräch mit Lothar Knessl', transcript for a memorial broadcast on Austrian radio (ORF) on 14 and 15 June 1999, pp. 2 and 4 (Universität für Musik und Darstellende Kunst Vienna, Sammlung Lothar Knessl).

[65]. Detailed discussion in FETTHAUER 2007, p. 205, and recently DÜMLING 2020, p. 67.

[66]. «[...] schwierigstes und kompliziertestes Werk»; memorandum [Schöll, early 1968] (PSS-GLC).

[67]. See SPRUYTENBURG 2011, p. 223, and Müller's letter of 22 March 1968 to Ligeti (PSS-GLC).

[68]. «[...] es ist mein bestes Stück bis jetzt. Sehr kompliziert»; Ligeti to Schöll, 16 August 1968 (PSS-GLC).

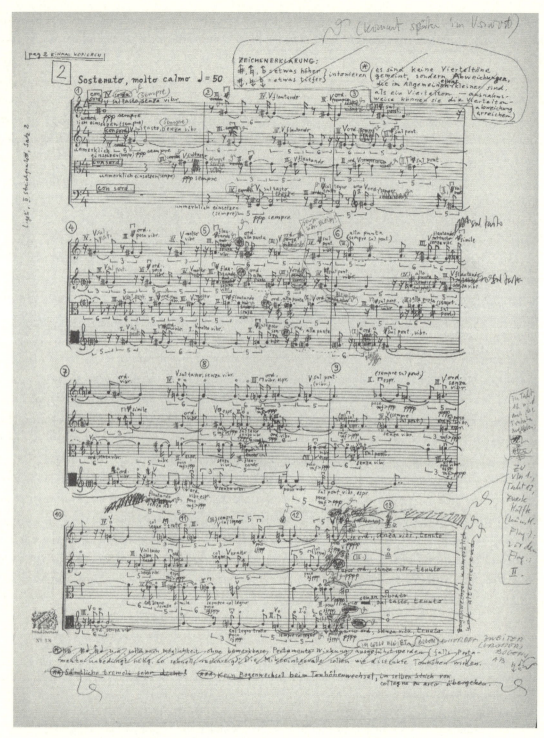

ILL. 1: György Ligeti, String Quartet No. 2. Blueprint of the fair copy with «touchups» (production master), Darmstadt, 9 Sept. 1968, p. [11] (PSS-GLC).

More than Printing Scores: Ligeti and His Post-1960 Publishers

Ill. 1 shows a page from the blueprint of the fair copy that Ligeti prepared as a production master in September 1968, with corrections and annotations. The basic layer of the musical text, written on preprinted string quartet manuscript paper, is the fair copy in black india ink, including annotations on the partial delivery in the left-hand margin. On top of this layer are the corrections, rapidly written in red ballpoint pen. They involve the dynamics as well as the notation and execution of harmonics and clarification of performance instructions, partly couched in additional annotations. There are also roughly a dozen «touchups» to the musical text that Ligeti wrote out afresh and delivered on separate sheets of manuscript paper. When this production master arrived at the publishers, the head of production responded, with amiable irony:

> While I dictate the acknowledgement of receipt of your corrected score, the desk and walls are bathed in a reddish glow reflecting the result of your extensive efforts. I believe it was worth re-examining the work; everyone involved stands to profit. But to reduce the shock to the graphic designer, we'll first carry out these touchups on the films and then present him with a new "manuscript"[69].

The performance score, produced in a combined process of printed music and manuscript, bears the copyright date of 1969. In June of that year Ligeti was promised the «responsible author's proofs»: «It need hardly be stressed how complex this not exactly simple operation had become for us with the extensive changes, or that our graphic designer and proofreader struggled valiantly at their task»[70]. The head of production then applied a bit a pressure, for the LaSalle Quartet needed offprints of the engraved score so as to assemble the material for the actual rehearsals[71].

Initially Ligeti, in consultation with first violinist Walter Levin, took great pains to determine suitable page-turns. But in the end the première, given on 14 December 1969, was played from copies pasted together individually from the score[72] (see Ill. 2). The proofreading

---

[69]. «Während ich die Empfangsbestätigung Ihrer korrigierten Partitur diktiere, liegt ein rötlicher Abglanz auf Schreibtisch und Wänden, der das Ergebnis Ihrer umfangreichen Bemühungen widerspiegelt. Ich glaube, es hat sich gelohnt, das Werk daraufhin durchzusehen, es wird allen Beteiligten gut zustatten kommen. Um den Grafiker aber nicht zu sehr zu schockieren, werden wir diese Retuschen zunächst auf den Filmen ausführen, um ihm dann ein neues "Manuskript" vorzulegen»; Müller to Ligeti, 20 September 1968 (PSS-GLC).

[70]. «Es braucht wohl nicht besonders hervorgehoben zu werden, wie kompliziert dieser an sich nicht ganz einfache Auftrag durch die umfangreichen Änderungen für uns geworden war, und dass sich unser Grafiker sowie der Korrektor redlich dabei abgemüht haben»; Müller to Ligeti, 3 June 1969 (PSS-GLC).

[71]. Müller to Ligeti, 16 June 1969, and Ligeti to Müller, 17 June 1969 (PSS-GLC). Despite Ligeti's voluminous explanations, it cannot be said with certainty whether separate parts were intended or whether marked-up offprints of the score were used from the very outset.

[72]. Performance materials in PSS, LaSalle Quartet Collection.

stage of the material used at the première is represented by the printed layer of the proof copy shown in ILL. 3. Ligeti, though «impressed by the quality of the handwriting», persevered with his revisions, particularly after rehearsing with the quartet. Not only did he correct misprints, he also altered the dynamics, reversed engraver's decisions, and optimized the appearance on the page.

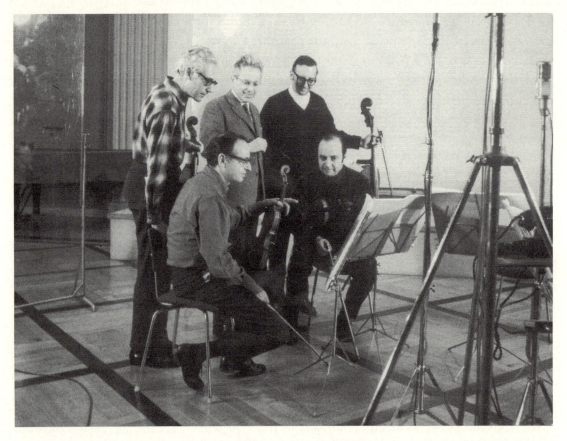

ILL. 2: György Ligeti in a rehearsal with the LaSalle Quartet, Munich 1970 (PSS-LaSalle Collection). «[Ligeti] could listen with extraordinary precision. He knew exactly what he wanted and simply never gave up. He was extremely critical, but very charming. He could say, for example, "The way you play that is absolutely marvelous, but it doesn't agree in the slightest with what I have in mind!"» (Walter Levin, in SPRUYTENBURG 2011, p. 261).

The publishers' original plan to present a printed study score for the première was dropped in view of the complicated proofreading stages. In any case the copyright and sales of the edition had to be postponed to December 1971, for LaSalle owned exclusive performance rights for two years. The Second String Quartet thus lay fallow while Ligeti communicated with Schott on finally issuing the First Quartet in print[73].

---

[73]. Memorandum (Schöll), 10 October 1969 (PSS-GLC).

More than Printing Scores: Ligeti and His Post-1960 Publishers

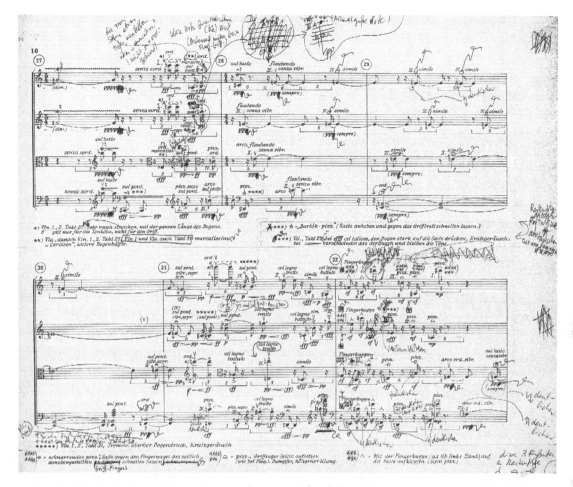

Ill. 3: György Ligeti, String Quartet No. 2. Advance proof with handwritten corrections, p. 10 (PSS-GLC).

After a second set of authorial corrections, Ligeti thanked the publishers for the «beautiful execution of the score» of his Second Quartet[74]. But he insisted on yet another set of proofs, to be mounted throughout with four systems per page[75]. Some six years after the première the study score finally appeared, with a bright yellow dustcover, in the series *Music of Our Time*. Schott's production department had passed their acid test, and Ligeti sealed his relations to the firm with charming insights:

> The one who is and was chronically behind schedule is me. I'm also aware
> of being a bit pedantic and often pose severe demands. But they always have to do
> with matters at hand. […] Time and again I've forced you into situations where you

---

74. «[…] wunderschöne Ausführung der Partitur»; Ligeti to Müller, 30 September 1975 (PSS-GLC).

75. See Ligeti, String Quartet No. 2, author's corrections 2 and 3 (14 August 1974 and 30 September 1975), and Ligeti to Müller, 8 November 1975 (PSS-GLC).

have to conjure up something for me at a moment's notice. For this, I'm grateful to you from the bottom of my heart. I can't imagine any better working relations than those we have. [...] Let's stick to it that each of us does what he can, and that each is allowed to make mistakes and fall behind schedule... So let's continue our good working relations... without apologies for normal human imperfections (though I have a hundred times more imperfections)[76].

Lost and Found: Pathways and Roundabout Routes to the Archive

Paul Sacher, a redoubtable conductor and impresario ideally networked with publishers and other exponents of New Music, had shown interest in Ligeti's music at an early date. The European première of *Ramifications* that he had programmed in his concert series never materialized owing to the above-mentioned scheduling difficulties. But in 1972 the Basle-based patron mounted the local première of *Lontano* with Francis Travis, and a few years later an all-Ligeti program with the same conductor. Shortly before opening his research institute for twentieth-century music, in April 1986, he performed *Apparitions* and *Ramifications*. At the end of that same year the scholarly coordinator of the Paul Sacher Foundation, Hans Oesch (1926-1992), introduced the new institution to Ligeti and expressed his personal desire to have the composer transfer all documents related to his creative work[77]. The resultant negotiations dragged on with many a snag and took more than thirteen years to reach a contractual agreement.

While Oesch took great pains as mediator until his untimely death, Ligeti clung to his pride, as did Sacher, and was unwilling to submit a direct offer. Then, in the early 1990s, the Swedish musicologist Ove Nordwall sold to the Foundation the manuscripts he had received from Ligeti as gestures of friendship. Ligeti was understandably offended, but still remained open to the thought that it would be better «for all the sketches and manuscripts to remain together»[78]. In June 1995 he traveled to Basle for an initial visit, which in turn ended in

---

[76]. «Derjenige, der chronisch im Rückstand ist und war, bin ich. Ich bin auch bewusst, dass ich etwas pedantisch bin, und oft hohe Ansprüche stelle. Es geht aber immer um sachliche Dinge. [...] Ich habe Sie immer wieder in Situationen gedrängt, wo Sie ganz schnell für mich zaubern mussten. Ich bin dafür Ihnen aus meinem ganzen Herzen dankbar. Ich kann mir auch keine bessere Zusammenarbeit denken, als wir sie haben. [...] Bleiben wir dabei, dass jeder von uns tut, was er kann — und dass jeder von uns sich auch irren darf und im Rückstand sein kann... Also setzen wir fort die gute Zusammenarbeit — ohne Entschuldigungen wegen normalen menschlichen Unzulänglichkeiten (wobei ich 100-mal mehr Unzulänglichkeiten habe)». Ligeti to Müller, 14 December 1975 (PSS-GLC).

[77]. Hans Oesch to Ligeti, 18 December 1986; see also Oesch to Ligeti, 5 March 1987 (PSS-GLC).

[78]. «[...] wenn alle Skizzen und Manuskripte zusammenblieben». Ligeti to Oesch, 13 May 1990 (PSS, business correspondence).

a stalemate. Sacher was about to enlarge his archive's premises and evidently let it be known that he could not immediately release the necessary funds. Ligeti responded by threatening to explore other options[79]. Following an acute crisis in the negotiations, everyone involved seems to have reflected on the priority of a single repository. Finally the contract was signed on 28 June 2000, and the first shipment and the official establishment of the György Ligeti Collection took place in November of that same year.

One peculiarity of Sacher's archival policy was, at first, not to regard a composer's papers as a finished arrangement, but to expand them with documents that cropped up later elsewhere. This desire finds expression in the term «collection» for the individual archives, and activities along these lines have been supported to the present day. To end this essay, the implications of his policy will be illustrated with a particularly significant example: the fair score of *Atmosphères*, whose ownership had remained with UE but had been marked «lost» since 1990[80]. Ligeti himself confirmed that it was missing when he handed over his manuscripts to the Foundation, and later remarked with surprising nonchalance:

> The scores of *Apparitions* and *Atmosphères* are lost. No one knows where they are. They must have been filed away somewhere. [...] A few years ago they were meant to be put on display in an exhibition, but UE replied that the manuscripts no longer existed. That's normal for publishers. [...] There's a lot of red tape in a big publishing company, and there was no love lost on these manuscripts. But it doesn't matter: *Apparitions* and *Atmosphères* have appeared in very nice printed editions[81].

Nine years after Schlee's death, and two after Ligeti's, the autograph turned up surprisingly at an auction[82], and the Foundation was able to acquire it for the Ligeti Collection[83].

The acquisition of parts of the Schott archive in 2019 also brought substantial additions to the Ligeti Collection. Besides the correspondence and production materials for a great many works, there were ten autograph fair scores of pieces dating from 1967 to 1974[84]. Thus, after

---

[79]. Ligeti to Albi Rosenthal, 22. November 1995 (PSS, business correspondence).

[80]. RICHART 1990, p. 15.

[81]. «Die Partituren von "Apparitions" und "Atmosphères" sind verschollen. Man weiss nicht, wo sie sind. Irgendwo wurden sie abgelegt. [...] Man wollte sie vor ein paar Jahren an einer Ausstellung zeigen, und die UE hat geantwortet, dass es die Manuskripte nicht mehr gibt. Das ist normal bei Verlagen. [...] Es gibt viel Bürokratie in einem grossen Verlag, und es fehlt auch die Liebe für diese Manuskripte. Aber es macht nichts. "Apparitions" und "Atmosphères" sind im Druck sehr schön erschienen». LIGETI – ROELCKE 2003, p. 104.

[82]. Christie's (London), *Valuable Manuscripts and Printed Books*, 4 June 2008, Catalogue 7540, pp. 158ff.

[83]. All that could be discovered about the manuscript's provenance was that it had passed through the hands of two private owners (oral information kindly supplied by Julia Rosenthal, 24 June 2008).

[84]. See MEYER – OBERT – ZIMMERMANN 2020. The fair copies of the works published by Peters already entered the collection in 2006. The materials remaining at UE were added as items on loan in 2021.

thirty years and several further additions, the collection has reached a state of completion that holds material for much research on a wide range of topics.

Translation: J. Bradford Robinson

Bibliography

Aigner 2021
Aigner, Thomas. 'Starthilfe im Westen: György Ligeti sucht um ein Rockefeller-Stipendium an', in: *Pässe, Reisekoffer und andere 'Asservate'. Archivalische Erinnerungen ans Lebe*, edited by Volker Kaukoreit *et al.*, Vienna, Praesens, 2021, pp. 131-138.

Beckles Willson 2011
Beckles Willson, Rachel. *Ligeti, Kurtág, and Hungarian Music During the Cold War*, Cambridge, Cambridge University Press, 2011.

Diederichs-Lafite 2001
Diederichs-Lafite, Marion. 'Auftakt', in: *Österreichische Musikzeitschrift*, LVI/2 (2001), p. 1.

Dümling 2020
Dümling, Albrecht. *Anpassungsdruck und Selbstbehauptung: Der Schott-Verlag im «Dritten Reich»*, Regensburg, ConBrio, 2020.

Fetthauer 2007
Fetthauer, Sophie. *Musikverlage im «Dritten Reich» und im Exil*, Hamburg, von Bockel, ²2007.

Herbort 1991
Herbort, Heinz Josef. 'Der Geburtstag der Geburtshelfer. Der Komponist Pierre Boulez über das Verlegen von Musik', in: *Die Zeit*, no. 47 (15 November 1991), p. 70.

Kapp 1996
Kapp, Reinhard. 'Gespräch mit Alfred Schlee', in: *Darmstadt-Gespräche: Die Internationalen Ferienkurse für Neue Musik*, edited by Markus Grassl and Reinhard Kapp, Vienna, Böhlau, 1996, pp. 181-202.

Kaufmann 1993
Kaufmann, Harald. *Von innen und außen*, edited by Werner Grünzweig and Gottfried Krieger, Hofheim, Wolke, 1993.

Knessl 1988
Knessl, Lothar. 'Interview mit Alfred Schlee' [50 Jahre danach], in: *Österreichische Musikzeitschrift*, XLIII/4 (1988), pp. 190-191.

More than Printing Scores: Ligeti and His Post-1960 Publishers

Kowalke 2001
Kowalke, Kim H. 'Dancing with the Devil: Publishing Modern Music in the Third Reich', in: *Modernism/Modernity*, VIII/1 (2001), pp. 1-41.

Krones 2001
Krones, Hartmut. '«Die Arisierungsbestätigung ist nun eingelangt...». Die Universal-Edition im Jahr 1938', in: *Österreichische Musikzeitschrift*, LVI/8-9 (2001), pp. 20-26.

Ligeti 2007
Ligeti, György. *Gesammelte Schriften*, edited by Monika Lichtenfeld, 2 vols., Mainz, Schott, 2007 (Veröffentlichungen der Paul Sacher Stiftung, 10).

Ligeti – Roelcke 2003
Ligeti, György – Roelcke, Eckhard. *«Träumen Sie in Farbe?» György Ligeti im Gespräch mit Eckhard Roelcke*, Vienna, Paul Zsolnay, 2003.

Marx 2016
Marx, Wolfgang. '«Weil die Texte oft mehr beachtet werden als die Musik». Zur Relevanz und Verlässlichkeit kompositorischer Selbstauskünfte am Beispiel György Ligetis', in: *Studia Musicologica*, LVII/1-2 (2016), pp. 187-205.

Meyer – Obert – Zimmermann 2020
Meyer, Felix – Obert, Simon – Zimmermann, Heidy. 'Archiv des Verlags Schott Music in Mainz', in: *Mitteilungen der Paul Sacher Stiftung*, no. 33 (April 2020), pp. 5-10.

Petschull 1965
Petschull, Johannes. *Musikverlage in der Bundesrepublik Deutschland und in West-Berlin*, Bonn, Musikhandel Verlag, 1965.

Pohl 2007
Pohl, Rüdiger. *Das autobiographische Gedächtnis. Die Psychologie unserer Lebensgeschichte*, Stuttgart, Kohlhammer, 2007.

Richart 1990
Richart, Robert W. *György Ligeti: A Bio-Bibliography*, New York, Greenwood Press, 1990.

Rubin 1986
Autobiographical Memory, edited by David C. Rubin, Cambridge, Cambridge University Press, 1986.

Schreiber 2019
Schreiber, Ewa. 'The Structure of Thought: On the Writings of György Ligeti', in: *Trio*, VIII/1-2 (2019), pp. 18-43.

SPRUYTENBURG 2011
SPRUYTENBURG, Robert. *Das LaSalle-Quartett: Gespräche mit Walter Levin*, Munich, Edition text+kritik, 2011.

STEINITZ 2003
STEINITZ, Richard. *György Ligeti: Music of the Imagination*, London, Faber and Faber, 2003.

STEPHAN 1981
STEPHAN, Rudolf. 'Ein Blick auf die Universal-Edition: Aus Anlaß von Alfred Schlees 80. Geburtstag', in: *Österreichische Musikzeitschrift*, XXXVI/12 (1981), pp. 639-644.

ZIMMERMANN 2016
ZIMMERMANN, Heidy. 'Musikologische Sprachrohre: Harald Kaufmann und Ove Nordwall im Dialog mit György Ligeti', in: *Studia Musicologica*, LVII/1-2 (2016), pp. 161-186.

«Everything Is Chance»:
György Ligeti in Conversation with John Tusa,
28 October 1997

Joseph Cadagin
(University of Toronto, Jackman Humanities Institute)

The following interview[1] with Ligeti was conducted in 1997 by John Tusa, an arts administrator and broadcast journalist who spoke with major artistic figures on his monthly series for BBC Radio 3. The complete interview was unaired, though a handful of sound bites made their way into a 2014 radio documentary[2]. Tusa interviewed Ligeti again in 2001, and this time their discussion was broadcast and later published as a transcription[3].

At this late stage in his career, the seventy-four-year-old Ligeti had only left to compose the *Hamburg Concerto*, *Síppal, dobbal, nádihegedűvel*, and the last two Piano Études. Number 16, 'Pour Irina', had its premiere at the Donaueschingen Festival eleven days before this interview, in a recital that also included the premiere of Conlon Nancarrow's Study No. 48 for Two Player Pianos. While the Études naturally form the central topic of the interview, the revised version of *Le Grand Macabre* — which played in Salzburg just a few months prior — is an oddly absent talking point.

---

[1]. For the most part, this is a faithful, word-for-word transcription of Ligeti's interview. However, for the sake of clarity and conciseness, there are passages where I have corrected grammatical/factual errors, inserted missing words, rearranged the order of sentences, and cut digressions or redundancies. A copy of the original audio is archived in the György Ligeti Collection at the Paul Sacher Stiftung in Basel, Switzerland.

[2]. The documentary also features commentary from this collection's editor, Wolfgang Marx. See Hall 2014.

[3]. Cheevers 2001; Ligeti 2003.

Tusa's two-hour conversation with the composer took place when Ligeti was in London to accept a Gramophone Award for Pierre-Laurent Aimard's recording of the Piano Études[4]. Over the previous two decades, Ligeti had become increasingly in demand in Great Britain, with commissions coming from major British ensembles and institutions. The Southbank Centre's nine-concert 'Ligeti by Ligeti' festival in 1989 paved the way for the 'Ligeti Edition' on Sony Classical in 1996 — an ambitious recording project involving Esa-Pekka Salonen and London's Philharmonia Orchestra. In between the (ultimately unreleased) studio sessions with the orchestra, Ligeti would often vent his frustrations by listening to algorithmic peals of change ringing performed on the bells of St. Paul's Cathedral[5].

The theme of chance is a recurring leitmotif in Ligeti's circuitous responses to Tusa. Major turning points in his career he ascribes to mere coincidence: coming across a Ciconia record, stumbling on a notated page of Nancarrow's music, bumping into a colleague in the loo. However, one suspects that, even if events had transpired differently, Ligeti would have inevitably gravitated toward the rhythmic labyrinths of Nancarrow and Ars nova polyphony. Or, if he hadn't encountered pianist Eckart Besch in the toilets, the Horn Trio commission would still have arrived under other, less lavatorial circumstances.

How do we reconcile Ligeti's *indeterministic* dictum that «everything is chance» with his comments on *deterministic* chaos elsewhere in this interview? As an avid reader of mathematical and scientific literature, the composer was familiar with the principles of this experimental field. In a complex system (e.g. weather, turbulence, population, stock-trading, traffic), tiny variations in the initial conditions generate vastly divergent results that give the impression of disorder. But since such a system is governed by the interaction of multiple deterministic processes, its outcome is not completely random. When we plot the results three dimensionally, we find that no two points follow the same path. Yet all their trajectories lie within the same region, known as a «strange attractor» — an intricate, fractally repeating pattern that visualizes the order underlying a so-called «chaotic» system.

Are the happy accidents Ligeti recounts the product of chance or the inevitable consequences of whatever dynamical system controls his existence? After all, the composer makes a statement to Tusa that leans perilously close to biological determinism: «Life is some complex behavior pattern growing out from the deoxyribose nucleic acid». It's conceivable that Ligeti is using the word «chance» as a shorthand for the impossibility of making long-range predictions about a chaotic system, especially one as complex as life. The outcome —

---

[4]. Ligeti received the award on 27 October, and the interview was conducted the following day. My thanks to the composer's former assistant, musicologist Louise Duchesneau, for consulting her datebook.

[5]. STEINITZ 2013, p. 351.

though theoretically calculable if we could measure the initial conditions with exactitude — may as well be random. Astonishingly, years before he discovered the field of chaos, Ligeti independently reached this conclusion in a pair of essays on serial composition published in *Die Reihe* during the 1950s and '60s: «There is really no basic difference between the results of automatism and the products of chance; total determinacy comes to be identical with total indeterminacy»[6].

It's more likely that, despite the absolutist language of his phrase «everything is chance», Ligeti ascribes to the intermediary paradigm formulated by Karl Popper, a philosopher of science. In his 1965 lecture 'Of Clouds and Clocks'[7] (whose title Ligeti modified for his 1973 composition *Clocks and Clouds*), Popper addresses the uncomfortable implications of living in a world that is either pure chance or pure clockwork. He proposes an alternative model that assumes a flexible interplay between determinism and indeterminism, while also allowing human rationality and free will to enter the equation.

How does our insight into this universe of ideas — i.e. the literature on chaos, chance, and determinism Ligeti was probing — color our understanding of his art? The composer insists throughout this interview that, while he finds inspiration in science and mathematics, his music isn't created through algorithms or calculations. Still, we can locate instances where these extra-musical concepts align with Ligeti's aesthetic thinking. Popper, in particular, likely reinforced the composer's «predilection for simple order but developed in a crazy way». His characterization of passacaglia and chaconne forms in this interview even resembles a Popperian system — one that permits a certain degree of chance or freedom (the improvisatory melody line) within the context of a regularly repeating process (the ground bass).

At this point, we might be tempted to start drawing a web of associations between Ligeti's remarks on (in)determinism, his biography, and his frequent use of the passacaglia in its *lamento* variation. Many scholars have, alongside Tusa, heard a tragic «dying fall» in Ligeti's descending grounds. Could we also read the *lamento*, in its cyclical inevitability, as a musical expression of fatalism from a composer who (in a later interview with Tusa[8]) attributed his survival during the Holocaust to chance? Ligeti firmly, but politely, asks us not to speculate: «Real life, what you experience..., I would not put in connection with the music».

---

[6]. LIGETI 1965, p. 10. See also Ligeti's 1958 analysis of Boulez's *Structures Ia*: «Seen at close quarters, it is the factor of determinism, regularity, that stands out; but from a distance, the structure, being the result of many separate regularities, is seen to be something highly variable and chancy». LIGETI 1960, p. 61.

[7]. POPPER 1972.

[8]. LIGETI 2003, p. 189.

Joseph Cadagin

Interview

Piano Études: Book I

If I could take you back, György, to when you started the first book of piano studies. Did you have in mind to write a book of them?

No, no.

What happened?

The whole idea of these piano studies came how things happen — sometimes in a very awkward way. When I was sixty, it was in the year '83. I'm good friends with Boulez. He held a concert in Stuttgart on the radio with some of my pieces[9]. And less than two years later, he became sixty. And I thought, «You conducted my pieces so wonderfully. If I would conduct your pieces, it wouldn't be the right thing. I have no gift as a conductor». So then I thought, «I have to write for Boulez, for his sixtieth birthday, some piano pieces as a present. And they should be played on his sixtieth birthday, which happened to be in Baden-Baden». I was ready with the pieces, but the pianist was not ready, so they weren't played. But the first three pieces are dedicated to Boulez. In that moment, I had no idea about the totality.

Just a collection of studies growing out of that. I know you like to have the feel of the piano under your fingers.

Yes. It's tactile music, not only auditive. I am what is called «synesthetic», like Messiaen. Always imagining colors, forms, shape, volume, even certain movement, certain speed. And even gravity, smell. So all the senses are melded together. The beginnings of these pieces are very simple ideas, mostly a kind of canon. And then I develop them with my ears, but always in feedback with my ten fingers on the piano. (But I couldn't play the pieces on the level of Pierre-Laurent Aimard, because I don't practice.)

And your interest in combinations of meters and rhythms — I know this is something that goes back a long way with you. These inform and inspire all sorts of things in the piano writing in these studies, don't they?

---

[9]. Stuttgart Radio Symphony Orchestra concert on 18 May 1983 celebrating Ligeti's sixtieth birthday; the program included the Chamber Concerto, Horn Trio, *Ramifications*, choral numbers, and the three harpsichord works. See RICHART 1990, pp. 189-190.

«Everything Is Chance»: György Ligeti in Conversation with John Tusa

Not only piano writing. For instance, in several of these pieces, the inspiration is the *mbira*, or *likembe*, or *sanza* — the lamellophones in African cultures, which you play usually with three fingers. I have one that I got as a gift from Zimbabwe. (I was invited to come to Harare, but I didn't go.) I'm deeply interested in African music. There are different African cultures — I'm speaking now of south of the Sahara. But they have a common denominator: it's very complex rhythm and no meter, in fact. And symmetrical and asymmetrical grids of pulses at the same time. So this kind of tension between symmetry and asymmetry, which, at the same time, exists in the European tradition coming from the mensural notation, dividing a unit in two or in three.

Six beats is two groups of three or three groups of two.

Exactly — it's called «hemiola». But it was much more complex in the times of Machaut to Dufay. I began to be very interested in the music of this time, since there are recordings and since I could see the transcriptions. Willi Apel did the Chantilly Codex, for instance[10]. There are a lot of still unknown, wonderful composers like Solage, Senleches, Galiot, Suzay (I have to avoid name-dropping here) between Machaut and Dufay. And the greatest may be Ciconia.

These things happen by chance. I think it was in the late '70s, I bought a Thomas Binkley record in the EMI Reflexe series of early music. It was a record with Ciconia, mostly three-part works[11]. Due to the several (especially British) consorts, we know these pieces very gradually. It's mainly French music, in fact, but better-known in London today. And it was such a chance that it began to appear on record. I became so very interested in Ciconia. And then when I'm interested in music, I want to see scores. I had some photocopies from libraries. And then I began reading about other names. It's a chain reaction.

One name leads to another. You make discoveries, yes.

They were absolutely unknown for me, and I began to be very interested in this very complex metrical and rhythmical world, which began before Machaut with Vitry, in fact. But the great composer was Machaut. Then came afterwards a lot of people who survived the terrible disease in the middle of the 14th century.

The Great Plague.

Like Machaut, they survived, or were born just after and made wonderful and complex music — difficult music. Wouldn't be in business today. There were always very small circles.

---

[10]. APEL 1950.
[11]. BINKLEY 1972.

And we owe this, for instance, to the popes in Avignon and to the King of Aragon in Barcelona. It's just chance.

Going back to the studies, could I ask you how the first one works? What does the pianist have to do?

The first study, you mean 'Désordre'? This was one of the most difficult. I had the idea to have two different tempi. No, more than this. To have certain patterns that are in order, and then they became shifted — and whether it's possible to do it with a living pianist. Nancarrow did it for player piano. This is also a very strong influence. For myself, I discovered the existence of Nancarrow by chance in 1980. I had never heard about him. Very few people knew.

No one had.

Yes, in the United States. Elliott Carter knew him, and John Cage knew him. Merce Cunningham choreographed some dances. There were a couple of European people knowing about him. So in this case, I was a kind of a public-relations person for Nancarrow. I saw a score in a catalogue of an exhibition of mechanical instruments in Berlin. I wasn't there, but by chance, I saw the catalogue. It was a page of a score of Nancarrow written in normal notation, but piano music which nobody can play.

One of his studies for player piano.

Yes, and I was amazed at this music — this kind of rhythmical *folie* I never could imagine. It's not possible to be performed by human beings. But a mechanical player piano can do it. So the name Nancarrow was in my brain, but I had no possibility to hear something. This was in February '80. And half a year later, in the summer of '80, I was in Paris by chance. I always go to Fnac, because, like Tower Records in London, they have a lot of records which in Germany you cannot find. And of course, I went there to buy Messiaen. I was interested in his piano music, and I found it. And then, of course, vanity took me to look after my name, and it's in the section 'Contemporary Music', of course. (Messiaen already was in the normal alphabetical classical, but I was still contemporary — still am.) I looked whether they had records of my music. Yes, they had. And because it was alphabetical — L, M, and then there were two Nancarrow records! I bought them. If I hadn't seen the score, this name would say nothing.

Nancarrow was last in Europe when he was a fighter on the republican side in Spain against Franco, being an honest American communist. (In '36/'37, outside of the Soviet Union, you could believe in communism. Inside, not anymore. But this nobody could know outside.) So this music made a terribly deep impression on me. «Oh! People here in Europe have to hear. Invite Nancarrow». He was about seventy, living in Mexico City. I had no idea about where and how. Everything is chance. There is in Graz this Musikprotokoll im steirischen Herbst.

«Everything Is Chance»: György Ligeti in Conversation with John Tusa

Yes, the autumn festival.

It was by chance I knew somebody who ran this, Peter Vujica, because I was invited to this festival with some pieces. And I told him, «Why don't you invite Nancarrow?» «Who is Nancarrow?» I explained about him. And he invited him, and he came[12]. We had no possibility to perform on player piano. But there were these two records and some more recordings on tape. Some people were very amazed; other people had absolutely no interest for this kind of music, as it happens always. I introduced Nancarrow and gave a lecture in German about him.

And then, very gradually, he became known in Europe. Schott Publishing, which by chance is the company where I have most of my scores, owns this small recording company Wergo for modern music. I persuaded the director to publish all the Nancarrow pieces. So there exist now five CDs, which is not everything, but almost everything. So I contributed a bit for the knowledge of him, because I was totally enthusiastic.

You asked me about my first study — I could *never* write it without the knowledge of Nancarrow. But it's not Nancarrow music. It has to do with Nancarrow, but it also has to do with the hemiola tradition in Chopin, Debussy, and Brahms. And in mensural notation, where it comes from dividing a unit in three and in two at the same time. So six is the good number — three times two or two times three. This I knew from the piano literature. But then discovering for myself all this 14th-century music, which is much more complicated. You divide twenty-one in three times seven, and this kind of thing, which makes music to be very complex. I was always interested in complexity. And very much in the visual arts, like the Alhambra, the Islamic complex; the Book of Kells, the complex Irish ornaments; fractal geometry. This is one area, complexity.

Complexity growing out of something really quite simple.

Life is some complex behavior pattern growing out from the deoxyribose nucleic acid, an extremely complicated molecule made from very simple units. In mathematics — fractal geometry or dynamic functions — you repeat a certain calculation many times. A million times, as many times as is possible with fast computers. And the result is something totally new. It's what's called fractal geometry, which has become a sport today.

I have a lot of knowledge of very complex rhythmic patterns in African music. For instance, xylophone-playing in Uganda: two people playing (in fact, there are usually three people or six people) on one xylophone at the same time, on both sides. And what they play is very simple. But the combination of the patterns, it's like the DNA molecule. It's a simple basis

---

[12]. Nancarrow made his European 'debut' in 1982 as part of the annual ISCM Music Days festival, which Musikprotokoll was hosting in Graz that year.

and a very complex result. This, combined with the thinking of Nancarrow, combined with 14th-century mensural-notation thinking, combined with certain mathematics, and the idea to transpose this kind of complexity in the two hands of one single, existing, live player — these are the Études. The first one, 'Désordre', is already in the middle of this total. If you listen to it, you don't understand — the pianist doesn't understand, he just plays.

His right hand is only on the white keys?

This is an idea coming from the *mbira* lamellophones, where you have the lowest metal tongue in the middle and the higher pitches alternating outward left and right. Sometimes the same pitch is on the left hand as on the right, sometimes it is slightly different. They have special tuning systems, and so on. It's spread over the whole area of Bantu-speaking peoples from Cameroon down to the southeast to Malawi, Zimbabwe, and Mozambique. And you have the possibility to play with two hands at the same time. That means with three fingers — usually on the right you have two fingers and on the left, one. You can play with two thumbs, also, having two different patterns, which fit together. It's what you call «interlocking». You find it in gamelan music. There are hypotheses that it's gamelan music going with the Indonesian colonization of the southern half of Africa, which might be true[13]. We know that Madagascar is Indonesian and Malaysian. It was a kind of colony. The language has a lot of similarities. But there is no evidence on the continent of Africa. But still, there are a lot of hypotheses that it could come from the old gamelan tradition of Java and Bali.

This interlocking, where one instrument or one player has a silence and another player plays a tone, is very common in different African cultures. If you take the *mbira*, the lowest sound is in the middle, and then left and right going up. There is a very wonderful hypothesis that this comes from two or more xylophone players sitting at the same instrument, *vis-à-vis*. So for one, the left hand has the lowest pitches and the right the high pitches, and for the opposite player, it is inverse. And this idea of two or more players on a xylophone is applied to one instrument for two hands. In fact, it's very similar music. This is an idea coming from the Austrian ethnomusicologist Gerhard Kubik, who became a very good friend in the meantime[14].

The idea was, I have on the piano no possibility for the two hands to play the same pitches like on the lamellophone — on the *mbira* — because the piano was constructed having the deep on the left and the high on the right. I have no symmetrical possibility. But I wanted to combine

---

[13]. JONES 1971; BLENCH 1982.

[14]. Kubik attributes the theory to fellow ethnomusicologist Arthur M. Jones, who was the chief proponent of the Indonesian-origins-of-African-music theory that Ligeti mentions earlier. See KUBIK 1983, p. 385; JONES 1973/1974.

two patterns. And I came to the idea that I can play with two hands at the same place by giving one hand the white keys and for the other, the black. So the idea is simply the topographical idea of the piano — it's not a musical idea. Then I decided, diatonic scale in the right hand, pentatonic in the left hand. And together they give the chromatic total. But not twelve-tone chromaticism — a different kind.

Following on from what you were saying, can I ask you about 'Touches bloquées', because that's another idea, isn't it?

I did it before in *Volumina*, in this organ piece in '61/'62. It begins with all the keys depressed, all the registers in the organ. Everything sounds together, and the releasing. This idea was partly my idea and partly Karl-Erik Welin's, the Swedish organist. We worked together, so I don't know whose idea it was — it doesn't matter. There are a lot of things which you do together, experimenting and so on. And a bit later, I read an interesting article in the German magazine *Melos* by the pianist Henning Siedentopf[15]. He wrote about some ideas — but not as a composer, as a pianist. Maybe we could reach very complex rhythmic patterns by depressing some keys, which was known since Schumann at the end of *Papillons*. But it was a different idea there, to release the keys one after the other, so we have harmonic spectra sounding then vanishing.

But in Siedentopf's article, the idea was to depress them silently, no sound. So it's not the Schumann effect for resonance. It's to produce gaps. For instance, in the left hand I depress some keys. I play, in the right hand, a very fast figuration on sounding keys and non-sounding keys. The non-sounding keys automatically will produce silence. It can be so intricate that a living pianist cannot do it on his own, but he can do it with this. So it's a kind of technical trick. You have a kind of 'negative music'.

I already used it in '76 when I wrote Three Pieces for Two Pianos. In the middle piece, there are always depressed keys in the left hand, and the right hand is playing. So the two pianists are like one pianist with two hands. But they can produce extremely complex rhythms. So this complexity didn't begin in '85 with the first étude 'Désordre'. It began much earlier. Also, my harpsichord piece *Continuum*, which is '68.

There are a lot of trends. You don't even know who works in which area. I wrote, maybe, the first piece of music which has very strong links with a whole new part of mathematics, which is chaos theory or dynamic systems or fractal geometry, which were developed during the '60s and '70s. I wrote the Kyrie of the Requiem in '64 at the same time when Edward Lorenz, a meteorologist in Cambridge, Massachusetts at MIT, published his first work on strange

---

[15]. SIEDENTOPF 1973.

attractors, absolutely opening a new world of geometry[16]. And this article was published in *Journal of the Atmospheric Sciences* at the same time that I wrote *Atmosphères*! So it's just by chance, but the same interest in complex patterns which are half disorder, half order.

People hearing you talk so interestingly about so many different things might get the wrong impression, I think — that somehow, your pieces are constructivist. Everything comes from a poetic or a musical idea, doesn't it?

Yes, it's not science. I'm deeply interested in science, in physics, and certain areas of math. I have a lot of ideas in music, but not on a mathematical basis. Now that I am becoming better known and older, I get a number of doctoral theses, especially from American universities. Everywhere, everybody finds the Golden Section — the Fibonacci numbers — in my music. Lendvai found it in Bartók[17]. He died in the meantime, but I used to be a very close friend with Lendvai in Budapest. I was in my late twenties, and he, too. I believed what he calculated in Bartók. Later, I became very skeptical. We have no hint from Bartók that he knew about it. After reading hundreds of studies and analyses of my music, everybody is finding the Fibonacci series. I really used it in my orchestral piece *Apparitions*, the first movement being influenced by Lendvai[18].

Anyway, I dare to announce my hypothesis: in places where there are very different relationships and proportions, you will always find what you want to find. So you find symmetry, asymmetry. And everywhere you will find the Golden Section. That means, the whole is in proportion to the larger part as the larger part is to the smaller part. It was used in Greek architecture. So it's not symmetry and not asymmetry — something in between. And it's a wonderful irrational number — the *most* irrational number. Some mathematicians proved this. More complex than *pi* and some other irrational numbers. And it's a wonderful mathematical idea which is objectively existing in the realm of mathematics, which is only in our culture. And you find it in nature in different plants. In the pattern of a sunflower, based on certain hormones which stimulate or slow down growing. It's a self-organization pattern, like a crystal. So in musical analysis, if a lot of very good and high-level musicologists write theses about finding everywhere the Golden Section in my music (I'm not aware of it, of course), they found it because they can find whatever they want to find, because it's complex.

---

[16]. The term «strange attractor» was coined by David Ruelle and Floris Takens in a 1971 paper and retroactively applied to the system of differential equations Edward Lorenz derived from a model for thermal convection in his 1963 paper. See LORENZ 1963; RUELLE – TAKENS 1971.

[17]. LENDVAI 1971.

[18]. LIGETI 1983, p. 43.

«Everything Is Chance»: György Ligeti in Conversation with John Tusa

Nonsense Madrigals, Magyar Etűdök

Could we talk a little bit about the «Nonsense Madrigals»? What made you go for these English texts?

Truth is always simple and by chance. My language is Hungarian. When I was a child, I only spoke Hungarian. This is a very small population of speakers — fifty million in the whole world, in Hungary a bit more than ten million. Hungarian, because of the structure of the language, has a very special tradition of poetry. I would go very far to say that maybe after Shakespeare, the greatest poet of all time is Sándor Weöres. I knew him very well (he died about ten years ago). He made a wonderful life's work of experimental literature on the basis of the possibilities of the Hungarian language, which is *not* a beautiful language. It's an *ugly* language if you listen to it. But it has a very special kind of syntactic structure, and you can use it in poetry in a very complex way. This is not chauvinistic, because I speak seven languages, so I can judge between different cultures a bit.

Compared with the number of the native speakers, it's a fantastically rich literature since the Renaissance times. And it happened that in Budapest, during the late-19th century and early-20th century, the Hungarian language combined with the tradition of assimilated Jews. There are a lot of Hungarian writers and poets who are not Jewish who combine linguistic possibility with the Middle European and Jewish traditions of very strong wit and sense of humor. It's a very special alloy between the Hungarian language, which has absolutely nothing to do with Jewish culture, and some Jewish writers, who were no longer Jewish believers. (I belong to this assimilated Jewish group. If you ask what I am, I am Hungarian speaking. But not knowing Jewish tradition, I belong to this.)

So especially in Budapest it developed. I think the most interesting period was between the two wars. It produced a fantastic, wonderful humorist, Frigyes Karinthy, whom you can compare to Jonathan Swift. He and his friends developed a nonsense literature and poetry called *halandzsa*, which, by chance, is very close to Lewis Carroll's nonsense poetry. So you can do it in English, and you can do it in Hungarian. (Maybe you can do it Chinese — I don't know about Chinese.) But in no other European language. Because English is a language composed from many different languages — Hungarian also. And the words become short, and substantives and verbs are the same word in English many times. This is very similar in Hungarian. So the possibility to make nonsense poetry in these two languages is easier. In German or in French, you cannot do it because you have endless prepositions and constructions. In English, you can develop a language that sounds like English, but it's nothing — like «Jabberwocky».

« 'Twas brillig, and the slithy toves. »

Exactly. And «kiszera méra bávatag», a Hungarian sentence which I cannot translate because it has no translation. It's Karinthy[19]. I think in the early '30s, when I was a child, Karinthy translated *Alice in Wonderland*, and I read it in Hungarian when I was ten years old in '33[20]. And this was a basic experience. So I would imagine that the Budapest Hungarian-Jewish humor is the closest to British understatement nonsense. I am very much attracted not only to Lewis Carroll (who was the most sophisticated, of course), but Edward Lear and a lot of other people in the Victorian age writing nonsense poetry. So this is the basis of the madrigals. The other basis is this Budapest tradition, and the other is the music of the 14th century.

So that in « Two Dreams and Little Bat», we have «The Dream of a Girl Who Lived at Seven-Oaks», «The Dream of a Boy Who Lived at Nine-Elms»…

And this is William Brighty Rands, a minor poet.

…and a sort of «cantus firmus» with «Twinkle, twinkle little bat, how I wonder what you're at».

This is Lewis Carroll. I use it as a *cantus firmus* in the old sense of a *cantus firmus* motet composition.

And the «Seven-Oaks» and the «Nine-Elms»?

They are sung simultaneously, like in motets — like in Machaut, and so on. But the music is not Machaut. The combination of 14th-century techniques, British 19th-century nonsense (it's not nonsense, but half-nonsense), and a certain peculiar Hungarian Budapest culture. I think really only Hungarian-speaking people who speak English can understand it, so not a lot of people.

Can I ask you briefly about the «Hungarian Studies» — the «Magyar etűdök». They came after you hadn't set any Hungarian for a very long time.

---

[19]. In Karinthy's humorous short story «Halandzsa», the «*halandzsa* man» (*halandzsa-ember*) gaslights café patrons with nonsensical phrases, including «kiszera méra bávatag». See KARINTHY 2001.

[20]. While Karinthy was a prolific translator, he never translated Carroll's *Alice*. Ligeti is likely confusing Karinthy with the author's contemporary, Dezső Kosztolányi, whose 1935 Hungarian translation of *Wonderland* was published when Ligeti was eleven or twelve years old. See CARROLL – KOSZTOLÁNYI 2013; CADAGIN 2020, pp. 27-37.

«Everything Is Chance»: György Ligeti in Conversation with John Tusa

In Hungary I did a lot of folklore — totally naïve. I didn't know about modern music, so I was influenced by Bartók and Kodály and so on. And then, being in the West, I used nonsense language in *Aventures* and *Nouvelles aventures*. But this is not Hungarian nonsense; it's *nonsense* nonsense you find in all language. Just emotional states and social relations — accepting something, being opportunist, being revolutionary. Disgust and joy. A lot of things. I have no idea how I came to this. And it has a lot to do with something which is not ready, which I have to begin. I would like to write *Alice* of Lewis Carroll in a kind of musical. I don't know what it will be.

But the «Magyar etűdök»? What made you go back to Hungarian? I suppose you were wanting to set Hungarian again after a long interval. These are quite constructivist pieces, aren't they?

The poems are from more than a hundred small poems by this very great poet, Sándor Weöres, who happened to be a close friend. He makes simple constructions out of Hungarian language. But this is only the 'garbage' of his poetry. He lived seventy-five years, and he has an output of a huge amount of poetry. He was forbidden in the Stalinist Rákosi time. And then in the '60s, he was allowed to publish again in Hungary in the Kádár era — in the half-soft dictatorship. (I wasn't there; I was already a refugee in the West.) And Weöres was a kind of *enfant prodigue* of Hungarian.

You know how we met? We quarreled. He hated Mozart. It was '47, after the war, but it was before the communist dictatorship. His poetry was published, and he was in very high regard in Hungary. I was twenty-four years old and a student in Budapest. I set three of his poems (you find it on record number four of the Sony Edition). But this is not his great poetry — his great poetry is not possible to use in music. Somebody told him there is a young student who made some interesting songs using his text. We had some common acquaintances. And then we met one evening in the apartment of a friend of his, Árpád Illés, a painter. We had wine, and I played for him and sang myself, and he was interested. And then we began to discuss, and we drank wine. Then we began to quarrel because he hated Mozart. For him, Mozart was nothing, and for me, Mozart was Mozart. And then in a situation with a lot of wine, we began shouting, and we began to fight. And we were drunk, all three. So I was very sorry. He was a very small gentleman — a Puckish figure — and I'm middle range, so I was much stronger.

He is one of the greatest poets, not only of Hungarian literature, but of all literature. Nobody who cannot understand Hungarian will believe this, but this is one of the existing truths. I was always very attracted to his poetry. He has a kind of mythological poetry. He invented religions, countries, planets, solar systems, and made something wonderful which has nothing to do with reality besides being totally poetic. I think my Piano Études are influenced by the poetry of Weöres. His poetry is highly constructivist, but without construction. It's free poetry using all the rhythmical and metrical possibilities of the language. Hungarian is amazing because you can write in the Greek and Latin meters. You can write in bars — four plus four. You can use every rhythmical possibility because you are not bound to prepositions. You can put a whole sentence in a word by agglutination. So the way Weöres thought in poetry and language, I am thinking in music and feeling in the piano keys. Maybe he was one of my main teachers.

The sound of Hungarian is important to your music, even piano music?

Yes, I'm very deeply bound to the Hungarian language. It's very good to know a lot of cultures, a lot of languages, because you have the relativity. This is a good side of being a refugee or an émigré, because it has very sad aspects. But it has an aspect that you regard your own language as one of the many possibilities.

But going back, you asked me why I chose Weöres. I always was attracted by these constructions in his very small poems. It's experimental, close to Joyce. Weöres also has a side that is close to René Char. Only, René Char, being French, comes from this half-abstract French tradition of Mallarmé. Whereas in Hungarian, everything is very concrete. You can take these words in your hand. So a part of Weöres' poetry is nonsense, but a nonsense having a totally clear content. And I use some of these small, half-nonsense poems for a chorus.

The first étude is extremely constructivist in the tradition of Machaut. It's a very complex mirror canon with diminutions and with *prolatio maior*, *prolatio minor* — all the educated stuff which I studied in early-Renaissance or late-medieval music. This is very abstract, totally constructivist. Also, the influence of Boulez, of *Structures*, is very strong in it. It's also a humoristic piece making fun of the serious constructivism of my composer colleagues who believe, still, in this utopia of avant-garde — a 'constructivist avant-garde'. We have, also, a '*de*constructivist avant-garde', which is John Cage.

I think of you still as a modernist, I suppose.

Some people consider me a traitor of modern music. Take my two small harpsichord pieces, which are pastiche, or the Horn Trio, which, in fact, was considered a criminal act.

Sort of retro, 'neo'.

Oh yes, *super* retro. But I'm not in the company of Arvo Pärt and John Adams. Oh, I like them. But I'm trying to do something which is *my* music. Whether you call it 'retro' or 'postmodern' or 'modern', I don't care.

«Everything Is Chance»: György Ligeti in Conversation with John Tusa

Horn Trio, Violin Concerto

Can I just ask you about the Horn Trio and perhaps a little bit about the Violin Concerto? I remember the Horn Trio came at the end of a period for you which had not been very productive. It was after the opera. Would you like to say something about what was in your mind?

Yes, a four years' gap. I was lost — today, also, I am lost — because I belong to the so-called avant-garde. In the late '50s and early '60s, I wrote these polyphonic-cluster pieces. And then already in the early '60s, during the composition of the Requiem, I began to be very skeptical of total chromaticism. I don't like the attitude to develop a cliché and repeat it and have a trademark. I try to change after every piece.

Sing a new song?

No, it's more like a science. If you solve the problem — it can be mathematic, it can be physics or biology or whatever — you develop a certain theory and you try to falsify it, and it seems that it's verified. And then after solving one problem, you have hundreds of new problems which you didn't know would arise. So this is the whole history of science. And I'm very close to scientific thinking. But I don't want that people should make the mistake to think that I use it. I don't use science. I know a lot about mathematics, but I don't use calculations, I don't use computers.

The Horn Trio puzzled so many people. They thought, «Oh my, what's he doing? He's going back to Brahms».

In fact, it's written «Hommage à Brahms», because Brahms wrote this wonderful horn trio. If you would know the story: Things are always very simple and very complicated at the same time. I was asked by Mario di Bonaventura, an American conductor, to write two concerti — a piano concerto for his brother, Anthony (which finally I did after seventeen years), and a horn concerto for Barry Tuckwell. I had a lot of contact with Barry Tuckwell and was thinking how to write it. And I am very slow, so in the meantime, Bonaventura told me that we will no longer work with Barry Tuckwell. And I was sad.

Then by chance, I was in the loo at the Hamburg Conservatory of Music (I used to be a teacher there), pissing at the same time as Eckart Besch, quite a good pianist in Hamburg. He didn't know about my plans for a concerto. At this moment, it was the early '80s. And Besch told me he's playing the Brahms trio with the best German horn player, Hermann Baumann, and an excellent violinist, Saschko Gawriloff. So Besch asked me if I would consider writing a horn trio that can be played with the Brahms one. And I told him spontaneously, «I could consider it because I was thinking about a horn concerto, but the sponsor is not sponsoring it anymore. So, do you have a sponsor for the horn trio?» «Yes. There will be a Brahms commemoration».

So I told him I have a lot of horn ideas, and I like the instrument and studied the technique. (I cannot play it, but I know how it works.) And then from Hamburg, those three people gave me a commission. But it was a prescribed condition that I use a Brahms theme, because it's for the Brahms commemoration. I thought, «This I cannot do. I will use a Beethoven theme!». That's from the 'Les Adieux' Sonata.

The «Farewell» motive.

Which is originally, in thinking, for two horns. But in Beethoven it's played by the piano, and my trio begins with the violin playing double stops. So it's kind of ironical — not doing Brahms, but making a bow in this direction. Brahms is not one of my favorites. The B-flat major Piano Trio[21] is wonderful music, and the two Sextets for Strings are wonderful. But he's not a main composer for me. They wanted a Brahms theme or a motive, and I thought, «I can use one tone — whichever C, you find it in Brahms». They didn't like my answer, and then I was asked to write a dedication, «Hommage à Brahms».

Something in the Horn Trio derives from your long-standing interest in different kinds of tunings. Would you tell us something about that?

I believed in total chromaticism in the late '50s and early '60s and began to grow skeptical. I knew a bit about meantone tuning — having the possibility of eight natural major thirds. I began to be bored with equal temperament. It's not beautiful. All these major thirds on the piano are ugly. And you cannot stand them once you hear the real ones. I heard them because I worked in '57/'58 in the electronic-music studio in Cologne. We had a lot of studies about Fourier synthesis and analysis. I produced there a lot of pure, natural spectra. And then in '72, I was a guest lecturer at Stanford University in California. After two months, I began to listen to things in the library. And it was a Henry Cowell piece (I don't know the title) based on natural tuning[22]. I had no knowledge about the book of Henry Cowell, *New Musical Resources*[23].

---

[21]. Brahms never composed a piano trio in this key. Ligeti is likely referring to the Piano Trio in B major, Op. 8.

[22]. While Cowell theorized on alternative tuning systems, he seldom experimented with them in his compositions. A notable exception is the 1931 *Rhythmicana*, which employs the «rhythmicon», an electronic instrument especially designed for Cowell by Leon Theremin. The instrument's pitches, which are tuned to the overtone series, pulsate at rates that are rhythmically analogous to natural harmonic ratios. In 1971, Stanford composition professor Leland Smith programmed a computer model of the rhythmicon for the world premiere of *Rhythmicana*, performed by the Stanford Symphony Orchestra on December 3. The following month, Ligeti took Smith's place while the latter was on leave from Stanford. Records indicate that Ligeti checked out the score of *Rhythmicana* during his stay. The recording he heard in the library was most likely a tape of Smith's rhythmicon realization. See SMITH 1973; GALVÁN 2007, p. 127.

[23]. In a 1993 article for *Neue Zeitschrift für Musik*, Ligeti mentions the 1969 edition published by Something Else Press. See COWELL 1969; LIGETI 1993, p. 28.

«Everything Is Chance»: György Ligeti in Conversation with John Tusa

I heard that some old, original, American composer close to San Diego, Harry Partch, built in all his life a lot of instruments with special tunings. I decided to visit Harry Partch. I couldn't drive a car to Encinitas, north of San Diego where he lived. By chance, somebody drove me there. And Harry Partch had no idea. He had no telephone, even no doorbell — just knocking and going inside. He lived there thanks to Betty Freeman, who helped a lot of American visual artists and composers. And he had these amazing instruments. Not only could I see them, I could play them. And in ten minutes, this opened my ears to what you can do with natural harmonies.

This was in '72. In '68, I wrote *Ramifications* for two groups of strings in quarter tones, but having no knowledge of the existence of the Charles Ives quarter-tone pieces for two pianos. So this is everything by chance. But quarter tones or sixth tones are boring; some alternative harmonic thinking is more interesting. From Harry Partch, I got this influence of thinking in natural harmonics. And the horn is the ideal instrument, because you can produce high harmonics. Without the Horn Trio, I would never write the Violin Concerto. Without the knowledge of the Harry Partch instruments, I would never write the Horn Trio. Without the knowledge of a lot of gamelan music from Java and Bali, I would never have the idea to go out from the system, which I did in the Violin Concerto.

So the sound has become, in a sense, «dirtier».

In a sense, «dirtier». In another sense, closer to natural harmonies. When I forget the modulation in major and minor tonalities, I can use alternate systems, because I'm not depending anymore on equal temperament. So I can produce certain new kinds of harmonies which are half «dirty» and half much cleaner than on the piano. I listen to a lot of gamelan music, especially the wonderful court tradition from Solo or Surakarta, in the middle of Java. The other is Jogjakarta, which is a slightly different tuning system. And the wonderful world of xylophone and lamellophone tunings in Africa. And pygmy singing, which is halfway between equal pentatonic (equal dividing of the octave, which you find on xylophones) and natural harmonics. So it's a kind of compromise. This is the way how I compose — no system, but somehow based on very different systems.

So the instability of tuning in the Violin Concerto, it's a fascinating area for the listener to appreciate, isn't it? With those instruments — the ocarinas, the slide whistle. It gives the concerto a sort of fragility. It sounds dangerous, as if something is going to slip.

Iridescence, shimmering. Which always interested me, already in the cluster pieces, in *Atmosphères* in '61 — the idea of static sound shimmering. At one time, I did it with moving chromatic clusters. And much later I did it with this half-clean, half-dirty tuning. So it's chaos and order. I have certain ideas which are always there. But, you know, I'm not thinking — I'm just doing. I have colleagues who make big, elaborate systems or use calculations. I appreciate it, but I am very far from this. I have a lot of knowledge of sciences, of mathematics, and of different cultures and so on — visual arts. But I don't use it deliberately; I use it indirectly.

Passacaglia and Chaconne Forms

Why are there so many passacaglias and chaconnes in your music? I'm interested in inherited forms that have always fascinated you.

It's something which goes back to several different influences. You will be very amazed if I tell you: spiderwebs. I was, as a three-year-old child, very much afraid of them. And I still have a spider phobia, but also a fascination for spiderwebs. And spiderwebs have repeated patterns, but are not totally ordered, because the wind blows, and insects are flying in. The spider has a certain program in the nervous system — how to build a regular web. Have you heard about the interesting experiments in the late '50s in Sweden[24]? Some insect scientist gave drugs to spiders. I saw the photos in '57 at the Darmstadt Summer Academy, with drunk spiders who make totally crazy web structures. Having a system which is regular, but destroying the system.

If you play a passacaglia or a chaconne — very elaborate, like the Bach chaconne for violin solo — it's simply a harmonic pattern which you repeat. But you repeat it always with a different pattern of rhythmical imagination. Building a huge «building» from this very simple pattern which is always repeated — eight bars repeated, no difference. This is also in African music. You have cycles, always of the same length. But inside, it is very richly ornamented. If I go back to poetry, to certain fixed forms like the sonnet, you have certain rules. Or *haiku* in Japanese. You have numbers of syllables; you have to maintain them. But inside, you can put every kind of riches.

So I think mainly because of my predilection for simple order but developed in a crazy way, the passacaglia or chaconne idea is very appealing to me. I played piano with a violinist — Corelli's *La Follia* chaconne. It's so simple, and it's always different. This is one of the sources. Then I was very fascinated with certain passacaglias. (What is the difference between a passacaglia and a chaconne? We leave that to the musicologists.) You find a wonderful example in Monteverdi's 'Zefiro torna'. It's a four-times-three motive, and then you shift it with hemiola structures. It becomes very rich. And I liked when I heard this for the first time — it was the Raymond Leppard recording of all the madrigals, which is a joy[25]. And then I heard, from Leppard and

---

[24]. Ligeti is likely thinking of the German-born pharmacologist Peter N. Witt, who resettled in Switzerland (as opposed to Sweden) after the Second World War. See WITT 1954.

[25]. LEPPARD 1971.

«Everything Is Chance»: György Ligeti in Conversation with John Tusa

also Harnoncourt, very different elaborations of the end of *Poppea*, when Nero and Poppea sing this very cynical love song. Nero is in love, and Poppea wants only glory. And it's the same form — repeating, having a ground.

And in English music, beginning with *Sumer is icumen in* and then going through Elizabethan time, you have a lot of this round ground. By the way, in English culture, I am deeply impressed by the change ringing you can hear at St. Paul's and everywhere[26]. When I first heard it, it was at an American church in West Berlin. Later I read books about it. When I heard it going Sunday at ten o'clock to St. Paul's in London, it was fascinating listening the whole hour. This is the same idea, having a simple pattern and then changing it.

There's another source of my predilection for passacaglia forms. You have 'shoes' and 'laces'. In a passacaglia or chaconne, you have to bind the shoelaces very tightly. This kind of order, which is not clockwork, is a bit inexact. But it's 'bound'. My preferred part of mathematics is topology and the science of different knots. And then my very deep interest in textile patterns, which I share with Morton Feldman.

But coming back — another thing. In my childhood, I couldn't speak Romanian, couldn't understand Romanian. But in Romania, there is a tradition of these women who will sing and cry when somebody is dead. You have it in different cultures, in many countries in Asia and Europe. But this is not real sorrow, because they are paid women. Professional sorrow, but with real crying — like in cinema. They're actors. In the Carpathian Mountains you find Romanian and you find Hungarian versions. The melodies are very different. In Romania, I heard it as a young boy. It's called *bocet*. In Hungarian, it's *sirató*. I heard this wonderful *bocet*, which is a repetition of a pattern which is always a fourth. So let's say F going down to C. Not chromatic.

And always descending?

Always descending, repeating, and always a bit different. And you find the same pattern in Andalusia in the extremely elaborate flamenco *cante jondo* — this descending, mostly Phrygian ending with a minor second. Very close. There are hypotheses why they are similar. Maybe it's gypsy tradition — gypsy migration from northeast India, going through Iran to Turkey and the Balkans until Ukraine, where you find this. And during the other gipsy migration in the 14th and 15th centuries, a part went through Iran, Arabia, through Sinai to Egypt (therefore «gypsies») and North Africa to the south of Spain.

---

[26]. Ligeti is referring here to the English art of change ringing, in which a set of church bells is rung in non-repeating sequences. Depending on the number of bells, a band of ringers may cycle through a complete 'extent', which consists of every possible permutation (a total of $n!$ permutations, where n equals the number of bells). St. Paul's Cathedral houses a set of twelve bells, which (as of this writing) are rung for a half hour before the three Sunday services and for four-hour peals on special occasions.

You find it not only in *bocet*, but in other kinds of Romanian folksong, especially in the north in Maramureș, close to what is Ukraine today[27]. It's a Romanian musical culture called *hora lungă* in a very small area in the northern Carpathians. *Hora lungă* is absolutely close to *cante jondo*. And it's Romanian, not gypsy. It is always on descending patterns, and always certain repeating figurations. I applied it in my Viola Sonata in the first movement, which is called 'Hora lungă'.

And you find it in old Galician Jewish klezmer music in the same area — the Ukrainian border. What is gypsy and what is not gypsy? We don't know. It's a total melding of cultures. My own experience with Romanian traditions (not *hora lungă*, because this I knew later, but what I heard in this *bocet*) and the passacaglias of Monteverdi and Purcell, combined with the idea of spiderwebs and the repetition of simple patterns in an irregular way — this explains my interest in passacaglia.

Your music has a dying fall, and I think you've now explained why. The descending so often gives a feeling of lamentation.

I don't think that I have a predilection for this kind of falling. Take may Piano Études 'L'escalier du diable' and 'Coloana infinită', which are always ascending — not at all descending. Don't make generalizations about going down.

Sometimes, when one has been immersed in your music, one speaks in very bald terms. It's actually very sad. One sometimes wants to know if there's something you can point to in this heightened expressivity.

Real life, what you experience (and I experienced a lot of very bad things in the Nazi times and communist dictatorship, also), I would not put in connection with the music. There were very sad people like Pergolesi writing very light, optimistic music. I don't think that Mozart was really sad. He wrote some pieces of the deepest melancholy, like the G-minor String Quintet or the C-minor Piano Concerto. No, I wouldn't dare to combine the descending passacaglia bass, which is a baroque tradition, and this association of chromatic descent with sorrow. I don't think in this kind of — was it Matteson who developed this kind of affect theory[28]? Stravinsky wrote that there is no expression in music. But still, in his music there is a lot of expression, *malgré lui*. We won't go into these speculations.

---

[27]. BARTÓK 1975.
[28]. MATTHESON 1739.

«Everything Is Chance»: György Ligeti in Conversation with John Tusa

Piano Études: Book II

Can you just say a little bit about 'L'escalier du diable' and 'Coloana infinită'?

I got one of these hundreds of theses or dissertations on my music by someone who examined the column of Constantin Brâncuși in Târgu Jiu, Romania. This is big — thirty meters. It gives the idea of being infinite — asymptotical to being infinite. (Wherever infinity is, it can be very close or very far away. This is another very deep mathematical problem, because we can find zero, but we cannot find infinity.) And this was an article, a study. I was so amazed. He gave the proportions: sixteen-and-a-half units in the Brâncuși column in Târgu Jiu, finding the same proportions in my étude — sixteen-and-a-half cycles[29].

You play with two hands going certain successions which are like in the C-minor étude of Chopin, Op. 25 No. 12 — always spanning the whole piano. Also, Op. 10 No. 1 in C major has the same idea. There the movement goes up and down all the time in waves. I had the idea — it's more a piano-technical idea — to go up with both hands playing a certain figuration which fits a certain harmony. And when I am with the right hand at the top of the piano, the right hand crosses the left hand, which is a technique very well known from Scarlatti. So I begin now with the right hand lower than the left hand. After a while, when I am in the middle of the keyboard, I go with the left hand lower again. This fellow found in it sixteen-and-a-half, exactly like in the Brâncuși. I don't know whether it is true in my study because I don't know from where you count it. So it's a very shaky idea. It's a musicologist's idea[30].

But the idea of these two studies, going all the time up, comes from a different piece which I wrote before, which is always going down. It's 'Vertige' — the irregular canons in chromatic scales. But always chromatic scales in different harmonic combinations of the two hands, which always go down. And the idea comes from acoustics — the Roger Shepard infinite scale. We never met, but he was also at Stanford University when I was. But in fact, I had no

---

[29]. Ligeti misrepresents the analogy set up by musicologist Volker Rülke in an essay published the year of this interview. Rülke makes no claims that 'Coloana infinită' corresponds exactly with the proportions of Brâncuși's column, which consists of fifteen stacked rhomboidal units, with an additional half-unit at the base and another half-unit on top (a total of sixteen units, as opposed to the sixteen-and-a-half Ligeti remembers). Rather, the analogy is a more flexible one that likens the étude's eighth-note chains (*Achtelketten*) to Brâncuși's individual units. The right hand's opening chain — about half the average length of the chains that follow — acts like the half-unit base of the column in Târgu Jiu. Likewise, Rülke draws a parallel between the étude's final ascent, which seems to imply «the lower edge of a chain that extends beyond the keyboard», and the topmost half-unit of Brâncuși's sculpture. See Rülke 1997.

[30]. Again, Ligeti seems to have mistakenly read this argument into Rülke's analysis, which keeps careful count of the number of eighth-note chains in the étude. While Rülke identifies an important formal juncture between the sixteenth and seventeenth chains (bar 27), he makes no explicit claim that this point is meant to correspond to the number of units in Brâncuși's sculpture. See *ibidem*, pp. 152-153.

knowledge about him. I became very good friends during the '70s with Jean-Claude Risset, who is in Marseille, and he produced ever-falling computer simulations. So it's the same idea. I transposed this to the solo piano in 'Vertige'.

It also comes from visual arts — Maurits Escher. And based on the Penrose steps, this endless up- or down-going staircase based on the optical trick representing a three-dimensional object on a two-dimensional plane. And this gave to Escher these wonderful ideas of his false perspectives. Escher's mathematics is like my mathematics — I use it, but not deliberately. There's a wonderful book from a Dutch mathematician, Bruno Ernst, who knew Escher and discussed with him[31]. You know this picture *Print Gallery*? It's a recursive structure. For this we have to go into projective geometry. Escher was not a mathematician; he was a craftsman. I feel very close to his thinking, not to his aesthetics. I admire more really great art, and this was a kind of high-level craft in Escher. (Me, too, maybe.)

When I was listening to 'Der Zauberlehrling', I thought it must be the German for «sorcerer's apprentice». Am I right?

Of course. This is the Goethe poem, but only the title. It's not program music. Like how Debussy gave the preludes titles afterwards with some poetic connotations, 'Zauberlehrling' is a sort of connotation because it's a very fast movement. Dividing in two, dividing in four, and so on — bifurcation. It's also an idea from scaling geometry and Mitchell Feigenbaum. Afterwards, I gave this piece the name of 'Zauberlehrling' because in the Goethe poem, there are two spirits and then more and more, and you cannot get rid of them. And the idea of my piano étude is totally farfetched — something else. There are certain xylophone pieces form Malawi which I heard in the collection of Gerhard Kubik, who lives partly in Malawi. Very complex xylophone music. And my idea was to have similar ideas from the xylophone put on the piano — not the same music, it's not folklore.

Do jazz pianists interest you?

Yes, the good ones. I think that I have a deep love for two 'not good' pianists — neither Duke Ellington nor Thelonious Monk was a great pianist. But as musicians, they are the most wonderful. Also, the virtuoso people like Art Tatum, the blind genius. The other blind genius is Lennie Tristano, but this is different — not high technique. And not a blind but a seeing pianist, Oscar Peterson, with the super speed. And this whole world of bebop and so on. Not only the piano — also Dizzy Gillespie and Charlie Parker.

---

[31]. ERNST 1976.

«Everything Is Chance»: György Ligeti in Conversation with John Tusa

But coming back to piano, there are two good pianists who make a lot of kitsch. But wonderful pianists: Herbie Hancock and Chick Corea. In one record, they play together half composed, half improvised (that's jazz always)[32]. And there are amazing polyrhythmic combinations of the two pianos. This was also a strong influence on me. I would dream of Chick Corea and Herbie Hancock playing my pieces for two pianos, but there's no improvisation in it. But my really favorite jazz pianist is Bill Evans, who is a poet — close to Arturo Benedetti Michelangeli and to the Murray Perahia and Pierre-Laurent Aimard culture of sound on piano.

Bibliography

Apel 1950
French Secular Music of the Late Fourteenth Century, edited by Willi Apel, Cambridge (MA), Mediaeval Academy of America, 1950.

Bartók 1975
Bartók, Béla. *Maramureș County*, edited by Benjamin Suchoff, translated by E. C. Teodorescu, The Hague, Martinus Nijhoff, 1975 (Rumanian Folk Music, 5).

Binkley 1972
Johannes Ciconia, Thomas Binkley – Studio der Frühen Musik, EMI Reflexe 1C 063-30 102, 1972.

Blench 1982
Blench, Roger. 'Evidence for the Indonesian Origins of Certain Elements of African Culture: A Review, with Special Reference to the Arguments of A. M. Jones', in: *African Music*, vi/2 (1982), pp. 81-93.

Cadagin 2020
Cadagin, Joseph. *Nonsense and Nostalgia in the Lewis Carroll Settings of György Ligeti*, unpublished Ph.D. Diss., Stanford (CA), Stanford University, 2020.

Carroll – Kosztolányi 2013
Carroll, Lewis. *Évike tündérországban*, translated by Dezső Kosztolányi, Budapest, Napkút Kiadó, 2013.

Cheevers 2001
'György Ligeti', in: *The John Tusa Interviews*, produced by Tony Cheevers, BBC Radio 3, 4 March 2001.

Cowell 1969
Cowell, Henry. *New Musical Resources*, New York, Something Else Press, 1969.

---

[32]. Chick Corea and Herbie Hancock released two duet albums: *An Evening with Herbie Hancock & Chick Corea: In Concert* (1978) and *CoreaHancock* (1979). The latter features Bartók's two-piano arrangement of the 'Ostinato' movement from Book vi of *Mikrokosmos*.

ERNST 1976
ERNST, Bruno. *The Magic Mirror of M. C. Escher*, translated by John E. Brigham, New York, Ballantine Books, 1976.

GALVÁN 2007
GALVÁN, Gary. *Henry Cowell in the Fleisher Collection*, unpublished Ph.D. Diss., Gainesville (FL), University of Florida, 2007.

HALL 2014
'Clocks and Clouds: An Adventure Around György Ligeti', on: *Sunday Feature*, produced by Alan Hall, BBC Radio 3, 25 May 2014.

JONES 1971
JONES, Arthur M. *Africa and Indonesia: The Evidence of the Xylophone and Other Musical and Cultural Factors*, Leiden, E. J. Brill, ²1971.

JONES 1973/1974
ID. 'Letters to the Editor', in: *African Music*, v/3 (1973/1974), pp. 96-97.

KARINTHY 2001
KARINTHY, Frigyes. 'Halandzsa', in: *Humoreszkek II.*, edited by Károly Szalay, Budapest, Akkord, 2001 (Karinthy Frigyes összegyűjtött művei, 4), pp. 65-67.

KUBIK 1983
KUBIK, Gerhard. 'Kognitive Grundlagen afrikanischer Musik', in: *Musik in Afrika*, edited by Artur Simon, Berlin, Museum für Völkerkunde, 1983, pp. 327-400.

LENDVAI 1971
LENDVAI, Ernő. *Béla Bartók: An Analysis of His Music*, London, Kahn & Averill, 1971.

LEPPARD 1971
Monteverdi Madrigali: Libri 8-9-10, Raymond Leppard – Glyndebourne Opera Group, Philips 6799 006, 1971.

LIGETI 1960
LIGETI, György. 'Pierre Boulez: Decision and Automatism in *Structure 1a*', in: *Die Reihe 4: Young Composers*, edited by Herbert Eimert and Karlheinz Stockhausen, translated by Leo Black, Bryn Mawr (PA), Theodore Presser, 1960, pp. 36-62.

LIGETI 1965
ID. 'Metamorphoses of Musical Form', in: *Die Reihe 7: Form – Space*, edited by Herbert Eimert and Karlheinz Stockhausen, translated by Cornelius Cardew, Bryn Mawr (PA), Theodore Presser, 1965, pp. 5-19.

«Everything Is Chance»: György Ligeti in Conversation with John Tusa

LIGETI 1983
ID. 'György Ligeti in Conversation with Péter Várnai', in: *György Ligeti in Conversation with Péter Várnai, Josef Häusler, Claude Samuel, and Himself*, translated by Gabor J. Schabert, Sarah E. Soulsby, Terence Kilmartin and Geoffrey Skelton, London, Eulenburg, 1983 (Eulenburg Music Series), pp. 13-82.

LIGETI 1993
ID. 'Rhapsodische, unausgewogene Gedanken über Musik, besonders über meine eigenen Kompositionen', in: *Neue Zeitschrift für Musik*, CLIV/1 (January 1993), pp. 20-29.

LIGETI 2003
ID. 'György Ligeti: «The cogs have to mesh, exactly»', in: *On Creativity: Interviews Exploring the Process*, by John Tusa, London, Methuen, 2003, pp. 183-199.

LORENZ 1963
LORENZ, Edward N. 'Deterministic Nonperiodic Flow', in: *Journal of the Atmospheric Sciences*, XX/2 (1963), pp. 130-141.

MATTHESON 1739
MATTHESON, Johann. *Der vollkommene Capellmeister*, Hamburg, Christian Herold, 1739.

POPPER 1972
POPPER, Karl R. 'Of Clouds and Clocks: An Approach to the Problem of Rationality and the Freedom of Man', in: *Objective Knowledge: An Evolutionary Approach*, Oxford, The Clarendon Press, 1972, pp. 206-255.

RICHART 1990
RICHART, Robert W. *György Ligeti: A Bio-Bibliography*, New York, Greenwood Press, 1990.

RUELLE – TAKENS 1971
RUELLE, David – TAKENS, Floris. 'On the Nature of Turbulence', in: *Communications in Mathematical Physics*, XX/3 (1971), pp. 167-192.

RÜLKE 1997
RÜLKE, Volker. '*Die Unendliche Säule*: Überlegungen zum Verhältnis von Musik und bildender Kunst anhand zweier Werke von Constantin Brâncuși und György Ligeti', in: *Semantische Inseln, musikalisches Festland: für Tibor Kneif zum 65. Geburtstag*, edited by Hanns-Werner Heister, Hamburg, Von Bockel, 1997, pp. 143-155.

SIEDENTOPF 1973
SIEDENTOPF, Henning. 'Neue Wege der Klaviertechnik', in: *Melos*, XL/3 (May/June 1973), pp. 143-146.

SMITH 1973
SMITH, Leland. 'Henry Cowell's *Rhythmicana*', in: *Anuario Interamericano de Investigación Musical*, no. 9 (1973), pp. 134-147.

Steinitz 2013
Steinitz, Richard. *György Ligeti: Music of the Imagination*, London, Faber & Faber, ²2013.

Witt 1954
Witt, Peter. 'Spider Webs and Drugs', in: *Scientific American*, cxci/6 (1954), pp. 80-87.

Abstracts and Biographies

Benjamin R. Levy, *Condensed Expression and Compositional Technique in György Ligeti's «Aventures» and Beyond*

György Ligeti's works *Aventures* and *Nouvelles Aventures* are complicated and at times almost self-contradictory pieces, hovering at the fringes of comprehensibility. The quick juxtapositions of contrasting material in these works can be alienating, shattering any continuity; yet the fragments that remain point tantalizingly towards a wider, yet unrealized context, partially hidden from the audience, but unveiled by a study of the composer's sketches held at the Paul Sacher Foundation. The network of associations this music entails touches not only on emotional states, but also on traditional genres of music, the visual arts, and literature — including the works of Gyula Krúdy and Franz Kafka. Moreover, once these connections are recognized, they inform similarly constructed passages in later works — including works as different as the Chamber Concerto, *Ramifications*, and *Le Grand Macabre* — creating a chain of intertextual references that originates in Ligeti's music of the early 1960s but extends for decades thereafter.

Benjamin R. Levy is Associate Professor of Music Theory at the University of California, Santa Barbara. He holds degrees from Washington University in St. Louis (BA in Music and Classics, 1999) and the University of Maryland (Ph.D. in Music Theory, 2006). His research interests focus on modernist and contemporary music and on connections between music, literature, and the arts. He has published widely on the music of György Ligeti, including *Metamorphosis in Music: The Compositions of György Ligeti in the 1950s and 1960s* (OUP 2017, Finalist for the Society for Music Theory's Wallace Berry Award) and 'Shades of the Studio: Electronic Influences on Ligeti's *Apparitions*' (*Perspectives of New Music*, xlviii/2 [2009], pp. 59-87, winner of the SMT's Emerging Scholar Award). He is currently working on English translations of *The Schoenberg-Webern Correspondence: Selected Letters*, for inclusion in Oxford University Press's series, *Schoenberg in Words*.

***

Britta Sweers, *Listening to «Lontano»: The Auditory Perception of Ligeti's Sound Textures*

When György Ligeti composed micropolyphonic works such as *Atmosphères* (1961) and *Lontano* (1967), he revolutionized established compositional thinking due to the shift from melodic-harmonic thinking towards a thinking in which timbre and sound color dominate. Especially *Lontano* has been framed by a large range of associative suggestions related to poetry and art, while also having been described in spatial terms associated with the idea of frozen time. This, however, deviates from associations mentioned by listeners unfamiliar with these theoretical Ligeti discourses. Falling back on two auditory experiments, this article explores the dichotomy of these discourses and auditory perceptions, as well as psychoacoustic issues in the case of *Lontano*. As I argue here, an adequate analysis of Ligeti's works needs to combine discursive, score-based, aural, and acoustic perspectives more strongly for a more comprehensive understanding. This, however, renders the listener and his/her imaginary musical perception a stronger authority over pre-determined descriptions and terminology that could, rather than support, restrict a listener's perception of the works.

BRITTA SWEERS is Professor of Cultural Anthropology of Music at the Institute of Musicology (since 2009) and she was Director of the Center for Global Studies (2015-2019) at the University of Bern (Switzerland). She is President of the *European Seminar in Ethnomusicology* (ESEM) since 2015. Having studied at Hamburg University (Ph.D. 1999) and Indiana University (Bloomington; 1992/93), she was Assistant (2001-2003) and Junior Professor for Systematic Musicology and Ethnomusicology at the Hochschule für Musik und Theater Rostock (Germany) from 2003 to 2009. She is Advisory Board Member of the Mariann-Steegmann-Foundation and is also co-editor of the *European Journal of Musicology* and the *Equinox* book series 'Transcultural Music Studies'. Ligeti-related publications include *Lontano – "Aus weiter Ferne": Zur Musiksprache und Assoziationsvielfalt György Ligetis* (1997, with Christiane Engelbrecht and Wolfgang Marx) and 'György Ligeti' (2016) in the online encyclopaedia *MUGI. Musikvermittlung und Genderforschung: Lexikon und multimediale Präsentationen*.

***

PIERRE MICHEL –MARYSE STAIBER, *Rediscovering the Meaning of Words with Hölderlin: About «Drei Phantasien» by György Ligeti*

The *Three Fantasies* for mixed choir after Hölderlin (1982) form a kind of 'bridge' between the very typical choral pieces of the 1960s/70s, *Lux Aeterna* and *Clocks and Clouds*, and György Ligeti's later development. Here, for the first time in a very long period, Ligeti renewed his acquaintance with poetry by confronting himself with one of the most outstanding German poets, who, moreover, made a great impact on the minds of composers during this very period (see Luigi Nono and Wolfgang Rihm among others). In this period of questioning and artistic crisis that shook the Ligeti generation, the use of meaning in vocal music was, so to speak, a challenge: to get away from aerial vocal polyphonies without truly comprehensible texts (except for a few phrases from the «Mass of the Dead») in these works that quickly became famous, to return to poetic texts of the highest quality by finding suitable means (which were, moreover, in full evolution at the beginning of the 1980s) for this new confrontation between canonical-type polyphonies or heterophonies and the question of «making a text heard». To explore this new path in Ligeti's work, which was followed by several choral pieces or pieces for vocal ensembles with texts, Pierre Michel and Maryse Staiber propose a multidisciplinary musicological and literary approach that they have already developed around other composers and poets (Wolfgang Rihm and Paul Celan, Paul Méfano and Paul Éluard or Yves Bonnefoy, etc.). This essay will also make it possible to better acquaint the English-speaking public with the context of German poetry and the profound references of these poems, as well as the musical specificities of this important work.

PIERRE MICHEL taught at the Strasbourg Conservatory before taking up lectureships at the University of Metz and then at the University of Strasbourg in 1998 (where he was appointed Professor in 2008). He had met Ligeti at the Acanthes-Academy (Aix-en-Provence) in 1979, and the composer supported his project of writing a book on his music: the result was the first volume to be published in French in 1985 (Éditions Minerve, Paris), with interviews made in Vienna in 1981. He also published several other papers on the Chamber Concerto and *Le Grand Macabre*, produced a web documentary on the Trio for Violin, Horn and Piano for UOH (Université Ouverte

Abstracts and Biographies

des Humanités) in 2016, and recently participated in a complete online issue of Ligeti's Ten Pieces for Woodwind Quintet. He translated an important part of the second French volume of Ligeti's writings entitled *L'Atelier du compositeur* (Éditions Contrechamps, 2013). Michel published articles and books about several composers and has edited French editions of writings by composers such as F. Busoni, G. Amy, T. Murail, H. Zender, and W. Rihm.

MARYSE STAIBER is Professor of German Literature at the Université de Strasbourg (France). Her publications concern the relationship between poetry and music, especially Wolfgang Rihm's works on poems by Paul Celan (in cooperation with Pierre Michel), the composer Hans Zender revisiting Cabaret Voltaire (in *Unité – pluralité: la musique de Hans Zender*, Pierre Michel, ed. by Marik Froidefond & Jörn Hiekel, Paris, Hermann, 2015), and Paul Méfano's works on poems by Yves Bonnefoy ('Paul Méfano et la «voûte chantante»: les compositions de Paul Méfano sur des poèmes d'Yves Bonnefoy', in: *Paul Méfano. Les chemins d'un musicien-poète*, ed. by Pierre Michel et Gérard Geay, Paris, Hermann, 2017).

***

MANFRED STAHNKE, *The Dove and the Bear: 'Galamb Borong' and the Connection to 'Ars Subtilior'*
This essay focuses on Ligeti's thinking with regard to rhythmic-metrical parameters as it developed in his composition class in the 1980s, demonstrating the origin of these ideas and analysing his compositional processes. This includes references back to his work in the 1950s, relating it to the emergence of new approaches as they evolved from 1980 onwards in his class. The composer's thinking was influenced by the 'Nancarrow complex' as well as the 'Ars subtilior' and non-European musical concepts (such as Salsa or music from Africa and Indonesia). Ligeti's seventh piano étude 'Galamb borong' (related to the Balinese 'gamelan barong') can serve as an example of Ligeti's striving for a non-mechanistic, somewhat improvisatory, free-flowing rhythmic world which is completely different from the first étude 'Désordre'. In 'Galamb borong' Ligeti develops melodic forms whose rhythmic asymmetries remind of a kind of improvisation not unlike the notated quasi-improvisations of the ars subtilior music. These parallels will be demonstrated through a comparison of rhythmic forms within melodic structures in Ligeti's étude with the Ars subtilior ballad *Angelorum psalat*. In *Angelorum psalat* an additive pulsation of free-flowing forms is created through an expansion of the existing musical notation while the étude achieves similar effects through ever-expanding or -contracting pulse patters independent of metric structures.

MANFRED STAHNKE studied with Wolfgang Fortner, Klaus Huber, György Ligeti and Ben Johnston composition, and with Hans Heinrich Eggebrecht and Constantin Floros musicology. In 1983 he was appointed a Lecturer at the Hochschule für Musik und Theater Hamburg; in 1995 he was made a full-time Professor for composition. As a keyboard player he travelled with his group CHAOSMA worldwide, presenting new forms of microtonality and hybrid forms of avant-garde music. Stahnke's works have a strong basis in microtonality and pulsative rhythms, as well as in improvisational practices. Among them are string quartets, orchestral pieces and operas. He semi-improvises as a viola player in the Hamburg-based group «TonArt». Currently he composes viola music in semi-Persian scales or semi-Bohlen-Pierce music for strings. Many of his pieces can be found at BabelScores, Paris. Stahnke has published several books, among them *1001 Microtones* (2015) and *Mein Blick auf Ligeti / Partch & Compagnons* (2017). He is chair of the music section of the Freie Akademie der Künste Hamburg.

***

Abstracts and Biographies

Peter Edwards, *Analysing the Concerto for Violin and Orchestra: Apparitions of the Past and Future*

In an interview conducted shortly after the completion of a revised version of his Violin Concerto in 1992, György Ligeti describes the «[l]ayers upon layers of conscious and unconcious influences [...] connected together to form an organic, homogenous whole» in the Concerto. Among the many sources of inspiration, he mentions African music, fractal geometry, 'Ars subtilior', Conlon Nancarrow and non-tempered tuning systems. This chapter explores Ligeti's remembering vision and transformation of past influences and experiences into new and complex ideas. Through an analysis of select compositional, thematic and expressive features in the Concerto, the chapter will seek to engage with the processes of transfomation of both explicit and implicit influences in Ligeti's compositonal vision, and how we as listeners might identify with this vision. This gives cause to reflect on ways in which the compositional process might be analogous to notions of the listening experience as the constitution of the past in the present.

Peter Edwards is Associate Professor at the Department of Musicology, University of Oslo. He has published in *Music Analysis*, *Music & Letters* and in edited collections on topics that intersect aesthetics, music analysis, cultural studies and critical musicology. His monograph *György Ligeti's «Le Grand Macabre»: Postmodernism, Musico-Dramatic Form and the Grotesque* (Routledge 2017) examines Ligeti's creative process, the sketches for the opera, and the significance of the opera in the wider context of modern and postmodern aesthetics. Peter is also a composer and guitarist.

***

Ewa Schreiber, *Listening (to) Ligeti: Tracing Sound Memories and Sound Images in the Composer's Writings*

The text discusses György Ligeti's sound memories related to his childhood and youth spent in Transylvania and Budapest. A number of contexts which accompany them most frequently is identified. These are: the local soundscape, multiple languages and identities, limitations linked to musical education, changing sound carriers and elapsing time as well as endangered sounds and existential fear. The aim of the article is also to answer, at least hypothetically, the question of how the sound memories contributed to Ligeti's creative imagination. They can be found in multiple associations jotted down as sources of inspiration in the initial compositional sketches. They also influence Ligeti's interpretation of the works of other composers (including Béla Bartók, Anton Webern, Gustav Mahler and Charles Ives whom he included in his artistic genealogy) especially in the context of musical space and transforming the sounds of nature. Measuring time also acquires its sound representation in Ligeti's music and the problem of language permeated his artistic biography from the earliest works. In the case of Ligeti the identity-shaping and performative role of his sound memories seems evident. Memories not only play an identifying role, but also enable a fuller characterisation of the medium of sound itself. In the composer's narrative sound generates complex and changing meanings, associations and emotions, imposes its presence, materiality, immediacy and particularity. This brings it closer to the rich experiences that Ligeti's compositions themselves leave in their interpreters and listeners.

Ewa Schreiber is Assistant Professor at the Department of Musicology of Adam Mickiewicz University in Poznań (Poland). She graduated in musicology and philosophy at Adam Mickiewicz University and defended her Ph.D. in musicology there. Her main research interests include the aesthetics of music (the theory of tropes, such as irony and metaphor, applied to music and musicological discourse), sociology of music and the musical thought of contemporary composers (György Ligeti, Witold Lutosławski, Helmut Lachenmann and Jonathan Harvey among others). In 2012 she published her monograph *Muzyka i metafora. Koncepcje kompozytorskie Pierre'a Schaeffera, Raymonda Murraya Schafera i Gérarda Griseya* [Music and Metaphor: The Compositional Thought of Pierre Schaeffer, Raymond Murray Schafer and Gérard Grisey] (National Centre for Culture, Warsaw). From 2020, she is the editor-in-chief of the journal *Res Facta Nova: Studies in Contemporary Music*.

***

MÁRTON KERÉKFY, *'Functional Music' and «Cantata for the Festival of Youth»: New Data on Ligeti's Works from His Budapest Years*

Perhaps the most formative period for György Ligeti's professional career were those eleven years during which he was active at the Liszt Academy in Budapest from September 1945 to December 1956. The first ground-breaking study devoted to this period of the composer's life and work, written by Friedemann Sallis, was published in 1996. Relying on a large body of archival sources but also on existing work lists by Ove Nordwall and Pierre Michel, Sallis compiled a catalogue of Ligeti's composed works and published writings up to 1956, analysed several key works from this period, and also made an attempt to set out their historical context. Since the publication of Sallis' book, a significant body of compositional sources from Ligeti's early years (including manuscripts of works formerly considered lost) has become available for research in the Ligeti Collection of the Paul Sacher Foundation. Yet a considerable part of Ligeti's juvenilia and early biography is still under-researched or unexplored, with several works remaining unpublished or being missing. It is owing to this that most of the information on this period in even more current literature stems from the composer's recollections rather than from facts supported by historical sources.

MÁRTON KERÉKFY is Research Fellow at the Budapest Bartók Archives, Editor of the *Béla Bartók Complete Critical Edition* and Editor-in-Chief at the music publishing company Editio Musica Budapest Zeneműkiadó. He studied musicology and composition at the Liszt Academy of Music in Budapest and received his Ph.D. in musicology from the same institution. He has published articles on the music of Ligeti and Bartók in, among others, *Tempo*, *Studia Musicologica* and *Mitteilungen der Paul Sacher Stiftung*. He translated into Hungarian and edited Ligeti's selected writings (2010) and was co-editor of the volume *György Ligeti's Cultural Identities* (2017). His book *Folklorism and Nostalgia in the Music of György Ligeti* explores the influence of East European folk music in Ligeti's music (forthcoming). Since 2019 he has been President of the Hungarian Musicological Society.

***

BIANCA ȚIPLEA TEMEȘ, *Mourning in Folk Style: Ligeti's Reliance on Romanian Laments*

As a Transylvanian, Ligeti witnessed until 1945 (when he moved to Budapest) a special model of cultural exchange between Romanians, Hungarians, Germans, Jews, and other ethnic groups. He therefore became familiar with the rich and varied folk music of the region, turning into a 'polyglot' in terms of musical idioms from a very young age. While the impact of these folk traditions was thus very strong due to his childhood and youth spent in Transylvania, later on Ligeti had the chance to study this heritage in depth when he returned to Romania in 1949-1950 to spent a few months in Bucharest, but also in Cluj where he had started his musical training. In Bucharest,

Abstracts and Biographies

Ligeti transcribed and studied folk music from the entire Romanian territory at the Folklore Institute, an experience which had visible consequences throughout his career as a composer. One of the folk genres which impressed him the most was the Romanian 'bocet' (dirge), a folk lament also studied by Bartók in his ethnomusicological journeys in Transylvania. Pieces such as Ligeti's piano étude 'Automne à Varsovie' or sections of his Piano Concerto rely on this powerful melodic resource. According to the composer's words, a part of his Requiem is woven as «a heterophony of bocete». Symbols of mourning as well as tribute to the victims of the Second World War, the Romanian folk laments become an encoded musical weeping in his scores, conferring a transcendental dimension to Ligeti's oeuvre.

BIANCA ȚIPLEA TEMEȘ is Reader in Music Theory at the Gheorge Dima National Music Academy in Cluj-Napoca. She earned two doctorates (University of Music in Bucharest; Universidad de Oviedo, Spain) and served until 2016 as head of the artistic department at the Transylvania Philharmonic. Her books have been published in Romania (the most recent *Seeing Sound, Hearing Images*, edited together with Nicholas Cook, *Folk Music as a Fermenting Agent for Composition – Past and Present*, edited with William Kinderman, and *A Tribute to György Ligeti in His Native Transylvania, nos. 1-2*, edited with Kofi Agawu). Her articles have appeared in leading journals in Romania, and abroad, her present research focusing mainly on the music of Ligeti, Kurtág, and contemporary Romanian music. She has participated in many conferences organised by prestigious institutions, and since 2010 she has been visiting professor at various institutions in Spain, Italy, Poland, Germany, and the U.S. and Heidelberg and received a research grant from the Paul Sacher Foundation, where she explored the Ligeti collection. In 2016 she became the founder and the artistic director of the Festival *A Tribute to György Ligeti in his Native Transylvania*.

***

JULIA HEIMERDINGER, *György Ligeti's Film Music beyond Stanley Kubrick*

Although György Ligeti has never composed film scores, his music has quickly found its way into the movies when it first appeared in Stanley Kubrick's space epos *2001: A Space Odyssey* in 1968 and later in *The Shining* (1980) and *Eyes Wide Shut* (1999). While these iconic movies have been widely examined in musicological literature, this chapter gives an overview of various employments of Ligeti's works in films beyond Kubrick up to today, including feature films, documentaries, TV series and shorts. Even though Kubrick's influence is still clearly discernible in some respects, the range of uses has broadened over the decades and holds some surprises, like the coupling of *Atmosphères*' piccolo-passage with Bruce Lee's battle cry in *Fist of Fury* (HK 1972), for example. In all, a crystallisation of favourite works and excerpts can be observed, and the selection and coupling of effective bits and pieces matches Ligeti's own commentaries on his compositions remarkably often.

JULIA HEIMERDINGER is a Senior Scientist (postdoc) at the Department of Musicology and Performance Studies at the University of Music and Performing Arts Vienna. Among her research areas is film music, especially the use of avant-garde music in film. She has given lectures and published a monograph (*Neue Musik im Spielfilm*, Saarbrücken 2007) and various articles on this topic, among them: '«I Have Been Compromised. I Am now Fighting against It»: Ligeti vs. Kubrick and the Music for *2001: A Space Odyssey*', in: *The Journal of Film Music*, III/2 (2011), pp. 127-143, or 'I Sing the Body Electric: Elektroakustik im Film', in: *Filmmusik und Narration*, edited by M. Gervink and R. Rabenalt, Marburg 2017, pp. 231-248.

***

Abstracts and Biographies

VITA GRUODYTĖ, *Letters from Stanford: György Ligeti to Aliutė Mečys*

Aliutė Mečys (1943-2013), an artist of Lithuanian origin, was not only the initiator of the libretto and the set designer of the premiere of Ligeti's opera, *Le Grand Macabre* (1978, in Stockholm) but also his confidante, his artistic advisor and his friend for many years. With both artists living in Berlin, they did not have what one might call an epistolary link. They had, however, a short yet intensive correspondence period at the time when Ligeti was invited to teach at Stanford University in the United States (in 1972). These letters, few (and perhaps incomplete) but often quite long, were saved after Aliutė's death. Fortunately, this correspondence includes not only the composer's originals sent to Aliutė, but also the drafts of her own answers to Ligeti (the originals having been destroyed by the composer). This correspondence is rich in its writing. It offers details about the musical compositions on which Ligeti worked at the moment (including *Le Grand Macabre*), his reflections, his personal life at the time; it also provides a unique insight into Ligeti's views on American society, its cultural scene, and about their German counterparts. Core excerpts from the letters translated into English, accompanied by a contextualising commentary, will offer the reader the pleasure of discovering new nuances in the thinking of one of the most important composers during the second half of the 20th century.

VITA GRUODYTĖ is a Researcher at the Lithuanian Academy of Music and Theatre (Vilnius). After Doctoral Studies with Tempus Programme at Helsinki University, she gained a Ph.D. in musicology from the Lithuanian Academy of Theatre and Music in 2000 with a Doctoral thesis entitled *The Phenomena of Space in the Music of the 20th Century*. She was Researcher at the Lithuanian Museum of Music, Theater and Cinema, at the University of Klaipeda (Lithuania), and supervised research at the Invisible College of the Soros Foundation in Vilnius. She is a Member of the Lithuanian Composers' Union and a correspondent of the Lithuanian cultural magazine *Fields of Culture*. Her research focuses on aesthetics and the history of 20th-century music, cultural and political influences in contemporary music, and in particular on the emergence of a national identity in Lithuanian music.

***

HEIDY ZIMMERMANN, *More than Printing Scores: Ligeti and His Post-1960 Publishers*

György Ligeti's first works composed in the West were published with Universal Edition in Vienna (*Apparitions* and *Atmosphères*), before he switched to Peters/Litolff (*Aventures*, *Volumina*, Requiem). Since 1967 he worked exclusively with Schott Music Publishing in Mainz. Recently Schott's large Ligeti archive was transferred to the György Ligeti Collection at the Paul Sacher Foundation. It offers interesting insights into a collaboration stretching over several decades. The extensive correspondence covers the genesis of most works of this period, yet documents related to revision and (partly quite lengthy) production processes show how Ligeti also revised earlier works, how he commented on and improved both notation and score layout very meticulously in order to ensure the best possible conditions for an adequate performance. This chapter will look at selected compositions (both string quartets, the piano etudes and early choral pieces) to demonstrate how Ligeti consciously influenced the publication of his music. Especially with regard to works from his Hungarian period Ligeti used the opportunity for a final revision of his scores. The essay will also address issues around the estate and the Ligeti Collection at the Paul Sacher Foundation. In preparation of the Ligeti centenary his main publisher, his executors and the Paul Sacher Foundation are preparing the publication of works that so far have never appeared in print. The goal is to make Ligeti's entire compositional oeuvre available by 2023.

Abstracts and Biographies

HEIDY ZIMMERMANN has been a member of the research staff at the Paul Sacher Foundation since 2002. She is the curator of more than twenty Collections, among them the archives of Igor Stravinsky, György Ligeti, and György Kurtág. She has published numerous articles on twentieth-century music (especially on Stefan Wolpe, Klaus Huber, and György Ligeti) and co-edited several books, such as *Jüdische Musik?* (Cologne, Böhlau, 2004), *Edgard Varèse: Composer, Sound Sculptor, Visionary* (Mainz, Schott, 2006), and *RE-SET. Rückgriffe und Fortschreibungen in der Musik seit 1900* (Mainz, Schott, 2018).

***

JOSEPH CADAGIN, *«Everything Is Chance»: György Ligeti in Conversation with John Tusa, 28 October 1997*

In this unaired interview for BBC Radio 3 conducted by John Tusa in 1997, Ligeti examines his musical output of the last decade-and-a-half, including Books I and II of the Piano Études, the *Nonsense Madrigals*, *Magyar Etüdök*, the Horn Trio, and the Violin Concerto. Discussion of compositional craft (piano techniques, alternative tunings, passacaglia and chaconne forms) is supplemented by the composer's colorful anecdotes about his colleagues and his reflections on the reception of his music. Exhibiting his usual intellectual virtuosity, Ligeti expounds on an encyclopedic range of influences, both musical (African thumb piano and xylophone, Ars nova polyphony, Conlon Nancarrow, folk laments, jazz pianists) and non-musical (complexity, fractal geometry, Victorian nonsense literature, Sándor Weöres, M. C. Escher). Running like a leitmotivic thread through his circuitous responses is the theme of indeterminism. Though Ligeti was fascinated by the experimental field of deterministic chaos — which posits that there is an underlying order to apparently random systems — he consistently attributes major turning points in his career to the pure whimsy of chance.

JOSEPH CADAGIN received his doctorate in musicology from Stanford University, with a dissertation on Ligeti's nostalgic interactions with the works of Lewis Carroll. His research focuses broadly on opera and vocal repertoire after 1960, with a special interest in settings of *Alice in Wonderland*. As a music journalist, he regularly contributes features and recording reviews to *Opera News* magazine. In 2019-2020, he was awarded a Fulbright grant to conduct research at Ligeti's alma mater, the Liszt Ferenc Academy in Budapest. From 2021-2023, he held postdoctoral fellowships at the University of Toronto's Jackman Humanities Institute and New Europe College in Bucharest, Romania.

Index of Names

A

Abbate, Carolyn 11
Adams, John viii, 260
Adés, Thomas 93
Aimard, Pierre-Laurent 248, 250, 269
Alexandru, Tiberiu 165
Almén, Byron 11
Altdorfer, Albrecht 28, 62, 64
Antunes, António Lobo 185
Apel, Willi 74, 251
Arany, János 146
Arató, Pál 146
Arom, Simha 72-73, 76
Arrabal, Fernando 214
Artaud, Antonin 214
Åstrand, Christina 108
Audiberti, Jacques 214
Auer, Leopold 118
Auer, Soma 118

B

Bach, Johann Sebastian 14, 77, 188, 217, 264
Bart, Jean-Yves 49
Bartók, Béla 76-77, 119, 125, 141, 163, 165, 172, 182, 220, 226, 256, 259
Bauer, Amy 63, 118, 127, 129-130, 163, 168, 170, 172
Baumann, Hermann 261

Baumann, Max Peter 72
Beckles Willson, Rachel 114, 118, 128, 135, 227
Beethoven, Ludwig van 95, 118-119, 170, 191, 262
Berei, Mária 146
Bergmann, Hjalmar 219
Berio, Luciano 227-228
Berlioz, Hector 193
Bernard, Jonathan W. 4, 124-125, 127
Bernstein, Leonard 116
Bertini, Gary 94
Besch, Eckart 95, 248, 261
Beurmann, Andreas E. 39, 44
Bihari, János 144
Binkley, Thomas 251
Borodin, Aleksandr 29-30
Bosch, Hieronymus 202, 207
Boulez, Pierre vii, 95, 227-228, 236, 249-250, 260
Bourbaki, Nicolas 75
Bradbury, Ray 186
Brahms, Johannes 61, 95, 253, 261-262
Brăiloiu, Constantin 76-77, 165
Brâncuși, Constantin 267
Breazul, George 165
Breughel, Pieter 202
Brockhaus, Immanuel 38
Bullerjahn, Claudia 30

Index of Names

C

CADAGIN, Joseph 247
CAGE, John 126, 188, 191, 208, 214, 229, 252, 260
CARDEW, Cornelius 7
CARROLL, Lewis 257-259
CARTER, Elliott 252
CELAN, Paul 59
CHAPLIN, Charlie [Charles Spencer] 186
CHAR, René 260
CHIN, Unsuk 93
CHOPIN, Fryderyk 253, 267
CHOWNING, John 73
CHRISTOU, Jani 188, 191
CICONIA, Johannes 72, 248, 251
CLAIR, René 186
CLASS, Olivier 49
CLENDINNING, Jane Piper 60
COLETTE, Gabriele-Sidonie 214
COREA, Chick [Armando Anthony] 269
CORELLI, Arcangelo 264
COWELL, Henry 262
CROSTEN, William L. 210, 218
CRUMB, George 182, 191
CSERMÁK, Antal 144
CUNNINGHAM, Merce 252

D

DADELSEN, Hans-Christian von 75
DALÍ, Salvador 174
DAUER, Alfons 76
DÁVID, Gyula 141
DEBUSSY, Claude 35, 74, 82, 125, 193, 253, 268
DELIBES, Léo 116
DE NIRO, Robert 186
DEPARDIEU, Gérard 184
DERZSI, Sándor 148
DESPLAT, Alexandre 180
DEVECSERI, Gábor 141
DE VITRY, Philippe 251
DIBELIUS, Ulrich 33-34, 63
DI BONAVENTURA, Anthony 261
DI BONAVENTURA, Mario 261

DICAPRIO, Leonardo 187, 192
DONIZETTI, Gaetano 9
DUCHESNEAU, Louise 72-73, 113, 248
DUFAY, Guillaume 88, 251
DUKAS, Paul 116
DURAS, Marguerite 189

E

EDWARDS, Peter ix, 93
EICHENDORFF, Joseph von 95
EIGEN, Manfred 73
EIMERT, Herbert 226
ELEKES, Dénes 145
ELIADE, Mircea 172
ELLINGTON, Duke [Edward Kennedy] 268
EÖTVÖS, Peter 95
ERNST, Bruno 268
ESCHER, Maurits Cornelis 75, 268
ESSEN, Gerd Wolfgang 202
EVANS, Bill [William John] 269

F

FÁBIÁN, Imre 140, 152
FARKAS, Anna 151
FARKAS, Ferenc 122, 144, 152
FEIGENBAUM, Mitchell 268
FELDMAN, Morton 188, 191, 209, 265
FERNEYHOUGH, Brian 73
FIBONACCI, Leonardo 256
FIENNES, Sophie 189, 190-192
FLOROS, Constantin 33, 50, 63, 73, 81-82, 163
FRANSSENS, Joep 182
FREEMAN, Betty 263
FREUD, Lucian 207
FUNK, Vera 52
FURTSEVA, Yekaterina Alexeyevna 212
FURUKAWA, Kiyoshi 74

G

GAINSBOURG, Charlotte 184
GALIOT, Johannes 251
GALLOT, Simon 143-145, 107, 261

Index of Names

Gentele, Göran 200, 212, 214, 221, 223
Georgescu-Stănculeanu, Lucilia 165
Gerő, Ágnes 144
Gesualdo, Carlo 104
Ghelderode, Michel de 202
Gillespie, Dizzy [John Birks] 268
Glass, Philip viii, 191
Goethe, Johann Wolfgang von 206, 211, 217, 268
Gombrich, Ernst 75
Gottschalk, Dietrich Diederichs 202
Grinberg, Anouk 184
Gruodytė, Vita xi, 199
Gubaidulina, Sofia 182, 188, 191
Günther, Ursula 72-73, 88

H

Hacks, Peter 216
Hamilton, Richard 75
Hancock, Herbie 269
Hanna, Vincent 187
Häusler, Josef 33, 192
Háy, Gyula 213-214
Heimerdinger, Julia x, 32-33, 39, 179
Heinrich, Rudolph 199
Herms-Bohnhoff, Elke 203
Hidi, Péter 144
Hindemith, Paul 231
Hitler, Adolf 122
Hocker, Jürgen 184
Hoffnung, Gerard 217
Hofstadter, Douglas R. 75
Hölderlin, Friedrich ix, 49-51, 63, 67-69
Holliger, Heinz 49
Huber, Klaus 73
Hufner, Martin 36
Huxley, Aldous 123

I

Ichiyanagi, Toshi 128
Illei, János 148
Illés, Árpád 259
Illiano, Roberto xi

Ionesco, Eugène 213-214, 218, 234
Iștoc, Lucia 165
Ives, Charles 125, 127, 263

J

Jagamas, János 145, 147
Jain, Gora xi
James, Montague Rhodes 183
Járdányi, Pál 140
Jarre, Jean-Michel 29
Jarry, Alfred 218
Johnson, Julian 128
Johnston, Ben 71, 73
Jones, Arthur M. 254
Josephson, Nors S. 79
Joyce, James 260
Jurašas, Jonas 202

K

Kadosa, Pál 140
Kafka, Franz 18
Kagel, Mauricio 217, 229
Kahane, Mariana 165
Kapp, Reinhard 236
Karbusický, Vladimir 202
Karinthy, Frigyes 257-258
Kármán, Vera 144
Kaufmann, Harald 33, 216
Keats, John 28
Kenderessi, Zoltán 151
Kerékfy, Márton x, 125, 135
Kevebázi, Lajos 151
Kiefer, Anselm 189, 190-192
Kiss, Ferenc 144
Kiss, Lajos 140
Kleiber, Erich 116
Klemperer, Otto 116
Klenjánszky, Sarolta 150
Kligman, Gail 165
Knessl, Lothar 237
Koch, Lothar 223
Kodály, Zoltán 143, 151, 259

Index of Names

Koo, Joseph 180
Körmöczi, László 148-149
Kotlári, Olga 144, 146
Kowalke, Kim 236
Kreutziger-Herr, Annette 72
Krúdy, Gyula 11, 13, 16, 18, 128
Krützfeldt, Werner 74
Kubik, Gerhard 73, 76, 254, 268
Kubrick, Christine 183
Kubrick, Stanley x, 27, 36-37, 179-180, 183-185, 187-188, 190, 192
Kuczka, Péter 154, 156
Kugler, Ema 182
Kunst, Jaap 72, 81
Kunze, Tobias 81
Kurtág, György 141, 162

L

Lakatos, Sándor 146
Lampsatis, Raminta 202-204
Lanthimos, Yorgos 188
László-Bencsik, Sándor 142
Lavelli, Jorge 214
Lavotta, János 144
Lear, Edward 258
Lee, Bruce 180
Lehel, György 144
Lendvai, Ernő 256
Leonhardt, Gustav 214
Leppard, Raymond 264
Levin, Walter 239
Levy, Benjamin R. viii-ix, 3, 128, 184
Lichtenfeld, Monika 33, 62-63, 114
Ligeti, Gábor 113-130
Ligeti, Mária 143
Ligeti, Vera 143, 156, 200, 208, 228, 235
Lins, Darel Valença 185
Liszt, Franz 193
Litolff, Henry 229
Lobanova, Marina vii
Lorenz, Edward 255-256
Lowry, Lynn 186

Lück, Rudolf 229, 230
Lunch, Lydia 182

M

Machaut, Guillaume de 75, 251, 258
Maciunas, George 128
Mahler, Gustav 125-128, 188, 193
Mallarmé, Stéphane 260
Mandelbrot, Benoît 81
Marbe, Myriam 168, 170
Marceau, Felicien 214
Marshak, Samuil 148
Marx, Wolfgang xii, 223, 247
Mârza, Traian 165
Máthé, Jolán 146
Matheson, Johann 266
Mayröcker, Friederike 213
McCauley, Neal 187
McQuiston, Kate 183
Mečys, Aliutė xi-xii, 199-200, 202-204, 206-208, 211-214, 216-217, 220-222
Mehta, Zubin xi, 219-222
Meissner, Roland 30
Meizl, Ferenc 144
Melis, György 144
Melles, Károly 151
Merkley, Paul 183
Meschke, Michael 200, 212-213, 218, 223
Messiaen, Olivier 250, 252
Mészöly, Miklós 149
Meynert, Monika 220, 221
Michelangeli, Arturo Benedetti 269
Michel, Pierre ix, 49, 135
Mihály, András 140
Moll, Dominik 184
Monk, Thelonious 268
Monteverdi, Claudio 216, 264, 266
Morabito, Fulvia xi
Morresi, Alessandra 173
Mozart, Wolfgang Amadeus 259, 266
Müller, Anton 232-233, 239, 241
Müller, Wolfgang 213

Index of Names

N

Nagy, Géza 149
Nancarrow, Conlon 71, 248, 252-254
Nemescu, Octavian 163
Nicola, Ioan R. 165
Niculescu, Florin 117
Nono, Luigi 49, 69, 189, 191
Nordwall, Martin 149
Nordwall, Ove 33, 135-136, 149, 200, 212-214, 218, 223, 228, 232, 234-235, 242

O

Ockham, William 80
Oesch, Hans 242
Oldfield, Mike 29
O'Neill, Lorcan 190
Oresme, Nicole d' 80
Orff, Carl 231
Ozawa, Seiji xi, 221-222

P

Pacino, Al [Alfredo James] 187
Paganini, Nicolò 107
Palm, Siegfried 183
Papp, Tibor 141
Parker, Charlie 268
Pärt, Arvo 191, 260
Partch, Harry ix, xi, 71, 73, 101-105, 263
Penderecki, Krzysztof 182, 188, 191, 230
Perahia, Murray 269
Pergolesi, Giovanni Battista 266
Péteri, Lóránt 128
Péter, Loránd 146
Petersen, Peter 73
Peterson, Oscar 268
Petrenko, Kirill 37
Petschull, Johannes 229-230, 232, 234-237
Piranesi, Giovanni Battista 28
Platt, Christopher 27
Popper, Karl 77, 249
Preobrazhensky, Sergei 138, 148-149
Purcell, Henry 266
Pustijanac, Ingrid 126

R

Rácz, József 146
Raics, István 140-141
Rákosi, Mátyás 122, 151, 156, 259
Rands, William Brighty 258
Rarichs, Karl 235
Rauhe, Hermann 74
Ravel, Maurice 94, 214
Reich, Steve 77, 191, 217
Reiche, Jens Peter 73
Richter, Peter 73
Rihm, Wolfgang 59, 67, 69
Riley, Terry 77, 217
Rimsky-Korsakov, Nikolay 94
Rîpă, Constantin 174
Risset, Jean-Claude 73, 268
Robertson, Robbie 188
Rodericus ix, 72, 78-81
Roelcke, Eckhard 113, 235-236
Roig-Francoli, Miguel 101
Rosenthal, Albi 243
Rosenthal, Julia 243
Ross, Alex 190
Rossmannt, Karl 18
Rózsavölgyi, Márk 144
Ruelle, David 256
Rülke, Volker 267

S

Sacher, Paul 236, 242-243
Saint-Saëns, Camille 116
Sala, Massimiliano xi
Sallis, Friedemann x, 135-136, 139-141, 143, 145, 147-148
Salmenhaara, Erkki 33
Salonen, Esa-Pekka 248
Sárközy, István 141
Scarlatti, Domenico 267
Schaeffer, Pierre 43
Schafer, Raymond Murray 38, 115, 126
Schlee, Alfred 227-230, 235-237, 243
Schneider, Albrecht 39, 44, 73
Schneider-Schott, Heinz 230, 232, 235

Index of Names

Schnittke, Alfred 188
Schoenberg, Arnold 35, 119
Schöll, Klaus 232
Schreiber, Ewa ix, 113, 234
Schubert, Franz 119, 188
Schumann, Robert 95, 255
Schütz, Hannes 76
Schweinitz, Wolfgang von 73
Scorsese, Martin 188, 192
Scovell, Adam 182
Senleches, Jacob [Jaquemin] de 72, 78, 251
Seress, Magda 151
Shakespeare, William 213, 218, 257
Shepard, Roger 267
Shostakovich, Dmitry 108
Siedentopf, Henning 255
Sierra, Roberto 72
Siklós, Albert 119
Simon, Artur 76
Sirató, Charles 173
Smith, Leland 218, 262
Solage 72, 78, 251
Spitz, Veronika 145
Stahnke, Manfred ix, 71, 78
Staiber, Maryse ix, 49-50
Stalin, Iosif 151, 156
Stein, Leonard 221
Steinitz, Richard 3, 95, 152, 163, 173-174
Stern, Isaac 220
Stockhausen, Karlheinz 120, 226, 228
Strauss, Richard 119, 193
Stravinsky, Igor 78, 94, 231, 266
Strecker, Ludwig jr. 232, 237
Strecker, Willy [Wilhelm] 237
Strobel, Heinrich 227-228
Stroe, Aurel 163
Stuckenschmidt, Hans Heinz 228
Sümegi, Zoltán 144
Suzay (Susay), Johannes (Jehan) 251
Sweers, Britta viii, 27
Swift, Jonathan 257
Szabó, Ferenc 140

Szabó, Iván 141
Szegedi, Ernő 147
Székely, Endre 140
Szendy, Peter 121
Szentpál, Olga 142
Szervánszky, Endre 140
Szirtes, George 11

T

Takens, Floris 256
Tardos, Béla 140
Tatum, Art 268
Taussig, Anna 236
Taylor-Jay, Claire xii
Tekeres, Sándor 146
Țiplea Temeș, Bianca x-xi, 161
Theremin, Leon 262
Thomas, Ernst 231-232
Tomek, Otto 226
Tornyos, György 143
Travis, Francis 242
Tristano, Lennie [Leonard Joseph] 268
Tuckwell, Barry 261
Tusa, John xi, 247-249

V

Varèse, Edgard 191
Várnai, Zseni 120
Vásárhelyi, Zoltán 141
Vaszy, Victor 122
Végh, Sándor 116
Veress, Sándor 140
Vetési, György 142
Vitry, Philippe de 80
Volk, Arno 234
Vujica, Peter 253

W

Wagner, Winifred 237
Walter-Leister, Hellos 199
Webern, Anton vii, 119, 125-126, 226, 229
Wehringer, Rainer 44

Index of Names

Weishappel, Rudolf 216
Weissmann, Adolf 227
Weisz, Miklós 230
Welin, Karl-Erik 255
Weöres, Sándor xi, 50-51, 129, 214, 257, 259-260
Wessel, Erich 199
Widmann, Jörg 190
Witt, Peter N. 264
Wörner, Karl 231

Y

Young, La Monte Thornton 77

Z

Zakariás, Gábor 143
Zemp, Hugo 72
Zhen, Chen 180
Zille, Heinrich 209
Zimmermann, Frank Peter 108
Zimmermann, Heidy xi, 143, 225
Žižek, Slavoj 191
Zöller, Karlheinz 223
Zsombor, János 148